The GARDEN of BETRAYAL

The GARDEN of BETRAYAL

Lee Vance

Alfred A. Knopf   New York   2010

THIS IS A BORZOI BOOK
PUBLISHED BY ALFRED A. KNOPF

Scripture taken from *The Message* by Eugene H. Peterson, copyright © 1993,
1994, 1995, 1996. Reprinted by permission of Nav Press Publishing Group.

Library of Congress Cataloging-in-Publication Data
Vance, Lee.
The garden of betrayal / by Lee Vance.—1st ed.
       p.   cm.
ISBN 978-0-307-26977-5
1. Kidnapping—Fiction.   2. Life change events—Fiction.   3. Energy
consultants—Fiction.   I. Title.
PS3622.A58595G37 2010
813'.6—dc22   2010000370

Manufactured in the United States of America
First Edition

For Cynthia, Zoe, Nikki, and Matthew

Judas, his betrayer, knew the place because Jesus and the disciples went there often. So Judas led the way to the garden . . .

JOHN 18:2–3

The GARDEN of BETRAYAL

New York City, 2003

Snow settled on a dark, open-air parking lot. A large man wearing slick leather shoes and a new camel-hair overcoat shuffled carefully across the slippery surface, arms extended for balance. He kept his head down, cognizant of the security camera on a tall pole at the far end of the lot. The red BMW was parked where it was supposed to be, and the freshly cut key opened the door with ease. Still warm, the engine started instantly. Driving slowly across the lot, the man edged the car into traffic beneath a pink neon motel sign. He turned right and then pulled up to the curb. Two more men wearing navy watch caps and oilcloth jackets opened the rear doors and got in, sinking low in the seats.

"Nice coat," one sneered at the driver. "Looks real good on a putz like you."

"Somebody owes me three hundred bucks," the driver replied irritably. "The only use I got for this thing is to shammy the car."

"Knock it off," the third man ordered. He mumbled slightly, speech impeded by a decade-old facial burn that had left him with a shiny, puckered band of grafted skin stretched taut from the corner of his mouth to his right ear. "Take Tenth all the way, and don't speed."

"We got diplomatic plates," the driver said. "We can do whatever we want."

"You'll do what I tell you," the scarred man said. "Don't speed."

"Stop," Claire said, lifting her hands from the piano's keyboard for the fifth time in as many minutes.

Kate lowered her violin. Dark like her mother, and still carrying her baby fat at ten, she looked like a sullen Raphael cherub.

"Play it for her again, please, Kyle."

Kyle turned from the living-room window, where he'd been watching snow swirl through the treetops in Riverside Park below. He was tall for a twelve-year-old, and had his own violin cradled in his arms. Looking from his mother to his sister, he saw Kate's lower lip protruding tremulously, the way it always did when she was getting upset.

"I'm kind of hungry," he said. "Maybe we should take a break."

"I'd like to hear Kate play this passage correctly first," Claire insisted. "You're neither of you babies anymore."

Kate drew back her arm and threw her violin bow the length of the room.

"I don't have to practice all night just because you're angry at Daddy," she shouted, bare feet booming on the parquet floor as she stomped away.

Claire closed her eyes and exhaled loudly. Kyle took a step toward her and then glanced after his sister. Yolanda was in the front hall. She was dressed to go home, with a brightly patterned scarf tied over her hair, but she pocketed her gloves with a sigh and started after Kate, motioning for Kyle to go to his mother. He nodded gratefully and turned away.

Claire was slumped forward from the waist, forehead touching the music on the rest. Ebony hair, gathered in a bun, shone blue above her delicate neck. Setting his violin aside, Kyle moved behind her and began massaging her shoulders gently, the way he'd seen his father do.

"There's no reason for you to cancel your performance," he said. "You've still got plenty of time to get to the theater. I can look after Kate."

"I know," she murmured. "But your father's on a plane. It's one thing for me to call in sick. It's another to get up from the piano and walk out in the second act of *Giselle* because I have to rush home for some reason."

The muscles in her upper back felt as if they were carved from stone. He pressed a little harder, using the heels of his hands. He didn't want to hurt her.

"You worry too much," he said. "We're neither of us babies, you know."

She laughed, and he felt her relax a bit.

. . .

The man in the camel-hair coat dropped off his companions, circled the one-way system, and then parked the BMW in front of a hydrant on Eighty-sixth Street between Riverside Drive and West End Avenue, nose pointed toward the park and the Hudson River beyond. He lifted a walkie-talkie from the passenger seat and squeezed the transmit button.

"Check," he said.

"Check," came the reply.

A block north, on the corner of Eighty-seventh and Riverside, the man with the burn dropped an identical walkie-talkie into an exterior pocket of his jacket. Reaching into the opposite pocket, he removed a Christmas card and held it out to his companion.

"What?"

"Look at the picture."

"I've got the goddamned picture memorized."

"Look at it again."

The second man took it, careful to mask his resentment. Tilting the card to the streetlight overhead, he studied the glossy photo glued to the front. A family of four gathered in front of a piano, the woman and boy almost the same height. It was the woman they were interested in.

"How much longer?" he asked.

"Fifteen minutes," the man with the burn said. "Twenty at the outside. She's punctual."

Snow melted on the picture, and the second man rubbed it dry against his pants. His pulse quickened as he imagined the evening ahead. The woman was good-looking.

"Kate's taking her bath," Yolanda announced, bustling into the living room with her coat on. "And now I really do have to get going."

Claire rose from the piano bench and kissed Kyle on the cheek. He'd gained an inch on her in the last month or two, and she had to tip up her chin.

"Thanks," she said to him. "Now scoot so I can talk to Yolanda."

Both women watched as he walked away. Kyle had a high, serious forehead like his father, and pale, watchful eyes.

"Skinny as a pole," Yolanda observed. "I remember the same about my Guillermo. They get all stretched at that age."

"He wears his pants half a dozen times and he's outgrown them." Claire dropped her gaze and began toying with her wedding ring. "Is Kate okay?"

"She's fine."

"I didn't mean to be so tough on her."

"Tough," Yolanda scoffed. "My *abuela* taught me my catechism with her Bible in one hand and her stick in the other. Kate's trouble is that she's *simpática*, like her brother. I'm not even through the front door and they both know whether I got a seat on the bus or had to stand the whole way. Any bother in the house and the two of them are as miserable as wet cats."

Claire winced at the mention of bother, cheeks flushing slightly. Yolanda pulled her scarf from her sleeve and began retying it over her head.

"Now, you listen to me for one minute. You need someone who can stay late if you're going to be working nights now. I'll ask around if you want. It won't be any trouble at all for me to find another situation."

"God forbid," Claire said, shocked. "You're part of the family." She hesitated and then covered her face with a hand, her voice choked. "I'm just feeling so frustrated. It's really hard to make the transition from teaching back to performing, and this job is a big opportunity for me. But nobody's ever going to hire me again if I get a reputation for being unreliable."

"Mark didn't know he had to travel?"

"A colleague in London got sick. He's flying over to deliver his speech at their big European energy conference."

"And what was it that other time, a few weeks ago?"

"Vienna," she responded, a note of defensiveness in her voice. "An unscheduled meeting with some people from OPEC."

Yolanda's worn brown face creased as she smiled.

"Seems like it's always going to be something. I been with you eight years and I never know if he's coming or going."

"So, maybe it was a mistake for me to start performing again," Claire said tentatively. "Maybe I should have waited until Kate was older."

"Maybe this and maybe that. Work's important. For a man, and a woman." Yolanda caught Claire by the wrist and shook her arm gently.

"You're lucky. You got a good man, and good kids, and a good job. The only mistake you made was not finding someone who could stay late."

"You're half right," Claire said, smiling and leaning forward to embrace Yolanda. "I'm lucky—with Mark, and with the children, and with this opportunity. But Kate and Kyle would never forgive me if you left us. I'll figure something out."

More than an hour had passed, and the man in the camel-hair coat fidgeted restlessly behind the wheel of the BMW. The weather worked in their favor, limiting the number of pedestrians who might get a good look at him, but it was well past time for them to be gone. He yearned for a cigarette. Whoever owned the car was a smoker, and the smell was driving him to distraction. He'd had to quit after Desert Storm, when weeks spent in the burning oil fields had permanently damaged his lungs. But nothing eased a long wait like a smoke.

A hundred yards north, his companions were equally impatient. Only two people had come out of the apartment building on the opposite corner: an older Hispanic woman with a scarf tied over her hair and a black man with a German shepherd on a leash. The man with the burn looked at his watch again. She hadn't ever been this late before. He'd checked her performance schedule—curtain-up was in less than half an hour. He wondered if she might have left early because of the weather.

"Ten more minutes," he said.

The second man stamped his feet against the cold and swore. Bad beginnings made bad endings, and the woman was only the first of two jobs they had that evening.

"*No*," Kate and Kyle screamed together, heaving couch pillows at the TV while Claire laughed. They'd finished dinner and snuggled up on the couch to watch *Titanic,* but the opening credits had barely finished rolling when the picture changed to a Latin man in a white tuxedo, lip-syncing a song in Spanish as he danced on top of a taxicab in Times Square. Much as they'd begged Yolanda not to change the channel on the cable box when the VCR was recording, she frequently forgot.

"I'll run to the store and rent it," Claire said, setting aside the blanket on her lap.

Kyle glanced outside. The wind was blowing harder, raising long plumes of spindrift from the snow-laden window ledges.

"Let me," he said, getting to his feet.

Claire looked over her shoulder to check the time on the kitchen clock. Kyle had started moving around the neighborhood by himself only in the last year.

"I could use the fresh air," she said.

"Liar," he teased. "You hate the cold. And you said it yourself—I'm not a baby anymore."

Claire bit her lip and nodded.

"Take your phone."

"I'll be right back."

An iron-and-glass door swung open on Riverside Drive, and Kyle emerged from his apartment building. He was wearing a green knit school hat that rode high on his head and a Gore-Tex parka that belonged to his father. The sleeves were bunched behind the elastic cuffs and the shoulders drooped, but he liked wearing it. Digging his hands into the pockets, he touched a folded piece of paper and removed it. A list was jotted in his father's hand: Rashid, Azikiwo, Statoil, Petronuevo. Some of the words he recognized, and some he didn't. Rashid was an old friend of his dad's who worked for OPEC, and Statoil was the Norwegian state oil company. Azikiwo and Petronuevo were unfamiliar to him. He mouthed the words, liking the sounds. Everything about his dad's job was cool. He wanted to be just like his father when he grew up.

He put the paper back into the pocket, stepped out from beneath the building's awning, and headed south. Two men were standing on the corner of Eighty-seventh Street. The streetlight overhead illuminated the side of his face as he hustled past, head down against the wind. One of the men turned, staring at Kyle as he walked away.

"That's the boy," the man with the burn said.

"What boy?" the second man asked.

"The son, you fucking idiot. I thought you memorized the picture."

"Her," the man protested. "Not the kid. You never said anything about a kid."

"But she didn't show. Now we have to improvise."

The man with the burn took the walkie-talkie from his pocket, whispered into it urgently, and hurried after Kyle. His companion hesitated a moment and then followed. He was in too deep to object.

The driver of the BMW lowered his passenger window as Kyle approached. Woman or kid, he didn't see any difference.

"Excuse me," he called politely.

Kyle took a step toward the car and bent forward uncertainly.
"Yes?"

The man with the burn closed in from behind and tapped Kyle behind the ear with a sap. The second man caught him as he sagged, his green hat falling to the ground. When the BMW drove away a moment later, the boy was wedged between the two men in the rear.

The wind caught the hat and sent it tumbling down the mouth of a storm drain. It reached the river an hour later, where the tide was running toward the harbor and the Atlantic Ocean beyond. Come daybreak, the hat was miles offshore, never to be seen again.

Seven Years Later

1

I woke early and listened to Claire breathe. She had her back to me, but she didn't sound like she was sleeping, so I rolled onto my side and used one hand to gently massage her neck and shoulders. Some mornings she ignored me, some mornings we made love, and some mornings she wept. After a few minutes of no response, I got up and got ready for work.

The kitchen was dark and cold. I flipped on the under-counter lights, opened the valve on the softly clanking radiator, and then set out the usual weekday breakfast for Claire and Kate—fruit, cereal, and yogurt. On Fridays I add a chocolate croissant, cutting it in half for the two of them to share.

Frank, the night doorman, had a taxi waiting by the time I got downstairs. He said good morning and solemnly handed me a few pieces of mail addressed to my son. It was a shock when I first received mail for Kyle about a year after he disappeared—a solicitation from some preteen magazine. I spent the day thinking about it and then knocked on the door of the building super, Mr. Dimitrios. Tears in his eyes, he admitted that he'd been intercepting junk mail addressed to Kyle for the past twelve months and turned over a shoe box full. I made myself go through it—Reggie Kinnard, the detective working with us, had mentioned that the psychopaths who kidnap children will occasionally amuse themselves by sending mail to the victim's family. There wasn't anything unusual in the box. A friendly representative of the Direct Marketing Association, who I spoke to on the phone, suggested I simply scrawl the word "deceased" on everything and return it to the post office. Instead, I had Mr. Dimitrios continue intercepting it, so Claire and Kate wouldn't see it, and arranged for Frank to pass it along. These days, it's all solicitations for acne products and CD clubs and summer-job programs and magazines like *Maxim* and *Outside*. The kind of stuff any nineteen-year-old might receive. The kind of stuff Kyle might actually be interested in, if he's still alive somewhere.

I stopped to pick up the papers at an all-night newsstand on Seventy-second Street and then went to work. There's always someone at the office when I arrive, no matter the time—the hedge fund I rent space from trades twenty-four hours a day. There are only about sixty employees, but they occupy an entire floor of a Midtown office building, the northern half of which is a single large unpartitioned trading room. One corner of the room is taken up by the fund's namesake, a midnight blue 1966 Ford Shelby AC Cobra that sits on a low dais, halogen spotlights reflecting off its mirrorlike finish. The car had proved too large for the elevators, so Walter Coleman, the fund's founder, had arranged to have it hoisted by a crane after workers cut a garage door–sized opening into the side of the building.

When Walter's son, Alex, first suggested setting me up as an independent energy analyst a year and a half after Kyle vanished, I was hesitant. I needed the money, but I didn't know if I was capable of committing to a job the way I had before, or if I could be successful as a freelance pundit even if I did. My entire career had been on the sell side, peddling research on oil companies to clients of the investment bank I worked for. Eighteen months out of the market, and lacking the institutional connections that had made people want to talk to me, I was afraid I wouldn't be able to deliver anything of value. Save one or two old friends, I was right to think that my former sources would abandon me but wrong to worry that it would matter. Cobra was the granddaddy of the hedge-fund community, progenitor of multiple generations of firms that gossiped and fought and generally behaved like an extended family. Alex and his father made a few calls on my behalf, and suddenly I had a dozen clients, all funds that Wall Street was clamoring to do business with. Pretty soon there wasn't a sell-side guy on the Street who wouldn't drop everything for me, anxious for a favorable mention to my clientele. And as I grew more influential, my old sources started reaching out to me again. Business prospered. Even the recent market crash had been a blessing in disguise, the clients who went under replaced by newly de-levered and deeply chastened survivors desperate for genuine ideas and analysis to supplant their soured credit strategies.

The biggest plus was that I rarely had to travel anymore. The traditional asset managers I'd covered had kept me on the hop across America and Europe, demanding my physical presence as an act of fealty, and dinner and a nice bottle of wine as tribute. It had been tough with a young family. I regularly kissed Claire and the kids good-bye on a Sunday night, knowing I was committed to spending the rest of the week in a series of barren hotel rooms and that I was leaving her to deal with most of the parenting alone. I missed being with them and felt bad about abandoning Claire, but—God help me—I never backed away from an assignment, craving the success, and the recognition, and the monetary reward. My new job let me be home most nights, my hedge-fund clientele indifferent to face time and insistent on buying their own meals, but the sad reality was that no amount of time now would ever make up for what I'd lost.

My office is on the southern half of the floor, around the corner from the trading room. After grabbing a cup of coffee from the kitchen, I settled in at my desk and went through the business and international news. I pay attention to bylines and keep track of reporters who seem particularly insightful or well connected; I'm wary of Wall Street group-think, and journalists are surprisingly easy to cultivate. There's always something they haven't been able to write, or want to write, or already wrote but don't feel they fully understand. And with more than twenty years' experience with the energy markets, I'm a great guy to bounce things off. I understand the industry upside down, am free with information, and never publish anything of my own—although I can be cajoled into dictating the odd market piece when a friendly reporter is in a bind. GAS PRICES SET TO SOAR AGAIN or TEN OIL STOCKS SMART INVESTORS OWN NOW. In return, they ask questions of people my Wall Street connections might not have access to, feed me tidbits they haven't figured out how to hang a story on yet, and give me early warning of big stories that might have market impact. Everyone wins.

At about eight, I banged out a two-page market update to my client base, telling them what they should be watching out for. I stood, stretched, and gave myself fifteen minutes to stare out the window next to my desk. The window was what made me decide to co-locate with Alex and Walter. It might even have been what persuaded me to try life as an independent analyst. It faces due south onto Park Avenue, and at almost any time of day I can see hundreds of people on the street below.

I was on a plane to London the night Kyle vanished. As we taxied to the gate at Heathrow, a stewardess bent forward and told me that a customer service manager would be meeting me on the jetway. I was too groggy to suspect anything other than the faux-warm handshake and stilted chitchat that airline management occasionally bestow on frequent business travelers. I recall hoping he'd brought a courtesy cart so I wouldn't have to make the long walk to Immigration.

The next twelve hours are pretty much a blur. I remember the physical impact of hearing that Kyle was missing, as if I'd had the wind knocked out of me and couldn't recover. I remember sitting hunched in my seat on the long flight back to New York, feeling as if I were falling and falling, with the ground nowhere in sight. Most of all, I remember the look on Claire's face when we met at the police station—the grief that persuaded me the nightmare was true, and the guilt that's never vanished. It wasn't until later that I began wondering what might have happened differently if I'd been home.

Amy, my assistant, walks in on me occasionally when I'm staring out my office window and makes gentle fun of me for being so entranced. It helps me think, I tell her, feeling bad about the lie. The truth is something I can only just bear to admit to myself. Claire and I never discussed the evening Kyle vanished in any detail, but I read the statement she made to the police and the description she gave of the clothes he was wearing. Despite all the years that have passed, I'm still searching the crowd below for a tall twelve-year-old in an oversized parka and a green knit school hat.

2

I was reading an industry rag at my desk when Amy stopped in to say good morning. She was holding a manila envelope in her hand and smiling.

"Guess what I have?"

"Hmm. . . " I said, tapping my finger against my chin. Amy's forty, married, and on the vestry of her church. She was wearing a simple navy dress and had her auburn hair done up in a prim bun. "A ticket to Vegas. You're leaving me to take a job dealing blackjack at the Bellagio."

"As if," she scoffed. "The only job I'd be willing to take in Las Vegas would be at a mission."

"Like what's-her-name in *Guys and Dolls*. The one who ends up with Marlon Brando."

"Jean Simmons," she said, reddening slightly. Amy was a big fan of old movies. "I liked her better in *Elmer Gantry*. And *Guys and Dolls* was set in New York. None of which has anything to do with anything." She reached into the envelope and extracted a BlackBerry with a dramatic flourish. "Ta-da!"

"My new phone?" I asked, puzzled by the flourish.

"Better. Your *old* phone."

I'd been feeling like a dope all weekend because a bike messenger had half knocked me down outside my office on Friday as I returned from a late-afternoon meeting, and a stranger had caught my arm to steady me. It hadn't occurred to me to check my pockets until I was riding the elevator upstairs. I figured the stranger had mistaken the bulky device for my wallet and lifted it.

"You're kidding. Where'd it come from?"

"Lobby guard gave it to me on my way in. Some guy came in off the street Saturday afternoon and turned it in. Said he spotted it under the newspaper machine on the corner and saw your business card taped to the back."

I took the BlackBerry from her and examined it. It looked fine. I pressed the power button. The screen lit up for a moment, flashed a low-battery warning, and then went dark again.

"Amazing," I said, snugging the unit into its charging cradle. "Maybe it just fell out of my pocket when I stumbled. Hard to believe someone actually returned it."

"Not so hard to believe," Amy chided. "New York is full of nice people."

"You get the guy's name?" I asked, thinking I should send him a bottle of scotch.

"Guard said he didn't leave it." She leaned forward and dropped her voice to a husky whisper. "This is when you thank your assistant for having remembered to tape your business card to the back of your three-hundred-dollar phone."

"Geez," I said loudly. "It sure is lucky that I have an assistant terrific enough to remember to tape my business card to the back of my three-hundred-dollar phone. Thanks so much, Amy. I don't know what I'd do without you."

"Waste half a day trying to load your contacts onto a new phone before losing your temper and yelling at me to call the tech guys." She sniffed. "I'll call AT&T for you and get it reactivated. You need anything from the storage room?"

"Nothing, thanks."

She left, head shaking in mock disapproval. I made a mental note to buy her some flowers when I went out to get lunch, thinking I could pick up something for Claire at the same time. Claire loved flowers.

I'd settled back in with my magazine when my desk phone rang. Amy wasn't back yet, so I picked it up and said hello.

"*As-Salāmu 'Alaykum*," a reedy voice said. Peace be upon you.

"*Wa 'Alaykum As-Salām*," I responded, recognizing the caller immediately. And on you be peace. It was Rashid.

"You're well?" he asked.

We'd spoken less than twelve hours previously, but Arabs are big on ritual. The first lesson of doing business with Middle Easterners is that nothing can ever be rushed.

"Very. And you?"

"Alive, *al-Hamdulillah*."

It was the answer I expected. Rashid was in acute renal failure, the result of a lifelong battle with diabetes and lingering complications from a kidney and pancreas transplant a few years back. He was being treated as an outpatient at New York–Presbyterian. His Viennese doctor's first suggestion had been a hospital in Houston, but Rashid was uncomfortable taking up residence in the first city of the American energy industry. He'd been head of the office of the secretary-general of OPEC for going on twenty years before his recent medical leave, and there was no love lost between his employer and the Texas oil and gas tycoons whose overseas reserves had been nationalized by OPEC's membership. New York had been the obvious second choice.

"Praise God," I said, echoing him.

"I'm hearing word of a problem at Nord Stream."

Nord Stream was a pipeline that was being built beneath the Baltic Sea to deliver Russian natural gas to Germany. I checked my news screen and didn't see anything.

"What kind of problem?"

"I don't know."

I hesitated, wondering if he was being completely honest. Rashid was my oldest and best source, as well as a close friend, but he routinely held back more than he shared. He usually let me know when he had information he couldn't discuss, though. I was about to press him when a sudden beeping caught my attention. A headline had scrolled up on my screen: EXPLOSION REPORTED AT NORD STREAM PIPELINE TERMINUS. The terminus was in Russia, near Saint Petersburg.

"Reuters just now posted a story saying there was some kind of explosion," I said.

"I see it."

I clicked on the headline, but there weren't any details yet.

"Let me make a few calls. I'll get back to you when I know more."

"Thanks. *Me salama*."

"Alla y'salmak."

I punched another line on my phone and called Dieter Thybold, a friend at Reuters in London.

"It's Mark," I said when he answered. "What's up with this pipeline explosion?"

"No idea yet," he replied tersely. "I can't even confirm that there was an explosion. But something strange is going on."

"Strange how?"

"Today's the day of the terminus construction completion ceremony. A lot of reporters and dignitaries are visiting. The whole site went quiet twenty minutes ago. Nobody can get hold of their people. And we just got word a moment ago that the Russians have closed their airspace between Saint Petersburg and the Finnish border, and that there's been a huge increase in encrypted radio traffic out of their military bases at Pribilovo and Kronstadt."

"So, how do your people know there was an explosion?" I asked, my adrenaline beginning to pump.

"There was a camera crew shooting the ceremony. The footage should be on air any minute. You can see the tiniest hint of a flash in the last frame of the video before it goes dark."

"Satellite views?"

"Too cloudy. I've got to go."

"Wait. You're thinking terrorism?"

"It's hard not to, isn't it? But we haven't got any facts yet."

"Stay in touch."

I turned on CNN after I hung up, listening for updates as I speed-typed an e-mail to my clients and Rashid. The newly completed terminus was doing only light duty while the attached pipeline was still under construction, a bare fraction of the capacity used to route gas locally, but an attack there would rattle the markets, an ominous portent for the future. Energy infrastructure was a soft target. A systematic campaign against refineries or pipelines or storage facilities could do an enormous amount of economic damage. The likely reactions were a knee-jerk spike in energy prices, weakening global equity markets, a steeping yield curve, and a declining euro. I wrote URGENT in the subject line and hit the send button. Alex Coleman was in my office thirty seconds later.

"You think this is serious?" he demanded.

Alex looked terrible, rough patches of psoriasis visible on his hairline and bluish circles beneath his eyes. He'd had a difficult time during the recent market turmoil. In truth, he'd been having a difficult time for years. I could guess what his positions were from the sweat soaking his shirt beneath his arms.

"I don't know anything more than what I put in my e-mail."

"You have a hunch?"

"Half the countries that used to make up the Soviet Union are furious about this pipeline, and they'd all like to see Russia take it in the neck. I think this is bad."

"Shit."

He rushed out just as CNN cut to a special report. It took only a few seconds to figure out that they didn't know anything more than I did. I grabbed my phone and started dialing.

Two hours later I was holding my phone to my ear impatiently, waiting for Dieter to pick up again. Equity markets were tanking and oil prices had gapped higher, but nobody knew a damned thing. Rashid was unavailable, having responded to my original e-mail with a note of his own saying that he'd be at the hospital all day and asking to be kept up to speed electronically. My phone turret was lit up like a Christmas tree, every one of my clients frantic for information, and I had nothing to tell them.

I stood to relieve my cramped muscles and turned to face the window. It was snowing, fat, lazy flakes drifting from a gunmetal sky and melting as they touched down. I'd come to hate the snow, just as I'd come to hate everything else about New York, the occasional cell phone–returning Good Samaritan regardless. But Claire and I could never move. Our apartment on Riverside Drive was the only home Kyle had ever known—the only home he'd know to come back to.

"Mark," Dieter said into my ear, sounding rushed. "I'm sorry, but I still don't have anything else to tell you."

"Don't hold out on me," I insisted. "You must have twenty guys working on this. You've got to know something."

"The Russians have everything shut down, but the prevailing wind is from the west, and we were able to get a stringer south of Vyborg before he hit a police roadblock. There's a lot of smoke in the air. That's all I've got."

I started to ask another question, but he was already gone. I hung up and smacked one hand down on my desk in frustration.

CNN had obtained the footage Dieter referred to in his first call. I watched on one of my desktop monitors as they began running it for the twentieth time. It opened with an establishing shot: frozen marshes, snow, and the bleak gray waters of the Gulf of Finland. The shot tightened as it panned to the terminus. It was nothing much to look at—squat scrubbing and absorption towers, low brown buildings to house the compressor equipment, an antennae-festooned central control station on tall stilts, and endless miles of dull blue pipe and valves. There was no housing—according to the CNN commentator, the workers commuted from Vyborg, thirty miles to the east, or from Hamina, in Finland, thirty miles to the west. The shot tightened further as a group of heavily bundled dignitaries began emerging from a building that was probably a dining hall. Jacques Pripaud, the head of Banque Paribas, was one of the first out the door. His expression seemed consistent with having eaten at a Russian cafeteria. He was closely followed by his counterpart at Deutsche Bank. I pulled my yellow pad closer and turned the volume up a little, hoping the commentator might identify more of the unknown faces this time around. I already had twenty-two names written down, including the chairmen of four of the largest banks in Europe, a Russian deputy prime minister, the mayor of Saint Petersburg, and the German foreign minister. The pipeline had been hugely controversial in Europe, implying an energy dependence on Russia that made people old enough to remember the Cold War queasy. All the businessmen and politicians who'd supported it had turned out to wave the flag.

The camera followed closely as the men trooped across an icy parking lot to a white canvas tent. Inside was a gang of valves, one of which had a gilded control wheel attached to it. The diameter of the attached pipe was way too small to be anything other than some kind of secondary line, but then the entire act of turning a valve by hand was pure theater—everything in the facility was automated. A microphone on a stand stood to the left of the pipe gang. The Russian deputy prime minister tapped on the microphone a few times to settle the crowd, took a sheaf of folded papers from his pocket, and opened his mouth. The screen flared orange for a tenth of a second and then went black.

"Shoot." I drummed my fingers on my head, trying to think of who else I could call. CNN had frozen the last frame of the footage on the screen, and my attention drifted to the small yellow credit on the bottom-right corner that read COURTESY OF EURONEWS. I didn't usually bother with broadcast journalists, but I remembered that someone I knew had gone to work at Euronews a few years back. I willed my mind blank and the name suddenly popped into my head: Gavin Metcalfe. He was a Brit who'd worked at the *Economist,* but he'd quit to take a job as a producer with Euronews because they were headquartered near the French Alps. He and his wife were big skiers. Typing the name into my address book, I saw two numbers, both with U.K. country codes. I punched the intercom button on my phone.

"Amy, have you got an updated number for Gavin Metcalfe? M-e-t-c-a-l-f-e. Used to be in London, but I think he's in France now."

I heard her fingers clicking on her keyboard.

"I have a work and a cell, but they're both U.K."

"Same. Do me a favor, please. Call the main switchboard at Euronews in Lyon and ask for him."

"Will do."

I hung up and dialed the cell phone number anyway, figuring there was some chance he'd kept it. The call kicked directly into voice mail, a generic prompt suggesting I leave a message. Hoping the number hadn't been reassigned, I explained why I was getting in touch and then followed up with a quick text from my own cell. My intercom flashed as I pressed the send button.

"It's weird," Amy said. "No one's answering. . . ."

"Hang on," I interrupted. My BlackBerry was ringing. I picked it up and checked the display, seeing the London number I'd just tried. "Gotta hop. This might be him."

I hung up the intercom and lifted the BlackBerry to my ear.

"Mark Wallace."

"Open a browser window on your computer," a voice answered. There was a rushing sound in the background that I couldn't identify.

"Gavin?"

"Don't interrupt. I'm in a car, and I haven't got much time. You want to know about Nord Stream, right?"

"Right," I confirmed, my excitement building.

"So, do what I tell you. Open a browser window and type this in the menu bar: F-T-P colon backslash backslash euronews dot net back-slash . . ."

I pecked carefully at the keyboard as he dictated a URL that was about fifty characters long, interrupting several times when I wasn't sure what he'd said. Gavin had some kind of impenetrable northern accent that made all his vowels sound the same. He told me to press enter, and I did.

"It wants a username and password," I said.

"The username is *extérieur,* all lowercase. Password *baiselareine.* Bloody frogs having a go at me every time I turn around."

I entered both, my high school French sufficient to translate the juvenile slur. I heard someone else on his end of the line as I pressed the enter key. It sounded like a child.

"I see a bunch of folders. You're with your family?"

"On our way to the airport. Click the folder labeled *archive,* and then click the one inside that with today's date, and then click the one inside that named Nord Stream."

"Done."

"You'll see two files—EsatIIB135542 and EsatIIC141346. Clicking on either will download it to your desktop. They're big files, but our server's hooked directly to the Internet backbone, so the limitation will likely be on your side."

"What are they?"

"Video. The first is the raw footage you've been seeing on television. The second is something else entirely."

I clicked the second. We were connected to a dedicated fiber-optic cable as well. A dialogue box indicated that I had ten minutes to wait, the file transfer speed a number I'd never seen before.

"Give me a hint," I said, wondering what the hell was going on. "I'm under a lot of pressure here."

"You?" he sneered. "I've had the effing DGSE in my face all afternoon."

"Remind me who the DGSE are?"

"French foreign intelligence creeps. Jackbooters. They turned up just after we released the first footage and put a lid on us. I went out for a cigarette and kept going. If I wanted to work for fascists, I would have taken a job with Murdoch."

"So, what's the second file?"

"It's what it isn't that bears thinking about. It isn't our footage. We had one cameraman and one reporter on the ground, and we lost them both in the initial blast. I'm inside the airport now, on the ring road. I'm going to have to hang up in a moment."

I scribbled the words "initial blast" on my yellow pad. I had to stay focused.

"Who shot the footage, then?"

"Our satellite truck kept running after our lads went off the air. Someone pirated one of the frequencies, and their feed uploaded automatically. We didn't even realize we'd received it until an hour ago."

"Does it show what happened?"

"Yes."

"Is it bad?"

"It makes the guys who did 9/11 look like a bunch of shit-arsed kids. Be sure to watch the whole thing."

"Will do," I agreed, wondering fearfully what I was about to see. There was just one more question I had to ask. "Has anyone else got this yet?"

"No. I hadn't figured out who to give it to. I want it distributed, but I don't want my name mentioned. You understand?"

"You're fleeing the country, Gavin," I said, feeling obliged to point out the obvious. "It's not like they aren't going to figure it out."

"There's a difference between suspecting and knowing. I have your word?"

"Of course."

"Fine, then. And listen, Mark—I'm going to need a job. Something in Dubai might be nice. I'm sick of the bloody winters. You know people there?"

"I do. Give me a shout when you want me to make some calls. And thanks."

He hung up without saying good-bye. The dialogue box indicated that I had seven minutes to wait. I typed another urgent e-mail, warning my clients and Rashid that I'd had tentative confirmation of a major terrorist action and that full details were to follow shortly. The Dow was down one hundred points when I hit the send key. By the time Alex and Walter showed up in my office, it was down two hundred and fifty, and my phone turret was pulsing like it was going to explode.

"What the hell is going on?" Walter demanded. He had a raptor's profile—aquiline nose, deep-set eyes, and short-cropped white hair. Part of his legend was that pressure only ever made him meaner. Alex looked as if he'd been run over.

"Two minutes," I said, bristling at Walter's tone. Gratitude for his professional help had never reconciled me to his habit of acting as if the entire world should jump when he spoke. I nodded toward my screen. "I have video of what happened. The guy who gave it to me said that it's bad. He mentioned an 'initial explosion,' implying there's been more than one."

Amy stuck her head in again.

"Sorry," I said, before she could open her mouth. "I can't speak to anyone right now. E-mail bulletins only for another half hour at least. Hang on."

The file completed downloading, and I dragged a copy to the folder where I kept documents for client access.

"I'm writing a big video file to the public drive. As soon as it finishes, e-mail the address to Rashid and then to everyone else on the prime distribution list."

"Right," she said, closing the door.

"Can we get on with this?" Walter snarled.

I clicked on the file irritably. My media player opened, and a second later the screen filled with an image I couldn't identify, the lower half shiny gray metal and the upper a blurry blue tube. The field of view began shifting smoothly upward, and suddenly I got oriented.

"The camera's mounted on one of the scrubbing towers," I said. "It was pointed straight down, maybe so nobody would notice it."

"Whose camera?" Walter asked.

"My contact didn't know. Pirates, he said."

The camera scrolled up until the Gulf of Finland was just visible at the top of the screen and then began tracking to the right. Alex pointed to the screen.

"What's that?"

Four metal struts reached skyward, the ends blackened and twisted. Dark smoke was spewing up between them.

"The control tower," I replied, horrified. Even with the terminus performing only minimal duty, there would have been at least three or four guys in the control tower.

The camera kept panning, and the white marquee where I'd last seen the Russian deputy prime minister about to speak—or what was left of it—came into view.

"Jesus Christ." Alex gasped.

Flaming scraps of canvas surrounded a charred rectangular area that looked like an airplane crash site. Burned corpses and scattered body parts became distinguishable as the camera zoomed in. A few survivors crawled on the ground, blood seeping from appalling wounds. Alex grabbed hold of my garbage can and threw up. I felt I wouldn't be far behind him. Walter started to leave.

"Wait," I managed to say. "My contact said I should watch until the end."

"Why?"

"I don't know."

"Can you speed it up?" Walter asked impatiently.

"I think so."

I clicked my mouse on the appropriate button and the video began playing at ten-times speed. Walter lifted my phone without asking, reeling off a litany of crisp orders while I tapped out yet another urgent e-mail with trembling fingers. Six minutes later—an hour of elapsed real time—the Russians had four military helicopters and fifteen or twenty fire trucks and ambulances on the ground, and another pair of helicopters circling overhead. The parking lot I'd seen earlier had been converted into an emergency triage zone, with dozens of coveralled medics working on the injured.

"Stop," Walter ordered.

I'd already moved my mouse to the pause button. A pale red *X* had suddenly appeared in the center of the screen, a column of similarly colored numbers superimposed to the far left.

"Play," Walter said. "Half speed."

I watched curiously as he bent closer to the screen. The camera swung slowly toward the helicopters and the emergency vehicles. Walter tapped the changing column of numbers on the left with one finger.

"Distance and azimuth," he declared crisply. Walter had been an army officer in Vietnam. I hadn't, but I had a sudden dread of what to expect. "Speed it up again."

The camera lingered fractionally on each of the landed helicopters and on the larger pieces of emergency equipment, the central *X* blinking repeatedly. Each time the X blinked, it left behind a red dot. The camera pulled back for a wide view, and I felt my heart in my throat. The blow wasn't long coming.

Every one of the emergency vehicles and helicopters exploded simultaneously. A fraction of a second later a rolling wave of synchronized explosions took out the triage zone. No one on the ground had a chance. Alex retched again.

"Mortars," Walter announced. "Some targeted, some pre-positioned. Probably on the roof of one of the buildings. They must've anticipated where the emergency workers would set up. Who the hell are these guys?"

I shook my head numbly as the camera rose higher, pointing at the sky. The pale red X changed to blue, as did the column of numbers on the left. It panned left until it located a hovering helicopter and then zoomed in. The blue X began flashing.

"I don't believe it," Walter said, sounding amazed for the first time since I'd known him.

A streak of white smoke appeared on the lower-right side of the screen. The helicopter burst into flames, heeled over onto its side, and fell from the sky. The camera swung left again with the same terrible mechanical precision. A second helicopter came into view, fleeing to the east. A second later, it too fell out of the sky in flames, taken down by a second missile. Walter rapped his knuckles on my desk, and I looked up at him, stunned.

"There's nothing we can do from here. We need to focus. What's the opportunity?"

I forced myself to look at my market screens. The Dow was down five hundred points, oil was up eight dollars a barrel in the front month, the long bond was getting crushed, and the euro had fallen three percent against the dollar.

"Short second month oil and buy back two-year," I said, surprised to discover that my brain was still functioning. "This has no immediate impact on energy supply, and short-term demand's only going to be forecast weaker if the market keeps tanking this hard."

"Good," he said, turning to Alex. "What are your exposures?"

Alex didn't respond. He was still staring at my computer screen. The camera had zoomed all the way out and was doing a slow pan. The horizon was empty, save for bellowing plumes of black smoke, and the ground was a sea of fire.

"Alex," Walter repeated sharply.

"I'm the wrong way around," Alex confessed dazedly, running one hand through his hair. "I was positioned long the market and I'm short volatility."

"So, what are you going to do?"

"I don't know, Dad."

"I see." Walter turned on his heel and walked out. Alex hesitated a moment and then followed him.

I began typing another e-mail, searching for words to describe what I'd just seen.

3

I was on a conference call with a group of fund managers late that afternoon, going over pretty much the same points I'd been covering all day. My voice was hoarse, and I was scanning headlines while half listening to repetitive questions, struggling to stay in front of the news. Everything I knew was already in my written bulletins, but I'd learned long ago that people are more likely to believe things if they hear you say them.

"It depends," I said, in response to a question about who might be responsible. "If the completion ceremony was just a target of opportunity, with the primary intent of killing a bunch of diplomats, then your guess is as good as mine. It could have been Islamic fundamentalists seizing the moment, Chechens working off old grievances, or some other terrorist organization. But if the goal was to make a statement about the pipeline per se, then it seems reasonable to ask who has motive. The countries most unhappy about the Nord Stream pipeline are Ukraine, Poland, the Czech Republic, Belarus, and Slovakia. They all stand to lose the transit fees they've been earning from the existing pipelines that pass through their territory, and—more to the point—they all become significantly more vulnerable to energy blackmail from Russia."

"Natural gas is cheap now," one of the listeners interrupted. "Why can't the Ukrainians and the Poles and the rest of them just buy from someone else?"

I stifled a sigh. My clients were financiers, accustomed to moving money and securities around the world at the tap of a computer key.

Logistics was as esoteric a subject to them as mortgage-backed securities had been to everyone else prior to the housing meltdown.

"First," I said, intent on correcting as many misapprehensions as possible, "natural gas is only cheap now because the economy tanked. And because it's cheap now, a lot of companies have canceled exploration and development projects. All of which means that prices are likely to go to the moon as soon as demand picks up again."

"Is that a prediction, mate?" an Australian voice asked.

"Absolutely. Second, the ex–Eastern Bloc countries can't buy from someone else, because gas moves most economically through pipelines, and the only producer their pipelines connect with is Russia. Nobody's going to invest the money to change that anytime soon, because pipelines are expensive, and eastern Europe isn't that big a market. The Russians have been over a barrel for the last decade, because the routing of the existing pipelines meant that they couldn't interrupt delivery of gas to eastern Europe without also interrupting delivery to western Europe. The Nord Stream pipeline changes that by making a direct connection to Germany under the Baltic Sea. And the Ukrainians and the Poles and all the other former Soviet clients and republics that have been trying to put distance between themselves and their former master are keenly aware of the fact that it's difficult to ignore a neighbor who can turn off your lights and heat."

"The speaker of the Russian Duma accused the Ukrainians on Moscow radio," someone else said. "How likely does that seem to you?"

"Russia bit the bullet on western exports and turned off Ukraine's gas twice in the last five years, once in January 2006 and once in March 2008, because of arguments over subsidized pricing. The ultranationalists in the Ukrainian coalition government made some ugly threats at the time. That puts them at the top of everyone's suspect list."

"So, you think they did it?" the same voice demanded.

"My opinion is that who actually did it isn't important in the short run. What matters is how the Russians react. They're going to be under enormous pressure to hit back hard and fast, and as the United States learned to its detriment in Iraq, intelligence has a way of providing the answers politicians want. Which raises the question of how NATO will respond if Russia threatens military action against one of the former Soviet republics."

A message from Alex popped up on my screen as two callers began arguing with each other about the likelihood of the Ukrainians having sponsored the attack. *Drink?* it read. I checked my watch. It was only a little past four, and I still had a huge amount of work to do. I hadn't been out with Alex in a while, though, and I knew how he must be feeling. There are no secrets on trading floors—Alex had gotten creamed. I wavered a moment and then typed back: *Fifteen minutes.*

"I have time for two more questions."

"What's your best trade?" another voice asked.

"The slope of the forward price curve. Let's take a look at the ICE closing prices for Brent . . ."

Alex was at his desk in his office, typing something on his computer. I tapped on his door and then took a seat, waiting for him to finish. He'd changed his shirt, but he still looked like hell. I was always taken aback to notice how worn and bloated he'd become—in my mind's eye, I always saw the skinny, engaging kid I'd first met a decade ago, a kinetic-market wonk with short-cropped hair and black-framed glasses who bore a passing likeness to Buddy Holly and wore his khaki pants too short. I'd been a top-ranked Wall Street analyst at the time, and Alex had been a recent college grad trying to make a go of his own small fund. Walter, a major client, had leaned on me, insisting that I spend time with him. Alex overcame my initial reluctance by being smart and entertaining. We fell into the habit of talking regularly—about work, and other things. Protective of my constrained time with Claire and the kids, I rarely invited professional acquaintances home, but I liked Alex enough to extend an invitation. He'd been a hit, charming Claire with his interest in the arts, and Kate and Kyle with a repertoire of simple card tricks and a willingness to play hide-and-seek. I remember thinking that he was exactly the kind of vivacious, intellectually curious young adult I hoped my own children would become. Claire insisted that I invite him back so she could fatten him up a little, but his luck had already begun to turn bad, and the return visit had been postponed and eventually abandoned.

"Tough day," I said.

"For lots of people." Alex pushed his glasses up with one hand to massage raw-looking indentations on either side of his nose. "What's the death count now?"

"North of three hundred." The only good news I'd received all day was a follow-up text from Gavin, saying that he and his family had made it back to England safely.

He winced.

"And here I am feeling sorry for myself because I got my socks blown off by the market. It puts things in perspective, doesn't it?"

Yes and no. Tragedy put unimportant things in perspective, but genuine pain was tougher to mitigate. Alex had been born with enough money to support any lifestyle he chose, but the only thing he really wanted was his father's approval. He'd been working at it as long as I knew him, and the harder he worked, the more it eluded him.

"How bad did you get hurt?" I inquired, thinking it was marginally less awkward than not asking.

"Drink first," he said.

We rode the elevator down together and walked around the corner to Pagliacci, an upscale restaurant-cum-lounge that was usually deserted at this time of day. The wallpaper, the cocktail napkins, and the bar menu were all decorated with clowns; even the light fixtures had clown faces stamped on the brass escutcheons. The place gave me the creeps, but Alex liked it for some reason. The barman saw us come in and reached for a bottle of Stoli. He settled a half-full highball glass in front of Alex as we took stools at the empty bar, then tipped his chin at me.

"Amstel."

Alex gulped at his glass three times, and the barman hit him again.

"You want to talk about it?" I ventured.

"Let me ask you a question," he said, staring down at the bar. "I've been hearing guys in the office call me Eddie behind my back. What's that about?"

Walter had named his firm after a classic American muscle car, the Ford AC Cobra. His first few apprentices who'd spun out on their own had followed suit, calling their funds Mustang and Charger. It caught on. When Alex briefly ran his own fund, he'd named it Torino. Like the Cobra, the Torino was a Ford.

"No idea," I said.

"You could do me a favor."

"What's that?"

"You could not lie to me."

I took a deep breath and let it out slowly. Five years back, when I'd been foundering, Alex was the one who'd persuaded his father to throw me a lifeline. I was indebted to him. I didn't want to hurt him, but I didn't see that I had any choice.

"Eddie comes from Edsel."

He nodded and took another swallow of his drink. The Ford Edsel was Detroit's most infamous mistake, a hugely touted vehicle that had failed utterly.

"That's funny," he said. "The Edsel was named after Henry Ford's kid, right?"

I nodded.

"Who came up with that?"

"I don't know."

He swiveled on his stool to face me.

"Didn't I already ask you not to fucking lie to me?"

I picked up my beer and took a sip, meeting his gaze levelly. I really didn't know who'd come up with it. Jokes and nicknames swept across trading floors like wildfires, and you rarely learned the source. What I did know was that there were a lot of guys who resented Alex because he was the boss's son, and because anyone else with Alex's track record would have been out on his ass years ago.

"I'm sorry," he apologized a few moments later. "I'm kind of a wreck right now."

"Don't worry about it."

The barman cutting limes a few feet away was obviously listening, so I suggested we move to a table. Alex had his glass refilled first. Less than ten minutes after walking through the door and he was on the equivalent of his fifth drink. We settled in a corner beneath a clock with oversized clown feet swinging side to side like a pendulum. A polka dot–painted arm protruding from the side rocked back and forth in time with the feet, perpetually threatening to launch a cream pie.

"You know what sucks?" Alex asked, elbows on the table as he rubbed his scalp with both hands.

"What?"

"That you're such a hard guy to whine to."

I gave him a smile to acknowledge the humor in the remark. It was something I'd noticed—people were self-conscious about complaining around me. Almost no matter their difficulty, my hardship trumped theirs.

"I just wish . . ."

"What?" I asked, as he trailed off.

"I made mistakes back when I had Torino. My dad says that mistakes are contagious."

His mistake had been trying to launch his own fund fresh out of graduate school, the way Walter had launched Cobra when he left the army. But where Walter succeeded, Alex had failed, as almost anyone his age would. His confidence had never recovered.

"You can't change the past," I said, repeating a truth I struggled to accept every day.

"Maybe not," he mumbled. "But it's like that butterfly thing. Everything might have been different."

I leaned back in my chair unhappily. It was something I'd seen before—guys who got smacked around by the market, and who became obsessed with some specific event or decision that had gone the wrong way. Like the former high school quarterback who'd be playing in the pros if only the coach had let him pass more the night the college scout came around, they became convinced that everything would have worked out fine if it hadn't been for that one unlucky moment. It was a level of delusion I hadn't seen Alex descend to before, and if he'd been anyone else, I would have finished my beer and walked out on him. I'd spent too much time with drunken traders to have any patience for their particular brand of self-pity. Alex was different, though. It wasn't just that I was grateful to him. I cared about him, if only because he so clearly needed to be cared about. I wanted him to be happy.

"Listen," I said, reaching out to nudge his shoulder. "Can I be honest with you?"

"Of course," he answered stiffly.

"You've been giving this job your best shot for years. Maybe it's time to admit that the hedge-fund business isn't what you're cut out for. Look at me: I'm a smart guy, but I realized long ago that I don't have the constitution to pull the trigger every day. And look at the people who are successful—a lot of them are just riding for a fall. Fifty percent of everything is luck. You know that. So why continue to beat yourself up?"

"You think generating return is about being lucky?" he demanded acidly.

"You think luck isn't important?" I countered.

"For most guys. But what about people like my father? The ones who never blow up?"

Walter had thrived during the financial implosion, hoarding Treasuries and relentlessly shorting the banks. His success had burnished his already immaculate reputation to a godlike sheen.

"The ones who haven't blown up yet, you mean. Read some history. Napoléon looked pretty good until he took off for Moscow. Anybody can roll snake eyes."

Alex opened his mouth and then visibly bit back an angry reply, taking another slug from his glass.

"You should be focused on the political stuff," I advised. "There's a big opportunity for you there."

He shook his head dismissively.

"Why not?"

"I'd prefer banging cocktail waitresses," he muttered sarcastically. "That was the job Fredo got, wasn't it?"

Alex was being both stubborn and stupid. Walter and his circle had left Washington alone until the late nineties, when a handful of congressmen made a halfhearted attempt to regulate hedge funds in the wake of the Long-Term Capital Management disaster. Once politics caught their interest, it hadn't taken them long to figure out that it wasn't dissimilar to the other arenas they played in, save that the trick was pushing money into the game without breaking any rules, as opposed to taking it out. They had a lot of money, and they were very good at working around the rules. Walter's latest stratagem was to channel his coterie's largesse through a new, ostensibly independent public advocacy group: Americans for Free Markets. He'd suggested that Alex become the group's first CEO. Alex—predictably—had interpreted the offer as a vote of no confidence in his trading abilities, and sunk deeper into his funk.

"You're not thinking about this right," I said, wishing I could cut through the bitterness and disappointment to the Alex I used to know. "You could become very influential."

He shrugged and drained his glass, rattling the ice cubes at the barman. I kept quiet against my better judgment, wondering if I was going to have to carry him home.

"That reminds me," he said, when the barman had left. "I'm supposed to invite you to the NASCAR lunch tomorrow."

NASCAR was the extant political organization, an informal club that Walter and his protégés had first convened fifteen years earlier to coordinate their initial forays into Washington. The decidedly less high-minded name was an acronym of its closely held mission statement: Never accommodate stupid congressmen and regulators.

"Why me?" I asked.

"Senator Simpson is going to be in. His handler, Clifford White, called today and asked if you could join. The senator has some new thoughts on energy policy."

Simpson was tipped as an early favorite for the Republican presidential nomination. It surprised me that he'd break bread with Walter and his cronies in the current political climate, but a moment's reflection led me to wonder whether it mightn't be a shrewd move. The newspapers would likely be vilifying someone else by the time the election rolled around, and the big money for national campaigns always came from Wall Street.

"Any other guests?" I asked.

"Nikolay Narimanov. White invited him as well."

Narimanov's name was more of an enticement to me than Simpson's. The wealthiest and most successful of the Russian oligarchs who'd risen from the ashes of the Soviet Union, Narimanov had built an energy empire that spanned the globe. I'd been following his companies for years, but I'd never met him.

"That's kind of unusual, isn't it?"

"I'm just the messenger boy. Yes or no?"

Meeting Narimanov wasn't an opportunity to pass up.

"Yes."

"Okay, then."

We sat in silence while Alex drank some more. The clown clock struck the hour overhead, hands spinning rapidly in opposite directions. Alex suddenly lurched toward me, spilling vodka onto the table.

"Tell me," he pleaded, voice thick. "How do you do it?"

"Do what?" I asked, realizing he was about to cry.

"Not despair."

I laid one hand on his as a tear trickled down the side of his face. After Kyle disappeared, I'd had panic attacks, bouts of crushing chest pain that dropped me to my knees and left me gasping for air. It had taken three separate cardiologists to persuade me that there was nothing physically wrong. The severity of the attacks had lessened through time, but I still felt the tightening in my chest when I got overloaded with work or family stuff.

"Everyone despairs. Trust me. What's important is to find a reason to keep going. A job you enjoy, or a girl. A family . . ."

"You had something special. It doesn't work out for everyone that way."

I half closed my eyes, waiting a moment for the emotional pain of the thrust to dissipate. It was true. Claire and I had had something special, with each other and with the kids. Alex was the product of a bitter divorce, one that had left him and his mother estranged from his father and laid the groundwork for his obsession. I took a deep breath and plunged on.

"Sometimes it does, and sometimes it doesn't. But it makes me sick to see you beating yourself up because you think you're letting Walter down. You're his son. You shouldn't have to grovel for his affection."

Alex rubbed his hairline again, nodded without meeting my eye, and threw back the rest of his vodka.

"You're right," he slurred. "I'm his son." He got up, almost overturning the table. "I have to go now."

"Back to the office?" I asked apprehensively.

"No." He flapped one hand at me vaguely. "I have to be somewhere. I'll see you tomorrow."

I trailed a few feet behind as he staggered out the door and flagged a taxi. He fell into the rear seat and slumped sideways as it drove away. Rubbing the back of my neck with one hand, I realized my underarms were damp with sweat. I hadn't known he was drinking this heavily. The barman stared silently as I approached.

"How much do I owe you?"

"He has a tab."

It figured. I dropped a ten on the counter for my beer anyway.

"How often does he get like that?"

The barman shrugged, perhaps reluctant to talk about a valued customer.

"Maybe you should consider cutting him off."

"Maybe," the barman replied. "But he'd only go someplace else. And I'm not the one making him unhappy. You ever think about that?"

4

I headed back to the office, needing to get caught up on e-mail and to prepare some notes for my next day's bulletin. Late afternoon is a productive time for me, the sole quietus in the global trading day. New York is done by four, the Asians don't get going until eight, and Sydney and Melbourne—the only open financial centers—are too small to generate much activity. Absent the blinking phone lines and beeping market data screens and the constant background cacophony of rage and glee from the trading floor, I can concentrate.

An hour later, I threw my pen onto my desk and gave up. Alex was on my mind, but more than that, the images I'd seen earlier were haunting me. Hundreds dead, and every one of them somebody's child. A voice in my head noted bitterly that at least these families knew what had happened to their loved ones and could grieve accordingly. It was a hateful, self-pitying thought, and I did my best to push it away as I packed my briefcase. I wanted to be home with Claire and Kate.

It was dark and cold out, but the sky had cleared. Cobra kept a line of Town Cars waiting from five to midnight despite the straitened economy, and Walter—ever gracious when it came to small things—allowed me free use. I stepped into the lead car and told the driver my address. He handed me a copy of the afternoon *Post* and then jockeyed his way into the dense traffic. The pipeline explosion dominated the first ten pages of the paper, and I was identified by name as the source of the Nord Stream video in two separate articles. Both mentioned that I'd declined comment. My reticence had been more than a desire to protect

Gavin—I wasn't interested in garnering publicity on the back of a tragedy.

There was a time when I'd thought very differently. Back when I was a Wall Street hotshot, I'd been as calculated in my pursuit of column inches as any scheming politician. Every war, every natural disaster, every refinery fire or tanker accident, was an opportunity for me to elevate my professional profile by pontificating on TV and in the press, explaining what the event meant to the energy industry and speculating as to what might happen next. It shames me to recall that I never took a moment to sympathize with the people afflicted, instead taking pride in my "objectivity." The single great lesson of my adult life—and one I'd give anything not to have learned so well—is that we're all vulnerable.

I set the *Post* aside and shifted restlessly in my seat. As always at this time of year, the avenues were choked with suburbanites intent on seeing the Christmas tree at Rockefeller Center or the animatronic store windows on Fifth Avenue. A surprising number were still driving massive, fuel-guzzling SUVs. Looking out the window at the noxious clouds of automotive exhaust, I found myself wondering what the world would look like in fifty years. It's not just global warming—everyone in the energy business knows there isn't anywhere near enough oil and gas in the world to meet long-term demand under any realistic economic scenario. It's a strangely obvious issue that doesn't get much play, perhaps because the constituencies that might naturally address it are too busy focusing on the quixotic objective of reducing consumption. Energy demand fluctuates with global GDP, but in the long run, no number of power-efficient fluorescent bulbs are going to offset skyrocketing use from developing nations. Every single available drop of oil and molecule of gas is going to be consumed by somebody, somewhere, unless there's a lower-cost alternative, and the sooner we figure out that alternative, the less painful the inevitable transition is going to be. No matter what happens in the future, though, I strongly doubt there will be anything like a Cadillac Escalade, save perhaps in a museum.

Rashid called as my car entered Central Park. We worked our way through the usual preliminaries and then spent a few fruitless minutes probing each other on Nord Stream. Neither of us had anything more to tell the other.

"What's your interest here, anyway?" I asked. OPEC dealt with oil, not natural gas. And to the extent its members also exported gas, their customer was Asia rather than Europe.

"Nothing specific. A couple of Middle Eastern banks are in the Nord Stream financing syndicate. One lost its European head today. And the senior people in the Kingdom get edgy whenever there's a terrorist event. They like to be kept informed."

The Kingdom was Saudi Arabia, and their concern was easy to understand. Fifteen of the nineteen September 11 hijackers had been Saudis, a fact that made the royal family nervous as hell about political repercussions. The Saudis lived in a bad neighborhood, and they needed America for security.

"Is there any reason to think Saudi nationals were involved?"

"Not that I know of," he said. "I have to answer a call on my other line. Stay in touch."

I slipped my phone back into my jacket pocket, inclined to accept his explanation at face value. Rashid's position with OPEC made him dependent on the goodwill of the more influential member states, which was the primary reason he swapped information with me. It helped him to be in the know about matters of interest to his constituents.

I tipped the driver a five when we finally got to my building, spent a couple of minutes bemoaning the Knicks with the doorman, and then rode the elevator up to my floor. The elevator car is antique mahogany banded by brass, the lower panels scuffed and scratched by generations of strollers and scooters and teenage roughhousing. As always, my eyes were drawn to a ding beneath the operating panel that an excited Kyle had left with a carelessly handled baseball bat when he was eleven. I touched the ding sometimes, when I was alone. The junk mail the super intercepted made me sad, because it reminded me of all the things I'd never get to do with my son—to teach him to shave, or to visit colleges with him, or to slip him a little extra money so he could take a girl to a concert and a nice dinner. But the ding in the elevator made me happy. He'd gotten three hits the morning he made it, and his coach had awarded him the game ball. It had been a great day, one that I liked to remember.

I could hear Claire on the piano as the elevator approached our floor. A violin began playing with the piano as the elevator doors opened, and then a second violin joined, contrapuntal to the first. The performers were likely Claire, Kate—and who? Opening my apartment door, I saw an NYU backpack on the floor and abruptly recalled something Claire had told me a few days ago—that she, Kate, and a college kid from NYU were scheduled to perform together in a holiday recital at Memorial Sloan-Kettering Cancer Center, the hospital where Claire was the volunteer director of the arts program. Hanging up my coat, I headed for the living room.

The black Yamaha baby grand I'd given Claire as a wedding gift had been rolled out of the corner where it usually sat. Claire was on the bench, leaning slightly forward as she played. Her shoulders were pulled back, her torso balanced over her hips and her forearms precisely parallel to the floor. Both the piano and the bench were custom-built; Claire suffered near-constant back pain if she wasn't seated correctly. Facing her were Kate and a tall, skinny Asian boy wearing wire-rimmed glasses. Kate had lost her baby fat as a teen, and her hair had lightened, but she still had Claire's Mediterranean coloring and full features. The combination gave her a slightly exotic look, like a blond Roman. She'd grown as well, towering over her mother and only a few inches shy of my six feet. Despite her height and her slim, womanly figure, she'd seemed a child to me until recently. Something had changed, and it wasn't just that we'd been filling out college applications together—there was a new maturity to her, a poise she hadn't had before.

Claire's head was turned from me, but Kate spotted me and wiggled the pinky finger on her bow hand. The boy smiled politely. I nodded to both of them, loosened my tie, and settled on the couch to listen. They were playing a Bach concerto. Assuming they played straight through, it had about ten minutes to go.

My eyes drifted back to Claire. Hearing her piano from the elevator had reminded me of our early days together. We met at a SoHo gallery opening that a colleague had cajoled me into attending. His girlfriend was the artist. I'd stationed myself next to the small buffet, trying to look like I was waiting for someone, and counted down the minutes until I could leave without offending anyone. A slender, dark-haired woman walked up and scrutinized the food on the table. She had on black jeans, a black T-shirt, and black ballet slippers. It was a downtown ensemble, more austere than I usually found attractive, but her forearms were toned and graceful, and I noticed that she had delicate wrists. She put her hands on her hips and frowned, pale lips drawn down into an exaggerated moue.

"Problem?" I asked, surprising myself by speaking.

"The amaretto cookies are gone."

Most of the amaretto cookies were in my stomach, a casualty of my boredom. I made a hasty attempt to change the subject.

"You come to a lot of openings here?" It came out sounding like a line, and I winced.

"Yes. I know the owner. I watch the gallery for her sometimes." Her gaze flicked down my body and back to my face. I'd arrived straight from work, dressed in a boxy Brooks Brothers suit, duty-free Hermès tie, and scuffed loafers. "Banker, right?"

"Is it that obvious?"

"Pretty much. Plus, Anna's dating a banker," she said, naming my colleague's girlfriend, "and you look like you got roped into attending by a friend of the artist."

"There's a specific look for that?"

"More of a behavior. The biggest clue is hanging around the buffet table alone and eating all the amaretto cookies."

She delivered the line deadpan, and I couldn't tell if she was flirting or genuinely annoyed.

"Busted," I said lightly. "What can I do to make it up to you?"

She folded her arms and tipped her head to one side.

"Are you being polite, or do you really want to know?"

I had the strong sense that she was about to tell me to fuck off back to Wall Street, but I liked her directness and the casual once-over she'd given me, and the way her black jeans rode low on her narrow waist, so I fed her the straight line anyway.

"I really want to know."

"There's a biscotteria on Mott Street that bakes everything fresh."

Mott Street was in Little Italy, only a couple of blocks away. I did a quick check of the room, working hard to keep a stupid grin off my face. The gallery was full, the opening a success.

"Mark Wallace," I said, offering her my hand. "I don't think anyone's going to miss us. We could walk over there now, if you'd like."

"Claire Rossi," she answered, smiling demurely. "Now would be lovely."

I expected the biscotteria to be a bare-bones bakery with a couple of Formica tables and an apron-clad proprietor, but the place she led me to was an immense pastry palace, with marble counters, an espresso machine that looked like a church organ, and tuxedoed waiters who sang opera. All the staff knew her, and we were serenaded twice. It would have been awkward if she hadn't been so clearly enjoying herself.

"I was at Juilliard with the owner's son," she explained, after a small man with a huge mustache sang us the Toreador song from *Carmen*.

"You're a musician?"

"A pianist."

"Is that something you always wanted to do?"

She nodded.

"Why?"

Her eyes narrowed quizzically.

"I mean, was there a pianist you really admired when you were young, or did one of your parents play, or did you have a great teacher, or something like that?"

She smoothed her hair, not making eye contact. I had the sense I'd misstepped, but I didn't know how.

"I'd love it if you played for me sometime," I said, trying to get the conversation back on track.

"For you?" she asked, with a hint of her previous assertiveness.

"As a swap. I'll do something for you."

"What?"

"Whatever you want."

She laughed, and I felt relieved.

"You have any talents?"

"Beyond analyzing financial reports and building spreadsheets?"

"Right. Beyond that. I build my own spreadsheets."

"Guy stuff. Opening jars, hanging shelves, burning breakfast."

"Hmm . . ." She took a pen from her purse and scribbled something on a napkin. She pushed it toward me and stood up. "I'll think about it. I have to go now. Give me a call sometime."

I stayed to finish my coffee, toying with the napkin and wondering how soon I could phone without seeming too eager. Her sudden departure had left me edgy and heated. I called the next morning. We went on a second date, and a third. I was working a hundred hours a week, but sleep soon became less important to me than being with her. I saw her giggly, and tender, and tearful, and passionate. But she never offered to play for me, and—much as I wanted to—I never asked again, convinced she was still thinking about it, for reasons of her own. Her gift on the two-month anniversary of our visit to the biscotteria was a key to the Chelsea ballet studio where she was employed evenings, and the murmured information that she stayed on to practice most nights, after the dancers went home.

I left my office at midnight the next day, catching the E train from the World Trade Center to Twenty-third Street, winding my way north and west through deserted warehouse blocks to a drafty industrial building on the West Side Highway. The sound of her piano echoed down the stairwell like a beacon, and my heart pounded as I climbed toward it. Opening the door to the studio, I saw her on the bench and abruptly understood why she'd been puzzled by my question about becoming a pianist. She played as if transported, hands confident and face rapturous. She'd been born to be a pianist. The joy her music elicited in me was tainted by fear. Her deepest self was rooted in a world that a nonmusician like myself could never fully appreciate. She noticed me at the door, and the piano fell silent as she rose to greet me.

We made love on a blanket on the hardwood floor. After, we sat up against the wall in the dark, the blanket wrapped around us like a cloak. The entire western wall of the studio was glass, and we could see out over the highway and the abandoned piers to the Hudson River beyond. The lights of Hoboken glinted on the turbulent water, and the passing tugs and barges looked like toys. We shared small secrets, whispering for the pleasure of feeling conspiratorial.

"Not so much," I said, when she asked if I'd been lonely as a boy. We were both only children. "I invented a baseball game that I used to play with dice, my team against historical teams or whoever was in town to play the Yankees. I kept box scores and statistics, and was always tinkering with the rules to try to make the probabilities work out like the real game."

"It sounds like you were lonely."

"Maybe," I admitted. "What about you?"

"Pretty much the same. I was always daydreaming. My big fantasy when I was twelve was that I was married to a famous cellist and that we had a child who was a prodigy on the violin. We toured Europe as a family trio, and everywhere we went, people applauded and threw flowers. I had a whole schedule of performances worked out, that I took from a library book about Jenny Lind."

Her recollection crystallized the apprehension that had been weighing on me since I'd opened the studio door—that she'd be happy only with someone who shared her passion and ability. I was afraid to ask what she daydreamed about now.

"Jenny Lind," I repeated, to fill the uncomfortable pause in the conversation. An indistinct memory came back to me. "The Swedish Canary?"

"The Swedish Nightingale." She dug an elbow into my ribs. "One of the greatest sopranos ever. Philistine."

"Sorry," I said, feeling her breast warm against my arm as I warded her off. My desire was rising again. "And what about the kid? Boy prodigy or girl prodigy?"

"I could never decide. If it was a girl, I was afraid she'd be prettier than me. But if it was a boy, I wouldn't have anyone to go to the bathroom with, and the idea of going by myself in a foreign country scared me."

I managed a laugh, screwing up my courage as I nuzzled her neck.

"No one could be prettier than you. But you have a bigger problem now."

"What's that?"

"You're dating a guy who's never played anything except a kazoo."

I held my breath as I waited for her reply. She kissed my face, hands roaming gently.

"Maybe a boy and a girl, then," she sighed. "Both on the violin, so they can practice together. And a husband to applaud and throw flowers."

"And teach them about baseball?" I asked, elated.

She nodded.

"I can do that," I said, pulling her closer. "Nobody throws flowers like me."

An uncomfortable tightness in my chest was just dissipating when the concerto finished. Claire struck a bittersweet Picardy third and then held the major chord with the right pedal as Kate and the boy drew their bows downward in unison, echoing her. I waited for the reverberations to die, took a measured breath, and then stood and clapped enthusiastically. Claire smiled discreetly in my direction before starting to tidy her music, but Kate tucked her violin beneath one arm and bowed low, sweeping her free hand up and out with an operatic flourish. Straightening with a grin, she tapped the boy on his shirtfront with her bow.

"This is Phil," she said. "He goes to NYU." She pointed the bow toward me. "And this is my dad."

Phil winced and rubbed his chest before extending a hand to me, grimacing at Kate in mock reproach. She rolled her eyes and gave him a sidelong smirk that instantly tripped my father alarm. I hadn't really had to deal with boys much yet—Kate wasn't particularly social. I'd quietly been rooting for her to meet someone she liked, concerned that she might be keeping close to home because she thought Claire and I needed her, or because she was afraid of exposing herself to another loss. Shaking Phil's hand, though, I realized I wasn't entirely ready for the reality of a guy in my living room—particularly someone older than her.

"NYU's a great school," I said. "What year are you in?"

"Sophomore," he answered. "Kind of."

"Phil took a year off to travel," Kate explained, "but he'll be a junior next semester because he's been taking a heavy course load and he had a bunch of AP credit."

Which made him nineteen or twenty, two or three years Kate's senior. I let the thought roll around in my head, trying to decide how I felt about it. He seemed like a nice enough kid—no visible tattoos or piercings, a decent violinist, and a hospital volunteer. I was wondering what his father did for a living when it occurred to me that I was getting ahead of myself.

"We're done, right?" Kate asked, addressing her mother.

"Yes," Claire answered. "The only thing you need to work on are the arpeggios in the first ritornello. The transitions could be a little crisper. Otherwise, *bravissimo.*"

"*Bella signora,*" Phil said, kissing his fingers. "*Grazie molto.*"

Kate flashed him another smile and then settled her violin in its case.

"I'm going out for a few minutes," she said casually. "I'll be back in time for dinner."

"Going out where?" Claire asked, looking up from her music with a troubled expression.

"Java Joe. Phil's laptop is acting kind of wonky, so I'm going to take a look at it for him. I think his registry's messed up—maybe a bad cluster on the hard drive or something."

Kate was a self-taught computer whiz who kept herself in pocket money by tending to our neighbors' networks and hardware. And Java Joe was where all the neighborhood teens hung out. Still, there was a breathy undercurrent to her voice as she said Phil's name that made the feeling I had before come back stronger.

"It's a school night," Claire said. "What do you think, Mark?"

Kate flushed, her expression stormy, but she almost never answered her mother back. She looked at me instead. I made a show of checking my watch, frowning to indicate that I shared Claire's concern. One of the first rules of parenting was never to undermine your spouse. But it was a bridge I'd had to cross before. Kate was seventeen. No matter how difficult for Claire, or for me, we had to let her grow up.

"It's six-thirty. I don't think it'll be a problem as long as you're home in time to set the table. Say an hour from now?"

"Mom?" Kate asked.

Claire bit her lip and nodded.

"Take your phone."

"I'll be right back."

The front door banged thirty seconds later, and Claire and I were alone. Walking around the piano, I began folding the music stands.

"You think she likes him?" I asked, when I couldn't bear the silence any longer.

Claire shrugged, eyes fixed on her keyboard.

I tucked the music stands behind a curtain drape and gazed out across the treetops toward the Hudson. A tug was nosing a barge upstream, fighting against the current. Claire's silences frightened me. Half the time I didn't know what touched them off, and I never knew how long they'd last. She'd brighten suddenly, as if emerging from behind a cloud, and we'd have a couple of good days, days that reminded me of what things used to be like. But inevitably the cloud would return.

A movement on the street below caught my attention, and I saw Phil and Kate on the corner. They were standing beneath a streetlamp, in a puddle of light. He touched her arm and said something that made her laugh. She tipped up her face, and he kissed her.

"I'm scared, too," I said, turning to look at Claire. "Every time she leaves the apartment. But Kate's going to be in college next year. It's normal for her to want to be more independent, and to start having relationships."

"And what about us?"

The question surprised me.

"What do you mean?"

Claire shook her head and began playing. A nocturne: Chopin, op. 9, no. 2. It was an old favorite, a piece she used to play in the evenings after we put Kyle and Kate to bed. I'd slump on the couch with a glass of wine, exhausted from work, and travel, and baths, and pajamas, and endless rounds of "Baa Baa Black Sheep." She'd glance up occasionally to smile at me as she played, and I'd remember the offer I'd made her at the biscotteria: whatever she wanted. It had been a good deal for me, and I'd wondered at my luck, right up until the moment when my luck ran out. I turned her words over in my mind as I listened to the familiar music. What about us—after Kate was gone? It was something I worried about. More than anything else, it was Kate who kept the cloud at bay.

I glanced out the window again. Kate and Phil were still embracing. I looked back to my wife. Her shoulders were hunched, the way they got when she was hurting. I felt a pang of guilt, remembering that I'd forgotten to buy flowers. Kate's relationship with Phil was something I'd have to think about later. Right then, I needed to do what I could to ease Claire's pain.

5

I was at the office the next morning, buried in fallout from the previous day, when the intercom buzzed. I'd slept badly and was feeling tired and irritable.

"What's up, Amy?"

"Theresa Roxas calling on your direct."

"Don't know her," I replied testily, assuming she was a journalist. The press had been hounding me nonstop, intent on learning where I'd obtained the Nord Stream video.

"She claims Alex sent you an e-mail introducing her."

"Hang on."

I grabbed my mouse and scrolled through my in-box. I'd received more than a hundred e-mails overnight and had time to get through only about a third of them. Sure enough, there was a note from Alex in the middle of the stack, the subject line THERESA ROXAS. I noticed it had been sent just after three a.m. and hoped he hadn't stayed up all night drinking. Alex stopped by most mornings to say hi, but it was after ten and I hadn't seen him.

"Found it," I said, clicking on the e-mail. "Is Alex in today?"

"I don't know. Would you like me to check?"

I took a moment to read the e-mail before responding: *Theresa Roxas will be contacting you today with some important information.*

It wasn't notably terse by trading-desk standards, and it certainly seemed lucid, but the late hour and indistinct mention of "important information" made me a little suspicious. The energy markets attract all sorts of lunatic conspiracy theorists, and I was constantly getting calls from people anxious to persuade me that international Zionists secretly controlled OPEC, or some similarly paranoid nonsense. I didn't have time to waste on a crazy woman Alex had met in a bar.

"I'll pick up," I said reluctantly. "And yes, please try to get hold of Alex for me. I'd like to speak to him."

"Will do."

I switched to my direct line.

"Ms. Roxas? This is Mark Wallace."

"Theresa," she said, pronouncing it the Spanish way. I could hear voices in the background, as if she was calling from a public place.

"Theresa," I repeated. "Thanks for calling. Alex sent an e-mail saying you have something to tell me."

"Yes. But I don't want to talk on the phone. I'd prefer to meet in person."

I rubbed the bridge of my nose wearily. There aren't that many things you can't talk about on the phone. Maybe she was still at the bar and needed someone to come settle the check.

"Do you mind my asking how you and Alex know each other?"

"We're old friends."

I waited, but it was all she had to say on the subject.

"My schedule's really very difficult right now," I said, doing my best to sound regretful. "Are you sure you can't give me a preview?"

"You're familiar with seismic reprocessing?"

The question caught me off guard. Energy companies had been using seismic studies—effectively, terrestrial sonar—since the early 1930s, to help them find oil and gas. Seismic reprocessing was a more recently developed technique that took advantage of computational advances to reanalyze old data, revealing originally unobtainable detail. It wasn't a subject many people knew about.

"Generally," I admitted cautiously.

"And you're aware that Aramco did extensive seismic work at Ghawar in the 1950s, and again in the 1970s?"

Aramco had been the original name of Saudi Aramco, the Saudi Arabian state oil company. And Ghawar was Saudi's largest oil field— the largest oil field in the world. Now she had my complete attention.

"Yes."

"So, we should meet."

I felt a little dizzy, exhaustion vanquished by excitement. Ghawar's geology was the most fiercely guarded secret in the energy markets, because the Saudis didn't want the market to know how much oil they were capable of producing. Information was power—if prices were low, the Saudis could hint at shortages. If prices were high, they could talk about bringing more capacity on-line. Reprocessed seismic data would go a long way toward shedding light on the truth of their situation, by revealing how much oil they'd started with. I counted to three, willing myself to calm down. The chances that someone I'd never heard of had gotten hold of Saudi secrets and picked me to share them with were slim to none.

"I'm not an engineer," I cautioned, making another stab at drawing her out. Experience had taught me that people tended to talk more freely when they thought you didn't understand them. "If you have technical data, I'll need help interpreting it."

"Interpretation won't be a problem," she said flatly. "Are we getting together or not?"

I realized I wasn't going to learn anything more on the phone. I glanced at my in-box unhappily—another four e-mails had arrived while we'd been speaking. But I couldn't risk missing out on a scoop of this magnitude. I had to hear what she had to say.

"Absolutely. When and where?"

"Now would be good. I'm at Café Centro, in the MetLife Building."

"Fifteen minutes," I said, abandoning any pretense of reserve.

"I'll be seated. The table's in your name."

The line clicked and went dead. I shouted for Amy and then grabbed my keyboard. Better I knew who Theresa was before we spoke. Google returned eight hits for "Theresa Roxas," four of them a MySpace page for a sultry Philippina baton twirler. I tried "Theresa" and "Roxas." A hundred and sixty-five thousand hits, the first half-dozen for a Catholic school in Mexico. I was fuming at Google and trying both of Theresa's names and words to do with the oil industry when Amy finally joined me.

"Sorry," she said. "I've been trying to locate Alex. Lynn hasn't heard from him, and he isn't answering his cell. I just left a voice mail asking him to call you."

Lynn was Alex's assistant and also Amy's neighbor in Brooklyn. They were members of the same church.

"Try his home, please," I said, pointing toward my phone. "Speed-dial seventeen."

"The machine," Amy announced a few seconds later. "You want me to leave another message?"

I nodded unhappily and shoved the keyboard away, frustrated by my inability to learn anything useful. Rising, I put on my suit coat.

"I'm going to go meet this Roxas woman," I said, as Amy settled the receiver back onto its cradle. "Keep trying Alex's home and cell. I'd like to talk to him as soon as possible."

"I will. And don't forget you have lunch at the Palace hotel with Senator Simpson."

"Shit." I had forgotten. My day had been a mess before I heard from Theresa, and it seemed it was only going to get worse. I shook my head, tempted to swear again, and noticed Amy frowning.

"Sorry. I've got a lot on my mind."

Amy dropped her eyes to my shirtfront and reached out to straighten my tie.

"I could call the super at Alex's building and have him go up and knock on the door. Maybe Alex isn't hearing his phone for some reason."

It was delicately put, but I knew her well enough to read between the lines.

"You mean because he's home sleeping off a drunk?" I asked quietly.

Amy nodded.

"Lynn came and spoke to me. She's worried. She thinks it's time for someone to have a word with his father."

I sighed, imagining what a conversation with Walter on the subject would be like.

"Are people talking about it on the trading floor?"

"Not yet," she said, eyes still lowered. Amy was as uncomfortable with gossip as she was with swearing.

"I feel like a jerk. I should've spotted it sooner."

"Don't be so hard on yourself," Amy said, sounding a little abashed by her own forwardness. "It's only gotten bad recently. And you can't always be looking out for other people's problems."

" 'Therefore do not worry about tomorrow,' " I recited, " 'for tomorrow will worry about itself. Each day has enough trouble of its own.' "

"Matthew six," she said, looking surprised and delighted. "Amen."

It was a verse I'd learned in family therapy. The only way I knew not to worry about tomorrow was to abdicate responsibility for my life, or to stop caring about the people I loved. Neither seemed like a good idea. I liked Amy, though, and—regardless of what Matthew had to say on the subject—I knew she worried about me.

"Amen," I repeated.

6

Café Centro is a big place, with intricately patterned stone floors and multiple dining areas separated by rows of brown leather banquettes and gleaming glass panels. Located right next door to Grand Central Terminal, it's always busy. I gave the maître d' my name, and he led me on a serpentine course toward a table in the far corner. A woman who looked to be in her early thirties was sitting alone, reading the *Financial Times*. She had on a crisp white blouse, a tight black skirt, and smoke-colored nylons. Her hair was done up in an elaborate French twist—a term I knew only because I'd helped Kate attempt one once—and she had a turquoise leather portfolio leaning against her chair leg. Delicate half-glasses perched on the tip of her nose. The overall effect was of a Latin Audrey Hepburn playing a Wharton business school grad. Every guy in the place was surreptitiously checking her out. She set down her paper as I approached and offered me her hand.

"Theresa Roxas."

"Mark Wallace," I answered, feeling slightly dazzled. Up close, she looked even better.

She lifted a small silver pot to fill two cups with steaming coffee as I sat down, and then nudged one toward me.

"Congratulations on the Nord Stream story. Your name's in all the papers."

"Thanks."

She lifted her cup to her lips and blew on it lightly, eyes fixed on my face. I had the sense she was waiting for me to elaborate, and wondered if my first instinct had been correct. Maybe she was a journalist, and everything she'd told me had been a calculated ruse to draw me out.

"I'm sorry to seem brusque," I said, "but if you've been reading about me in the paper, you must realize that I'm unbelievably busy right now. So, if you have information for me, I'd really appreciate getting to it."

She held my gaze for another long moment, sipping from her cup. Setting the coffee down, she bent and retrieved her portfolio from the floor. One of the side pockets contained a clunky white iPod without headphones. She took it out and put it on the table in front of me.

"There's no backup copy of this data," she said. "You need to be careful."

I lifted the iPod and turned it over, seeing a fun-house version of myself reflected on the silvered back. Flipping it faceup again, I tentatively pressed the central button on the front. I wasn't even aware you could put data on an iPod—I thought they were only for music.

"You need to connect it to a computer."

"Right." I dropped the iPod into my pocket, hoping I wasn't blushing. "I have a couple of questions, if you don't mind."

"Such as?"

I hesitated, unsure where to begin. Everything about our encounter felt wrong. The vast majority of unsolicited tips I'd collected in my career had been from drunk guys bragging about their importance or from disgruntled staff looking to nail their employers. Outside of the movies, beautiful women didn't disclose confidential information in fancy restaurants.

"I'm still interested in knowing how you and Alex are acquainted."

"I lived in New York briefly when I first got out of college. I was taking graduate classes at Columbia. Alex and I met at a party and became friends."

Her tone was cool, but I got the sense she was suggesting they'd been more than just friends. It was possible. Alex had been a very different person ten years ago, and the Buddy Holly look had been surprisingly effective with the ladies. He always seemed to have a good-looking girl hanging around back then.

"Graduate classes in what?"

"Operations research."

She'd surprised me again. OR was a complex branch of math that dealt with decision making, usually the exclusive purview of the pocket-protector set. Based on her appearance, I would have pegged Theresa as a French lit major.

"Is that your field?"

"No. I took an MS in petroleum engineering from Texas Tech and then went to work for Halliburton. They sent me to Columbia for six months to brush up my analytic skills."

"Which would make you an expert in reprocessed seismic analysis."

She shrugged. It was an impressive résumé, if it was true. Alex could presumably vouch for her later, but I figured there was no harm in a quick test.

"Maybe you can help me out. I've had to skim through a number of seismic studies, and I've never been completely clear on the difference between pre-stack time migration and depth migration."

"Because you're not an engineer."

It was my turn to shrug. Not being an engineer didn't mean I hadn't picked up a few things.

She shook her head, looking put-upon, and took a sip from her cup.

"It's a question of the vertical axis and the traveltime approximation. Any assumption of rays within a vertical plane qualifies as time migration. Is that good enough for you, or would you like me to elaborate?"

Any elaboration would be beyond me. Her qualifications didn't have a direct bearing on the information she'd given me, but I felt my pulse quicken. Every true thing she said made her more credible.

"That's perfect, thanks." I topped off both our cups and then tapped the iPod through my jacket pocket. "So, what am I going to find on this?"

"Reprocessed seismic, daily and life-to-date production figures by well, bottom-hole and wellhead pressures from drill date to present, saltwater injection volumes, current and historical produced mixture percentages, well rotation schedules, onsite GOSP capabilities, and some other stuff."

"For Ghawar?" I asked, stunned.

"For every oil field in Saudi Arabia. I gather you were only playing dumb when you said you didn't know how to analyze this stuff, right? Because the official Saudi depletion estimates are in there, too, but I wouldn't want you to start with them. They're pretty much worthless. It's better if you do your own work."

I was speechless. Any single subset of the data she'd mentioned would dramatically enhance understanding of Saudi production capacity. Collectively, it was the intelligence coup of a lifetime, one that would paint a precise picture of the biggest and most secretive oil economy in the world. It was way, way, *way* too good to be true—and I'd been around long enough to know what that meant.

"And this comes from where?" I demanded.

"An acquaintance. I can't tell you any more than that. Alex said you knew a lot of people in the industry, though. You should be able to confirm enough bits and pieces to get yourself comfortable. You can ask clever questions, like the difference between time migration and depth migration."

The sarcasm was justifiable. And she was right—I knew people. But only one who might be able to confirm this kind of information: Rashid.

"Can you at least tell me how your acquaintance got hold of it?"

"He—we'll say it's a he—was hired to do a consulting project for Saudi Aramco. The project required some poking around in their databases, and he found a back door into their confidential data. An administrative password on a server that had never been changed from the default."

The Saudis must have monster information security, but it was the kind of mistake that was just prosaic enough to be plausible. I had to be careful, though, because I wanted to believe so badly.

"Which brings me to my next question," I said.

"Why you?"

"Why anybody? The Saudis are going to go berserk when this information hits the street, and they can hire the best IT people in the world to help them figure out where it came from. This acquaintance of yours is asking for a world of trouble. Why would he do that?"

"He's covered his tracks." She tapped the *Financial Times* on the table in front of her. "And he reads in the newspaper that you're a guy who knows how to keep his mouth shut. You do know how to keep your mouth shut, don't you? Because let me be very clear—I don't want my name mentioned to any third parties in connection with this information. This is between me and you."

"And Alex," I added, wondering if she actually had an acquaintance or if she'd turned up the information herself.

"And Alex. Speaking of which, I prefer not to give you my contact details. If you need to reach me for any reason, you can go through him."

"So, I gather Theresa Roxas isn't your real name?" I said, realizing why I'd come up empty on Google.

"Does it matter?"

"No. But you didn't answer my question. Why would the guy you know take this kind of chance?"

Theresa—or whatever her name was—picked up her portfolio and her newspaper and stood.

"Take a look at the data," she said. "I think you'll understand."

7

I could tell there was something going on in the market as soon as I stepped out of my office elevator. The din of the trading floor rises and falls in pitch with the level of tension, like the sound of the wind in the rigging of a ship. There wasn't enough urgency for whatever storm was looming to have hit yet, but the clipped expectancy in the voices suggested that everyone was fixed on the horizon. I turned toward the noise automatically and then reversed myself. The iPod was burning a hole in my jacket, and I had only an hour before lunch with Senator Simpson. Whatever was happening—or about to happen—in the market would have to wait.

Amy hung up the phone as I approached, looking harried.

"Did Alex call you?"

"No. Did you speak to him?"

"No. But he sent Lynn a text confirming that he'd be at lunch."

I pulled my phone from my jacket pocket and checked it, thinking maybe he'd contacted me directly. Another two dozen e-mails and a single text, but from Kate, not Alex: *library freezing chaucer boring buy me sushi and hot green tea?*

Kate had been spending a few hours a week at the main midtown library, on Forty-second and Fifth, working on her senior English project.

"Nothing yet," I said, simultaneously thumb-typing *sorry can't today stay warm love xox* to Kate. "Is there some kind of news out?"

"The French and the Russians issued a joint statement announcing that they're going to work together to catch the terrorists. Your phone's been ringing off the hook. Everybody wants to know what you think."

It figured. The NATO allies, led by the United States, had issued a communiqué overnight, condemning the Nord Stream attack but urging Russia to exercise restraint. The Russians had responded predictably, suggesting that NATO piss up a rope and pointing out that the United States hadn't exercised restraint when it invaded Afghanistan after 9/11, or when it mustered up a transparently flimsy "coalition of the willing" to take out Saddam. Confronted with an opportunity to knife the United States and suck up to Russia—where French companies were bidding on a number of enormous oil and gas construction projects—the Palais de l'Élysée had also responded predictably. The irritating thing was that Bush had so tainted us internationally that we'd ceded the moral high ground. It hurt not to feel superior to the French.

"All right. I'll read through the news and then try to get something out ASAP. Do me a favor and get in touch with Rashid, please. Tell him I'd like to meet with him in person—tomorrow morning, if possible." I turned toward my door and then spun on my heel. "You don't know how to get data off an iPod, do you?"

"An iPod?" Amy asked, looking confused.

"Yeah." I took it out of my pocket and showed it to her.

"No idea. You want me to call Frick and Frack?"

Frick and Frack were tech support for the floor, a pair of chubby, balding fifty-year-olds with identical ratty ponytails who'd worked for the National Security Agency before joining Cobra. Walter had been a demon on security ever since a guerrilla financial Web site hacked his positions and published them. He'd been short a bunch of illiquid biotechs, and his competitors had squeezed him mercilessly. Frick and Frack—actually Fred Ricker and Frank Ackerman—had been hired shortly after the debacle to implement new security protocols.

"I don't think so," I said. "Theresa" had made me a little paranoid about security myself. I didn't want anyone to see the data she'd given to me until I'd decided when—and whether—to release it. I thought for a moment, trying to figure out who else might be able to help.

"Do me a favor?" I said to Amy.

"What's that?"

"Find a Japanese take-out menu and order in a bunch of tuna rolls and some green tea."

. . .

I'd just finished an e-mail suggesting that my clients buy French oil services companies and short the German and English when Kate showed up. She was wearing blue jeans and a navy peacoat over an ivory Shetland sweater, and her nose was red with cold. I pressed the send key and got to my feet.

"Hey," I said, leaning over my desk to give her a kiss. "You have the cable?"

She pulled a hard plastic clamshell container from her coat pocket and held it out of reach.

"You have my sushi?"

"Amy ordered. It should be here any minute."

"Excellent." She stripped off fleece gloves, lifted a pair of scissors from my desk, and set to work on the package. "This is a seriously high-rent district. I had to pay twenty-nine ninety-five for a stupid piece of wire. That's almost thirty-three bucks with tax."

I took three tens and three singles from my wallet and laid them in front of her.

"So, how do we do this?"

"Simple," she said, setting down the scissors and deftly extracting the cable from the mutilated plastic. "Give me the iPod."

I handed it to her, and she snorted derisively, flipping the unit over to study the microscopic printing on the back.

"Second- or third-generation," she said, fitting one end of the cable to an attachment point on the bottom. "At least five years old. It'll be a miracle if it still functions. The half-life of these things is only about six months, which—surprise, surprise—is about as long as it takes Apple to roll out a new model."

I smiled mechanically as she attached the other end of the cable to a concealed port on the side of my monitor, thinking she seemed a little too bright and sarcastic. Whenever Kate got hyper and sharp-tongued, it meant something was bothering her. Maybe that was why she'd wanted to have lunch with me.

"Hmmm," she said, touching the iPod's face. "It powered up at least. That's good." Pocketing the cash I'd set out for her, she came around the desk and took hold of my mouse, clicking first on the Windows start button and then on the My Computer icon. "Even better," she said, using the pointer to highlight a rectangular gray drive symbol on the screen. "For a second there, I was afraid that we might have to mount it on a Mac. Some early iPods weren't natively compatible with Windows." She double-clicked the drive symbol and an Explorer window opened, revealing dozens of folder icons with cartoon zippers running down their left side.

"So, what've we got?" I asked.

"About nine gig of compressed files," she said, clicking on folders randomly. "Mainly Excel spreadsheets and a handful of PDFs. The best thing would be if I copied everything to your computer and then extracted it. That way you'd have a backup in case the iPod bricks."

I hesitated. My computer was attached to Cobra's network, which meant—what? I was in the business of publishing information, not concealing it. I'd never particularly had to worry about security before.

"Can I get it backed up on CDs instead?"

Kate shook her head.

"Not easily. The files are going to be, like, twelve to fifteen gig when they're inflated, which would be twenty to twenty-five CDs. You could get it on two or three DVDs maybe, but I'm guessing you don't have a dual-layer burner here?"

"Not that I know of."

"You want to move the information around with you, or you're worried about somebody snooping?"

"More snooping," I admitted.

"I could encrypt everything."

"Is that effective?"

"Oh, yeah," she said. "There's a lot of excellent military-grade encryption software out there. You'll have to deal with a really long, random password, but I can write it down for you so you don't have to remember it. Just don't leave it taped to the underside of your keyboard."

"Great," I said, impressed, as always, by her tech know-how. "How long will it take you?"

"Forty-five minutes to an hour maybe, depending on how fast the iPod transfers data. Why? You going somewhere?"

Her voice caught as she asked the question. Something was definitely bothering her. If this Phil guy had hurt her, I was going to kick his skinny ass.

"A lunch I can't get out of, but that's not for half an hour yet. You want to talk?"

She fidgeted with my mouse, dragging files from the iPod to a new folder on my computer. I waited, giving her time.

"I got an e-mail from Sophie Reyes this morning."

I struggled with the shift of context for a second. Sophie was the daughter of an old work acquaintance of Claire's. She and Kate had gone to preschool together, before Sophie and her parents had moved to San Francisco. They still visited New York regularly, though, and the mothers and daughters had lunch together once or twice a year.

"Is everything okay?"

She shook her head, her lower lip quivering.

"What is it?" I asked gently. "What happened?"

Kate cleared her throat and touched a hand to her face. I got to my feet and gathered her into my arms just as the tears began flowing.

"Shh," I whispered. I waited for Kate to calm down a bit and then guided her back to one of the chairs in front of my desk, handing her a box of tissues and sitting down next to her. She blew her nose and dabbed at her eyes.

"I spent the whole morning trying to decide how to tell you," she choked. "I don't want to make things worse."

"Just say whatever you feel like saying. You're not going to make anything worse by telling me. I promise."

She took a deep breath and let it out slowly, damp tissues bunched in her fist.

"Sophie's mother got a new job, as the artistic director of the San Francisco Ballet. Sophie wrote to say how excited she was to learn that Mom was going to audition for the orchestra."

"The ballet's coming to New York on tour?" I asked, confused.

"No. I checked. But their resident pianist is retiring at the end of this season. They're looking for someone new to start in September."

An old joke came to mind for some reason, about a woman who won the lottery and rushed home to tell her husband to pack his bags. "What should I pack? Warm stuff or cold stuff?" he asked excitedly. "Who cares?" the woman replied. "Just get the hell out."

"I don't know what to say," I stammered. "You're telling me that your mother's planning to leave me."

Kate shook her head forcefully, seeming more composed with her secret out.

"No. That's why I was worried about telling you, because I knew you'd jump to the wrong conclusion. I'm betting Sophie's mother asked Mom if she was interested, and Mom said yes without really giving it much thought. It's a good thing, in a way. It means Mom's interested in her career again. You always told me how important her career was to her, when you first met."

Kate was trying to twist the facts, to make the blow less painful. A surge of anger gave way to a feeling of panic. I'd told Claire the truth the previous evening. I was scared, too. And the thing I was most scared of was another loss. Kate or Claire. They were all I had.

"She said yes to an audition for a job in San Francisco, and she hasn't mentioned it to me. That has to mean something."

"But not that she wants to leave you. I think she's scared."

"Of what?"

"Of spending so much time alone in our apartment next year, after I go to college." Kate reached out for my hand. "Everything there reminds her of Kyle. She needs to let go. To really let go. To leave New York and put all the bad associations behind her."

"She told you that?"

"Not in so many words. Sophie's note was what pulled it together for me." Kate squeezed my hand. "You need to talk to her, Dad."

"And say what? That I have a sudden urge to move to San Francisco?"

"Maybe." Kate ventured a smile. "There's less snow."

I disentangled myself gently and stood up, moving to the window.

"What was the line from that eighties flick we watched a few weekends ago? *Buckaroo Banzai*? 'No matter where you go, there you are.' Moving to San Francisco isn't going to change anything."

"It might if you let it."

I stared down at the street below, my chest aching.

"I'm not the one stuck in the past, Kate."

"For Christ's sake, Dad," she shouted. "Are you fucking kidding me? You treat Mom like an invalid, you have this conspiracy with the doorman to hide Kyle's mail, and every time we ride up or down the elevator, you moon about the dent in the paneling. It's not just the apartment she needs to get away from."

Turning, I saw Kate was leaning across my desk, her cheeks blazing.

"So, you think she should leave me?" I asked, overwhelmed at this onslaught.

"No. Don't you get it? It's not you she needs to get away from. It's your never-ending obsession with what happened to Kyle."

I felt like my chest was going to burst.

"How can I not be obsessed? I'm the one who flew off that night to give some stupid, goddamned speech. I should've been there. . . ."

"That's right. You should have been there. And if you were, you probably would have walked to the video store with Kyle, and nothing bad ever would have happened. But don't forget that I was the one who wanted to watch the movie, and Yolanda was the one who taped over it, and Mom was the one who let Kyle go out by himself, and Kyle was the one who insisted on running the errand. It was everybody's fault. We're all guilty, and we all have to get over it."

I turned back to the window, trying to calm myself.

"None of us are ever going to forget what happened," Kate continued softly. "That's a given. But if you can't at least try to put the past behind you—to move beyond your guilt and help Mom move beyond hers—then I think you're right. I think Mom's going to leave you."

8

I was running late by the time I finally left for lunch, Kate's words ringing in my ears. Walking north on Park Avenue, I pressed the heel of one hand hard against my breastbone, fighting the pain the way a runner fights a cramp. There was another mantra I'd picked up in family therapy—you can do only as much as you can do. I'd always interpreted it to mean that I couldn't completely protect my loved ones, no matter how hard I tried. For the first time ever, it occurred to me that maybe the limitation was within myself, and that the thing I couldn't do was to ease my wife's pain by letting go of my missing child.

An Asian girl who looked to be about Kate's age approached me on the corner of Forty-seventh Street, offering me a leaflet about Tibet and asking politely if I'd be willing to send an e-mail to my congressperson. She looked apologetic when I met her eye, perhaps recognizing how upset I was, but I made an effort to smile and took the leaflet from her hand. I know how difficult it is to be ignored when you're trying to attract attention to an issue that's desperately important to you.

In the immediate aftermath of Kyle's disappearance, I'd spent feverish hours devouring books and articles about missing children, trying to learn everything I could about who took them, and what happened to them, and—most important—how they were found. There's an entire fraught literature on the subject, and innumerable sad organizations and support groups. The cardinal rule is to publicize the disappearance as widely as possible and to reach out to the community for help. The police had hung posters throughout our neighborhood, appealing for information, and the local news led with the story the morning after Kyle's disappearance, following up with smaller stories and articles in the paper over the next couple of days. But bad things happen all the time in a city the size of New York. A few media cycles later and Kyle was lost in the clutter. I bought a series of prohibitively expensive ads in the *Times* and the *Post* and the *Daily News,* desperate to keep my son's face in front of as many people as possible. Riding the subway home from One Police Plaza on day seven, though, I noticed that only a handful of riders were reading newspapers, and that at least a third of those were papers in languages other than English. It occurred to me that there were millions of people only a short train ride away who would never have any idea what my son looked like—or even that he was missing—regardless of how many quarter-page ads I purchased.

The next morning, I had the employment office at Columbia University post a notice offering top dollar to students with language skills who were willing to hang posters and hand out leaflets. I hired twenty-five teams of two, insisting that the students work in pairs for safety. Most of the kids tried to refuse the money when I explained what I wanted, but I made them take it. It was only fair. We produced dual-language versions of the police posters in Spanish, Cantonese, Russian, Korean, Bengali, Arabic, Urdu, Portuguese, and half a dozen other languages, and then they—and I—hit the subways, guided by an ethnological map of the city that I'd found online.

Claire and Kate and I were already in family therapy. I talked about my work with the Columbia students—about how much better it made me feel to be actively doing something, and to be meeting strangers every day who cried for our loss and promised to do whatever they could on our behalf. Claire was in bad shape at the time, cycling between uncontrollable weeping and prolonged periods of near catatonia. Kate spoke up, saying she wanted to come with me. I was hesitant because she was so young, but the therapist sided with her, pointing out that she felt the same need to do something for Kyle that I did, regardless of her age. I started taking her with me on short jaunts after school, and then on slightly longer trips on weekend mornings. Pretty soon I was taking her with me as often as I could.

There was a garbage can on the corner of Forty-eighth and Park a hundred yards beyond the Asian girl. I glanced in out of habit and saw a mound of crumpled leaflets. It didn't surprise me. Ninety percent of the leaflets I'd handed out had ended up in the nearest garbage can as well. I knew, because I used to check. It made me despair sometimes. But when you really care about something, it's impossible not to do whatever you can, if only to keep your own sense of hope alive. I folded her handout and put it my pocket. An e-mail wasn't much to ask.

The Columbia kids fell away as summer approached. I didn't blame them. We'd already hit every neighborhood in the city twice. Kate and I kept going. The leafleting had become an act of solidarity, with each other and with Kyle. We ranged increasingly far afield, hanging posters and distributing handbills throughout Westchester, Connecticut, and New Jersey. We even went to Boston and Washington. We talked in the car on our travels—about serious things and not-serious things. And when we weren't talking, we listened to audiobooks, and we followed the New York sports teams on the radio, and we worked on crossword puzzles, Kate reading the clues aloud. The time together was a gift, the only thing that kept me sane.

Eighteen months passed somehow. Alex took me to lunch, learned I was verging on money difficulties, and arranged for Walter to offer me work. Shortly thereafter, Yolanda—who'd been acting as the other functioning adult in our household—announced that she had to move home to the Dominican Republic to care for her sister. I'd been able to balance the time spent leafleting and the time with Claire, but the new job made it difficult. I curtailed the leafleting but refused to give up entirely. Giving up meant acceptance. Claire had begun volunteering at Sloan-Kettering, and Kate and I used the time when she was at the hospital to resume canvassing locally. And then Kate began making excuses not to accompany me, and I realized one day that she'd had enough. It was understandable. She was thirteen, with interests of her own. My choices were to continue alone, spending less time with Claire and Kate, or to stop. I stopped. It was one of the hardest decisions I ever made. Stopping felt like a breach of faith and deepened my sense of shame.

A liveried doorman greeted me as I entered the Palace hotel. There was a round red sofa in the center of the ornate lobby, and I sat down to rest for a moment before heading toward the dining room. I abandoned the leafleting because it had been the right thing for the family I had left. It was time to abandon my denials as well. I'd put a halt to Kyle's mail, and give up my vigil at the office window, and move to San Francisco, if Claire wanted me to go with her. And I'd hide my shame. I closed my eyes, trying to steady my breathing. My son was dead. Claire and Kate were alive. I had to be strong for them.

9

I checked in for lunch with a somber plainclothes security agent who examined my ID carefully before finally admitting me to the private room where Senator Simpson was scheduled to hold forth. It was a long, narrow, high-ceilinged chamber, paneled in dark mahogany and illuminated by lead crystal chandeliers—an old New York setting, like something from an Edith Wharton novel. A number of the people already seated around the enormous oval table in the middle glanced toward me as I entered. Apart from the room, the only thing reminiscent of a turn-of-the-century power lunch was the fact that everyone was male. Other than that, the attendees were too young, too casually dressed, and too ethnically diverse. It was a typical hedge-fund group, hyperkinetic forty-year-olds in blue blazers and open collared shirts, wearing ten-thousand-dollar watches and compulsively checking BlackBerrys held in their laps. The crowd was a fair bit smaller than it had been at my last lunch with this group. The survivors looked aged but unbowed.

I nodded to the room and then spied Alex. He was sitting at the far end of the room, an empty chair to his left. I sat down next to him just as Walter rose to his feet and began tapping a glass with his butter knife. Walter, as always, was impeccably turned out in a pin-striped Savile Row suit and a discreet club tie.

"You okay?" I whispered to Alex.

He touched a finger to his lips and pointed toward his father, not making eye contact. He reeked of stale alcohol. I made an effort to set aside my problems with Claire and focus on Alex.

"I met with your friend Theresa this morning. We need to talk."

Walter tapped his glass more loudly, frowning in my direction. "If I could have your attention, please," he said. "And if the serving staff would leave now."

I settled back in my chair impatiently as half a dozen tuxedoed waiters finished straightening cutlery and scurried for the exits. Food was already on the table—a cold seafood salad for most, special dietary options for a few. The kosher meals came on disposable plates and were elaborately wrapped in plastic, like bouquets from an expensive florist.

"Gentlemen," Walter said. "We have a number of guests today, none of whom require any elaborate introduction. Seated next to my son, our late arrival, Mr. Mark Wallace."

I gave a small wave, figuring his only purpose in mentioning my name was to reproach me for being tardy. Walter was obsessively punctual. A few people clapped and gave me a thumbs-up for the Nord Stream scoop.

"On my left, Mr. Nikolay Narimanov."

A frisson of interest crackled through the room, even the most determinedly blasé of the hedge-fund managers looking up from their BlackBerrys. Narimanov, a powerfully built man in his late fifties, attired simply in a black turtleneck and an expensive-looking leather jacket, was an oddity in this group—a nonfinancial guy who was every bit as wealthy and successful as his lunch companions but who'd made his money in the real world, like the proto-industrialists who'd dominated the American economy back when Wharton had written her novels. I'd wanted to meet him for ages. He sat motionless, enduring the scrutiny of the room impassively.

"Second to my right," Walter continued, "the former assistant secretary of commerce, Mr. Clifford White."

You could almost feel the temperature drop. White—Senator Simpson's campaign manager—was a lawyer and a political fixer, exactly the kind of backroom Washington hack the hedge-fund types normally despised. His one brush with notoriety had occurred during his Poppy Bush–era confirmation hearing, when a Democratic member of the Banking Committee acidly inquired of the chairman precisely how many rocks the majority party had been forced to turn over before they'd found him. The ensuing ruckus had briefly made White a minor-league Republican cause célèbre, a Bork light. White smiled tightly.

"And finally, to my immediate right, our guest of honor today, Senator Joseph Simpson."

The senator tipped his head to acknowledge a smattering of grudging applause. Most Wall Street conservatives are actually Libertarians, which means they loathe the Christian Coalition crap that Simpson and all the other Republican candidates feel compelled to pay lip service to. Pragmatic to the core, though, the conservative fund managers present knew that a candidate like Simpson—a Reagan-like proponent of free markets and minimal taxes—was probably the best they could hope to elect, regardless of his hectoring family-values cant. The applause terminated abruptly as White, not Simpson, rose to his feet.

"A point of order before the senator speaks," White began. Someone to my left coughed the word "dickhead" loud enough to draw a reproving look from Walter. A handful of people laughed. White cleared his throat irritably.

"Senator Simpson would like to consider this a working session. To that end, he intends to explore certain policy positions that he hasn't yet publicly advocated, and he is dependent on your discretion. . . ."

Yada yada yada. Senator Simpson was about to kiss the asses of the guys who could raise the really big bucks for him, and he wanted them to know he was secretly more their ally than he could ever say in public. I could sense the antagonism in the room building. White was trying to bullshit a room full of guys whose primary skill in life was to see things as they were and to act accordingly. Glancing away from White, I caught Narimanov looking in my direction. He nodded slightly, and I nodded back, wondering if he knew who I was. One funny aspect of my profession is that you often don't know the people who are most familiar with your work. In the old days, when I had a broader distribution, I was always meeting people who greeted me as if I were a close acquaintance, and who were eager to resume intellectual arguments I hadn't realized I'd participated in. Jarring as it could occasionally be, it was an effective icebreaker. It would be helpful if Narimanov turned out to be a closet fan. Like everyone else in my line of work, I was weak on Russia and really needed a top-level source.

"And now," White said, making an ill-judged attempt at a ring announcer's cadence, "the esteemed senior senator from the great state of Wyoming and, God willing, the next president of these blessed United States, Senator Joe Simpson."

White turned to Simpson and began clapping enthusiastically. His applause echoed in the otherwise silent room, and he trailed off after a moment, sitting down, red-faced. You had to wonder about a guy so utterly unable to read his audience, although I gathered White wasn't unique. I'd heard brutal stories about these lunches over the years—pretense, hypocrisy, and obfuscation were chum in the water, and more than one overly slick or mealymouthed candidate had been savaged.

Simpson rose leisurely and surveyed the hostile faces around the table. A tall man with a weathered, cigarette-cowboy look to him, he was frequently photographed in a string tie with a turquoise clasp and tended to poll well with female voters despite his conservative politics. I had a sudden conviction that things were about to get really ugly.

"Has it occurred to you," he asked, smiling easily, "that I might not like you, either?"

He paused, the deathly silence that White's introduction had generated gradually giving way to a ripple of appreciative laughter. Much to my surprise, he'd said exactly the right thing. Straight talk was red meat to this crowd.

"My father was a rancher," he continued, a barely perceptible down-home twang to his words, "and the only time I ever bumped into financial folk as a kid was when the local bank manager would come around and inquire after our 'delinquent payments.' I learned a lot of words listening to that banker—words like 'delinquent,' and 'arrears,' and 'foreclosure.' It was quite the education."

He paused again, and I took a quick look around. Everyone present was leaning forward and paying attention. Maybe the entire purpose of White's introduction had been to make Simpson seem sincere by contrast. Either way, there was no doubt that the senator had a knack for connecting with people.

"I wanted to continue that education, so I went off to college and then to law school. And my ultimate objective was to get myself to Washington, where I could persuade the government to work harder for honest folk like my father, and like the neighbors I'd grown up with. So, after I graduated, I took a job with the Bureau of Land Management in the U.S. Department of the Interior, one of thirty fresh-minted lawyers they hired that year alone. And I thought I had all the answers. I had a whole bunch of New Deal ideas about programs the government should institute—about things the government should *mandate* for rural America's benefit. But much to my surprise, the day I started work at the BLM was the day my real education began. And what I learned was that everything the government touched became corrupt and bloated and snarled in red tape. I observed it time and again, firsthand, in every conceivable kind of circumstance, and I struggled mightily to integrate what I was seeing with my youthful big-government leanings. And then one day, like Paul on the road to Damascus, I saw the light. I came to realize that, as our esteemed president Ronald Reagan used to say, the nine most terrifying words in the English language are: 'We're from the government, and we're here to help.'"

He was in a groove now, having segued seamlessly into what sounded like a pretty standard stump speech. He held forth on the evils of big government for a few minutes, mainly battering the Democrats and the decisions of our current president but also careful to disavow Republican follies, such as the infamous Alaskan Bridge to Nowhere. Realizing perhaps that his audience had a limited attention span, he wisely circled back to his starting point just as the energy started to leave the room and eyes began drifting back to BlackBerrys.

"So, it seems an irony that I'm a politician, the very thing I profess to dislike, and the very thing all of you so clearly despise. But let me tell you something I learned as a boy back home on the range—there's a delicate balance in nature, and everything and everyone has a role to play. Coyotes are pests, but they keep down other pests, like rats and mice and rabbits. Financiers can be predatory, but they're an instrument of market discipline, and they're necessary if we're going to get our economy going again. And politicians—well, maybe we can talk the truth sometimes, and tell people that more isn't always better, that wishes are never fishes, and that strength and dignity are possible only when people accept responsibility for their own lives."

There was some spontaneous applause despite the fact that he'd just compared his audience to animal pests, and it occurred to me that I might actually be listening to the future president.

"Let me turn now to the reason I'm actually here today, which is to share some thoughts on the economy. I recognize that you all probably know more about this subject than I do, so I'm going to work my way though some introductory material quickly and then get straight to my point."

I listened carefully as Simpson sped through a coherent overview of our current precarious economic situation. He had his facts and figures correct, which gave him a leg up on most politicians.

"What, then," he concluded, "is the greatest long-term threat to our collective hope of rebuilding American prosperity for the generations to come? The Democrats are focused on a declining manufacturing base, the export of middle-class jobs, and rising income inequality. All important issues, I admit, although I differ on the appropriate policy response. But, ultimately, all trees in the forest. Where does America's greatest *strategic* vulnerability lie? What is it that's the actual lifeblood of our economy?"

"Energy," I said, abruptly understanding why I'd been invited to lunch.

"Thank you, Mr. Wallace," Simpson said, nodding in my direction. "That's exactly right. Energy. The *only* production input that drives every single sector of our economy. The *only* input that drives every single sector of the *global* economy. We Americans currently import more than a third of the energy we consume. And rising demand for that same energy from countries like China and India means not only that energy prices will spiral ever higher in the future but also that the countries possessing that energy will increasingly have the luxury of deciding precisely who they're willing to sell to—and who they aren't."

I glanced at Narimanov, who had his eyes half shut. Simpson seemed to be working toward a variant of the argument that had been advanced against the Nord Stream pipeline—that energy dependence gives energy exporters too much political sway. I wondered again why Narimanov was here, and where Simpson was actually headed.

"Slow down a minute," one of Walter's more cantankerous protégés interrupted. "You're not suggesting an Apollo program or a Manhattan Project to make us energy independent, are you? Because we can vote for Al Gore if we want that. Jack taxes even higher, keep domestic growth in the toilet, and all walk to work in the snow while a bunch of Poindexters at some government base in Florida or New Mexico flush trillions down the toilet on solar bicycles."

I'd half warmed to Simpson, and hoped he'd point out that both the Apollo program and the Manhattan Project had been resounding successes.

"Never," Simpson said vehemently, disappointing me. "I've already told you my view of government-sponsored initiatives. The markets will cope just fine if oil and gas prices increase smoothly through time. But *only* if the markets are given a chance to work freely. And therein lies the critical rub—of the top fifteen energy-exporting countries in the world, exactly two treat hydrocarbons as a free-market good. The other thirteen—a group that includes Iran, Venezuela, Angola, and Nigeria—have all demonstrated their willingness to use their energy resources as a political weapon. So I ask you gentlemen: What happens when one or more of these countries attacks our economy by not selling us their energy? Or, more important, how should we position ourselves in anticipation?"

Three or four people tried to answer simultaneously, their replies uniformly skeptical in tone. Walter rapped his glass with the butter knife again, hard, and everyone fell silent.

"A little more decorum, please, gentlemen," he commanded sharply. "I'd like to hear from Mark first." He turned to face me. "How about it? Do you buy the senator's scenario?"

"Personally," I said, leaning forward, "as an American and a father, my biggest economic fear for the next generation is runaway inflation on the back of unsustainable deficits and bankrupt entitlement programs." My remark drew murmurs of approval. Inflation is to financiers as garlic is to vampires, and books about the Weimar Republic had become de rigueur reading in the hedge-fund community. "Still, the senator raises an interesting point. We're not really vulnerable in the sense he suggests until global demand for oil and gas has met or outstripped supply, but it's only a matter of time until that happens. . . ."

"Bullshit," someone said, repeating the coughing trick. It was an audience that turned on a dime and never cut anyone any slack, but I had too much experience with them to be intimidated by heckling.

"Bullshit yourself," I shot back. "There's only so much oil and gas in the world. It's going to happen."

"When?" Narimanov asked. There was a rustling around the table as people turned to look at him again.

"Hard to say," I replied carefully, wondering why he'd asked the question. His company did business in dozens of different energy markets around the globe. If anything, he could probably answer the question better than I could. "Short-term, demand fluctuates with the economy, giving us the boom-and-bust cycles that make cities like Houston go broke every ten to fifteen years. Longer-term, though, demand tends to increase at something slightly greater than the population rate, which is pretty much reflective of ongoing development in the Third World. The great unknown is supply."

"Worst case," Walter prompted.

"Worst case . . ." I began. I fell silent mid-sentence, struck dumb by a sudden appreciation of an enormously unlikely coincidence. The real answer to the question lay in the supposedly unknowable Saudi data that Theresa claimed to have given me that very morning. My brain raced as I struggled to understand what the coincidence might mean. Something fishy was going on, and I didn't like it at all. Alex rapped me on the leg beneath the table as Walter frowned.

"Worst case is that we've already passed global peak oil production," I managed, regurgitating an analysis I'd expounded a hundred times before. "The Saudis claim to be able to produce another three to four million barrels a day, which represents most of the excess capacity in the world. But no one really knows, because they won't share their production data." I ran a hand through my hair, trying to stay focused. "There's a school of thought that holds the Saudis are lying—to us, and maybe to themselves—and that global oil production is set to turn sharply lower in the near future. Anyone interested in the technical argument should read up on Hubbert peak theory. There's a lot of literature."

A number of people were taking notes on their BlackBerrys, and I paused to let them catch up, stealing a glance at Alex. He was staring down at his untouched lunch and chewing a cuticle intently. My gut told me I'd been right to suspect Theresa. She'd lied to me. About how she'd got the data, or about why she'd given it to me, or about whether it was genuine. The timing of our meeting was too great a coincidence not to have something to do with this lunch. Maybe she was secretly trying to further Simpson's candidacy, or maybe she was trying to torpedo him. Either way, I was betting that Alex knew something was wrong. It was why he'd been avoiding me. It hurt to think he might have tried to mislead me.

"If the Hubbert theorists are correct," I continued, "then Senator Simpson's right to think that we're looking at trouble. It's going to take the United States twenty years—minimum—to transition away from our current energy paradigm, and our economy will be enormously vulnerable in the event of any shortage."

"Relax," the guy who'd coughed "bullshit" earlier interjected. "Energy's a commodity. If we buy less from Nigeria, we buy more from Mexico. It's just a matter of price."

"Two observations," I snapped, annoyed by his ignorant condescension. "First, there are lots of different types of crude oil, and our refining infrastructure is geared to a very particular mix. It's not that easy to replace Nigerian sweet with Mexican sour. Second, you have to remember that we're talking about government sellers, and governments aren't just interested in money. They're also interested in things like weapons, technology, and political influence. China did a big-guns-for-oil deal with Saudi in 2006. And we've already seen an example of exporters clubbing together for political purposes, in 1973, when the Arab nations boycotted the United States and other Western countries because we supported Israel in the Yom Kippur War. Back then, though, the Arabs didn't have anywhere else to sell their oil. Things might have turned out a lot worse if China and India had been lifting oil throughout, and if yuan and rupees had been flowing into Arab bank accounts."

There was a pregnant pause as everyone present digested my argument, and I half regretted having been so forceful. I shouldn't have let myself be provoked. It was still a low-probability scenario, and I hadn't figured out what Simpson was advocating as a response.

"Okay, then," Walter said, addressing himself to Simpson again. "Assume for the moment that you're right to be concerned. What do you suggest?"

"Let's start by turning back the clock," he answered. "Post–World War II, one of America's biggest strategic imperatives was to secure our oil supply by keeping the Soviet Union out of the Middle East. Six different American presidents saw the need to address the issue. Roosevelt, Truman, Eisenhower, and Carter all affirmed a commitment to military action against the Russians if necessary. Nixon and Reagan extended that policy beyond the Soviet Union, committing us to intervene against any external threat to the region—from China, say, or from India. But as your associate Mr. Wallace has already pointed out, only Nixon faced the kind of problem I'm talking about here today, back when the Arabs boycotted us in 1973. And what was Nixon's response?"

Simpson looked at me expectantly.

"The Emergency Petroleum Allocation Act—" I began.

"EPAA was a tactical measure," Simpson interrupted, "intended to deal with the immediate shortage. What *strategic* action was Nixon contemplating if the boycott hadn't collapsed when it did?"

"An invasion," I answered uneasily. "Schlesinger, Nixon's secretary of defense, told the U.K. ambassador that the United States wasn't willing to abide threats by 'underdeveloped, underpopulated' countries, and that if the embargo didn't end, America would send troops to seize oil fields in Saudi Arabia, Kuwait, and Abu Dhabi. Of course, Nixon was also in the middle of Watergate, and falling down drunk half the time. . . ."

"It was the only option America had at the time," Simpson said dismissively. "And it's the only option we'd have today."

"So, let me see if I understand you," I said, pissed off at having been used as his straight man. "You're planning to run for president on a platform of invading *more* of the Middle East?"

He gave a patronizing laugh.

"Of course not. Three Democratic presidents and three Republican presidents committed America to defending our Middle Eastern energy supply against disruptions external to the region. My policy will build on those precedents to make clear that we'll also intervene against disruptions *internal* to the region. The best war is the one that's never fought. The Arabs would never have dared boycott America in 1973 if they'd known we'd respond militarily."

It was an argument I'd heard before but never from a mainstream politician.

"So, if the Arabs don't want to sell their oil to us, we'll just take it, correct? What exactly do you call that policy?"

"I call it energy security," Simpson riposted silkily. "And I think the time for it is now."

White popped to his feet before I could respond, a greasy smile on his face.

"Questions?" he said.

The room erupted.

10

Walter calmed the crowd with another forceful application of his butter knife, insisting that anyone who wanted to speak raise his hand. White, moderating, proceeded to deliberately ignore me—not that it mattered much. Simpson was mainly ducking the questions, seeming to have said as much as he wanted to say. The tone of the questions reflected a pretty even split in the audience—half sounded as if they thought Simpson was on the right track, and half sounded as if they thought he was a dangerous lunatic. Walter kept quiet, not giving anything away. I knew which camp I was in. America was going to have to transition from oil and gas at some point—far better we begin addressing the issue now and try to avoid the implicit moral hazard. Because no matter what Simpson might argue, American insistence on unfettered access to oil and gas wouldn't just be about busting boycotts. When the supply and demand curves crossed, and genuine energy shortages arose, it would be about maintaining an automobile-oriented lifestyle at the expense of heat, food, and potable water for the developing world. It was a choice I didn't want to have to make.

Alex got up and left the room just before White brought the session to a close, leaving his suit jacket on his chair. I followed a moment later, brushing past the security staff and searching left and right for the men's room, where I assumed I'd find him. I wanted a word in private, to get to the bottom of the Theresa Roxas business. Someone touched my arm from behind, and I turned to find myself face-to-face with Nikolay Narimanov. I'd been so worked up that I'd forgotten about him.

"Mr. Wallace," he said, offering me his hand. "I'm an admirer of your work."

He had a strong grip and an incongruous hint of a Scottish burr.

"Thanks," I said. "Call me Mark, please. I wasn't aware that you read my work. Do you mind my asking who's been forwarding it to you?"

"Friends send me things of interest. I hope that's not a problem."

I was a little taken aback by how good his English was. I'd read that he'd been the Soviet equivalent of a scholarship student—a bright kid from the butt end of nowhere who'd gotten fast-tracked to a top engineering program after he won a regional math competition. My line of work brought me into contact with a lot of foreigners who'd learned English as part of a technical secondary education. They were rarely so fluent, no matter how much exposure they had to the language later in life.

"Not at all," I said. "I only wish I'd known sooner that we had a connection. It might be interesting to talk from time to time."

"Perhaps a word in private now? I have my car. I can give you a lift."

"That'd be great," I said, making a spur-of-the-moment decision to let Alex go for the time being. He couldn't avoid me for long, and the opportunity to get to know Narimanov was too compelling to pass up. "Let me get my coat and briefcase."

He lifted a finger, and a bulky bodyguard I'd mistaken for another of the senator's security staff snapped to attention.

"My associate will retrieve your things. Shall we?"

He led the way out a side entrance, through a courtyard, and to Madison Avenue beyond. Three black SUVs with tinted windows were parked in the shadow of Saint Patrick's Cathedral. The rear window was open in the last car, and I could see two guys sitting backward in the third row of seats with unzipped gym bags in their laps. I wondered if Narimanov carried a diplomatic passport and what kind of strings he'd had to pull to get permission to ride around New York City in a heavily armed motorcade.

Yet another large man opened the rear door of the center car, and we both got in. The interior was crammed with electronics—flat screens, keyboards, and telephones, all professionally mounted and ready to hand.

"Nice," I said, as the door closed. My experience of billionaires was that they liked to have their toys complimented.

"Functional," Narimanov replied offhandedly. "So. Senator Simpson's associate, Mr. White, reached out through a mutual acquaintance to suggest I attend today. Why do you imagine I was invited?"

The pleasantries were over.

"He didn't tell you?"

"I spent a few minutes with Senator Simpson and Mr. White before lunch. The senator told me that he is a great admirer of the Russian people. He wanted to know if I played tennis."

I laughed and then gave the question some thought. Narimanov hadn't been invited because of his money. Simpson was evidently willing to run the risk of cozying up to the hedge-fund community, but no mainstream politician would be dumb enough to take money from a foreign national or a foreign-controlled company.

"You're plugged into the Kremlin," I said tentatively. "Maybe Simpson wants you as a back channel to your government, to give them a window on what he's thinking."

"My conclusion exactly," Narimanov said. "But why?"

It was a tougher question. Russia had become a major energy exporter since the collapse of the Soviet Union, so their only stake in the game was political.

"Pushing his plan will mean trouble with Europe and Asia," I ventured. "They're not going to like the idea of America formally asserting a first call on Middle Eastern oil and gas. Maybe he wants Russian support?"

"Again, my conclusion. In exchange for what?"

"I don't know," I admitted, having exhausted my ingenuity.

"Nor do I."

"You could ask."

"If I wished to be a messenger. It's not always a desirable role."

I took his point. Politics was a means for businesspeople, not an end. The front door opened, and the bulky bodyguard got in the passenger side, handing my coat and briefcase back to me.

"Where to?" Narimanov said.

"Forty-sixth and Park, if it's not out of your way. I could walk as easily."

"It's not a problem."

The bodyguard murmured something into his sleeve, and all three cars pulled away from the curb simultaneously. Narimanov craned his neck to look up at the cathedral as we passed beneath its spires. I took advantage of his distraction to pose a question of my own.

"How do you think your government is going to respond to the Nord Stream attack?"

"Do you know the word *'laldie'*?" he asked, still gazing out the window.

"No. Is it Russian?"

"Scottish. I spent a year on an offshore rig in the Sea of Okhotsk when I was in my twenties, apprenticed to a Glaswegian chief engineer. When a worker reported drunk, he'd give them a *laldie*—a thorough beating with a pipe wrench. It sent a message."

"And you think Russia's getting ready to give someone a *laldie*?" I asked, catching his drift.

"Russia and our new allies, the French. Most definitely."

"The Ukrainians?"

"I'll let you know if I hear."

"Will you?" It never hurt to ask.

"Perhaps," he said seriously, turning away from the window to look at me. "In exchange for your candid opinion of Senator Simpson's proposal."

I knew he was just jerking me around, but I liked the fact that we were talking. Any dialogue was a good start.

"It's a bad idea. We'd only be postponing our problems. And creating categories of haves and have-nots reduces the likelihood of global cooperation on other fronts, which is important if we want to spread the cost of next-generation energy projects or tackle ecological issues. China has a lot of dirty coal they can burn if their backs are to the wall. Not to mention the fact that any genuine energy shortage would be an enormous drag on global growth, which would inevitably hurt our economy anyway. The whole notion is stupid."

"And your suggestion?"

"Big science is something governments have done well. Nuclear, wind, syngas, solar, and fuel cells are all promising. At a minimum, Washington should be making carbon-based energy more expensive, to spur research on alternatives. The real difficulty is that there's no sense of urgency, both because the economy is weak right now and because nobody really knows when the oil and gas are going to run out."

"Agreed," he said crisply. "Your work gives you access to information, as does mine. I suggest we collaborate."

"Collaborate on what?" I asked uncertainly.

"On understanding precisely when the oil and gas are going to run out. I can bring information on Russia, Africa, and certain areas of the Middle East to the table."

It was a fantasy offer, but I had to be straight with him.

"I'd love to collaborate. But we both know that it all comes down to Saudi Arabia."

"The Saudis have employed a number of foreign workers in their oil fields over the years. Syrians, Iraqis, Palestinians, Indians, and others. I've made a point of collecting as much information from these workers as possible. Fragmentary, of course, but voluminous nonetheless. Perhaps you have other fragments?"

The people he'd mentioned were all denizens of countries with strong governmental ties to Russia. It occurred to me to wonder how much of the information he was referencing had flowed to him directly and how much had come through intelligence contacts. Not that it particularly mattered to me who he associated with. Reliable fragments were exactly what I needed to spot-check the information I'd gotten from Alex's friend.

"I do," I said firmly. "Quite a few. And some OPEC contacts who might help me confirm the big picture, if we can put it together."

"We're agreed, then?" he asked gravely.

I felt a flush of professional excitement. Narimanov would be one of the biggest sources I'd ever reeled in, second only to Rashid.

"We are."

He offered his hand again, and I shook it.

11

Narimanov and I parted after hashing out some details and exchanging contact numbers. It was going to take him a few days to assemble his data, which was fine by me. Assuming Alex could explain why Theresa had picked this particular moment in time to seek me out, and persuade me that she was a credible source, I'd likely need at least that much time to make a stab at parsing her information. I wondered if I was right to think Alex hadn't been completely honest about her, and—if so—whether it had anything to do with how upset he'd been the previous day. One possibility was that Walter had leaned on Alex to further whatever agenda he had regarding Senator Simpson. I knew how vulnerable Alex was to Walter's demands, but it still pissed me off to suspect that he might have tried to use me.

I found a sealed envelope in my center desk drawer when I arrived back at my office, and a note from Kate inside. She'd successfully transferred and encrypted the files from the iPod and written down the password for me. I refolded the note and stuck it in my shirt pocket, the professional buzz I'd felt in Narimanov's car fading as I was reminded of my conversation with Kate. I rubbed my forehead with both hands, trying to decide what to do next. Claire was at Sloan-Kettering all afternoon, and would be attending a concert at Carnegie Hall with Kate later that evening. Better I get her by herself somewhere quiet than rush into a conversation when she was distracted. Maybe a night away this coming weekend. There was an inn we'd gone to in Connecticut a few times when the kids were little. And the delay would give me time to figure out what I was going to say to her. Fragments of my talk with Kate ricocheted around my brain. What if Kate was wrong and Claire had a very specific plan mapped out? One that didn't involve me?

My news screen beeped, and I glanced at the flashing headline. A German wire service was reporting that the French and Russians were mobilizing special forces troops. There wasn't any detail, and no one else had reported it. The markets gapped lower on the story and began trading skittishly on light volume. I picked up my phone, tempted to call Narimanov and ask him if he'd heard anything. I tapped the handset against my palm, hesitant. I hated to call as a supplicant. Better I have something of value to share with him first—which brought me right back to the Saudi data. The French and the Russians would have to wait, I decided. There was nothing more important than figuring out exactly what Theresa had really given me.

"I'll be in Alex's office," I told Amy, as I walked by her desk.

"You'll be alone. I heard from Lynn that he called to say he was taking the afternoon off." She lowered her voice meaningfully. "Evidently, he's not feeling well."

I sighed. Nothing shy of a kidney transplant was supposed to keep you out of the office when the market was moving. Holing up with a hangover was an invitation to an ass-kicking from Walter, or worse.

"Try him on his cell again, please."

"Will do. You've been getting a lot of calls. Do you want me to start putting people through?"

The core dilemma of my business was that my clients paid me to be responsive, but the more time I spent talking to them, the less time I had to work, and hence the less I had to say of value.

"No, but let me know if anyone's really insistent and I'll try to get back to them. Were you able to get in touch with Rashid?"

"I just heard back. You're on for breakfast at the Four Seasons Hotel tomorrow morning. His room at eight-thirty."

"Thanks."

I headed back to my desk and sat down again, half wishing I could curl up in the knee space and hide. I had too much going on, and too much to worry about. The best cure for anxiety was to stay busy, I reminded myself. Pulling Kate's note from my pocket, I set to work decrypting the files she'd copied from the iPod. Absent a conversation with Alex, my sole option was to slog through the information as best I could, and to hope like hell I wasn't on a snipe hunt.

Seven hours later, I'd just about managed to assemble the data into an intelligible order. The sheer quantity was overwhelming, let alone the complexity, and a handful of the key technical reports were written in French. Alex hadn't called back. It was lucky that Claire and Kate were out at the concert—it meant I could work through dinner without feeling guilty. Amy had ordered in some pizza for me before she left, and the cold remains were sitting in a box on my credenza.

Theresa had cautioned me not to believe any of the management information, and the raw data were way too granular for me to reach any off-the-cuff conclusions, so my next step was to employ a multivariate model of oil field decline that an acquaintance at the Colorado School of Mines had written a few years back. Loading the model was tricky, painstaking work that involved a number of easy-to-screw-up volume and density conversions. I was copying figures between spreadsheets when my cell phone rang, the caller ID blocked. I ignored it. My office phone flashed a few seconds later, and then the cell phone rang again. I picked up, thinking it might be Alex calling from the bar at Pagliacci.

"Mark Wallace."

"It's Reggie. How you doing?"

"Not bad," I said, taking off my reading glasses and rubbing my eyes. Reggie Kinnard was the NYPD detective who'd been working with us on Kyle's disappearance since day one. He checked in every couple of months to let me know that he'd updated this or that database, but mainly, I suspected, simply to let me know that he hadn't forgotten. We usually had a drink somewhere, or a cup of coffee. I liked him, and was grateful to him for his continued efforts. It mattered to me that he was still trying. "How about you?"

"Hanging in there. Where are you?"

"At the office."

"You didn't answer."

"I'm kind of busy."

"Too busy for a beer?"

"I wish I could. I'm buried."

I heard the sound of a match being lit, suggesting he'd already had at least one drink. Reggie had been a smoker for as long as I'd known him and was always trying to quit. Liquor was his undoing. He exhaled loudly, and I imagined him enveloped by a blue cloud. Roughly the size of a Division 1 offensive lineman, Reggie was a dark-skinned black guy with a square, immobile face, a graying fade, and a permanently mournful expression.

"Joe Belko retired today," he said.

Joe was Reggie's partner, a twenty-year veteran of the major case squad. In the five years they'd been working together, I'd rarely heard Joe talk about anything except fishing. It didn't surprise me to learn he'd pulled the pin. He and Reggie specialized in abductions and disappearances, usually working in concert with the FBI and the state police. I had the sense that Joe, like Reggie, had seen a lot more than he'd ever wanted to.

"That must be tough. They got someone new lined up for you?"

"Not yet. The guys upstairs want to talk to me about riding a desk. If I were going to sit around with my thumb up my ass all day I'd want to get paid some serious money, like that hot-rod crowd you hang around with."

I gave him the laugh he was looking for.

"So, can I take a rain check and call you next week?"

He sucked on the cigarette again. I felt bad about letting him down. Childless and long divorced, Reggie didn't seem to have much of a social life.

"It really would be better if we talked tonight."

I felt a funny catch in my chest, abruptly aware of how still the office was. The only noise was the buzz of the fluorescent lights, a barely audible siren a dozen blocks away, and Reggie's muted breathing through the receiver.

"You have something to tell me?"

"It may be nothing. Don't get yourself too excited."

I got to my feet and grabbed my suit jacket from the back of my chair.

"I'm coming to you," I said. "Right now. Tell me where you are."

The address Reggie gave me was a Second Avenue dive in the low sixties, near the Roosevelt Island tram. I entered the small bar beneath a green neon sign with a flashing shamrock. It was a drinker's place—no jukebox, no cutesy decorations, no waitresses. Just bare walls, a linoleum floor, and a battered tin ceiling. Half a dozen guys were crowded together near the door, watching a silent hockey game on a flyspecked, undersized television. Reggie stood alone at the far end of the room, wearing a gray three-piece suit and a pale yellow tie. He tapped a knuckle on the scuffed counter as I approached and attracted the attention of a tubercular-looking barman.

"Jimmy and Guinney," he said. "Times two."

I pulled out my wallet and dropped a twenty on top of the small pile of money in front of him. The barman served up the whiskey and made change, waiting for the heads to settle on the Guinness. Reggie clinked his glass to mine and we both threw back the shots in a single go.

"So, tell me," I said, feeling the whiskey smolder in my gut.

Reaching into his breast pocket, Reggie extracted a folded sheet of paper.

"An e-mail," he said. "Sent directly to me. It came in last night."

I unfolded the page with shaking fingers and scanned past the detailed header information, hunting for the body of the message. It was only two sentences long:

Kyle Wallace was left in the trunk of a red BMW M5 with diplo-matic license plates. The car was last seen in a lot at 125th Street and the Hudson River.

My hands sank to the bar, the page suddenly too heavy to support.

"Jimmys again," Reggie said, as the barman served up the Guinness. He touched his pint glass to mine, and I automatically lifted the black liquid and took a sip.

"We've had tips before," I said, choking slightly on the bitter beer. "Dozens of them. They never amounted to anything. What makes this different?"

"Maybe nothing," Reggie said, extracting his Marlboros and lighter from a jacket pocket. He shook out a cigarette and began tapping the filter against the top of the box as the barman poured more whiskey.

"You can't smoke those in here," the barman protested with a soft Irish lilt. "It's against the law."

Reggie flipped open his jacket and exposed his gold badge.

"We'll have a right fecking riot, we will," the barman said, glancing over his shoulder toward the men watching the TV.

"Give it a rest," Reggie told him, lighting up. "Nobody's here to get healthy."

The barman looked as if he might argue and then walked away, muttering beneath his breath.

"Maybe nothing, but maybe something," I said, keeping my eyes on his face.

He nodded slightly, turning his head to blow smoke away from me.

"Let me explain. The police get tips from four kinds of people." He stuck the cigarette in a corner of his mouth and began counting on his fingers. "First, the vindictive types. The neighbor's got a barking dog and they want to get even, so they make up some bullshit story and try to get him in trouble. That doesn't fit here, because there isn't any accusation. Second, the wackos. The wackos want attention, so they call on the phone and show up in person and claim that they're the real Son of Sam, or that they did whatever's on the front cover of the *New York Post*. A lot of them we know already, because they keep coming back. But their tips are never anonymous—they want the attention. Third," he continued, moving on to another finger, "you got your sick bastards. The sick bastards are in it for the fun. They want to confuse the cops or torment the families. Their tips are anonymous, but there's never anything you can really check out. It's always that they saw the person you're looking for on a bus in France, or—"

"You can check out the car," I interrupted. "There can't be that many red BMWs with diplomatic plates."

"Correct." He flicked some ash to the floor and took another sip of beer. "First thing I did. Makes it easier that it's an M5—that's a high-end, limited-production car. Seven years ago, there were exactly four M5s in the entire country with diplomatic plates—three black and one red. The red one was registered right here in the city, out in Queens. It was stolen the same night that Kyle vanished."

I swayed slightly, my knees weak, and felt Reggie's arm around my shoulders.

"Steady," he said. "You okay?"

"Yeah." I straightened and took a deep breath. Everyone in the room except the barman was smoking now, and the air already seemed impossibly close. I'd wanted closure for years, but the possibility of finally learning the truth terrified me. The truth meant the end of illusions.

"The car was registered to a Venezuelan diplomat named Mariano Gallegos," Reggie continued. "I got a request out for the case file. There might be something in it. And I'd like to talk to him if he's still in the country, but that could be tricky. Dealing with diplomats is a real pain in the ass."

"Maybe I can help," I suggested, hearing my voice quaver. "I'm meeting with a guy from OPEC tomorrow morning. He knows a lot of Venezuelan diplomats. He can probably make a connection for me."

"That'd be great," Reggie said encouragingly. "Keep me posted. *Sláinte.*"

We raised our whiskey glasses and shot the second Jamesons. My stomach turned over and I thought I might retch. Lifting the e-mail again, I scrutinized each word. *Kyle Wallace was left in the trunk of a red BMW . . .* The word "left" might mean anything.

"You have any thoughts about what might have happened?" I said, afraid to ask the direct question.

Reggie took a minute to scan the room. He looked tired, the way his ex-partner Joe Belko had always looked tired.

"Nothing good," he answered finally. "I'm sorry."

My vision blurred as tears welled. Silence built between us and rapidly became unendurable.

"So, tell me about the fourth type of person who tips the police," I said blindly.

"The fourth type are the people who actually know something. If it's not about a reward, and it's not about taunting the cops or the family, then it's usually about guilt."

"You think this is from the guy who took Kyle?" I asked, my voice breaking.

"No," he said, laying a hand on my arm. "I don't. Guys who commit a crime and feel guilty enough to own up to it almost always apologize. There's no apology here. So, assuming this isn't bullshit from some particularly clever sick bastard, my guess is that it's from someone who found out about the crime secondhand and feels bad about not coming forward."

"But not bad enough to identify him- or herself, or to tell us who did it."

He shrugged.

"Yeah. But this isn't necessarily the end of it—whoever wrote might get in touch again. It happens. The first contact is the hardest."

I studied the Internet gibberish at the top of the e-mail, my fear of the truth receding. Anything was better than more waiting.

"The FBI or somebody must be able to track this back to wherever it was sent from, right?"

"I wish." He flicked more ash onto the floor. "I already talked to our tech guys. The e-mail was sent through an anonymous remailer, which is a fancy name for a daisy chain of computers in parts of the world where they haven't got much in the way of disclosure laws. The particular remailer that sent this message is located on the Isle of Man, but the tech guys tell me that the message might have hopped from the sender to India to Africa to God knows where before it hit the last stop. They're going to take a stab at running it down, but they warned me not to expect much."

"So, what's next?" I asked, refusing to believe that we were at a dead end.

"Next I go looking for a red BMW M5." He took a final hit from his cigarette, dropped the butt to the floor, and ground it out with his shoe. "Seven years is a long time, but I broke in on auto crime, and I know a few tricks when it comes to finding cars. Farther south, we'd have to worry that it went deadhead on a banana boat to South America. Up north, though, most cars get chopped or reregistered under a fake vehicle identification number. If we find the car, we might be able to track it back to whoever stole it." He swept the change on the bar toward him, leaving a five-dollar bill. "Come on. I got my wheels out front. I'll give you a ride home."

I shook my head, feeling a little dizzy.

"I'd rather walk awhile. I could use the fresh air."

"You sure?"

"Yeah."

"Okay, then. But call me if you got any questions. Don't worry what time it is. I never sleep much." He hesitated. "You going to tell Claire and Kate about this?"

I thought about it for a second. If Kate was right, and Claire really did want to put the past behind her, a false lead would be the worst possible thing for her, potentially destroying whatever emotional barriers she'd managed to erect. It might even be the final straw persuading her to flee—from New York, and from me.

"Not until we know more."

"Your call. But don't wait too long. You don't want to be carrying this around by yourself, and they're going to be upset if they discover you were holding out on them."

12

The heat of the whiskey dissipated rapidly in the cold night air as I walked south on Second Avenue and then west on Fifty-seventh Street. Long crosstown blocks carried me through the shuttered heart of Midtown, the brightly illuminated shop windows forlorn in the absence of daytime crowds. *Kyle Wallace was left in the trunk of a red BMW. . . .* By whom? And in what condition? Head down and collar turned up, I quickened my pace.

I figured out where I was headed only when I arrived. Carnegie Hall is at the intersection of Fifty-seventh and Seventh, a tan brick building that looks like an outsized college library. A uniformed usher told me the concert was due to end in half an hour. I crossed the street and sheltered in a doorway, knowing Claire and Kate would pass by on their way to Eighth Avenue, where they could catch a taxi uptown. Covering my face with my hands, I prayed Kyle hadn't suffered.

A rush of early departees signaled the end of the performance. I spotted Kate ten minutes later. She was wearing the navy peacoat she'd had on earlier, but she'd switched from jeans and sneakers to dark slacks and fancy leather boots with a low heel. She had hold of Claire's arm with one hand and was gesticulating emphatically with the other as she made some point. Claire was wearing a long black dress coat, and she was nodding. Heads together, they looked almost like sisters. Attractive as Kate was, Claire had been wrong to worry all those years ago that her daughter might outshine her. She was still the most beautiful woman in the world to me.

I stepped back into the doorway, hiding in the shadow as they passed. I knew Reggie was right about telling them, but it wasn't time yet. I'd needed to see them, though, if only to remind myself that I hadn't lost everything. I watched until they disappeared into the crowd before turning and heading east, back to my office. It would be hours before I was physically exhausted enough to sleep. In the interim, I thought I might as well get some work done.

13

The alarm on my cell phone woke me at seven-thirty. I was sleeping on the couch in my den, where I'd bedded down a few hours before so as not to wake Claire. My head ached, and my stomach felt bloated—whiskey, beer, and cold pizza are a miserable combination. Scrabbling blindly on the floor by my head, I found the phone and pressed the central button, knowing it would give me another five minutes to snooze. A cricketlike chirping replied, announcing a low battery. I rolled onto my back, swearing. The phone had been in the charging cradle for hours before I left the office to meet Reggie, and the battery was practically new. I typed a semiliterate e-mail to Amy, asking her to pick up a replacement on her way to work. My phone was too important to me to risk having it give up unexpectedly.

I groaned as I sat upright. It had taken me until four to finish loading numbers into the depletion model. A dialogue box had popped up when I pressed the go button, estimating the run time at ten hours. I was impatient for it to get done quicker. A number of things in the raw data were disconcerting, and I was anxious to see the results.

There was a note on the coffee table in front of me. It was in Kate's handwriting: *You snore. Phil coming to dinner tonight. Can you make it? Please?* I smiled, glad she seemed excited and that she wanted Claire and I to get to know him better. I picked up the note, crumpled it into a ball, and tossed it toward the garbage can ten feet away, scoring an improbable basket. I hoped it was an omen—it had been a confusing couple of days, and I desperately needed some things to start falling into place.

. . .

The lobby of the Four Seasons Hotel in New York is done up like a memorial chapel, with soaring stone columns, a backlit onyx ceiling, and an altarlike dais at the far end. I climbed a flight of steps to the reception desk and told a clerk I was there to see Rashid al-Shaabi. He checked my identification against his computer and summoned a liveried security guard to escort me to the fifty-first floor. A Middle Eastern–looking man I didn't recognize was waiting when the elevator doors opened. He escorted me down a short hall, tapped on the only visible door, and then swiped a key card to unlock it. His jacket swung open as he extended his arm, and I caught a flash of a gun in a holster.

"Mr. al-Shaabi is supposed to be taking it easy," he said to me in a Brooklyn-accented whisper. "Don't let him overexert himself."

The door swung open to a suite that was all blond wood and earth-tone carpets, with sweeping views of Central Park and the Manhattan skyline. Rashid was sitting behind a desk in an alcove, talking on the phone in Arabic. He gestured for me to come in and then pointed to a silver butler's tray laden with coffee and Middle Eastern pastries. The coffee and pastries were for me—I knew he was allowed only tiny quantities of diuretics or sweets. I draped my coat over a chair, poured coffee for myself, and settled in front of his desk to wait.

Rashid was wearing a crisp white shirt with rolled-up cuffs, blue suit pants, and worn green house slippers. He looked terrible. Barely five feet tall and maybe a hundred and ten pounds on his heaviest day, he hadn't had any weight to lose when he'd taken his recent turn for the worse, but the wiry definition he'd had in his neck and forearms was gone, degenerated into a slack-toned frailty. When I'd last seen him, three or four weeks back, I'd been shocked by how aged he seemed.

"As-Salāmu 'Alaykum," he said, hanging up the phone and struggling to his feet.

We went through the whole ritual, kissing each other on both cheeks. He shook me by the shoulders as he inquired about my health, barely jostling me. In the old days he'd made my teeth rattle.

"And Claire and Katherine?" he inquired.

"Both fine. Thank you for asking."

"Bring them to see me," he ordered. "There's a Lebanese in the kitchen downstairs who makes proper *qatayef*. You know *qatayef*?"

I nodded. Crepes filled with cheese or nuts, ubiquitous at Ramadan.

"So, bring them," he said, giving me another feeble shake. "They'll eat. It would make me happy."

Rashid had met Claire and Kate exactly once, when he'd turned up at my apartment unannounced ten days after Kyle had vanished, bearing a tin tray filled with grilled lamb kebabs and rice. We hadn't had many visitors, save for family and police. Nobody knew what to do or say. He stayed an hour, weeping when I wept, and leaving only after I promised to call him if there was ever any help he could provide.

"I will," I said, realizing I'd been remiss.

"That's settled, then." He let go of my shoulders and glanced at his watch. "Excuse me for a moment. I have to go and take some medicine."

He didn't look strong enough to go anywhere. The effort of standing had raised a sheen of sweat on his forehead, and his breathing was rapid and shallow.

"Can I get it for you?"

He straightened slightly, looking offended.

"It would make me happy," I said, playing my trump card as a guest.

"In the bathroom," he acquiesced grudgingly, pointing with a finger. "Off the bedroom. There's a cup with the time written on it."

I followed a rust-colored carpet around a corner and down a narrow corridor. Both the bedroom and bathroom doors were open. Twelve paper cups were arranged neatly on a plastic tray to the left of the sink, each containing four or more pills and marked with a time in black felt-tip pen. It seemed incredible that someone of Rashid's size could even swallow that much medicine on a daily basis, let alone metabolize it. I searched for the cup labeled nine a.m., thinking ruefully that I'd best bring Claire and Kate soon.

Exiting with the medicine in hand, I noticed a mezuzah fastened to the frame of the bedroom door. It was a Jewish religious thing, an ornate, flattish metal container about the size of a pack of gum, with a verse from the Torah tucked inside. Every third doorway in my apartment building had one. I smiled, assuming a previous guest had left it behind and wondering if Rashid knew what it was.

"Tap water okay?" I called.

"Please. Not too cold."

I poured a large glass of lukewarm water in the kitchenette and carried everything back to the alcove, where Rashid had reseated himself behind his desk. There were six pills in the cup I handed him. He put the first in his mouth, closed his eyes, took a sip of water, and then swallowed with effort, repeating the procedure mechanically until they were all gone. It took him a good two minutes, and he looked even more exhausted when he was done.

"You okay?"

He nodded silently, eyes still shut.

"I noticed the mezuzah on the bedroom doorway," I said, hoping to cheer him up with a little banter. "Don't tell me you've converted?"

He sighed heavily.

"When you're as sick as I am, you'll try anything."

I felt uncomfortable until he opened his eyes and grinned, and I realized he was joking.

"Actually," he said, "it was my grandmother's. An old family secret. Don't tell anyone."

I smiled back, wondering if he was telling the truth. I knew his grandparents had migrated from Yemen to Saudi Arabia. Maybe a mixed marriage had been the reason. He took another sip of water, carefully set down his glass, and then looked up at me expectantly. Time for business.

"I have something fairly delicate to discuss with you, but before I do, I was wondering if I could ask you for a small favor," I said.

"Of course."

"Do you know a man named Mariano Gallegos? He was a member of the Venezuelan delegation to the United Nations a few years back, and he might or might not still be here in New York."

He frowned slightly and rubbed his wispy beard.

"I don't think so."

"I need to speak with him. No big deal, I just want to ask him a couple of questions. Is there any chance you could arrange an introduction?"

He pulled a pad toward him and scribbled on it.

"I'll see what I can do," he said.

"Thanks. I appreciate it." I hesitated a moment, uncertain how to broach Theresa's data. It had occurred to me that Rashid might get angry. In all our long acquaintance, he'd never done or said anything that wasn't in OPEC's best interest, and having Saudi secrets laid bare wasn't necessarily in that category. Best just to heave it out, I decided, and let the chips fly.

"A friend of a friend looked me up the other day. The friend knew a person who'd done work for Aramco. The friend gave me a computer hard drive that contained an enormous amount of internal Aramco information. Reprocessed seismic data, production figures, mixture percentages, you name it. Well by well, for every field in the Kingdom."

I paused, wanting to get a sense of his initial reaction before carrying on.

"Let me see if I have this straight," he said, steepling his fingers and tipping his head slightly to one side. "You have a friend who has a friend who has a friend. And this person gave your friend's friend a mass of highly confidential information, and then your friend's friend came to you out of the blue and gave the information to you. And you think this information might be credible."

"Stranger things have happened," I said, coloring a little.

"Not often."

"True," I admitted. "Which is why I'm here."

"You'd like me to vet this stolen data for you?" he asked, leaning forward slightly. "Based on confidential knowledge I may have obtained in my professional capacity as an employee of OPEC?"

It wasn't exactly how I would have put it, but it pretty much summed things up.

"Yes."

He tossed his hands skyward.

"Why would I do that?"

It was a question I'd anticipated. I extracted a sheaf of papers from my briefcase and handed them to him.

"What are these?" he demanded.

"Saltwater injection volumes and produced mixture percentages at Ghawar for the last five years. There's a summary on the last page."

He flipped to the end of the packet and glanced at the summary.

"So?"

"So, the mixture percentages are much lower than you'd expect, unless the wells were in serious decline."

"Don't embarrass yourself. Please. You're not an engineer. There are any number of technical reasons for low yields. Even if the figures are correct, it doesn't necessarily mean anything."

My head was throbbing slightly, and I wished I'd gotten more sleep. I had only one chance to pitch him. I didn't want to screw it up.

"I know. But hear me out for a second. The Aramco data I saw—"

"The supposed Aramco data you saw," he interrupted.

"Fine. The supposed Aramco data I saw contained a bunch of senior-management reports, including a few that had been explicitly written for OPEC. One was addressed to you by name."

"And?"

"And the numbers in the reports don't match the field data."

"Meaning your information is internally inconsistent, and thus inherently suspect," he said dismissively.

I didn't answer, giving him time to think about it. Rashid was a long, long way from being stupid. One possibility was that my information was incorrect. The other was that Aramco had lied to him, and lied to their political masters. Which—if true—raised the question of why.

"I'm tired." He sighed a few moments later, opening a drawer in the desk. He pulled out a handkerchief and used it to blot his forehead. "These pills are worse than my illness."

"I'll go," I volunteered immediately, starting to my feet. "We can talk more after you've rested."

"Stay." He waved me back into my seat. "It's nothing. I enjoy the company. You have a copy of this report that was addressed to me?"

I took it out of my briefcase and handed it to him. He flipped through a few pages and handed it back, his expression inscrutable.

"Let me explain something that may be difficult for you to understand," he said, draping the handkerchief over his head like a kaffiyeh. "The truth is that nobody knows how much oil the Saudis have, or the real condition of their fields. Not me, not the Saudi oil ministry, and not the king. The Saudi government twists OPEC's arm for the allocation they want, and then orders Aramco to produce that amount. Aramco does whatever they have to do to make it happen. If the minister or the king wants to know how much surplus capacity they have, or the exact quantity of their proved reserves, the head of Aramco reports whatever they want to hear and concludes by saying 'Inshallah'—God willing. And who can argue with that? If God wills the oil to come, it will come. If He doesn't, it won't."

"With all due respect, Rashid, I don't buy it. I've spent time with the Aramco people. There are a lot of smart engineers working there. I can't believe they don't know what's going on."

"Don't confuse issues of intelligence with issues of culture," he rasped irritably. "At the lower levels of the organization, I'm sure the smart engineers you refer to have made all the correct calculations. But it's not acceptable to pass difficult news up the line at Aramco, particularly in the form of a forecast. Because many of the senior people in the Kingdom—including the king—genuinely believe that there's a large measure of hubris in trying to predict the future. *Inshallah.* It will be what God wills."

"Which would be fine if the Saudis weren't sitting on most of the world's excess oil reserves," I said, watching the sweat bead on his forehead again. It was the kind of give-and-take he normally enjoyed, but I continued to worry that I was overtaxing him. "If the peak-oil people are right, and the Saudis are closer to running out of oil than anyone realizes, it means trouble for everyone."

He smiled grimly, mopping his face with the handkerchief from his head and then tossing it on the desk.

"You want my opinion?"

"Please."

"*Inshallah.*"

I half grinned, thinking he'd made another joke. As seconds ticked past without his elaborating, my grin faded.

"You're not interested in trying to prevent a global energy crisis?"

"Unless it happens in the next few weeks, I doubt it's going to have much impact on me."

We stared at each other in silence, and I wondered if I was listening to the drugs.

"I'm kind of at a loss here, Rashid," I said quietly. "You've always gone out of your way to be helpful to people, especially me. It's hard to believe that you genuinely don't care about preventing a catastrophe, regardless of whether you think you're going to be here to see it."

"There are a lot of things I care about," he responded gravely. "Some I can affect, and some I can't."

"You don't believe it would make any difference if the Western governments knew there was an oil crunch coming?"

"Frankly, no," he said, sounding more amused than regretful. "America and her allies are so in love with democracy, but all that really means is never making hard choices. Everyone's already aware that there's only so much oil, but the Western economic powers won't summon the political will to deal with the entirely predictable shortages until lines begin to form at your gas stations. And by then, as you and I both know, it will be years too late."

"They'd take the steps if they had definitive warning. We're talking about the end of the world as we know it. Genuine shortages mean famine and death and war. Those are issues that tend to focus the mind."

"Famine and death and war for whom?" he riposted sharply. "Not America. America will suffer, but it won't pay the full price. You're the only great military power left. You'll seize the Middle Eastern oil and gas fields and use what's left of the energy to manage a crash transition. The genuinely bad consequences will be reserved for the Third World—the places where famine and death and war never seem to focus anyone's mind."

It was a terse, brutal, and entirely accurate summary of what Senator Simpson's plan really meant. I wished Rashid had been present yesterday, when Simpson was trying to sell his idea as "energy security." The world Rashid was describing wasn't the one I wanted to leave my daughter.

"Is that the prevalent OPEC view?"

"More or less. The heads of the Arab Gulf States understand the danger of their 'special relationship' with America, but they're afraid of Iran and of the extremists in their own populations. The lesson of Kuwait wasn't lost on anyone. If it wasn't for Bush forty-one and the U.S. Marines, the emir and his entire clan would be just another group of deposed aristocrats cooling their heels in Paris or London and waiting for their money to run out. The kings and the emirs and the sultans need America for security, so they can continue looting their national treasuries in peace, but they all know they've done a deal with the devil. When push comes to shove, America will annex what it needs to annex, and the most the Gulf royalty will be able to hope for is generous severance. The devil always demands his due."

He was laboring for breath as he finished speaking.

"You're not well," I said, furious at myself for letting him become overexcited. No matter how important the issue, I'd been wrong to push him. "I'm sorry. Can I get you something?"

"Just more water," he muttered, collapsing back into his chair.

I fetched him some and then waited silently until his eyes closed and he began breathing more easily. I was halfway to the door when I heard his voice behind me.

"Send me your information. I'll look at it and let you know what I think."

"Thanks," I said, feeling a rush of gratitude. "I appreciate it. I'll get everything over to you later today."

I had my hand on the knob when he spoke a second time.

"Would you like some advice?"

I turned to look at him. His eyes were open, and he was smiling at me.

"Please."

"You should buy a nice piece of land somewhere remote and stock it with goats. Goats are easy to keep and very useful. The meat can be eaten, the hair can be woven into clothing, and the dung can be burned as fuel."

He was laughing quietly as I left.

14

Amy wasn't at her desk when I got back to the office, but my new cell-phone battery was on my desk, so I knew she couldn't be far. I checked my computer while I swapped out the battery, to see if the depletion model had finished running yet. No luck—the progress icon was still flashing. I tapped the top of the CPU a few times to hurry it along. Old habits die hard—tapping had made the TV work better when I was a kid.

I dropped the reassembled phone into the charging cradle and then scanned the news. The Ukrainians were still denying everything loudly, but the Russians and the French had gone ominously quiet. Nothing that required my immediate attention. I was starting to go through messages when I noticed Amy bustling my way, a concerned expression on her face.

"Morning," I said, stepping out from behind my desk to greet her. "What's up?"

"Morning." She glanced over her shoulder and then leaned toward me. "Alex is out again today," she whispered. "There's a rumor on the floor that Walter's closing his positions."

"What positions?" I asked apprehensively.

"All of them."

I started to swear, catching myself just in time. Having your positions closed is the trading-desk equivalent of having your epaulets ripped off. It meant Alex was out for good, his trading career over, at Cobra and everywhere else—with his track record, no one would be hiring. I was upset with him because I suspected he'd tried to mislead me, but I certainly didn't want to see him hurt. Although maybe it was for the best, I thought, as the initial shock wore off. I'd told him the truth the other day—he was a smart guy, but he wasn't cut out to be a trader. Relieved of the day-to-day pressure, he might be able to pull himself together, stop drinking, and get back in some kind of decent physical shape. And he'd still have Walter's political activity to manage. Or at least I hoped he would. There was some chance that he and his father had had a major falling-out, which would be another explanation for why he hadn't been back to the office.

"Has Lynn talked to him?"

"No. He didn't call in. She's on her way over to his place now, to make sure he's okay."

I wavered a moment, wondering whether I should get involved, before deciding I didn't have a choice. Alex was a friend. I had to help if I could.

"I want to talk to Walter. Set something up as soon as possible, please."

"Will do. And I don't know if you saw the message yet, but Reggie called a few minutes ago. He'd like you to get back to him on his desk number."

"Thanks."

Amy was wearing a bright red Christmas sweater with metallic candy canes embroidered on it, and the shimmering reflections made me feel nauseated. I was too old to get by on three hours of sleep, particularly after a couple of shots of whiskey.

"Can I get you some coffee?" she asked, sounding concerned. "You look kind of rocky."

"Maybe later," I said. The coffee I'd drunk at Rashid's hadn't gone down so well. I had enough acid working on my insides. "A little dry toast would be great."

"I'll see what I can rustle up."

I dialed Reggie's work phone. The cop who answered put me on hold, and Reggie picked up a minute later.

"Mark?"

"Yeah."

"Any luck with this OPEC buddy of yours on Gallegos?"

"He didn't know him, but he promised to make a few calls. I should hear back later today or tomorrow. Why?"

"Because the situation's a lot more complicated than I realized."

My hand tightened on the receiver.

"Complicated how?"

"The stolen-car report on the BMW is cross-referenced to a murder investigation."

"Whose murder?" I asked breathlessly.

"Gallegos's brother-in-law, a guy named Carlos Munoz, also a diplomat. He and Gallegos were married to sisters. Gallegos lent Munoz the car the day it was stolen. This guy Munoz sounds like a real prince. A bunch of complaints about him for sexual harassment, and a girlfriend out on Long Island who he liked to use as a punching bag. According to the file, Munoz drove out to see the girlfriend that afternoon, but she'd skipped town. Could be she finally had enough. So he drove back into the city, picked up a hooker, and took her to a motel on the Lower West Side. That's where his body was found. He caught three to the chest from a military forty-five. The girl vanished."

I exhaled slowly.

"Which suggests what?"

"Hard to know. One possibility is that Munoz is the guy we're looking for. There was a security camera in the parking lot. The tape showed him arriving with the hooker at five-thirty and driving away alone at six. Kyle left your place a little after seven-thirty."

"I'm confused," I said, making an effort to remain analytical. "Didn't you just tell me that Munoz was murdered at the motel?"

"Right. In bed and with his pants down, the way we all should be lucky enough to go. Second security camera in the lobby caught him when he arrived the first time but not leaving or returning. Parking-lot camera showed him arriving and leaving but not returning. Best our guys were able to figure, Munoz checked in, left by the fire stairs, propped the door open behind him, moved the car, and then came back in by the fire stairs. They reckon maybe he went out for cigarettes and left the car somewhere else."

"That make sense to you?" I asked incredulously.

"Nope. Sounds like a load of shit. I read enough files to be able to tell that the guys who caught the case mailed it in. Dead diplomat in a seedy hotel room; semen on the sheets; watch, wallet, and money clip gone.

He went walking on the wild side, and he got more than he bargained for. All she wrote. Nobody was interested in loose ends."

"So, what are the chances that he kidnapped Kyle before he was murdered?"

"Slim, in my book. ME made his time of death around nine, which doesn't give him a big window to have grabbed Kyle, ditched the car in Harlem, and found his way back downtown."

"This is weird," I said, wishing again I'd had more sleep.

"No shit."

"What do you think?"

"I don't know. Munoz's car key was still in his pants pocket. Maybe he really did just move the car around the corner for some reason and then some third party boosted it. Or maybe we're chasing a fairy tale. Bottom line, it makes me want to talk to Gallegos even more. He was interviewed at the time, but he made his brother-in-law out to be a saint. I'm reckoning he might know more than he said. So, let me know as soon as you hear back, okay?"

"Okay," I said unhappily. The last thing I wanted was more uncertainty.

"Hang in there," Reggie urged. "I'll talk to you soon."

Amy buzzed as I hung up.

"Walter's free now."

"Thanks. I'm on my way."

Walter's office was modest in the scheme of things, a ten-by-fifteen glass-walled chamber in the middle of the trading room, backed against the building's core. Guys on the floor called it the fishbowl, and nobody ever wanted to be in it, save at bonus time. Conversations about the market were held on the trading desks so everyone could listen. A summons to the fishbowl meant you were in for a reaming.

"Come," Walter said, beckoning with one hand as I tapped on his door. He turned the report he'd been reading facedown on an otherwise empty desk and fixed his pale blue eyes on me. One of his defining characteristics was that he was never distracted, always entirely focused on whatever he had at hand at the moment. Admirable in concept but disconcerting when what he was focused on was you.

"I'm worried about Alex," I said, figuring it was best not to beat around the bush. "He hasn't seemed well recently."

"I appreciate your concern," he replied curtly. "But Alex isn't twenty-two anymore. He doesn't need a minder."

"I'm not saying he does. He might need help, though. My sense is that he's been drinking heavily. Having his positions liquidated isn't going to improve his outlook."

Walter stared at me unblinkingly. I stared back, wondering if he was deliberately trying to intimidate me.

"Close the door and sit down," he ordered.

I did as he asked, chafing at his tone, as always.

"Every guy out there works his ass off to keep his job," he said, stabbing a finger toward the trading floor. "I can't play favorites just because Alex is my son."

"I'm not suggesting you should. I'm suggesting you reach out to him. Because he's your son, and because I suspect he's in a bad way."

I endured the stare for another few seconds, wondering what he was actually thinking. It was hard to believe he didn't care about Alex at all, even if they'd had a falling-out. He glanced down, nudging the upside-down report with a fingernail to align it more precisely with the front edge of his desk.

"I've expressed my concerns to Alex directly," he said hesitantly. "I don't know that there's anything more I can do at this point."

"You agree he has a problem?"

"It seems that way." He frowned. "His mother and I are worried."

The highlight of Walter's ugly divorce twenty years previously had come when Alex's mother submitted evidence from an animal psychologist asserting that Walter's negative energy made her Yorkie suicidal. The tabloids had a field day, leading Walter to temporarily relocate to London. The admission that he was discussing anything with his former wife was a better indication of his level of concern than his mild declaration.

"I'd be happy to talk to Alex about getting help," I offered, warming to him a little, father to father. "I'd like to know that I have your support, though. He values your opinion."

Walter's phone rang before he could reply. He picked it up, listened, and then held the receiver out to me.

"It's Amy. She says it's urgent."

"Sorry." I took the receiver from him and put it to my ear. "Amy?"

"Nikolay Narimanov is calling," she announced apologetically. "I tried to take a message, but he insisted I interrupt you."

"Narimanov," I relayed to Walter, covering the mouthpiece with one hand. "He wants to speak to me right away."

Walter raised his eyebrows, and I shrugged.

"Take it," he said.

"Put him through, please," I told Amy.

The phone clicked.

"Nikolay?"

"Mark. Your secretary tells me that I've reached you at a difficult time."

"I'm afraid so."

"Let me get straight to the point. I've been reflecting on our conversation yesterday, and I've decided that I don't want any of my confidential information put into the public domain, with or without attribution."

"Then there isn't much for us to talk about," I said, feeling simultaneously crestfallen and pissed off. Narimanov was theoretically only backing me up on Saudi, but I was counting on him as my primary source for Russia. "All of my prime clients see everything I'm working on at the same time. I can't do a special analysis for you and not share it with my other subscribers."

"I assumed as much, which is why I'd like to change the terms of my proposal. I'll buy you out. I'll capitalize your current income stream at a favorable discount rate and pay it down in cash over five years. In exchange, you agree to work for me exclusively for the same period."

I swallowed hard, running the numbers in my head. It worked out to three or four million bucks a year. Walter was staring at me quizzically.

"That's unexpected," I said, keeping my voice neutral. "I'll have to give it some thought and get back to you."

"Do. And think about this—working for me will give you access to information you won't be able to obtain elsewhere."

"I understand."

"Perhaps not as fully as you imagine. Here's a small sample: Russian and French paratroopers have just completed a clandestine assault on a Ukrainian ultranationalist paramilitary base north of Zhytomyr, about a hundred kilometers west of Kiev. Early reports are that they've seized evidence of Ukrainian involvement in the Nord Stream assault and captured two prisoners directly linked to the attack."

My jaw dropped.

"You're certain?"

"What?" Walter interjected. I waved him silent, intent on Narimanov's answer.

"Yes. There'll be a press release within the hour. Act quickly. And get back to me on my offer as soon as possible, please. I don't like to be kept waiting."

He hung up. I was too shocked to move for a second, and then I leaned over Walter's desk and punched a free line on his phone, dialing Amy.

"What's going on?" Walter demanded.

"News," I said. "Just listen."

Amy answered on the second ring. I cut her off mid-greeting.

"Open an e-mail to my full client list immediately."

Walter got up and moved to the door, poised with one foot in his office and one foot on the trading floor.

"Done."

"Subject line URGENT, all caps. Message body: *Reliable report received of successful Russian/French military strike in Ukraine. Evidence seized implicates Ukrainian ultranationalists in Nord Stream attack. Press conference expected soon. Look for capital markets to rally strongly and energy markets to decline. Detailed analysis follows.* You got that?"

"Got it."

"Hit send. I'll be at my desk in two minutes."

I hung up the phone and turned around. Walter was already out on the floor, barking orders to his trading staff. He looked calm and collected, like a battle-hardened officer directing troops in an attack. I guessed we were done talking about Alex. I closed the door behind me as I left his office. It was going to be another long day.

15

Amy popped in on me just before lunch. She had a plate in one hand and a steaming mug in the other.

"You got a minute?"

It had been a crazy couple of hours. The Russians and the French had staged a mind-blowing press conference about half an hour after I got the heads-up from Narimanov, replete with slick exhibits detailing the forensic evidence that had prompted them to act and capped by stark video footage of their combined forces carrying out a successful *Apocalypse Now*–style daylight assault on the Ukrainian paramilitary camp. It had been a heck of an impressive show, and both foreign ministers managed to sneak in backhanders suggesting that the United States could learn a thing or two about dealing with terrorism without laying entire countries to waste. The Ukrainians were screaming that they'd been set up and threatening to raise the issue of their violated sovereignty at the United Nations, but nobody was paying them much mind—even their former Soviet bloc allies were keeping quiet. The United States had been reduced to having a junior State Department spokesperson affirm that America supported responsible efforts to combat terrorism globally. Game, set, and match to the bear and the poodle. The markets reacted as I'd anticipated, and my in-box was stuffed with congratulatory messages from clients.

"Sure," I said, glancing at my computer screen for the hundredth time. The red progress icon on the depletion model was still flashing at the same infuriatingly leisurely pace. "Come on in."

"I have more toast," she said, setting the plate down on my desk. "You ready for some coffee now?"

The question made me realize how tired I was.

"Please," I said, stifling a yawn. I washed a bite of toast down with a sip from the mug. My stomach wasn't any happier, but I needed the caffeine. "Any word from Alex?"

"None. He didn't answer Lynn's knock. She's worried."

"She tell Walter?"

"She spoke to Susan. Susan promised to talk to Walter."

Susan was Walter's assistant.

"I'll stop by on my way home," I said, glancing at my watch. "Anything else?"

"Rashid called earlier to set up a meeting between you and someone named Mariano Gallegos. He said not to interrupt you."

"Good. When and where?"

"Tomorrow morning, nine a.m., at the Turtle Bay Diner on the corner of Forty-sixth and Second. I'm assuming you'll walk over?"

"Right. Do me a favor and let Reggie know also." She looked at me curiously, but I wasn't inclined to explain. "And one more thing." I scribbled a quick explanatory note and then took the iPod and the cable Kate had purchased from my desk. "Seal these in a Bubble Wrap envelope and have an in-house messenger run them over to Rashid, please."

"Will do. Also, you got a bunch more inquiries from prospective clients, and about a million calls from reporters."

Talk of prospective clients reminded me of Narimanov's offer to buy out my business and employ me exclusively. I didn't know him well enough to jump to any decision, but it was an intriguing opportunity. The money he'd mentioned would support a major upgrade in our lifestyle. And I could probably work for him from anywhere. New York, London—maybe even San Francisco. I wondered again how serious Claire was about moving, and whether her plans included me.

"Fill out background reports on the potential new clients, please, and e-mail me a list of the reporters." I needed to get back to the ones I was friendly with, even if I didn't intend to tell them anything.

"Okay. Also, I spoke to Claire. She ordered a lasagna from Butterfield, and she'd like you to stop and pick it up on your way to the Christmas concert at Sloan-Kettering tomorrow night. You want me to book a car?"

"What time does it start?"

"Potluck dinner at six o'clock and concert at seven o'clock." She waited for my answer. "Mark?"

My eyes had drifted back to my computer monitor. The progress icon for the depletion model had stopped flashing and turned green.

"Sorry. What?"

"I asked if you wanted me to book a car."

"That'd be great," I said, reaching for my keyboard. "Thanks."

I was working at the big table in the main conference room a few hours later when I heard someone enter. Lifting my head wearily, I saw Walter. I'd had another five or six cups of coffee in an effort to stay alert—my shirt was soaked with sweat, and my nerves were jangling. I was in a bad mood, in part because the results I was examining were so shocking, and in part because I couldn't figure out whether or not to believe them. If the data were false, someone had gone to a heck of a lot of trouble to make them look real, and to use me in some way I hadn't completely figured out yet. I wondered if Walter knew who that someone was. He was the only person I could think of who might have been able to persuade Alex to lie to me.

"Quite the display," he said, looking at the array of documents I'd taped to the long glass wall.

"I needed some space to spread out. You here to talk more about Alex?"

"To make clear that you're to keep me posted on any conversation you have with him regarding his personal issues." He did a slow tour of the wall, coming to a halt in front of a map occupying the central position. "Saudi Arabia?"

"Message received," I said. "Thanks for stopping by."

He touched one of the brightly colored 3-D representations of Saudi oil fields surrounding the map.

"And this is what?"

"Work."

"Hmm . . ." He bent closer, examining the legend on the lower-left corner of the colored printout. "Yellow is oil, blue is water, and green is sedimentary rock. Geological studies?"

I crossed my arms and stared at him. He moved left, peering at a spreadsheet.

"'Net yield by month in hundreds of thousands of barrels,'" he read. "I thought the Saudis didn't make public their production data?"

"They don't."

He turned from the glass wall to scrutinize me.

"More manna from Narimanov?"

There were two possibilities. Either he knew I'd received the Saudi information from Theresa, and was trying to play me for a fool, or he didn't. If he did, nothing I told him would be news. If he didn't, it was marginally more likely that Alex had been straight with me. I was tired of guessing at everything. I decided to find out which.

"No," I said. "Another source."

He whistled softly.

"You're kind of on a hot streak, aren't you?"

"Maybe. There are complications."

"Such as?" he asked, settling himself in an empty seat.

I got up to close the door and then sat down opposite him. It took me about five minutes to explain how I'd come by the data, referring to Alex as "my friend" and Theresa as "the expert." His face was a mask.

"The thing that's making me most uncomfortable is that Simpson's entire argument yesterday was predicated on assumptions about the very data that just fell into my lap. It seems like too much of a coincidence. I'm betting that there's something going on behind the scenes."

"Let me guess," Walter said, waving a hand at the documents taped to the wall. "The work you've done makes the senator seem prescient."

"A proper analysis would take weeks. But the short answer to your question is yes. My quick-and-dirty read is that the Saudis are likely to begin experiencing serious production declines in about five years. There's no way the Western economies can retool that quickly, which pretty much guarantees massive dislocation unless the United States adopts Simpson's plan or something similar."

I paused for a reaction, but Walter kept quiet. I wasn't sure what to think. He rarely showed emotion, so it was no surprise that he was taking the news calmly. I had to push harder to get him to show his hand. If he'd arranged for me to receive the data, he'd want me to believe it.

"My best guess is that the same source who gave me this information also fed it to Simpson, and—if so—that Simpson took steps to check it out. Simpson is on the Senate Select Committee on Intelligence. I'd love to know what the CIA or the NSA had to say."

I let the observation hang, waiting for Walter to volunteer a connection. He was plugged in, but not plugged in enough to do fact-checking with our intelligence agencies. If he suggested he'd look into it and then came back the next day to give me the high sign, I'd know something suspicious was going on. Walter pondered for a moment and then shook his head decisively.

"You've got this backward."

"What do you mean?"

"Think about it. That story you told me about how 'the expert' got hold of the data and decided to pass it along doesn't smell right, and you know it. That's why you're so suspicious, and why you're hell-bent on trying to confirm the information from other sources."

I nodded tentatively, wondering if this was some kind of double fake.

"So, what's your hypothesis?"

"Simple. This is the kind of data that *originates* in the intelligence community. Isn't it a lot more likely that the CIA or the NSA obtained the information in the first place, realized the potential ramifications, and then posted the Select Committee? And that Senator Simpson, who's running for president, saw an opportunity to pre-position himself as the candidate with the visionary policy?"

"But that would mean—"

"That Simpson leaked the data himself. Exactly. Or, more likely, his pet weasel White. Because otherwise the voters wouldn't know the senator was such a visionary, would they? And," he continued, holding up a finger to forestall any interruption, "having decided to leak it, who better to give the information to than someone close to me? That way he's really killed two birds with one stone. He shows up on Tuesday and hand-sells his energy security scheme to me and my associates, and you waltz in on Wednesday and tell me that he's right to be concerned. Simpson gets the data into the public domain and locks up big-money support at the same time."

It was a neat hypothesis, but there was a piece that didn't track.

"You're forgetting that the expert was introduced to me by a friend. It's a big stretch to think Simpson was able to find a pliable expert who happened to know a friend of mine."

Walter gave me a pitying look.

"Occam's razor," he said.

Occam's razor: Any explanation of a phenomenon should make as few assumptions as possible. I thought about it for a few seconds and felt sick.

"Simpson didn't find an expert who knew a friend of mine. He found a friend of mine who was willing to lie about knowing an expert."

"Simpson figured you'd be suspicious. An introduction from a friend gave the expert credibility."

Between the fatigue and confusion, I felt as though my head were going to explode. Walter's argument made sense, but the very fact of his putting it forth made it less likely that he was the one who'd asked Alex to lie about knowing Theresa. Which meant that White or Simpson had somehow gotten to Alex? How? In exchange for what? Walter read the emotion on my face and grinned.

"You know the old saying," he said. "If you want a friend on Wall Street, buy a dog."

I wasn't able to muster a smile.

"Well," he said, getting to his feet. "I think we both know what to do next. I'll talk to other members of the Senate Select Committee and see what I can learn. Even if we're right that Simpson leaked the data, it doesn't necessarily follow that it's true. It would be an elegant little political trick to release deliberate disinformation, just the sort of thing White might cook up. Any mention of imminent energy shortages in the press would be enough to scare the bejesus out of most Americans, no matter who subsequently denied it. And that alone would work mightily to Simpson's benefit. You talk to your 'friend' and see if you can get him to come clean. Let me know if you need any assistance."

"What kind of assistance?" I asked dully.

"Fred and Frank. They're pretty good at finding hidden connections."

Frick and Frack. They'd hinted to me in the past that they were available for work in the gray zone, trawling vulnerable computer systems for confidential information. Even if I thought they'd keep Alex's identity secret from Walter, I wasn't ready to sic them on him.

"I'll be okay on my own for now."

"Fine . . ."

There was a tap on the door. Walter opened it. Amy was standing outside.

"I'm sorry to interrupt," she said, "but Susan's looking for you. She needs to speak with you right away."

He turned his head toward me.

"Come see me tomorrow mid-morning and we'll compare notes. I'll have talked to some people by then."

I nodded, and he left.

"And Reggie wants you to call him on his cell," Amy continued, addressing herself to me. "He said it was important."

"Thanks."

She closed the door as I dialed Reggie's number.

"Mark?" he said, answering on the first ring. "Where are you?"

"At the office."

"Are you alone?"

"Yes," I said. "Why?"

"I hate to have to tell you this, but Alex Coleman is dead."

16

"I can't believe it," I said for the tenth or eleventh time. We were in Reggie's car, across the street from my apartment building. All he'd been able to tell me thus far was that Alex had been found dead in his bathtub.

"It's hard," he said. "I'm sorry. I know he was a good friend of yours." His phone rang and he checked the number. "This is my buddy at the Nineteenth Precinct. Give me a few seconds here."

I opened the car door and got out, needing the air. We were on the west side of the street, adjacent to the stone wall bordering Riverside Park. I sat down on a bench and buried my head in my hands, attempting to come to grips with what had happened. I was shivering despite the winter sun on my back. I'd tried to be a friend to Alex—to advise him as best I knew how, and to do what I could to bolster his confidence. Ultimately, though, we're all alone in the world, and there's a limit to how much any one person can do for another. I choked back a sob, thinking of Alex as I'd first known him—the intelligence, the warmth, and the promise that had never been fulfilled. Reggie got out of the car a few minutes later and sat down next to me.

"I have some details if you want to hear them."

"I guess."

He took a minute to light a cigarette.

"Time of death won't be officially established until the autopsy, but the tech on the scene makes it sometime early this morning, most likely between twelve and three. There was a half-empty fifth of vodka on the bathroom floor next to the tub and an open bottle of sleeping pills on the vanity. The immediate cause of death looks to be drowning."

"Jesus." I had an abrupt, vivid mental image of Alex's face staring up at me from beneath a rippling sheet of water. I shook my head violently, trying to clear the vision. "Did he leave a note?"

"You think it was suicide?"

"I don't know." An accident would be easier for Walter and Alex's mother to accept. "What do your guys think?"

"They're withholding judgment. The apartment's torn up pretty bad."

"Torn up how?"

"Like someone was searching for something."

A sudden thought jolted me upright.

"You're not suggesting he was murdered?"

Reggie shrugged.

"No sign of violence on the body, so it seems unlikely. Maybe he searched the place himself, looking for a hidden bottle or an old love letter. Drunks rip stuff up all the time. We'll know more when the medical examiner and the forensic guys report back." He started to take another hit from the cigarette and then flung it away irritably. A woman passing by with a dog gave him a dirty look. "The hard drive's missing from his computer."

"So, someone else was with him."

"Not necessarily."

I glanced over at him.

"Listen." He sighed. "A guy gets wasted and starts thinking about offing himself, maybe he begins to worry about what he's leaving behind. These days, everybody's secrets are on their computers. Did Alex have a technical background?"

"A master's degree in economics and an undergraduate minor in computer science."

"There you go. He must have known that it's tough to completely erase things from a hard drive. The safe thing to do if you want to cover your tracks is to pop the drive and get rid of it. We're checking trash cans in a ten-block radius."

"What kind of secrets are you talking about?"

"What kind of secrets does any guy have? Porn's always a good bet. He might have been into nasty stuff, like pictures of little kids."

I flinched reflexively.

"I'm just speculating," Reggie added quickly. "I'm just saying there might have been stuff he didn't want his parents or friends to find out about when he was gone. You never know."

Maybe his secret was that he'd done an under-the-table deal with a U.S. senator to help get him elected president. I rolled the notion around in my mind uneasily, unsure whether to mention it to Reggie. If Alex had been murdered, or driven to kill himself, the police needed to know everything. If he hadn't, I didn't want to drag his name through the mud with a lot of wild speculation. I felt as though I needed to talk things through with Walter.

"At any rate," Reggie continued, "that's all I have right now. The investigating officers will probably want to interview you at some point. I mentioned that you were a friend of his."

"That's fine," I said apprehensively.

"Good, then. I gotta run. You gonna be okay?"

"Yeah. I might sit here awhile, though."

"No problem. We still getting together with Gallegos tomorrow morning?"

With everything else going on, it had slipped my mind.

"Sure," I said, not wanting to postpone. "Meet at the diner?"

"Nine o'clock. You talk to Claire and Kate yet?"

"No. I'm waiting for the right moment."

I left unsaid that just then, I couldn't imagine when the right moment might be.

Dinner with Claire and Kate and Phil was a challenge. I didn't mention Alex's death, not wanting to cast a pall on the evening. I decided to tell them the next morning, before they had a chance to read about it in the paper.

Phil sat in Kyle's old seat at the dining-room table. The good news for the evening was that he wasn't shy. He got started on the year he'd spent traveling and told story after story about Third World misadventures, making Claire and Kate laugh. I smiled along as best I could. Claire had a second glass of wine and then a third, something she almost never did. Seeing her animated made my heart ache with nostalgia. Midway through dinner, I caught Kate looking at me with concern, which made my heart ache for a different reason. She was too young to be so finely attuned to unhappiness.

I quickly lost a game of Risk after dinner and retired to the bedroom, leaving the three of them to scheme cheerfully toward world domination at the kitchen table. I was dozing fitfully when Claire came to bed. She reached for my hand in the dark and pressed it to her breast. I unbuttoned the neck of her chemise slowly, desiring her but careful of her mood. She knelt upright and pulled the chemise overhead with a single fluid gesture, and then shifted sideways to straddle me. We made love silently, her head burrowed against my chest.

Afterward, I held her in my arms, my body spooned tightly to hers. I kissed her neck and tasted salt. Her breathing had slowed, but I could tell she was still awake. I felt like crying. I didn't want to lose her as well.

"I was offered a job today," I said.

"By who?" she asked sleepily.

"A Russian guy named Narimanov. He's a big oil tycoon, with operations all over the world. It would be doing pretty much the same thing I'm doing now but working for him exclusively."

"I thought you liked working with Alex and Walter."

"It's a lot more money," I said, wincing at the mention of Alex.

"Do we need more money?"

"Not really," I said. The last seven years had been good to me financially. I braced myself for the plunge. "But it got me thinking. Kate's going to be off to college next September. There's no reason for us to be tied down here. Maybe we should spend a year in Paris or Rome. You always told me there's a more robust classical music scene there, and you already speak a little French and Italian."

She stiffened slightly.

"Or somewhere else," I added quickly. "I was just thinking a change might be good."

"I already have a job, at Sloan-Kettering."

"It's a tough place to work," I said, pushing for her to confide in me. "You never think about leaving?"

She shook my arm off her shoulders and edged away from me.

"Claire?"

"It's late," she said. "We'll talk another time."

I lay in bed next to her, tears starting from my eyes. It felt to me as if she was already gone.

17

The Turtle Bay Diner had smudged plate-glass windows that wrapped around the corner of Forty-sixth and Second, and twin plastic signs announcing the name on both façades in faded sea green script. It looked like a neighborhood place, the kind that had been there for twenty or thirty years, and that nobody who lived or worked outside a five-block radius of it had ever noticed. I was reaching for the door handle when I heard Reggie's voice.

"Hey."

I glanced over my shoulder and saw his battered blue undercover car parked at the back end of a bus stop. He was in the driver's seat, leaning sideways to call out the open passenger window.

"What's up?"

"I just got word that I need to be in Staten Island ASAP. You think you can handle Gallegos by yourself?"

"I guess," I said, resting my forearm on the roof of his car.

He leaned over a little farther to get a better angle on me.

"You sure? You look kind of beat this morning. No offense."

"I didn't get a lot of sleep. And I had to tell Claire and Kate about Alex before they heard about it somewhere else. They were both pretty upset."

"I bet," he said, shaking his head. "What about you?"

"I don't know." I was grateful he didn't ask if I'd also told them about the Kyle e-mail. I hated keeping things from Claire. Our relationship was initially built on the idea that we were a nation of two, without secrets. But Kate's revelation and my conversation with Claire in bed had rocked me. I couldn't risk upsetting her further until I had a better sense of how to respond. "I feel like I could use a stiff drink."

"One of the first things you learn as a rookie cop on patrol—if you feel like you need a drink, take one."

"Great," I said, laughing despite myself. "That makes me feel a lot better about our police force. Any update on Alex or the missing hard drive?"

"Not that I know of, but I'm not sure I'd hear. His father has everybody from the mayor down on eggshells. I'm betting the coroner rules it an accident unless they turn up a note, and maybe even then. Families tend to resist suicide verdicts."

I understood how Walter must feel. It would be horrible to think your child was so unhappy that he deliberately took his own life.

"So, listen," Reggie continued. "Gallegos. Don't go barging in with a bunch of questions about his brother-in-law or he's likely to just clam up. Get him talking about himself first, and then work your way toward the subject when he seems comfortable."

"Is that from the police handbook?"

"Yeah," he said. "And if that doesn't work, smack him in the kidney with your nightstick."

"Fifty percent of my job is getting people to talk to me. I'll be okay."

"Try and find out as much as you can about the car, the motel, and the hooker. How often Carlos used it, where he usually went, and whether he was in the habit of picking up working girls. Also, if he had any enemies that Gallegos knew about."

"The cops must've asked those questions the first time around."

"The file's pretty skinny on what Gallegos had to say. I'm a little curious about that."

A bus pulled up behind Reggie's car and blasted its horn. Reggie hit the switch to activate the red emergency lights in his rear window and waved it around. I could read the obscenity on the driver's lips as he wrestled with the oversized steering wheel.

"You, too, buddy," Reggie said, watching the driver in the mirror. "And one more thing, Mark. Make sure to ask Gallegos his opinion about what happened. It's a question that a lot of detectives tend to forget."

. . .

The smell of bacon greeted me as I pushed the diner door open. The interior was long and narrow, with ten or twelve booths to the left of a central aisle, and an old-fashioned lunch counter to the right. It was about half full. A sullen, purple-mascaraed cashier was perched on a stool next to the entrance, the tendrils of a ragged spider plant trailing into her hair.

"One?" she said, reaching for a menu.

"I'm supposed to be meeting a guy named Mariano Gallegos. You know him?"

She snapped her gum and led me toward the rear of the restaurant. A man wearing a light brown suit and a maroon tie was seated in a booth, facing in my direction. He was pudgy, with a weak chin and thinning hair, and looked to have about ten years on me. He half stood as I approached and extended a hand.

"Mark Wallace?"

"Nice to meet you."

We shook hands and sat down.

"I know who you are and what you do," he said rapidly, fidgeting with a fork. "Pardon my saying so, but I think you've made a mistake. I'm a commercial attaché. I deal with contracts. Everything oil related is handled by a different section."

"I understand," I said, caught a little off guard by his abruptness. "But your name came up in conversation recently, and I thought it might be good to get to know each other."

"What conversation?"

"A conversation with a friend," I said, wondering why he seemed so edgy. "Relax, please. There's nothing to worry about."

The waitress approached with a tired smile to pour coffee and take our orders. Gallegos asked for an egg-white omelet. I stuck to coffee and toast. He glanced left and right as she walked away and then hunched forward.

"It was an assistant to the ambassador who told me you wanted to meet," he whispered. "My colleagues are aware that you work with some very influential people." He rubbed the thumb and first two fingers of his right hand together to indicate the type of influence he was talking about. "Everyone at the embassy is a patriot, but I'm instructed to tell you that if you're interested in information, certain arrangements could be made."

It was a pitch I'd heard a hundred times before. The energy business is the sleaziest corner of the financial universe—guys in my line of work get hit up for bribes the way investment bankers get leaned on to buy program ads for charity galas. The surprise was how uncomfortable Gallegos seemed delivering it. He had a death grip on the fork in his left hand, and I could feel the table vibrating as one or both of his legs shook. My snap read was that he was a mild-mannered, midlevel diplomat a few years away from his pension, and deeply unhappy to find himself so far outside his comfort zone.

"Listen," I said, as soothingly as I could manage. "Let me apologize. I'm not trying to get you involved in anything you don't want to be involved in. And I'm not here to ask questions about Venezuela's oil industry."

"Then what?"

Reggie's caution regardless, I wasn't about to be coy.

"Your former brother-in-law, Carlos Munoz. I'm hoping you can tell me more about him."

Gallegos looked blank for a few seconds and then shook his head.

"I have nothing to say."

"Why not?"

"Because it's a private matter."

He'd already solicited money once. My immediate reaction was to ask if a cash payment would make him feel better about sharing, but I sensed it would be a mistake. I noticed that he was wearing a wedding ring. I took my wallet from my jacket and opened it to a photograph.

"This is a picture of my son, Kyle. Seven years ago, the very same night that your brother-in-law was murdered, Kyle was kidnapped. He's never been found."

Gallegos flinched, murmuring something in Spanish. I caught the word *Dios.* He was a parent himself; I could tell.

"I need your help," I said. "Please."

"I don't understand what you want from me," he answered, sounding shaken.

"The police have information that suggests my son might have been in your car the night he disappeared. They say you'd lent the car to your brother-in-law."

Gallegos's face hardened.

"The police think Carlos had something to do with your son's disappearance?"

"Their best guess is that the people who stole the car from Carlos might have been involved."

It wasn't quite the denial it sounded like, but fortunately, he didn't seem to notice.

"The police are fools," he spat bitterly. "I wouldn't believe anything they tell you."

"What makes you say that?"

He sipped from his coffee cup and then sighed.

"Because they got everything wrong. Carlos was not the victim of a random crime. He was deliberately murdered."

I blinked. It wasn't the answer I'd been expecting. I was torn between a sudden hope that I was about to learn something important and a fear that Gallegos was delusional.

"Murdered by whom?"

He touched the picture in the open wallet I'd set down on the table.

"Everything I tell you is between us. You have to swear it on your son."

"Between us and the policeman I'm working with, a detective named Reggie Kinnard. He's a good cop. I trust him. Nothing you tell me will go any further without your permission. I swear."

He hesitated, and I was afraid I'd put him off.

"Fine," he said eventually. "Let me explain. Carlos and I grew up poor in the same neighborhood. We were scholarship students at secondary school together. He was captain of the football team, captain of the debate team, a natural leader. I was quiet, but he always had time for me because we'd known each other in short pants. After university, we married sisters. Carlos introduced me to my wife. The sisters are from an old Caracas family, and their connections were enough to get us both good jobs with the government." He touched his chest with a trembling finger. "Me, I've never had much ambition. A good book, a nice glass of wine, a fast car—that's always been enough. But Carlos was destined to be a great man. He rose rapidly. There were people who thought he might become president someday."

"You admired him," I suggested, uncomfortable at the discrepancy between the Carlos he was describing and the violent thug Reggie had told me about.

"Very much."

"So, what happened?"

Gallegos's eyes shone, and I had the impression that he was on the verge of tears.

"Carlos and I met for lunch the week before he was murdered. He was agitated and unhappy. I'd never seen him that way before. I asked what was wrong. He said that he and some of his political rivals had been offered a bribe—a very large bribe—to do something that wasn't in the best interests of Venezuela. The others had agreed, but he'd said no. Afterward, he had the feeling that these men were suspicious of him—that they thought he might use what he knew to embarrass them. He told me that he'd been falsely accused of harassing some women at work. He suspected that he'd been followed, and that someone was listening in on his phone calls. He believed it was all part of an effort to intimidate him, to suggest what life would be like if he didn't cooperate."

"How did he respond?"

"He hadn't decided yet. It was the last time we spoke. A week later, his wife called to say that he was dead."

"And you think these people had him killed."

"I'm certain of it. His rivals used his death to generate political capital. The Venezuelan papers went on at length about the 'criminal behavior' that led to his 'sordid demise.' Carlos was a reformer. Everyone like-minded had to distance themselves from him, no matter how suspicious they were of the circumstances."

The waitress put food on the table. We both ignored it. He seemed sincere, but I strongly suspected he was seeing his former brother-in-law through rose-tinted glasses. During my twenty-year career in the financial industry, I'd never met a guy wrongly accused of sexual harassment.

"And you told all this to the police?"

"No. None of it."

"Why not?"

"Because I got a call ordering me not to. You have to understand. I'm not brave like Carlos was. I had a wife, two daughters, a newly widowed sister-in-law, and four fatherless nieces and nephews. I did what I was told to do. I kept my mouth shut."

"Who called you?"

He shook his head wordlessly.

"I need to know," I insisted.

"I can't tell you," he said softly. "It's not right of you to ask. Things happen. You have no idea."

I was well aware that things happened. I had a sudden urge to grab him by the collar and bang his head against the wall. The fact that someone didn't want him spouting wild notions didn't mean the notions were true, but a name would have given me an avenue to investigate.

"You mentioned your sister-in-law," I said, struggling to keep the animus out of my voice. "What was her relationship with Carlos like?"

His eyes narrowed.

"You read the police report. You want to know if he was violent."

I was beyond apologizing.

"Was he?"

"It was all lies. Carlos never hit a woman in his life. He was a devoted husband." He smiled grimly. "Your next question is why a devoted husband kept a girlfriend."

"Yes."

"Americans are unreasonable about sexual matters," he said, flapping a hand dismissively. "Carlos cared for his family, but he had normal desires."

"You knew he was seeing another woman?"

"Of course. He told me when he first asked to borrow the car. The woman lived east of the city, on Long Island. They'd been seeing each other only for a few weeks, and he was planning to end it. It was nothing important."

"How often did he borrow the car?" I asked, reverting to Reggie's list of questions.

"Once or twice a week. He had a key."

"And always to drive out to Long Island?"

"As far as I know."

"Carlos was with a prostitute when he died. Did that surprise you?"

He grimaced.

"Men are men. But yes, it surprised me. Carlos was a romantic. He always had an infatuation for some girl. There's nothing romantic about a prostitute."

My cell phone chimed softly, indicating an urgent text message.

"Excuse me a second," I said, taking it from my pocket and checking the display. The message was from Amy: *Walter wants to see you in his office as soon as possible.* I swore softly, wondering what the hell he was doing at work the day after his son's death. *Twenty minutes,* I texted back.

"You have a problem?" Gallegos asked.

"It's nothing," I said, berating myself for having broken his flow. I needed to get as much as I could from him while he was still inclined to talk. "The bribe you mentioned. Did Carlos tell you anything more about it?"

"A little. He and his colleagues had been offered an opportunity to buy shares in an oil company. The oil company owned drilling rights that were worth more than the market realized. The idea was that everyone could buy the shares inexpensively and then make a big profit when the news came out."

"In return for what?"

"Carlos didn't say."

"You know the name of the company?"

"No. Nothing more than I've told you."

There couldn't have been that many oil companies whose stock prices had popped seven years ago because of hidden reserves. It was a lead, although I wasn't sure to what. I was about to thank him and say good-bye when I recalled Reggie's final question.

"Tell me," I said. "What exactly do you think happened that night at the motel?"

Gallegos lowered his head. When he looked up again, the tears I thought I'd spotted earlier were flowing.

"I think a brave man died for being honest."

We said our good-byes, and Gallegos disappeared into the men's room to pull himself together. I was paying the cashier when I glanced into the mirror behind the lunch counter and caught the eye of a man at the counter who was sitting with his back to me. He was wearing a baseball cap pulled low, but I could see a wide, shiny scar stretching from his mouth to his ear, as if he'd been badly burned at some point. I turned away quickly, feeling bad about having stared.

18

Activity on the trading floor was muted, everyone hunched over their screens or whispering on telephones. I rehearsed awkward condolences in my head as I walked toward Walter's office. His curtains were drawn—I'd never noticed that he had curtains, much less seen them closed. I could feel eyes watching me as I knocked on the door.

"Come," Walter called.

I entered, the words I'd prepared stopping on my tongue. There were two men in the room with Walter—one fortyish, sitting in front of his desk, and the other twenty years older, off to the left, with his back to the curtained glass wall. They could have been before and after models for a temperance brochure—the younger fit and fresh-faced, and the older beefy and with a broken-veined nose. Identical flat stares and a rumpled sameness to their suits made me suspect that they were members of Reggie's fraternity.

"Lieutenant Wayland and Deputy Chief Ellison of the NYPD," Walter intoned quietly, confirming my guess. The chief was the dissolute-looking one. "They have a few questions for you." He pointed to a vacant chair between the policemen. "Sit, please."

Neither cop extended a hand. I sat, my attention shifting back to Walter. He was as carefully dressed and groomed as ever, but the near-tangible intensity he always radiated had evaporated, his gaze directed into the mid-distance over my shoulder. For the first time, I noticed that he was getting old.

"I can't tell you how sorry I am," I said. "Alex was a good friend. Claire sends her condolences also."

Walter nodded stiffly, still not looking at me. The lieutenant cleared his throat and removed a memo pad from his inside jacket pocket, but it was the chief who spoke.

"Mr. Wallace," he rumbled. I swung my head one hundred eighty degrees, faked out. "Mr. Coleman and his family are in a difficult position here. They'd naturally like to grieve in peace, but, unfortunately, people tend to gossip when there's any ambiguity surrounding a death." He massaged a jowl, looking mournful about the base tendencies he'd described. "Our job today is to eliminate that ambiguity, to make things easier for the family. You understand?"

"I think so," I said, glancing toward Walter again. His eyes were fixed on his hands. Presumably, this was about nudging the coroner toward an accidental-death verdict instead of suicide.

"Let's find out," the chief said. "Lieutenant?"

The lieutenant flipped a few pages on his pad.

"You and Alex Coleman had a drink together Monday afternoon at a bar named Pagliacci," he said, pausing for confirmation.

"Right."

"The bartender said that Alex seemed upset. Can you tell us why?"

"He'd had a bad day at work."

The lieutenant pursed his lips and made a note.

"I see. And to the best of your ability to discern, did Alex express any feelings of depression or futility while you were together?"

It was a ludicrously pointed question, the answer he wanted obvious, but I hesitated, recalling Alex's drunken plea to know how I staved off despair and his flat dismissal of my suggestion that he consider any job other than trading.

"Mr. Wallace," the chief growled behind me. I turned my head again. "In a situation like this, the medical examiner requires that we ask very specific questions to shed light on the decedent's state of mind. It's tough, though, because he's really looking for a psychological evaluation, and most people aren't qualified to make those kinds of observations." He reached forward, laying a nicotine-stained finger on my arm. "You, for example. You're not a psychologist, are you, Mr. Wallace?"

"No."

"Then it's probably best not to speculate too much." He tipped his chin toward the lieutenant. "Ask the question again."

"To the best of your ability to discern," the lieutenant repeated, "did Alex Coleman express any feelings of depression or futility when you had drinks with him at Pagliacci on Monday afternoon?"

"No," I lied. If Walter and Alex's mother wanted an accidental-death verdict, I didn't see that it was my place to oppose them. "He didn't."

"You sat beside him the next day at lunch. Did he express any feelings of depression or futility at that time?"

"No."

"Did he talk about suicide on either occasion, or mention wanting to harm himself?"

"No."

"Are you aware of any incident that might have triggered suicidal thoughts between the time you last saw Alex Coleman and the time he died?"

I chanced another look at Walter, wishing I'd had time to discuss Alex's potential involvement with Senator Simpson before talking to the police—although on reflection, I doubted a relationship with the senator had been the precipitant the lieutenant was asking about. Alex died early Wednesday morning, just a few hours before Walter liquidated his positions. I was willing to bet their last conversation had been the night before, and that Walter had told Alex what he'd decided to do. Maybe Walter was just trying to mitigate his own feelings of guilt. He hadn't set out in life to intimidate Alex, but I wondered how he felt about all his accomplishments now that he'd lost his son.

"No," I answered softly. "I'm not."

"Good," the chief said. "I think we're about done here—"

"One more thing," the lieutenant interrupted, flipping another page. "Alex sent you an e-mail earlier this week, suggesting you meet with a woman named Theresa Roxas. Did you?"

"Yes," I said uncomfortably. It wasn't a surprise that they'd been able to recover his e-mail—copies of everything were kept on the server.

"We'd like to talk to Ms. Roxas. Do you have a contact number for her?"

"No."

He raised his face from his pad, frowning.

"Alex's e-mail said she had important information for you. Did she?"

"She had information," I admitted. "I don't know if it's important. I'm still checking it out."

I caught a flicker of movement from Walter out of my peripheral vision. He'd glanced up from his hands and was looking at me.

"So, how were you supposed to get back in touch with her if you had any follow-up questions?"

"Through Alex."

The lieutenant tapped his pencil on the pad, evidently uncomfortable with the turn my answers had taken. The chief kept quiet, not giving him any help.

"Did she say how they knew each other?"

"They were friends."

"Her name wasn't in his address book."

"Maybe it was on his computer."

" 'Was,' " the chief interjected quickly. "You just said 'Maybe it *was* on his computer.' Why not 'is'?"

Shit. I was an idiot. The last thing I wanted was to get Reggie in trouble for blabbing about the police investigation.

"Meaning that I'm in the information business, and that I talk to a lot of people. I heard that the hard drive was missing from Alex's computer. Maybe Theresa's contact information was on the hard drive."

"What's the name of this person who talked to you?" the chief demanded.

Shit. Shit, shit, shit.

"I'm not at liberty to say."

"I don't give a good goddamn what you think you are or aren't at liberty to say," he snarled.

I shrugged, furious at myself for screwing up. The chief turned to Walter with an apoplectic expression.

"Mr. Wallace is an employee of yours. Perhaps you could persuade him that it's in his best interest to answer our questions as completely as possible."

Not true. I was a consultant. I turned my head to Walter, wondering how he was going to handle it. He stared at me for a long moment and then spoke up.

"I want a private word with the officers. Mark, I'd appreciate your waiting outside."

"Of course."

"I don't think—" the chief began, but Walter silenced him with a gesture.

I stepped out, grateful for the break. Ignoring the inquisitive eyes still directed at me, I dialed Reggie on his cell phone. He answered on the first ring.

"Hey. What happened with Gallegos?"

"Later," I whispered, cupping the phone in my hands. "Listen. I screwed up. A couple of senior guys from your department named Wayland and Ellison were asking me questions about Alex, and I let slip that I knew his hard drive was missing."

"Shit."

"The chief wanted to know who told me, and I refused to say. He wasn't happy."

Reggie sighed.

"Chief's a little cranky before lunch with his buddy Jack Daniel's. Afterward, he gets mean."

"Sorry."

"Don't worry about it. I got a good balance in the favor bank. It's not the end of the world if you have to give me up."

"You sure?"

"Yeah."

"Okay. I gotta hop. I'm waiting outside Walter's office. I only got bounced so they could figure out how to lean on me."

"Understood. Where you going to be later?"

"Here, then Sloan-Kettering. Why?"

"I might have some news for you."

"You got a lead on the car?" I asked, my heart in my throat.

"Could be. Keep your phone on. And I want to hear about Gallegos."

"It's another weird story."

"My fucking epitaph. Stay in touch."

The door opened again thirty seconds later. Wayland and Ellison filed out, neither acknowledging me. Walter called my name.

"Let me explain—" I said, as I reentered the office.

"Don't bother," he interrupted. "I couldn't care less who you talk to in the police department. You got the Saudi information from this woman Theresa Roxas, didn't you?"

"Right," I said, not surprised he'd put the pieces together.

"And Alex was the friend who introduced you to her."

"Yes."

"And when we spoke yesterday and agreed that the friend who introduced you to the expert was probably working on behalf of Senator Simpson, you didn't see fit to tell me that your friend was actually my son."

His tone was withering. Any other time, I would have told him that my sources were none of his goddamn business. Today, it was understandable that he was upset.

"I wanted to give Alex a chance to explain things first. And then yesterday, after I heard what happened, I knew that I had to come tell you, but I didn't get the opportunity."

He glared at me as if I'd said something ridiculous, but I wasn't about to fall into the trap of defending myself when I hadn't done anything wrong. I let ten long seconds tick past and then tried to move beyond his accusation.

"So, what do you think Alex's relationship with Theresa Roxas means?"

He shot his cuffs and began straightening the tiny golden pigs he wore as cuff links. The pigs were a signature item, a reminder of the old Wall Street aphorism that bulls and bears make money but pigs get slaughtered. The fussing was a familiar signal that his mind was at work, and I took advantage of the break to resume my previous seat.

"I think it means that Senator Simpson—or more probably Clifford White, on the senator's behalf—reached an arrangement with Alex behind my back," he said calmly, when the links were perfectly aligned.

"What kind of arrangement?"

"I have no idea. And your failure to keep me properly informed means that I'll likely have difficulty finding out."

"Sorry," I said, hoping a generic apology might prevent another flare-up. I wasn't in the mood for histrionics. "What can I do to help?"

"You've done quite a lot for this family already. I have only one more favor to ask."

"Name it."

"I want you to pack up your stuff, get the hell out of my office, and never come back."

19

I was sitting at my desk ten minutes later, feeling poleaxed, when a message from a friendly client popped up on my screen: *Hearing Cobra terminated your contract because Walter thinks you're untrustworthy. What the hell is going on?*

I reached for my keyboard and then stopped, realizing that nothing I wrote would make any difference. It was true if Walter said it, and plainly he had. Short-term, I had nothing to worry about. My clients weren't lemmings; most would stick with me, if only because I'd been so hot recently. But they'd be more standoffish, so as not to offend Walter, and because something like this would give me a bad smell. Long-term, my relationships would deteriorate, and I'd get more cancellations. A year or two hence I might well be out of business. I sat quiet for a second, thinking about it.

The truth was that I didn't give a damn. I could always make money. Alex's death was a wake-up call, a reminder that the only important thing in my life was the people I loved. I picked up my phone and dialed home, tired of being clever. I'd come right out and tell Claire I knew about her audition in San Francisco, and make her understand that I'd do anything to be with her—that I loved her and couldn't be happy without her.

"Hello?" she answered.

"It's Mark. You busy?"

"I'm heading over to the hospital in a few minutes. I have rehearsals all day. Why? Is everything okay?"

"Not really. I need to talk to you."

She was silent for a moment, and I wondered what she was thinking.

"Come early tonight. Before the reception. I'll meet you in the Pediatric Pavilion at five o'clock."

"I love you."

"Five o'clock," she repeated distantly. "There are some things I need to talk to you about as well."

20

I took a minute to pull myself together and then buzzed Amy. She opened the door a few seconds later, dabbing at her eyes with a tissue.

"You heard?"

She nodded.

"What happened? Is it something to do with Alex?"

"In a way. It's a long story. I'm not completely sure how things are going to shake out for me yet, but I'll be leaving here immediately. You need to think about your own situation. I'd love it if you came with me, but I understand completely if you'd rather explore other options. You know what kind of reference I'll give you. It's your decision."

"'If you faint in the day of adversity, your strength is small,'" she said, attempting a smile. "Proverbs. I'll stay with you."

"Thanks," I said, touched by her loyalty. "I appreciate the confidence. How quick do you think we can get some cardboard boxes up here?"

"The warehouse just dropped off a stack. I was getting ready to purge files. You want help assembling them?"

"I think I can handle it. I'd prefer it if you lined up a moving company and began investigating short-term space. With a premium on speed, please. I'm as anxious for me to get gone at this point as Walter is."

The packing kept me busy well past lunch, in part because I'd been overoptimistic about my ability to assemble the origami-like boxes, and in part because everyone I knew was calling in to find out what had happened between me and Walter. I solved the box problem by asking Amy for a tutorial after mangling a few, and the other by simply telling everyone it had been personal. To the handful of clients who pushed harder, I let slip that Walter and I had fallen out over Alex, assuming it would get around the market quickly enough. It was the least damaging version of events I could circulate, and it had the advantage of being true.

Amy buzzed for the umpteenth time shortly after two. I left off wrapping a bunch of old deal mementos and punched the flashing line on my phone.

"Mark Wallace."

"I was disappointed not to hear from you this morning."

I recognized the voice immediately. Narimanov.

"It's been a difficult twenty-four hours."

"I read about Alex Coleman. You were close?"

"Very."

"I'm sorry. I was going to suggest we get together to discuss my offer further, but we can put if off if you like."

I wasn't much in the mood for business, but my circumstances made it stupid to discourage him.

"Get together when?"

"Three o'clock? My flat at the Time Warner Center?"

I double-checked my watch. I'd still have plenty of time before meeting Claire.

"Three o'clock works fine."

"Enter on Fifty-eighth Street. The doorman will direct you."

"I look forward to it."

21

The Time Warner Center is a slice of Hong Kong transplanted to New York City—a cramped, upscale mall topped by a generic luxury hotel and a host of overpriced, absentee-owned condos in linked towers, with a few million pounds of marble tossed in to make everything classy. Narimanov kept a penthouse, but I had the sense that he didn't spend much time there. The immaculate, Scandinavian modern living room I was shown to was entirely devoid of photos or other personal items, every throw pillow freshly plumped and perfectly placed. It made me wonder if the maids worked from brochures. I noticed a simple wooden chessboard on a table by the glass wall overlooking Columbus Circle. It was set wrongly, with the pieces randomly arranged behind the pawns. I walked over and began correcting it.

"You play?" Narimanov asked from behind me.

"Some." I turned to face him. He was wearing the same outfit he'd had on the other day—charcoal slacks and a black turtleneck—and he was carrying a manila envelope. I wondered if it contained an offer letter. "Years ago. When I was in college. I never wanted to spend time memorizing moves, so I never became very proficient."

"My objection precisely. Have you ever played Fischer Random Chess?"

"Never heard of it."

"It's a modern variant of a game called Shuffle Chess, codified in the mid-nineties by your eccentric former champion Bobby Fischer. You roll a die to determine the arrangement of the high-value pieces, eliminating reliance on memorized openings and combinations. There are nine hundred and sixty legal starting positions. We'll have to play some-time." He motioned toward the seating area. "It's good of you to come. Sit, please."

I sank down onto a white leather sofa and he settled in the matching end chair, tucking the envelope he was carrying between the seat cushion and the chair's arm. He leaned forward, muscled forearms resting on his knees and thick hands clasped loosely. Broad shoulders and typically Slavic features gave him the look of a Russian movie heavy, but there was a delicacy to his movements that saved his appearance from coarseness.

"Nice place you have here. Great views."

"My only instruction to my people was not to buy in any building that said Trump on it," he said wryly. "And this is what they came up with. Trump without Trump."

I smiled, liking him more and more.

"Drink?" he asked.

"Nothing, thanks. Before we discuss anything else, I want to thank you for the heads-up on the Russian/French attack. Russia's a big black hole to most analysts. I'm looking forward to learning more about it."

"Russia's a big black hole to me sometimes. The only thing the Russian people really learned from seventy years of Communism was the importance of keeping their mouths shut. I heard about the attack from a senior French oil executive, who heard about it directly from the general in charge. It's much easier to gather confidential information in France than in most other places. The Grandes Écoles graduates are all in bed together."

"So, what happens next?"

He shrugged.

"The French went out on a limb for Russia. Next, they'll want pay-back. That means preferential consideration for French companies bidding on Russian energy projects."

"A number of which you control," I said, deciding to probe how good-humored he really was. "I'm curious—how does that work exactly? You get a phone call telling you who to award contracts to?"

"In the old days," he replied easily. "Russia's become more Western-ized. We negotiate with carrots now, instead of sticks. The Kremlin has a list of things they want, and I have a list of things I want. Business gets done."

Liking him didn't mean I completely believed him. It had been only a few years since the Russian government deliberately broke the oil giant Yukos and sent its billionaire owner, Mikhail Khodorkovsky, to prison. The charge was tax fraud, but his actual crime—in the opinion of most Western observers—had been funding opposition political parties. Narimanov might negotiate with his government about some things, but there had to be times when they made him toe the line. I made a mental note to learn what I could about his political connections.

"And you seem to have done well by it. I'm flattered by your offer."

"And surprised that I followed up again so soon?" he asked shrewdly.

"A little," I admitted. "It's not a standard negotiating technique."

"Unless something's changed. I heard about your difficulty with Walter Coleman."

I made an effort to keep my face blank. I'd wanted to tell him the story myself. His having heard from someone else was bad, because it put me on the defensive.

"You invited me to your apartment to retract your job offer?" I asked, playing it cool. "That's equally nonstandard."

He laughed.

"Not at all. But I need to know what happened between the two of you if there's a possibility of our working together. Walter's very well regarded in the markets. I can't just ignore his judgments."

It was the reaction I'd expected. A public condemnation from Walter was a huge burden to be carrying around, regardless of my track record. Narimanov's offer entitled him to more information than I'd shared with my clients.

"Walter's son, Alex, directed me to some confidential market information," I explained carefully. "The source of the information is an open question, as is the nature of Alex's relationship with the conduit. Walter only found out after Alex died. He felt I should have kept him informed."

"Walter realized his son had a secret arrangement with some third party and was angry at you for not telling him?"

I nodded, impressed by how quickly his mind worked.

"I see." He tapped the tips of his fingers together, considering. "Is this about the Saudi Arabian oil field data?"

I felt the ground shift under my feet, wondering how the hell Narimanov knew about the Saudi data, and, more to the point, how he knew that Alex or I knew. The last couple of days spun by in my head at high speed as I tried to figure out what hidden connection Narimanov might have to the events that had transpired. Nothing leapt out at me.

"You're going to have to explain how you knew to ask that particular question," I said, as evenly as I could manage. "If there's a possibility of our working together, that is."

He grinned, apparently enjoying my discomfiture.

"I got a call from an acquaintance in Washington a few days ago, telling me that Alex Coleman had been asking questions about a trove of confidential Saudi Arabian information. He was insistent that the people he spoke to not mention his inquiries to his father."

"And these people kept the secret from Walter but told you. That seems odd."

"Why? I've made it known that I pay well for information that interests me. It's been an important element of my success. I get calls from all sorts of people, on all sorts of subjects. It's as I told you yesterday—I have access to information that isn't normally attainable."

"You get calls from people in the U.S. government?"

He gave me a condescending look.

"Of course."

I'd seen too much in my career to be shocked by corruption, but the notion of people in my own government selling information to foreigners pissed me off. And the realization of the extent to which Narimanov had manipulated me the first time we met pissed me off more. He hadn't even mentioned Saudi—I'd been the one to bring it up, thinking I was clever. I wasn't in any mood to be jerked around.

"I suppose we're done, then," I said, getting to my feet.

"What do you mean?" he asked, looking up at me.

"You approached me because you wanted to collaborate on an analysis of how much surplus oil there is in the world. You already have most of the information you need to figure out the answer, or you can get it from your friends in Washington. Either way, it doesn't seem that you have any real need of my services. It's been a pleasure meeting you. Good luck."

I took a step toward the door.

"Wait," he said. "Perhaps I've expressed myself badly."

"On the contrary—you've been remarkably clear. It's just that I don't like being toyed with."

He stood as well, his brow furrowed.

"I apologize," he said, looking me squarely in the eye. "You're correct that I should have been more forthright the other day, when we first spoke." He gestured toward the couch. "Please." ⋅

I sat down again, surprised and encouraged. Most guys as rich as Narimanov were constitutionally incapable of apologizing.

"The truth is that I don't have the information," Narimanov admitted, settling back into the end chair. "Alex only made inquiries. He didn't pass the data along. And I'm reluctant to fish for it at the source."

"You know what the source is?"

"I do. A U.S. agency most commonly known by three initials."

Which was consistent with Walter's theory. The information had been passed to Senator Simpson from the CIA or the NSA, and then Simpson had arranged to get it to me.

"And you're reluctant to fish for it why?"

"I draw the line at suborning state intelligence agencies, and at cooperating with them. Russia's, America's, or anyone else's. Intelligence agencies make bad friends and worse enemies. I troll exclusively in open waters—or at least waters that aren't too heavily restricted."

It was a smart policy, and his caution prompted me to take a step back and reconsider my own circumstances. I'd been around the block enough to know that I was okay publishing the Saudi data, regardless of the source. Any potential legal repercussions would attach to the person or persons who leaked the information, not to me. But my situation was different if I simply sold the information on to a foreign national. Morally, and maybe legally. I didn't want to become the kind of sleazeball that I'd been mentally condemning a few minutes ago, and I certainly didn't want to go to jail.

"So, what exactly are you suggesting?"

"Yesterday's offer stands. I buy you out, and you come to work for me exclusively. It's not just the Saudi data I'm interested in—I receive far too much information to process myself, and the people I currently employ frequently don't grasp the subtleties of what's important. I need someone like you—someone who can operate independently, and who I can trust."

I shook my head regretfully.

"It's still not going to work. I can't negotiate a private sale of something that originated in the U.S. intelligence community, particularly to a foreign national. Assuming I can verify the data, my only option is to make it public."

He frowned at the carpet for a moment and then looked up.

"How about this? The raw Saudi data and anything else you might receive from U.S. government sources constitute an exception to our agreement. You're free to publish through whatever channel you see fit, provided it can't be traced back to you or my operation."

It was a clever concession, and eminently workable. There were any number of competent reporters I could use as a blind to get stuff into the public domain. I felt a sudden rush of professional elation, excited by the offer for reasons that had nothing to do with Walter's disapprobation. Absent Alex, I didn't feel any emotional tie to my current situation. I respected my hedge-fund clients, but I didn't particularly like them. They were too self-absorbed, too focused on making money, and—perhaps—too much of an endangered species. A move now would be smart.

"Perfect. Assuming we go forward, where would you want me to locate?"

"Entirely your choice. I'll want to meet face-to-face at least monthly in London or New York, at my discretion, but otherwise you're free to set up shop wherever you'd like."

Which would let me accommodate Claire, if she wanted me to move with her to San Francisco.

"Great. I still need to run it by my wife, but I think we might have a deal."

"Excellent." He took hold of the envelope nestled against his leg and offered it to me. "A good-faith gesture. The bits and pieces I've been able to collect on Saudi independently, as promised. I'd be interested in hearing your preliminary conclusions as soon as possible."

I reached out and took the envelope eagerly. Unwinding the red thread sealing the flap, I saw that it contained three data CDs in purple-tinted jewel cases.

"Thanks," I said, deciding it was the right moment to do a little trolling of my own. "Tell me, did your guy in Washington tell you whether he thought the Saudi data was good?"

"No. Only that it had the correct provenance—which, of course, is a powerful recommendation in and of itself."

"True." I got to my feet. "Assuming no problem at home, I'll have my lawyer draft some terms and get back to you first thing next week."

He smiled.

"Welcome aboard."

22

I was standing outside Butterfield an hour later, waiting for the car that was supposed to pick me up, when my cell phone rang. I rested my right foot on top of a fire hydrant, balanced the heavy lasagna I was carrying precariously on my uplifted knee, and cautiously let go with one hand. The number on the phone display looked familiar, but I couldn't place it.

"Hello?"

"*As-Salāmu 'Alaykum.*"

Shoot. It was Rashid, calling through the switchboard at the Four Seasons. Not that I didn't want to talk to him, but this was an awkward moment for an extended hello. The tin tray sagged in the middle like an overtaxed seesaw as we executed the compulsories.

"Can I ring you back in a few minutes?" I asked, at the first polite opportunity.

"No need. I'd appreciate it if you came to see me tomorrow morning. Is that convenient?"

"Sure," I said, wondering if he had feedback on the Saudi data already. I'd sent it to him only the previous day. "Can I bring you anything?"

"Nothing, thank you. We'll have coffee in the lobby. At eleven?"

"At eleven," I confirmed.

I hung up just in time to save the tray from disaster. It was good that Rashid wanted to get together—it would give me a chance to ask him what he thought about my potentially working for Narimanov. I respected his opinion. A Town Car with livery plates cruised past, my name in the passenger window and the driver's head turned the wrong way. I shouted, waving an elbow like a chicken, and watched him go around the block. The burst of optimism I'd felt after my meeting with Narimanov had left me. It was time to go see Claire.

Memorial Sloan-Kettering occupies an entire block on the Upper East Side, near the East River. The original building was a brick box, but they added a modern tower with updated facilities a few years back. The Pediatric Pavilion—a dual-storied atrium featuring a twenty-foot-high kinetic wall sculpture—was the showpiece of the addition. I dropped the lasagna on a table set with steam trays and went hunting for my wife. I found her in a conference room nearby with Kate, Phil, and a handful of other youngish people I didn't recognize. The door was shut, so I hung around in the corridor, watching. A scruffy-looking kid asked a question, and Claire's answer made everyone laugh. She'd always been a natural with students. She noticed me through the glass wall and beckoned for me to come in, her smile fading.

"Okay, then," she said as I entered. "Six o'clock in the atrium and six-forty-five back here. And remember to spread out and talk to people during dinner, please."

There was a ragged chorus of assent as the volunteers got to their feet and began departing. I smiled at Kate, but she gave me a furious look and hurried away without saying anything. I couldn't imagine why she was upset with me.

"Hey," I said, planting an awkward kiss on Claire's cheek. "Something bothering Kate?"

"Not that I know of."

Her tone was clipped, and she wasn't making eye contact. I glanced at the clock. An hour suddenly seemed like an impossibly short time to cover everything we had to talk about. I took off my coat and draped it over a chair.

"Shall we sit?"

"I called you at the office this morning," she said, ignoring my suggestion. She was twisting her wedding ring on her finger. "It occurred to me that you might want to pass on the concert and spend the evening with Alex's friends or parents. Amy mentioned that you were at breakfast with Reggie and another man."

I could hear the question in her voice. Amy routinely posted Claire on my schedule, with my approval, but I wished to God she hadn't mentioned Reggie. It was exactly where I didn't want to begin.

"That's not why I'm here."

She looked at me quizzically, perhaps hearing something in my voice.

"Mariano Gallegos. Amy didn't know him. Is he a police officer?"

I couldn't think of any way to put her off without lying to her.

"Sit," I said gently. "Please."

She sat. I told her everything—about the e-mail, and the stolen car, and Carlos's murder, and my conversation with Gallegos. A single tear ran down her face when I related what the e-mail had said. I wanted to reach for her hand, but her shoulders were hunched and I was afraid she'd pull away.

"That's everything, except that Reggie mentioned he might have a lead on the car. He's supposed to call me later."

Silence fell. Claire hadn't asked any questions. Her head was bowed, and her hair was hanging down limply. She looked defeated. It was torture to see her suffering.

"I'm sorry," I continued. "And not just about keeping secrets. I love you, and the most important thing in the world to me is to be with you. I meant what I said last night—I think it's time for us to get away and make a fresh start." I hesitated, cautious of mentioning San Francisco, lest it sound like I was accusing her of something. "My sense is that you feel the same way but that you don't know how to tell me, because you don't know if you can start over with me. You can. We can. I swear it. I'll do whatever I have to do."

She took a deep breath and pushed the hair back from her face.

"And what about Reggie and these Venezuelan people?"

"Reggie doesn't really need my help. He's just keeping me involved. . . ." I trailed off, aware that I'd headed in the wrong direction.

"Because you want to be kept involved," Claire said, finishing my sentence.

"If it weren't for the fact that Kate is still in school," I said slowly, looking directly into her eyes, "I'd drive to the airport right now, and get on a plane with you, and never come back to New York, and never speak to Reggie again. Kyle's not coming back. I know that now. Being with you, moving forward with you, that's more important to me than the past."

She touched my cheek fleetingly, as if afraid I might burn her.

"I love you, too," she said. "I always have. Enough to know that you'll never stop being tormented, the way I've been tormented. . . ."

"It doesn't have to be that way," I said, pleading with her to believe me.

"Shh," she whispered, touching a finger to my lips. "Listen. After Kyle disappeared, I felt . . . panicked. All the time. Like I was frozen in that moment when I first hurried into the video store with Kate, and the man behind the counter told me he hadn't seen Kyle, and the woman next to me suggested I call the police. All those months when you and Kate were out searching and handing out the leaflets, I was trapped in that moment, and with that feeling, and I couldn't get out."

"I wanted to help you," I said, feeling tears on my face. "I didn't know how."

"I know. I'm not blaming you. Even at the time, I was glad you were doing what you were doing, and that you'd taken Kate with you. It was important for our family, and I felt terrible that I wasn't strong enough to help."

"I never judged you or thought less of you."

"No. You and Yolanda and Kate, you all took care of me. And then you went back to work, and Yolanda went home to the Dominican Republic, and I woke up one morning and realized that I had to get Kate off to school, and shop for dinner, and pick up the dry cleaning. And I felt better, because I had responsibilities, and I wasn't just thinking about Kyle all the time. That's when I decided to volunteer here at the hospital. Being here, helping people who needed my help—it keeps the feeling of panic away."

"And being with me makes the panic come back," I said, feeling as if my heart might break.

She nodded.

"Sometimes. More than I can bear. I'm sorry."

My phone rang in my coat. I ignored it, but Claire took the phone from my pocket and checked the display.

"It's Reggie," she said. "Answer it."

"I don't want to," I choked.

"You have to. I've thought about us a lot. The only way we can be together is if you're at peace, and the only way you're ever going to be at peace is to learn the truth."

She held the phone out to me. I wiped my face with my hand and took it from her.

"Reggie," I said.

"Hey. I'm out front. You got a minute to come outside and talk?"

I looked at Claire beseechingly.

"Go," she said. "For both of us."

23

Reggie's car was parked at a hydrant just outside the main entrance. I opened the door and climbed in, letting my head drop back against the rest as I sat.

"Something wrong?" he asked.

Everything, but I wasn't ready to get into it with him.

"Smells like puke in here."

"Gave a runaway a ride home this afternoon. Bought him a thirty-two-ounce orange Slurpee and a foot-long Snickers bar to keep him quiet. Live and learn. But you looked unhappy before you got in."

"Family trouble," I said, scrabbling for the window switch.

"With Kate?"

"Maybe," I replied, thinking of the angry look she'd given me. I lowered the window halfway and turned my face to the opening, inhaling a lungful of cold, fresh air. The car really stank.

"I saw her canoodling with some Asian kid on a bench down the block. They going out?"

"I guess so." I hadn't considered her relationship in quite those terms before. It was another subject I didn't feel ready to pursue. "So, what's up?"

He struck a match and lit a cigarette. It was the first time I could recall being grateful for the odor.

"I think I found the guy who stole the car."

I jerked upright, galvanized as if by an electric shock.

"You talk to him?"

"Not yet," he said, stuffing his crumpled pack of cigarettes and matches into a cup holder. "Tonight."

"So, what are we waiting for?"

He gave me a baleful glance.

"Who's 'we,' paleface?"

It was the punch line to an old joke, Tonto's reply to the Lone Ranger when he observed that they were both about to be killed by hostile Indians.

"There's some kind of problem because I'm the wrong color?" I asked, confused.

Reggie laughed.

"Nah. There's some kind of problem because you look like you work in an office on Park Avenue. The guy I found will be more talkative if he's scared."

"Trust me," I said forcefully, "I meet the person who might've murdered my son, and I'm going to look like what I am—someone who wants to fucking kill him."

He nodded, perhaps conceding the point.

"Which brings us to the second issue. You're involved here."

"And you aren't?"

The rebuttal popped out before I had time to think about it. Reggie chewed on it for a minute, one thumb drumming on the steering wheel, and I realized it had been exactly the right thing to say. He'd dedicated his life to finding people who were lost or taken, and he was honest enough with himself not to pretend it was just a job. He'd never given up on Kyle, because he cared.

He took a hit from his cigarette, sighed as he exhaled, and then dropped the car into gear. We made an illegal U-turn across four lanes of traffic and headed south on York Avenue. I kept quiet as we passed Rockefeller University, not wanting to accidentally dissuade him from his apparent decision to let me ride along. The sun was already down, and the Rockefeller campus was a floodlit oasis, a grassy fifteen-acre chunk of Harvard or Princeton transported to the Upper East Side. I fleetingly wondered where Kate would be at school next year—and where Claire and I would be, and whether we'd be together.

"You'll do what you're told, right?"

"Of course," I replied immediately. "Where is this guy?"

"Staten Island."

"How'd you find him?"

"Remember I told you that most stolen cars in this part of the world get reregistered with fake VIN numbers or chopped for parts?"

"Right."

"If you're going to reregister a car, the easiest way is to pretend it's coming in from out of state. That way there's no paperwork for the local DMV to match to." He clucked irritably as he made the left turn onto the descending ramp for FDR Drive. The highway was jammed in both directions. "I checked out-of-state registrations in the tristate area for the six-month period after Gallegos's car was stolen. A couple of potentials but nothing that really rang any bells. Again, it's lucky as hell for us that the M5 is limited production."

We reached the bottom of the ramp. The cars before us had alternated into traffic, but a shiny black Hummer with chrome running boards was refusing to give way, tailgating the vehicle in front of it. Reggie closed to within eighteen inches, the roofline of his beat-up Chevy level with the bottom of the Hummer's windows. Shifting his cigarette to his right hand, he popped open the driver's door and slammed it hard into the side of the Hummer. The driver screeched to a halt, and Reggie accelerated smoothly into the resultant gap.

"Somebody's going to take a shot at you one of these days," I said, glancing back over my shoulder. The Hummer owner was out of his car and walking around to the passenger side to inspect it. He looked perplexed. I could hear horns sounding behind him.

"Happened before. At any rate, the other thing I did was to go back through the records and look for chop-shop busts. There's usually a couple a year. Then I went through the seized property lists to see if anything matched the M5. Again, nothing really jumped out."

"That's not much of a surprise, is it? The detectives investigating Carlos's murder would have been looking for Gallegos's car also. They must have left some kind of flag in the system."

"True," he said, sounding offended. "But the department computer is three monkeys in an orange crate. You got to try the data a bunch of different ways to make sure you're getting good answers, and you got to be creative."

"So, what'd you find?"

"I'm getting to it," he muttered, checking his side-view mirror intently. I hoped he wasn't sizing up another victim. "Don't rush me.

The next thing I did was to pull the plate numbers of all the tow trucks owned by the busted chop shops."

"Why?"

"BMW and other high-end cars have good security systems. Sophisticated thieves don't bother messing with them. They just hook the car to a tow truck and haul it away."

"Your point being?"

He reached up and tapped the small white box Velcroed to his windshield below the rearview mirror.

"You matched the tow trucks to their E-ZPasses," I said, comprehension dawning. "Very clever."

"Not many chop shops cough up for Manhattan rent, and most vehicles leaving the city pay a toll or get clocked somewhere," he said smugly. "I figured it was worth a shot."

"You got a hit?"

"A flatbed truck belonging to an outfit called Frank's Foreign Cars, sole premises a piece-of-shit garage in Staten Island. The truck was clocked inbound on the Verrazano-Narrows Bridge around seven on the evening that Gallegos's car was stolen, and outbound around ten. Frank was busted for selling stolen parts six months later. The cops found a half-disassembled Porsche last seen in front of Nobu at his place. Belonged to one of the Yankees." He reached over me to open the glove box and pulled out a manila envelope. "Check it out."

The envelope contained a grainy black-and-white photograph. I expected it to be of a Porsche, but the subject was a toll plaza at night, shot from a height of maybe twenty feet.

"What's this?"

"Fourth lane from the left," Reggie said.

I counted with my finger. The vehicle in the fourth lane from the left was a flatbed truck, and it was hauling a dark-colored car. The car looked like a BMW.

"You got to be kidding me," I said breathlessly. "Where on earth did you get this?"

"Bridges and tunnels into the city are all covered by multiple security cameras. In the old days, they used to keep the tapes for a year. Post 9/11, they started digitizing everything and keeping it indefinitely. The E-ZPass gave me an exact time to check. Once the tech from the MTA queued up the right day for me, it only took a couple of minutes to find the shot."

"And that's an M5 the truck's hauling?"

"Looks like one," Reggie said. "The picture's not clear enough to be sure. Could just be a regular Five series. The tech who helped me out said the gray scale was consistent with a deep-red color. We can get a more scientific match later if we need to."

My hands started trembling. If this was the right car, and if what we suspected was true, my son, Kyle, was in the trunk of the car in the photo, dead or suffering.

"Hey," Reggie said softly, reaching over to take the photo from me. "Don't sweat it until we know more."

I took a couple of deep breaths.

"This guy Frank is still operating out of Staten Island?"

Reggie shook his head.

"Nope. Went to jail and got mixed up in a turf war between some skinheads and some Mexican Mafia. Took a shank in the yard. Dead before he hit the ground. But he had a sidekick named Vinny Santore, an eighteen-year-old kid. According to the detectives who worked the case, Vinny was the one who grabbed the cars and Frank was the one who broke them down. Vinny did two years up at the Mid-Orange penitentiary and another two on parole."

"So, we're on our way to see Vinny."

"Right."

"And you think he'll talk to us?"

"I got a few ideas on how to persuade him," Reggie said calmly. "Now, tell me about breakfast with Gallegos."

We ended up in a semi-industrial neighborhood in Staten Island. I'd been lost since the moment we crossed the bridge, but Reggie seemed to know where he was going. He pulled to the curb behind a green Jeep Cherokee and flashed his lights once before turning them off. A guy got out of the Jeep. I was surprised to recognize Joe Belko, Reggie's recently retired partner. Joe was a skinny white guy with a monk's fringe of gray hair, who looked like what he was—someone who spent a lot of time fishing with his grandkids. Reggie lowered his window as Joe approached.

"Hey," Joe said. If he was surprised at my presence, he didn't show it. He leaned into the car and offered me his hand. "Good to see you, Mark."

"And you. Retirement treating you okay?"

"So far." He glanced at Reggie and made a face. "Car smells like puke."

"I hadn't noticed. So, what do you think?"

"Vinny's working solo, and traffic's light. I think we're good."

"You got the gear?"

Joe nodded.

"Wait a second," I interrupted. "What's our plan here?"

"What I told you," Reggie replied. "To talk to Vinny."

"Officially?"

"Officially's not likely to be very productive," Reggie explained, speaking as if to a child. "Vinny has experience with the justice system. I show him my badge, he tells me to fuck off. I say I want him to come down to the station, he tells me to fuck off. I ask him what he knows about the car, he tells me to fuck off. And then I fuck off, because I got no leverage on him and don't know that I can get any. That's officially."

"What's unofficially?"

"Joe takes my badge and my car and holds down the front, so nobody bothers us. You and me go around back."

"The front and back of what?"

Reggie smiled.

"Let's go see."

Joe drove, Reggie in the rear seat. He slowed as we cruised past a decrepit-looking gas station. It had an attendant's booth the size of a garden shed and a single island of pumps. There was a discount beverage center to the left and a used-car lot to the right, both closed.

"That's him," Joe said, tipping his head toward the booth.

A shaggy-haired guy sat framed by a three-by-six glass window, racks of cigarettes surrounding him. It looked as though he was talking on a phone.

"What's behind?" Reggie asked.

"Lot of weeds and a chain-link fence. Fence backs onto a sheet-metal outfit, also closed. It's a good setup. There's an alley runs behind the beverage center."

I was starting to feel nervous, wondering whether I'd been smart to insist on coming. All the years I'd been watching Reggie break small rules, it had never occurred to me to wonder how far he really went.

"Relax," Reggie said, reading my face. "I'm not in the business of breaking legs."

Not breaking legs seemed like a small carveout in the grander category of kicking the shit out of people.

"I'm okay breaking legs if it's going to help us learn the truth," I said, hoping my bravado wasn't too transparent. "But what if Vinny gives us the guy who kidnapped Kyle? What if he is the guy who kidnapped Kyle? What are we all going to say in court when some defense attorney asks us what we did tonight?"

Reggie shrugged.

"Whatever we have to say. That's how the game's played."

Joe reached over to nudge my arm.

"Reggie and I worked a lot of cases together. Anything really bad was going to happen, I wouldn't be here. Just be cool and back him up."

I took a deep breath, realizing that I was in deep over my head.

"Fine," I said. "Let's do it."

The alley behind the beverage center was strewn with trash and alive with mysterious rustlings. I stuck close to Reggie, who was carrying a miniature Maglite in one hand and a wooden baseball bat in the other. He'd given me a pole saw with an extendable handle to carry, the kind used for trimming trees. We were both wearing black mesh trucker's caps pulled low. Reggie turned his light off when we got to the far end of the alley.

"Okay," he said, peering cautiously around the corner of the building. "Just a nice easy stroll now. No running. And when we get there, remember not to touch anything with your bare hands."

We crossed the open apron of pavement surrounding the gas station attendant's booth, the side of Vinny's face clearly visible through the wraparound window. He'd have seen us if he'd turned his head, but he was still absorbed on the phone. Thirty seconds later we were behind the booth and out of his sight line. A caged bulb shone overhead, making me feel exposed. Reggie took a black box the size of a paperback book from his coat pocket and touched a switch. An LED on the box glowed green.

"What's that?" I whispered.

"Cell phone jammer," he said, dropping the box back into his pocket. "Has an effective radius of about two hundred yards. Borrowed it from a SWAT guy." He pointed upward. "Landline connection there. I'm going to count to three. When I get to three, you cut the line."

"Got it."

I extended the saw and raised it to touch the phone line. Reggie took a two-handed grip on his bat and planted himself in front of the electric meter.

"One, two, three."

I jerked the saw downward as Reggie swung the bat overhead. The phone line parted and the electric meter crashed to the ground. Every light on the lot extinguished simultaneously. I was blind in the sudden darkness and could hear my heart thumping wildly.

"Now what?" I hissed.

"Shh. Now we wait."

My eyes adjusted enough to see. Reggie glanced at me and offered the bat.

"Take it and give me the saw," he murmured. "Don't make any noise."

We completed the exchange silently. Reggie leaned the saw against the cinder-block wall of the booth. Another minute passed. My palms were damp on the handle of the bat.

"What if he doesn't come?"

"He'll come."

I heard the door of the attendant's booth open. Reggie pulled his gun and pointed it skyward. A gray figure shambled around the right-hand side of the booth, an open cell phone held in his hand for illumination. Reggie caught him by his collar and swung him in a wide circle, smashing him into the cinder-block wall.

"What the fuck?" Vinny yelped.

Reggie jammed the gun under his chin, and Vinny got quiet. Close up, I could see that he was chubby and had bad skin. He was wearing sneakers and ratty jeans and a brown or black leather coat. He looked terrified.

"Vinny Santore," Reggie said. "Seven years ago, you made a bad mistake. You fucked with the wrong people. It took us a while to find you, but now you have to pay."

"I don't know what you're talking about."

Reggie banged him against the wall.

"You been inside, Vinny. You understand how things work. It doesn't matter what you know. It only matters what you did."

Vinny's eyes slid in my direction and then dropped to focus on the bat.

"Whatever it was," he stammered, "I can make it right."

Reggie banged him against the wall again.

"Too late to make it right. But you might be able to make it better. And if you make it better, there's a chance you get to go home in one piece tonight."

Vinny nodded as much as he could with the gun to his throat.

"What do you want from me?"

"Seven years ago, you swiped a red BMW M5."

"I swiped a lot of fucking cars. How am I supposed to remember that one?"

Reggie banged him against the wall more forcefully. Vinny's head bounced off the cinder blocks and onto the barrel of the gun, the impact to his larynx making him choke.

"There was something special about that car. You remember."

Eyes wild, Vinny looked back to me, maybe searching for an ally. I hoisted the bat to waist level.

"Diplomatic plates," he said.

"Good," Reggie said. "Where'd you grab it?"

"One hundred twenty-fifth and the river, on the West Side. There's a parking lot. I used to get high there sometimes before I went cruising, to calm myself down a little bit. Fucking car was just sitting there, man, totally cherry. I watched for a while to make sure it wasn't a setup and then figured what the fuck, you know? Fucking key was even in the ignition. It was weird."

"You put the car on the truck and did what?"

"Took it straight to Frank's."

"Was Frank there?"

"No. Frank only ever worked days. I drove the truck into his garage and left it there with the car still on top. Then I went out and got fucked up."

"And you're sure the key was in the ignition."

"One hundred percent."

Reggie released Vinny to rack the slide on his gun. He elevated the barrel and touched it to Vinny's forehead. Vinny's eyes crossed.

"First you don't remember anything, and now you're remembering too much," he said. "You must think I'm stupid."

"I swear," Vinny squeaked. "I remember. Frank called the next morning. I had a monster fucking tequila headache, and Frank was screaming at me. Calling me a stupid motherfucker and saying he didn't want to work with me no more. I didn't know what was going on. Frank was fucking fierce. I was scared. I thought he was going to fuck me up good."

"And did he?"

"No, man. He came around later that day, all fucking strange and spooky. Told me to keep my mouth shut about that car, forever. And I did, until right now. Never talked about it again."

Reggie lowered the gun and nodded thoughtfully.

"I reckon you've told me about half the truth, Vinny, and I appreciate it. So I'm not going to shoot you in the head." He lifted the gun again and pressed it to Vinny's chest. "I'm going to shoot you in the heart, so your mother can send you off in an open casket."

"I told you everything," Vinny wailed.

"You didn't. You saw what was in the trunk of that car, or Frank told you. You know why we're here."

Vinny looked as if he might pass out.

"I don't. I swear. I don't know anything about anything in the trunk."

"You're lying," Reggie insisted. He took a half step backward, extending his arm more fully. "I hate to shoot you like this, Vinny, because I'm wearing my favorite coat, and I'm going to get blood all over my sleeve when your heart explodes."

Vinny moaned, tears running down his face.

"Last chance," Reggie said.

A surge of furious despair brought me to life as I realized what was going to happen next. Vinny wasn't going to admit to knowing what was in the trunk, and Reggie wasn't going to shoot him. Vinny would realize that Reggie had been bluffing, and we'd never learn whatever else he might know. I remembered what Claire had said about our being together.

I swung the bat. I swung it as hard as I could, catching Vinny on the inside of his right knee. He crumpled to the ground, screaming. I drew it back to take a second swing and Reggie grabbed me by the shirtfront, his body interposed between me and Vinny.

"Where's my son?" I yelled, struggling to get past Reggie. "What did you do with him? Tell me, you little motherfucker, or I'll kill you."

Joe came running around the corner, flashlight in one hand and gun in the other.

"Jesus Christ," he said.

Reggie wrenched the bat from my hands and shoved me toward Joe.

"Get him out of here," Reggie barked. "Now. I'm going to clean this mess up as best I can."

24

Reggie and I didn't talk much on the ride back to Manhattan. He kept his police radio on and tuned to the Staten Island frequency. I heard the call for a patrol car to the gas station where we'd left Vinny, and a follow-up call for an ambulance. I rode with my head tipped against the passenger window, too emotionally spent to care. Reggie hung a left into Battery Park City after we emerged from the Brooklyn-Battery Tunnel, hopping the curb at the end of Liberty Street and following the footpath toward the North Cove marina. We parked shy of a flight of stairs, with a view of the river. He turned off his headlights and lit a cigarette.

"You and me have a problem."

I watched the lights of the Financial Center play on the water, listening.

"I'll admit I screwed up tonight. I shouldn't have let you come. That makes me stupid, because I let you get mixed up in something you shouldn't have been mixed up in. But you crossed a line back there. I'm not a goon, and I don't work with goons. I scare people, and I slap them around sometimes, but I don't ever hurt anyone unless they're trying to hurt me, and never if they're defenseless."

I straightened up in my seat, took a cigarette from his pack, and lit it. I hadn't smoked since college. The first inhalation made me flushed and dizzy. I exhaled and took another hit, feeling my nerves steady.

"I hear you, and I respect your opinion. But I'd be lying if I said I felt bad about what I did back there."

The statement was as much a revelation to me as it was to him. Reggie sighed.

"I'm not saying I don't understand the impulse. I deal with scumbags all the time, and it wouldn't make me lose any sleep to kick the shit out of most of them."

"So, why don't you?" It had never occurred to me that Reggie had any hard limits. I always assumed his methods adapted to meet the circumstances, regardless of what those circumstances might be. "Because it's illegal?"

"Fuck legal or illegal. That's for lawyers to worry about. At the end of the day, you're a good guy or a bad guy. Good guys try to help people; bad guys try to hurt people. And if you start hurting people to help people, then you've crossed the line. It's not that complicated."

"I'm a father, Reggie. I know you care, but Kyle's my son."

"Why I shouldn't have brought you along," he muttered, sounding angry at himself. "Who knew you'd turn into fucking Joe DiMaggio on me."

I took another hit from the cigarette, remembering the rage I'd felt when I swung the bat.

"Let me ask you a question. What happens if we find the car, and track it back to whoever kidnapped Kyle, but can't prove anything in court?"

"We find the guy, and I'll make the case. One way or another. That is what I do."

"Always? Every time?"

"No," he admitted. "Lot of random bullshit happens when you get into court. But the nice thing about scumbags is that they tend to do the same bad things over and over, so you almost always get another crack at them. I got a list. Some names I put on the list, some names I got from Joe, some names he got from his old partner. I know where they live, and I have the precinct cops keep an eye on them, and I watch the computer for crimes that fit their pattern. Most of them will end up in jail eventually. And the ones I don't put behind bars I'll pass along to my last partner, when it's time for me to retire. That's how things work."

"Not good enough," I told him, thinking about Claire again. "I need this settled. For me, and for my family. We find this guy and it looks like we can't make a case, I'm going to have to deal with it myself."

"And what about Claire and Kate?"

"What about them?"

"You can't take care of them from jail."

It was a testament to our friendship that he was able to home in on my vulnerable spot.

"True. But who's going to know?"

"Me."

"Right. But I'm not asking you to get involved. If and when the time comes, all you'll have to do is look the other way."

Reggie turned off the engine and opened his door.

"Come on," he said. "Let's walk."

We made our way to the river and then turned left onto the esplanade. The wind was up and the temperature had dropped. I flipped the cigarette away, buttoned my coat to the collar, and buried my hands in my pockets.

"Vinny tell you anything else?"

"Where Frank usually dumped the cars after he stripped them. In the swampland off the Arthur Kill, near Prall's Island, on the western edge of Staten Island. He gave me a pretty good description. I'll get a search team out there tomorrow."

"You think they'll be able to find the BMW?"

He shrugged.

"Cars last a long time in the water."

I wanted to ask about bodies but couldn't make myself say the words.

"Tell you what's bothering me," he continued. "Beyond your going vigilante. Vinny said the key was in the ignition."

"So?"

"So, when the homicide detectives searched the room where Munoz was murdered, they found the key to his brother-in-law's car in his pants pocket. Where'd the second key come from?"

I gave it a few seconds' thought and came up empty.

"No clue. I can ask Gallegos if Munoz had more than one copy."

"You think Gallegos was straight with you, right?"

"Absolutely," I said, remembering the expression on his face when I'd told him about Kyle.

"Which makes me wonder about the girlfriend out on Long Island, the one Munoz was supposedly smacking around. Detectives interviewed the girlfriend's neighbors. The neighbors said they heard a lot of fight noise coming from her apartment. Said she usually wore dark glasses and floppy hats but that they saw bruises on her face and arms. Doesn't sound right if Gallegos was telling the truth about his brother-in-law being a kind and gentle person."

"And the girlfriend would have had access to his keys," I said, beginning to understand what Reggie was thinking. "It's a big coincidence that she disappeared the same night he was murdered."

"Exactly. The file has fingerprints for her that they lifted from the apartment. I'll run a check in the morning, see if she's turned up in the system."

We reached the end of South Cove and stopped by the railing, facing south toward the Statue of Liberty.

"The big picture still doesn't make sense to me. What does any of this have to do with Kyle?"

Reggie tossed his cigarette butt into the water.

"Don't know yet. Police work is like that sometimes—you figure out the what before the why. All you can do is keep pulling at loose strings and see what happens. You think you'll be able to learn anything about that bribe Gallegos mentioned?"

"I got a decent shot at it. I'll start digging first thing tomorrow morning."

"Good." He turned to face me. "One more thing."

"What's that?"

"You get it into your head to do something wild, make sure you talk to me about it first. Because you're right that I wouldn't want to send you to jail, but you might be wrong about what I'd do. I've had to make a lot of tough calls in my line of work. I'd rather not confront that kind of decision with you."

"Agreed," I lied. If push came to shove, I was going to do what I had to do, with or without his approval.

"Then let's go get a drink. It's been a long night."

25

I was at the bar at Pagliacci with Alex and it was raining on us. Alex lifted his empty glass and rattled the ice cubes, water dripping from his sleeve. I turned to suggest that we leave and saw a third man on the stool beyond him, his face concealed by Alex's profile. There was something familiar about the man. I leaned forward and back, trying to get a better look, but Alex was always interposed between us. I was reaching over to tap the stranger on the shoulder when I felt someone tugging at my arm.

"What?" I demanded, coming awake abruptly.

I was lying on the couch in my study, where I'd bedded down again after a heavy drinking session with Reggie. Kate was standing over me, dressed in jeans and a brown V-neck sweater. She had my bathrobe under one arm.

"What time is it?" I asked, fumbling for my watch on the coffee table.
"Eight."
"Shouldn't you be on your way to school?"
"I don't have any classes this morning."

I opened my mouth to ask why not, and she touched a finger to her lips, shaking her head from side to side. Wondering what was up and whether it had anything to do with her odd behavior the previous night, I tossed off the throw blanket I'd been sleeping under and reached for my pants. She intercepted my hand and offered me the robe instead. I was too hungover to play games. I was about to snap at her when I registered her expression. She looked scared. I stood up and slipped the robe on over my T-shirt and boxers, tying the belt tight.

Kate led the way into the kitchen. The apartment was dark and quiet, and I noticed Claire's coffee cup in the sink. She'd told me she had an early charity breakfast when I'd called the previous night to post her on my trip to Staten Island with Reggie. I hadn't mentioned hitting Vinny. Claire's absence begged the question of who Kate thought might over-hear us. I felt an increased twitch of anxiety. It wasn't like Kate to be melodramatic.

She opened the steel service door to the fire stairs and motioned me to pass through first. The small landing was crowded by two gray plastic trash cans and a blue recycling bin, and the cement floor was gritty underfoot. Closing the door behind us, she squeezed past me and took a seat on the stairs. I sat down next to her, wrapping the robe beneath my legs. The stairs were just wide enough for us to sit at a right angle to each other, our inside knees touching.

"I know this is weird," she whispered, inclining toward me, "and I'm sorry, but there's something really strange going on. It's kind of compli-cated, so let me explain first and then you can ask questions, okay?"

"Okay," I said, trying to conceal my discomfort.

"Yesterday afternoon, I got home from school early and started downloading some music videos. Our Internet connection was all messed up, normal one minute and dead slow the next. I did a soft reboot of the modem and the router, but that didn't fix the problem, so I decided to restart everything manually."

I nodded, grasping the big picture if not the details.

"The equipment is up on the top shelf of the linen closet, and I was feeling around the back of the modem for the power cord when I touched something unfamiliar. There was a little metal box plugged into the port where the Ethernet cable from the router usually attaches, between the modem and the cable. It looked like an oversized coupling, or one of the little signal amplifiers the cable TV guys use. I'd never seen anything like it in a network setup before. I unplugged the box and hooked the cable directly to the modem again and everything worked fine."

"So, what was the box?"

"That's what I wanted to know. Little pieces of network kit like that always have a part number or a description on the case somewhere, but this didn't have anything stamped or printed on it, which also seemed strange. I took it back to my room and used a screwdriver to pry the faceplate off. The box had a microprocessor and some flash memory wedged inside, and the processor had a serial number. I searched the serial number on the Web and ended up in a bunch of hard-core hacker forums. The processor is a repeater, a chip that's designed to capture Internet traffic and forward it to some third location."

"What third location?"

"Any third location. In our case, to a server somewhere in the Cayman Islands."

"Wait a second," I said incredulously, her import penetrating. "Are you telling me we were bugged?"

"Exactly. Everything any of us have done on our home network the last couple of days—all our mail, all our chat, and all the Web sites we've visited—has been copied to this other server."

Much as I wanted to know who'd bugged us, and why, I had a more important question to ask first.

"Let me get this straight. This box you found was physically inside our apartment, right? Which means that whoever put it there had to be inside our apartment."

She nodded, her scared expression returning.

I was scared also, and confused, but more than either, I was furious. Someone had broken into my home. What would have happened if they'd bumped into Kate or Claire?

"I'm calling Reggie," I said, starting to stand up.

"Wait," she said, grabbing my wrist. "There's more."

"How can there possibly be more?"

"Sit," she urged. "Come on. I asked you to listen until I was done."

I settled next to her again apprehensively.

"I'm listening."

She let go of my wrist and sighed.

"After I figured out what the repeater was, I got really mad at you."

"At me? Why?"

"Because I read in the hacker forums that these things are mainly sold to employers snooping on employees, and to parents checking up on their kids."

It took me a beat to catch her drift.

"You thought that I was spying on you? Why would I do that?"

"I could tell you picked up on something between me and Phil when you met him the other day," she said, cheeks turning pink, "and that you were a little freaked out. I thought maybe you wanted to know what was going on between us, and didn't feel comfortable asking."

"You're right that I noticed," I admitted, reminded of how adept she was at reading me. "And that I'd been meaning to ask you about it. But I'd never spy on you. I trust you."

"I know," she said, nudging my knee with hers. "And I'm sorry for jumping to the wrong conclusion. But this was a pretty slick installation. Mom couldn't have done it—she doesn't have the tech skills. You have a bunch of smart network guys at work, though. I figured maybe one of them helped you."

I made an effort to set my anger aside and think about what had happened objectively. Frick and Frack certainly had the tech skills, but they operated only at Walter's behest. Was it possible that Walter was spying on me? Why?

"Do you have any idea when the bug was planted?" I asked, hoping the time line might shed some light on the situation.

"Some," she said. "But let me finish. I was really pissed at you all yesterday afternoon, and then after the concert, I decided to teach you a lesson. I hunted around on the Internet and found a program that let my computer emulate our modem."

"Remember who you're talking to here, please," I said, wary of her slipping into jargon. "Keep it simple."

"Sorry." She hesitated a moment, lips pursed. "What I wanted to do was hook the repeater up to my computer but trick it into thinking it was still attached to the modem. The repeater has a limited amount of memory. When it runs low, it has to send the information it's captured somewhere else. That's why our network was acting so strange when I was downloading the big video files—because the repeater kept interrupting to dump data to the remote server. By hooking the repeater directly to my computer, I was able to fill the memory with garbage and force a call to the server. And since it was communicating through my computer, I could see where the repeater had called."

Again, I only partly followed, but I caught the gist.

"Which is how you know the server is in the Cayman Islands."

"Right."

"And you can just find programs on the Internet that let you do stuff like that?"

"Pretty much. I needed some help to make it work with my configuration. I got started talking to a Hungarian guy named Gabor in one of the hacker forums, and I was able to persuade him to walk me through it."

"Able to persuade him how?"

"I sent him a picture of Vanessa Hudgens that I grabbed from a fan site and told him it was me," she said, looking a little embarassed. "We have a date this Sunday afternoon in Budapest. Lunch at his mother's house."

I didn't know what to say. She cleared her throat and carried on.

"Once the repeater made the connection, I was able to cut it out of the loop and communicate with the server directly. The fact that the server was in the Caymans shook me up—I'd assumed it would be in your office. My plan was to erase the files you'd copied and leave you a message telling you what I'd done, but I poked around some instead, and I found a folder filled with media files. I clicked on a few and played them." Her voice dropped. "They were all voice recordings of you, talking to different people."

I was confused again.

"This repeater thing was hooked up to our phone also?"

"No. The recordings were made in lots of different places, not just in our apartment. A bunch of them sound like you're talking to people at restaurants, or in the street."

"How's that possible?"

"I asked Gabor. He thinks someone reprogrammed your cell phone."

"You can do that?" I asked, stunned.

"A cell phone is just a simple computer and some memory attached to a radio. The computer has an operating system, like every other computer. All someone has to do is physically get hold of your phone and make changes to the operating system. Then the phone becomes a bug, like the repeater, recording everything you say and transmitting it to the server. You said you lost the phone last Friday, right? And that it was returned on Monday? That's more than enough time for it to have been reprogrammed."

Son of a bitch. I should have known better than to believe in cell phone–returning Good Samaritans in New York City.

"Have you noticed that your phone hasn't been holding a charge well recently?" Kate asked.

"I replaced the battery Wednesday morning, because it died overnight."

"The recording function can be programmed to be voice-activated, so it will capture everything you say, instead of just your calls. Gabor said hacking a phone like that makes it consume a ton of battery." She shook her head. "I'm going to have to send him some cookies or something. He was really helpful, and he's going to be upset when I don't show this weekend."

"Bottom line, our network's bugged, and my phone's bugged."

She nodded.

"And I'm guessing that we're out here on the fire stairs because you think our apartment might be bugged as well."

"It's possible. And I didn't want you to bring your pants or anything else, because we can't be sure that it's only your phone. Lots of small things can be microphones—a button, or your belt buckle, or something in your shoes. But the phone's the best, because you charge it up every night, and it can transmit over greater distances, and—"

"Because I carry it around with me everywhere," I said, finishing her sentence.

"So, what's going on?" she asked quietly.

"I wish I knew. You said you had some idea when the bugging started?"

"The oldest files on the server were from Sunday night, which means at least since then. It could be longer, if someone's been erasing stuff, but I don't think too much longer, or I would have noticed."

Sunday night. Before I generated the scoop on Nord Stream, before I met with Theresa Roxas, and before I had my falling-out with Walter. It didn't make sense. There wasn't any reason for anyone to have been that interested in me last week.

"Just to be clear, how sophisticated do you have to be to do something like this?"

She shrugged.

"It's like a lot of things in the tech world—simple in concept but tough to get right. I could probably do it if I had enough time, but whenever you monkey around with hardware at the BIOS level, or try to get different systems to communicate, you're going to have a million tiny problems to work through. Whoever did this seems to have gotten everything right, so I'm guessing they're experienced."

Her mention of experience brought Frick and Frack to mind again. But if Walter had been monitoring my conversations and my e-mail, he wouldn't have been surprised to learn that Alex had introduced me to Theresa Roxas. My head ached. I was missing something big—nobody would have gone to these lengths on a whim. There had to be some deeper pattern to events that I wasn't perceiving.

"Is that everything?" I asked.

"You were expecting more?"

We shared a weak smile.

"How much of this have you told your mother?"

"Nothing yet. She went to bed early. She seemed upset."

"I tried to get her to open up to me about San Francisco."

"And?"

"And it's complicated." I slapped my knees with both hands, attempting to project more confidence than I felt. "We can talk about that later. Come on. It's time to go."

"Go where?"

"To pick up your mother and move to a hotel until we figure out what's going on. Someone's already broken into our apartment once. I don't want to take any chances."

She nodded, her face troubled.

"There actually is one more thing. This probably isn't the right time, but I'd like to ask you about it."

"Shoot."

"These past couple of days, I've felt there was something important you weren't telling me. That's the other reason I thought maybe you were spying on me—because I had the sense you were keeping a secret. Is there anything else I should know?"

She looked at me searchingly.

"Kate . . ." I said, unsure how to begin.

She gasped, a hand flying to her face.

"It's about Kyle, isn't it?"

I wrapped an arm around her and gently lifted her upright.

"It's nothing definitive. Let's go find your mother. I'll tell you everything on the way."

26

Kate ran down the location of Claire's charity event while I threw on some old jeans and a pair of ratty tennis shoes, mindful of her caution about listening devices. The breakfast was at the Parker Meridien hotel, on West Fifty-seventh Street. I brought her up to speed on everything I'd been doing with Reggie as we rode downtown in a cab, again omitting the beating I'd given Vinny. Like Claire, Kate wept when I told her what the e-mail Reggie received had said.

The ride to the hotel took us about fifteen minutes. Kate went hunting for Claire in the hotel's reception rooms while I used a lobby pay phone to try Reggie's numbers. Both his office and cell kicked to voice mail. Recounting the morning's events to his machine, I felt my rage mounting again. Forget the eavesdropping—someone had broken into my home. I asked Reggie if he could enlist some forensics guys to dust for fingerprints and do whatever else they did. I wanted to catch whoever it had been, and to make sure they paid the price.

The Meridien was a good hotel, and convenient, so I booked a suite for the week, assuming that would give us enough time to have our apartment swept clean and figure out what had been going on. Kate showed up with her mother as I was pocketing the plastic room keys. Claire had dressed more Park Avenue than Upper West Side for the benefit, in a navy dress, black pumps, and a wide, black, patent-leather belt. Her hair was loose around her shoulders. She looked young, and vulnerable, and frightened. I reached for her hand. She took it and clung tight.

Our rooms were too contemporary for my taste, with odd inversely colored photographs of flowers on the walls, but they were also airy and light, with rooftop views of the southern skyline. We settled at an asymmetric breakfast table beneath an oversized close-up of a pale green rose while Kate reexplained the bugging.

"So, this has something to do with your work?" Claire asked, turning to me when Kate had finished. She looked pale but composed.

"It must, although I can't imagine what. I don't want either of you to be concerned, though. I have a call in to Reggie. He and I will figure this whole thing out and take care of it."

Kate glanced at her mother.

"You and Reggie are going to take care of it. So Mom and I should just hang around here at the hotel and wait. Maybe book a massage and a pedicure."

"That's not what I meant," I said, stung by her sarcasm.

"Isn't it?" Claire asked quietly.

I hesitated, afraid of getting them involved in anything dangerous, but recognizing that I'd made things worse between me and Claire in the past by being overprotective.

"I'm sorry. This is difficult for me. I worry about you both, and I want to protect you, and I feel guilty for having brought this into your lives."

"It's difficult for all of us," Claire said. "I think we should try to understand it together, as a family."

I was a little surprised to hear her be so forceful, and more than a little happy to hear her emphasize our being a family. It made me feel hopeful. Kate spoke up again before I could formulate a reply.

"Which brings us back to Mom's question," she said, looking at me. "Are we sure this has to do with your work?"

"As opposed to what?"

"As opposed to something to do with Kyle."

"I'm not following."

"I was thinking about what you told me in the cab. The e-mail Reggie got was sent through an offshore remailer. Your phone and the repeater in our house were both forwarding information to an offshore server. There's a similar level of technical sophistication. Maybe the e-mail and the bugging are related somehow."

I felt light-headed, as if I'd been sucker punched from behind.

"It's possible," I admitted.

"Has there been much going on at work?" Claire asked.

"A huge amount. Way more than I've had time to tell you about."

"So, Kate could be correct that the bugging has something to do with the e-mail about Kyle, but we can't rule work out."

"Right." I rubbed my forehead with my hand, trying to think. "Frankly, I have no idea what's going on."

Claire tucked her hair behind her ears, looking pensive. Kate slipped a rubber band off her wrist and handed it to her.

"The earliest files on the Cayman Island server were from Sunday night, correct?" Claire said, glancing from Kate to me as she pulled her hair back into a ponytail. "And you got your phone back on Monday morning."

We both nodded.

"So, it seems likely that the people who bugged us are interested in either something that happened this week or something that's supposed to happen soon."

"Probably," I said. "But I don't see how that helps. The e-mail and the work stuff all fall in the same time window."

"I have an idea," Kate said. "Maybe we should go through your entire week minute by minute and do what you do when you're working on a big project—write everything down on note cards, and tape it all up on the wall, and see if any connections pop out."

I didn't have any better suggestion.

"Sounds good," I said. "Let's get to it."

I took the creepy photographs down while Kate and Claire ran out for supplies. They came back with coffee, bacon-egg-and-cheese sandwiches, and enough note cards, poster paper, colored markers, and Scotch tape to document the entire Civil War. Our goal was to lay out everything that had happened by event, time line, and people involved. Two hours later we'd created a flow chart from hell, with dozens of boxes connected by lines and arrows that intersected everywhere. If there was a pattern in the data, it was well hidden. Pushing my chair back from the table, I leaned forward and rested my elbows on my knees. Tired and frustrated as I was, I felt buoyed by working together with Kate and Claire—particularly Claire. Her transformation was nothing short of incredible, a testament to the rejuvenating power of having something to do other than brood. It made me wonder if it had been a mistake all those years ago not to insist more forcefully that she accompany Kate and I on our leafleting. Maybe the activity would have taken her out of the moment she'd felt trapped in.

"I'm going to have to go soon," I said, rubbing my eyes. "I promised Rashid I'd meet him at eleven."

"Did Rashid know the Venezuelan guy who got murdered?" Kate asked.

"Maybe. I haven't asked him."

She drew a dotted red line from Rashid's name to Carlos Munoz's and labeled it with a question mark. I looked at the line and shook my head.

"Any relationship the two of them might have had is ancient history. We have to be careful of cluttering the picture with extraneous facts."

Kate glanced at Claire.

"It's hard to know what might be important," Claire said, shrugging.

"The problem here is that the only obvious link between everything and everybody is me," I said, circling my head to stretch my shoulders. "I broke the Nord Stream story, I received the Saudi data, I'm the one who was bugged, and Kyle was my son."

"My God," Claire gasped. "What if that's the connection?"

"What if what's the connection?" I demanded.

"You. You just said it. Kyle's your son."

My heart skipped a beat.

"Meaning?"

"Meaning we've always assumed Kyle was kidnapped randomly," she said tremulously. "That's what made things so difficult for Reggie and the other police, right from the beginning, because they didn't have any motive to work from." She rose unsteadily and took the marker from Kate's hand. "But look at the facts. Kyle was supposedly last seen in a car belonging to an OPEC diplomat, and that same diplomat was in trouble with his own people because he'd turned down a bribe of shares in an oil company." She touched Kate's written words with the tip of the marker as she spoke. "Don't you see? It's all your world. Maybe the connection we're looking for is you."

I couldn't breathe.

"We don't know enough to reach any conclusions," Kate protested vehemently. "It's not fair to blame Dad."

"This isn't about blame," Claire said, visibly struggling to stay composed. "There's more than enough blame to go around. This is about finding out what happened to your brother, and about protecting our family." I could feel her looking at me, but I couldn't meet her eyes. "What do you think, Mark?"

Thinking was beyond me. Claire reached across the table and took my hand.

"Stay with us on this," she pleaded. "We really need your help."

"You might be right," I managed, drawing strength from her touch. "Kyle might have been deliberately targeted. . . ." My voice faltered, and I began again. "Kyle might have been deliberately targeted because of something I was involved in. . . ."

"Why?" Kate asked.

"I don't know. But if we're right, those same people might still be out there, and they might be interested in me again for some reason. They could even be the people who broke into our home and bugged us."

There was a horrified silence as we all considered the possibility.

"I need to talk to Reggie," I said.

Claire squeezed my hand hard and then let go.

"No. I'll talk to Reggie. You have to go meet with Rashid." She leaned back and touched his name card on the flow chart. "He knows everybody and everything in the oil world. That's what you've always told me. You have to go ask him if he knows who took our son."

27

Claire's words thundered in my head as I staggered the three blocks crosstown to the Four Seasons. I couldn't think of anyone who had reason to attack Kyle to get to me, or even of a reason that seemed plausible. Revenge? To send some kind of message? But I hadn't been able to come up with a reason for anyone to spy on me, either. Claire was right—even if I'd never met him, Carlos Munoz was part of my world. It was only because the possibility of a connection between my work and Kyle's disappearance was too terrible for me to imagine that I hadn't realized it sooner. I did a sudden about-face on the corner of Madison, seized by a panicked urge to rush back to the Meridien and make sure that Kate and Claire were still okay. No one knew where they were, I reminded myself, and Claire had promised not to open the door to anyone other than me or Reggie. I turned again and resumed walking eastward. I had to go meet with Rashid. And what if he knew the truth of what had happened to my son, and withheld it for his own reasons? Over the years, the uncertainty had taken almost as brutal a toll on my family as the loss. I never would have believed Rashid was capable of anything so monstrous, except that so many things I never would have believed had already happened.

Lobby seating at the Four Seasons is on two low balconies flanking the somber central chamber. I climbed a flight of stairs and checked the western balcony first. I was retracing my steps when I glanced to my right. A man exiting the hotel through the revolving door looked back over his shoulder at me. I noticed a scar, or some other type of disfigurement, running from his mouth to his ear. I'd seen him somewhere else recently, but I couldn't place him.

"Mr. Wallace."

I shifted my gaze up, spotting the bodyguard who'd admitted me to Rashid's suite the other day. He was standing in the middle of the eastern balcony, leaning over the rail and beckoning to me.

"This way, please," he called.

I climbed the matching stairs on the opposite side of the lobby and saw Rashid at a table set for two in the far corner. The bodyguard took my coat and then escorted me toward him, whispering out of the side of his mouth.

"He was up all night on the phone. His doctors are very unhappy. Try to be as brief as possible, please."

I hadn't thought Rashid could look worse, but he did. His previous pallor had taken on a yellowish tinge, and his features seemed to have sunk, as if he were a balloon with a slow leak. I took his hand delicately, afraid of hurting him. The suspicions I'd had on the way over seemed absurd in his presence. Rashid was a friend.

"*As-Salāmu 'Alaykum,*" he said hoarsely. Peace be upon you.

"*Wa 'Alaykum As-Salām.*" And on you be peace.

"You'll have something to eat or drink?" he asked, gesturing toward the pastries and coffee on the table.

"Nothing, thank you."

He scratched his neck with the backs of his nails and sighed.

"Courtesy obliges me to insist, but then I'd have to take a bite of something myself, to shame you. And I can't bear the thought of eating just now. My sense of taste has entirely gone—a side effect of the drugs. Every meal is like working my way through a plate full of cardboard."

"I'm sorry."

"Don't be. It's my own fault, for being seduced by Western medicine. My people have a saying: There comes a time for every old man to ride his donkey into the desert." He walked his hand across the table and let it fall off the edge. "It's a different mentality."

Even in my agitated state, it hurt to see him so low.

"Old people here ride the Amtrak to Florida. That's kind of the same thing."

He laughed, as I'd hoped he would.

"Imagine me in Miami Beach." He lifted his water glass, pretending to make a toast. "Next year in Jerusalem."

I forced a return smile.

"That's always a popular line at OPEC meetings," he confided. "Delivered with and without irony."

"Listen, Rashid," I said, leaning toward him. "I have something very important that I need to ask you about."

"Excellent," he said, setting the glass down and crossing his legs. "Tit for tat, as ever between us. But I believe the possession arrow is in my quiver."

"Sorry?"

"Did I say it wrong?" he asked, sounding abashed. "I've been watching American basketball in the evenings, when I have difficulty sleeping."

"It's more of a pointer," I said, catching his drift. "There aren't any quivers involved."

He stroked his beard, looking put out.

"As you prefer. I have some preliminary reactions to your Saudi information, but before we get to that, I'd like to discuss the luncheon you attended with Senator Simpson."

I felt a sudden chill. I hadn't mentioned my meeting with the senator to him.

"Who told you I had lunch with Simpson?"

He shrugged.

"We exchange information, Mark, not sources."

"Not today," I said, struggling to keep my voice light. I felt irrationally certain that the knowledge must have come from whoever had bugged me. "Today I need to know your source."

"Business is business . . ." he began.

"To hell with business," I snapped, my nerves overstretched. I held up a hand, simultaneously taking a deep breath to calm myself. "I'm sorry. There's a lot more going on here than I've been able to tell you. I really need to know how you learned that I had lunch with Senator Simpson."

I could hear the bodyguard approaching, drawn by my outburst. Rashid waved him off and gave me a wan smile.

"It's I who should apologize. It's easy to be self-absorbed when you're ill. I heard about your falling-out with Walter Coleman. This must be a difficult time for you professionally."

"This has nothing to do with Walter."

He uncrossed his legs, seeming to gain strength as he sat up straighter. "Then what?"

"Please," I said, looking directly into his eyes. "If we've ever been friends. Just answer the question for me."

He returned my gaze for a long moment and then sighed.

"This one time," he said quietly. "As a token of respect for our long friendship. Everything I tell you to be held in strictest confidence."

I nodded impatiently.

"The French minister of foreign affairs flew to Riyadh yesterday morning, where he met with his Saudi equivalent. The minister had with him a transcript of certain remarks made by Senator Simpson at a lunch at the Palace hotel. I was asked to learn whatever I could about this lunch. I have a relationship with the officer in your Secret Service who coordinates protection for visiting Arab dignitaries. I called that officer and asked if he could obtain a list of the attendees at the senator's lunch, in exchange for certain considerations that don't concern you. He tapped some of his former colleagues and was able to get the information. Your name was on the list."

"The French minister of foreign affairs?" I said, bewildered. "Where on earth did he get a transcript of the lunch?"

"I don't have immediate access to French state secrets. Would you like me to call Paris and ask for you?"

The sarcasm was deserved, but it didn't lessen my interest in the transcript. My phone might well have been the source.

"Forgive me," I said. "I didn't mean to push so hard. I appreciate your candor."

"It's nothing," he said wearily, slumping back into his seat. "Friends don't hold grudges. Just tell me about your lunch with the senator."

I made an effort to concentrate, still preoccupied by the existence of the transcript but feeling I owed him a proper response.

"In a nutshell? America first when it comes to Arab oil, regardless of Arab preferences. Disagreements to be resolved by the U.S. Marines."

"Precisely what I heard from Riyadh," Rashid said, shaking his head mournfully. "This is very bad for Arab-American relations."

"Why? You said yourself that the Arab potentates all understand they've done a deal with the devil, and that America will eventually annex whatever it needs to annex. What difference does it make if Simpson says it out loud?"

"Every difference. You keep forgetting the importance of culture. Arabs are like Asians—face is more important than anything else. Tacit recognition of an inferior position is one thing. Having a bully rub your face in your inferiority publicly is quite another."

I nodded, trying to think of a way to work the conversation back to the transcript.

"I'm missing the French interest here," I said. "Are they just stirring up trouble?"

"I explained this to you the other day. The Saudis and the other moderate Arab leaders are allied with America only because they need protection—from the radical elements in their own societies, and from the rogue regimes in the region. If America isn't best able to provide that protection, or if U.S. policy makes the relationship unpalatable, then they'll form new alliances."

"Nord Stream," I said, the pieces clicking together despite my distraction. "The French are touting their success in the Ukraine and suggesting they take over America's Middle Eastern security role."

Rashid shrugged.

"We're almost ten years past 9/11, and America still hasn't found bin Laden. It's not a difficult argument to make."

"Nobody who's read a lick of history would ever trust the French."

"I agree. But it's not only the French. They've proposed a coalition—France, Russia, and a handful of other countries to be named later. A coalition is an attractive concept to the Arab leadership. It's much easier to treat with a superior force if you can potentially play the members of that force off against one another."

"And the quid pro quo?"

"Overtly? What you'd expect. A switch of primary reserve currency to the euro, munitions deals, preferential allocation of infrastructure contracts, and so forth. Covertly—"

"Control of the oil when it runs short. Exactly what Simpson wants."

"Precisely. But the French will be well mannered enough not to mention it."

"And they think America is just going to let this happen?"

"Your people are still pinned down in Afghanistan and Iraq, and your regional popularity has never been lower. What's your kinder, gentler Democratic president going to do when the Saudis and the Kuwaitis politely ask your forces to leave—declare war on the rest of the Arabian Peninsula? By the time America starts getting squeezed for energy, the French and their partners will be entrenched on the ground and have control of the oil fields locked up."

It was a disaster in the making for the United States. Right at that moment, though, I had other concerns.

"I hate to keep pushing the same question, Rashid, but did the French minister give any indication at all of how he obtained the transcript?"

"I can ask Riyadh. Why are you so interested?"

"It's a long, strange story, and before I tell it, I want to ask you something else. Were you acquainted with a man named Carlos Munoz?"

"The Venezuelan who was murdered a few years back," he said, toying with his beard again. "We'd met."

I heard a hushed conversation behind me and turned to see the bodyguard conferring with a uniformed hotel employee. The bodyguard took a cordless phone from the employee and approached our table.

"I'm sorry to interrupt," he said, offering the phone to Rashid. "A call from your office in Vienna. They say it's urgent."

"Forgive me a moment," Rashid said, accepting the phone and raising it to his ear. "Hello? Hello?"

I leaned toward the table to pour myself a cup of coffee. A hammer blow knocked me backward out of my chair. I was on the floor, lying beneath something heavy. The air was filled with smoke. I tried to get up, but the room began spinning, and I spiraled down into darkness.

28

A sharp, persistent noise summoned me back to consciousness. I opened my eyes and saw an ebony hand inches from my face.

"Come on," a voice said, as the fingers snapped again. "Wake up."

"I'm awake," I mumbled. "Where am I?"

"You tell me."

I was flat on my back and couldn't seem to turn my head. The ceiling was acoustical tile, and my view to either side was blocked by pale green curtains. I half recalled people lifting me, and asking me questions, and a siren.

"Hospital?"

"Right. Saint Luke's." The speaker moved into my field of view. He was a young black man wearing a white medical coat. He flipped on a penlight and shined it into my eyes. "You remember where you were before here?"

"Four Seasons Hotel."

"Good. Follow the light with your eyes. What's three times four?"

"Twelve. Why can't I move my head?"

"It's immobilized. I'm going to manipulate your arms and legs. You tell me if anything hurts."

He worked his way professionally from limb to limb, tapping my reflexes and bending my joints. Everything hurt, but not enough to deter him.

"You're a lucky guy," he said, when he was done. "You're basically fine, except for a mild concussion and a nasty piece of shrapnel in your forehead. You had a tetanus shot recently?"

"I'm not sure. What do you mean 'shrapnel'?"

"From the blast that knocked you out."

"What blast?"

"At the hotel. I don't know anything more about it."

He unstrapped whatever had been imprisoning my head and helped me sit up. The last thing I remembered was the bodyguard handing Rashid the phone.

"Where's my friend?"

"The big guy or the little guy?"

"The little guy."

"Came in a few minutes before you. Hold still. I need to get the shrapnel out of your head."

"Is he okay?"

"No clue," he said flatly, probing near my hairline with forceps.

"You're lying to me, aren't you?" I asked, studying his face.

He hesitated a moment and then nodded.

"Yes."

"Is my friend dead?"

He grabbed hold of something with the forceps and pulled. I felt blood trickling down my forehead; he mopped at it with a swab.

"Instantly. No pain. Big guy was less lucky than you, but he'll make it. I'm putting a butterfly bandage on this wound. You don't need a stitch."

"I'm going to be sick."

He held a cardboard basin for me while I threw up. When I was done, he eased me down to a prone position again and covered me with a blanket. My head was throbbing, but I knew I had to get in touch with Claire and Kate immediately.

"Do me another favor?" I said.

"What's that?"

"Bring me a phone."

"Can't. No phones in the ER. And you need to rest."

"Then call a cop named Reggie Kinnard for me and tell him where I am," I said, not wanting anyone else to know where Claire and Kate were.

"Got a dozen cops here already."

"Please."

He took a pad from his pocket and wrote down Reggie's cell number.

"Thanks," I said. "For everything."

"No problem. Now rest. You're still shocky. I'll be back in a minute."

I must have drifted off, because when I opened my eyes again, Reggie was standing over me.

"How you doing?" he asked.

"Not so good." I pushed myself up to a seated position and my vision swam. "Where are Claire and Kate?"

"Here. In the lobby down the hall. I was with them at the Meridien when I got the call from the doctor."

"I want to see them."

"Have to wait a little bit. You're still in a restricted-access area—no visitors."

"You have someone watching them?"

"Uniform keeping them company. Why?"

I heaved myself backward eighteen inches, so I could lean up against the headboard. Every muscle protested. I felt as if I'd been hit by a car.

"These people killed Rashid right in front of me." I choked back an involuntary sob. "I don't want to take any more chances."

"What people?"

"I don't know. I'm not sure of anything anymore. The people who bugged my house, maybe."

"We're talking about an Arab diplomat," Reggie said skeptically. "Could be any number of reasons for someone to hit him."

"No. No more coincidences. Everything that's happened recently is tied together somehow, and tied to Kyle as well. I can feel it. I just . . ."

A nurse entered through the curtain and gave Reggie a hostile look. He flipped open his coat to display the badge on his belt.

"Would you like some water?" she asked, offering me a plastic cup with a straw.

"Please," I said, suddenly realizing how thirsty I was.

I drained the cup while she checked my blood pressure and fussed with my bedclothes.

"He has to go," the nurse said, jerking her head toward Reggie.

"Soon," I promised. "We just have a few more things to cover."

She left, muttering unhappily.

"You have any details from the hotel?" I asked Reggie.

"You sure you want to hear?"

"Yes. I need to know."

He sighed.

"Had a quick word with a guy on the scene. Best our people can figure, someone rigged a phone with a shaped charge inside the earpiece. Rashid put it to the side of his head, and they detonated it by remote control."

I closed my eyes for a second, overwhelmed by a sense of unreality.

"You like to take a few minutes?" Reggie asked.

"No. I'm okay. What's a shaped charge?"

"Explosive designed to project force along a single axis. You were at a right angle to the axis because of the way Rashid was holding the phone, so you didn't catch much of it. Bodyguard was at a less oblique angle, so he caught more."

"So, Rashid was the only target?"

"Seems like. Else they would have used something with a bigger spread."

"Anybody get a good look at the guy who handed him the phone?"

"Security camera grabbed a decent shot of him. He was dressed like a hotel employee, but he doesn't work there. Feds will be able to check his picture against their digital photo records. Technology on that is pretty good now. They might get lucky."

I wiped sweat from my forehead, wincing as I inadvertently tugged at my bandage.

"Rashid was a good buddy of yours, wasn't he?" Reggie asked gently.

I shrugged, not ready to start down that path. Rashid had been a friend, a colleague, and a mentor. He was one of the few people I could talk to about almost anything, and he'd always been there for me. At the end, I'd suspected him of betraying me, and he'd died before I could ask him for help on the one thing that mattered to me most.

"I'd like to get out of here now."

"Doctors want to keep you overnight."

"No. Fix it for me, please."

He tapped a thumb against the side of his leg, frowning.

"Doctors aren't as suggestible as regular people. And we got another problem."

"I can't deal with any more problems."

"I hear you. But you're going to have to make a statement. Investigating officers will be here soon to talk to you. You have to decide how much to tell them."

"Why not everything?"

"Might be the right thing to do. But the department likes to keep things simple. You start talking about all that stuff you have taped to your hotel-room wall and their heads are going to spin. That whole cold-case thing is only on TV. Real life, the powers that be only worry about what's in the paper today and what's going to be in the paper tomorrow. First priority will be to nail a guy for doing Rashid. Beyond that, it might play either way."

"Meaning?"

"NYPD side of things is being supervised by Deputy Chief Ellison, guy you met in Walter's office."

"Great."

"Chief's not stupid, no matter how many pops he has in him, but he is political. He might assign a team of people to get to the bottom of this whole thing, or he might decide to leave well enough alone. It depends on what he thinks will work better for him with the mayor and the press."

"What do we care if he decides to leave it alone? We can still keep working on this thing ourselves unofficially. Right?"

"Not as easily," Reggie said, shaking his head. "It's one thing for me to be poking around outside my territory when no one's paying attention, but it's another for me to keep at something when I've been ordered to stand down. Chief doesn't let much slide, and I want to clear some more names off my list before I pull the pin."

"So, you're suggesting I keep my mouth shut about everything except the basic facts."

"It's a judgment call, but yeah, that's how I'd play it right now. We might be able to lean on the Feds later for some informal help, if we need it. I have good relationships there."

I crossed my arms and tucked my fists up into my armpits, struck by a sudden chill. There were too many powerful people in the mix for me to risk coming clean just yet—Senator Simpson, Walter, the Saudis. Any of them could bring intense political pressure to bear to orchestrate a cover-up, if necessary.

"Fine," I said, feeling shakier by the moment. "But I got to tell you— I can't take any more people dying. It seems like everything's been going sideways on me for a long time, and now it's all picking up speed."

"I been there," he said. "Lots of times. You just got to hang on."

One of the green curtains jerked sideways. I expected the nurse, but it was Deputy Chief Ellison at the foot of my bed, Lieutenant Wayland directly behind him.

"Irish Reggie Kinnard," the chief said. "As I live and breathe."

"Chief," Reggie replied evenly.

"He got that nickname in the four-one," the chief confided to the lieutenant sotto voce. "First year out of the academy. You know why?"

"Boozer?"

"No more than anyone else," the chief muttered irritably. "No, they called him Irish because he was old school, inclined to solve problems with a minimum of paperwork."

"New department these days," the lieutenant observed piously. "New rules."

Reggie laughed. The lieutenant looked angry, but the chief smiled.

"I been meaning to look you up," he said to Reggie.

"Why's that?"

The chief pointed his chin at me.

"Because I looked him up, and I learned that he's got a missing kid, and that you've been beavering away on it for the better part of the last decade. Very admirable. Makes the department proud. But I'm guessing that also makes you the guy who's been leaking confidential information on one of our priority cases to him. And that's not so admirable."

"*Fidelis ad Mortem,*" Reggie said. "My bad."

The chief kept smiling.

"Happens again and you're going to have a lot more free time to fish for stripers with your old partner Joe Belko, no matter how many pals you got on the community boards. You read me?"

"Loud and clear, chief."

"Good."

The chief turned to look at me, the lieutenant's head following as if it were attached.

"And what about you?" he asked.

"What about me?"

"Either you're the unluckiest son of a bitch in the city of New York or you're dirty in this up to your elbows."

I was tempted to tell him to fuck off, but I decided to follow Reggie's lead. I didn't feel strong enough to get involved in a pissing match.

"Unlucky, I guess."

"I see. And what can you tell me that might shed light on the untimely demise of the city's esteemed Arab guest Mr. al-Shaabi?"

"Zero. Rashid and I got together periodically to talk about the energy markets. He called yesterday out of the blue and asked me to stop by. We spoke for a while, and I woke up here."

"Spoke about what?"

"Ongoing production problems in Iraq, and how the rest of OPEC will respond."

"So, it's pure happenstance that I'm bumping into you on two separate murders in the same week."

"I thought Alex was an accident," I said, my mouth suddenly dry again.

"We have an expression in the department: Who the fuck knows? We say suicide, his rich and well-connected father says accident. We say accident, his father says maybe someone put him in the tub. I don't mind admitting that we're a little confused. You haven't had any more thoughts on Mr. Coleman's death, have you?"

"None. I wish I could help you."

"No link between Mr. al-Shaabi and Mr. Coleman that we should be aware of? Nothing you were working on with either of them that might have made someone unhappy?"

"No."

"Did Mr. al-Shaabi and Mr. Coleman know each other?"

"No. I'd been careful to keep my relationship with Rashid quiet, even from Alex, because Rashid hadn't wanted his employees to know that he spoke to me."

The chief nodded and turned to the lieutenant.

"What do you think?"

"I think he's a lying sack of shit."

"Mr. Wallace is a citizen," Reggie said, giving the lieutenant a look that would have made me take a few steps back. "Courtesy, professionalism, and respect. That's the new department, isn't it?"

The lieutenant glared back at him.

"Detective Kinnard's correct," the chief said mildly. "I apologize for Lieutenant Wayland's rudeness. But I incline toward his point of view." The chief came a step closer to my bed and touched his forehead. "That piece of shrapnel you caught. The doctor tell you what it was?"

"No," I said, confused by the change of subject.

"A splinter of Mr. al-Shaabi's skull. Doctor thinks maybe it's a tiny piece of his lachrymal." The chief lowered his finger and touched the bridge of his nose, next to his eye. "Little bone right here. Although how the fuck he could tell with all that mess, I got no idea."

I fought back the urge to vomit again.

"I mention it to make the point that you're involved here, Mr. Wallace. You're as involved as it's possible to be. And there's no skating away from that. The NYPD and the FBI and God only knows how many other agencies are going to be crawling all over this case and all over you. If I discover you've been lying to us, I'll do my best to nail you for hindering prosecution and get you three hots and a cot courtesy of the city. The Feds are doing some interesting things with conspiracy law. They might be able to get you on that as well. You understand me?"

"Perfectly," I managed.

"Good." He turned to Reggie. "Walk me to the elevator, Irish. You and me got a few more things to talk about."

I dozed restlessly for about ten minutes until Reggie came back.

"I got hold of Belko," he said. "He's on his way in from Queens. He'll keep an eye on Claire and Kate until we figure out some other arrangement."

"Thanks," I said. "So, tell me. The chief show you the carrot or the stick?"

"Chief's a stick guy. He read your file and wanted to know where I'd gotten with the e-mail. I gave him the abridged version and told him we had divers looking for the car in Staten Island. He's in your camp—he doesn't like all the coincidences. He suggested I use my relationship with you to win your confidence and find out what's really going on. Or else."

"You worried?"

"Not yet. Long as I can argue I'm working Kyle's case, I'm okay."

"Should I be worried?"

"About the hindering-prosecution thing or a conspiracy charge? No. That's a load of bullshit. But you're the one who has to be comfortable going down this road. Means a lot more strain on you personally. Be easier to punt the whole thing. I got a friend in the FBI you could talk to."

"FBI less political than the NYPD?"

He laughed.

"No such thing as a nonpolitical cop over the rank of sergeant—city, state, or federal. But the FBI's not pissed off at you yet."

"I'll take my chances with you." My eyes closed involuntarily, and it was an effort to open them again. "You said you knew what I meant before, when I told you how overwhelmed I was feeling."

"I've seen a lot of bad stuff over the years," Reggie said, shrugging. "It comes with the territory."

"So, why not just walk away? Transfer back to auto crime, or something less onerous."

It was a question I'd been wanting to ask him for a long time.

"I wish I knew," he said. "Seriously. I wonder about that all the time."

"I was thinking about walking away. I talked to Claire about it the other night. Get Kate settled in college and then relocate to Europe or the West Coast and try to put everything behind us."

"You don't feel that way now?"

"No," I said, feeling resolved. "I don't."

"Why not?"

"Because for the first time ever, I think we have a real shot at learning what happened to Kyle and finding the people who took him," I said, the words tumbling out of me. "And because I think these same people are responsible for what happened to Carlos Munoz, and to Rashid. It's all knotted together somehow. But mainly because I think these people came after me deliberately, and they might be coming after me again. I'm not going to rest until I find them and put them down."

Reggie nodded.

"Flip side of my philosophy. You don't hurt people who aren't trying to hurt you, but if they are, you hit back hard. Some things demand a response."

"Right," I said, my eyes closing again. "That's exactly right."

"Rest," he said. "I'll see what I can do about getting you out of here."

29

I slept another hour, waking when the same doctor turned up to peer into my eyes again and make me do more mental arithmetic.

"Your friend the cop says you're in a hurry to be released. That true?"

"You have many patients who aren't?"

He laughed.

"Issue is where they go. Some don't have anywhere, and others are afraid of a place worse than this. But I think you're okay. Tell you what—it's just after two now. You spend a couple of hours in the observation ward, and—if you stay stable—you can go home at five. The nurse there will explain what you need to do. Someone's going to have to stay with you today and tonight, and to wake you up every couple of hours to make sure you're still alert. Concussions can be tricky."

"My wife and daughter will love that."

"And you should consider talking to a counselor of some sort," he added in a more somber tone. "Priest, therapist, whomever. You've had a difficult experience today. You want a recommendation?"

"No, thanks. There's a family guy we go to sometimes. If I have a problem, I'll call him."

"Fair enough. Good luck to you, Mr. Wallace."

An orderly came to fetch me ten minutes later, moving my bed to a room with a glass wall that looked out onto a nurse's station. Claire and Kate were waiting for me. After the kisses and the tears, they wanted to know what had happened with Rashid. I asked Kate to summon Reggie and Joe from the waiting room, so they could hear the story at the same time. I was doing a good job of describing it all dispassionately until I got to the bodyguard handing Rashid the phone, and then I lost it. The nurse who'd carped at Reggie's presence earlier was watching through the window. She pounced, insisting I was emotionally exhausted and threatening to hold me overnight unless everyone left immediately. I made Claire and Kate promise to head straight back to the Meridien with Joe, and not to go anywhere without protection. Neither protested.

True to the doctor's word, the hospital began processing my release at five, but it was almost six by the time I'd finished all the paperwork. A cheerful orderly rolled me out the front door in the obligatory wheelchair and helped decant me into the front seat of Reggie's waiting car.

"Better," Reggie said, nodding approvingly as he scrutinized me. "You got some color back. Thought you might be done for when I first saw you this morning. You looked like fucking Casper."

"Thanks, I guess. Any more news on Rashid?"

"Nope," he said, pulling into traffic. The Meridien was only a few blocks away. "The guy with the phone came out of nowhere and disappeared into the same place. Hotel doesn't have a camera on the street, and the doormen don't remember seeing him. Feds didn't get a hit on his picture. They'll circulate it more widely, to Interpol and other international police forces, and wait to see what forensics on the bomb tell them. But right now it's a mystery."

"What about Staten Island?"

"I drove the area Vinny described with the search team this morning. That's where I was when you were trying to get hold of me earlier. Whole lot of swampland and no cell service. Haven't had any update yet, but I'm thinking it will take some time."

"So, nothing and more nothing."

His phone rang before he could respond. He answered it, his side of the conversation mainly grunts. I slumped in my seat for the rest of the short ride, staring out the window at Christmas lights. I was tired of being in the dark. It was past time for us to catch a break. Everybody made mistakes. We just had to figure out what mistakes the other side was making.

Claire and Kate fussed over me when I got back to the hotel room, insisting that I lie down on the couch while they pored over the home-care instructions I'd been given. Both seemed disappointed that Jell-O wasn't mentioned, as they'd had the hotel kitchen make me an enormous tub of it. I finagled my way upright by observing that I couldn't eat lying down and paid for my cleverness by being forced to slurp down a bowl of raspberry goop at the asymmetric breakfast table. The taste reminded me of having my tonsils out at age twelve. But it felt nice to be taken care of by them.

"So," I said, setting my spoon down resolutely, "have we made any more progress?"

"A little," Reggie answered. Joe had left to run errands, but Reggie was sprawled on the couch I'd vacated. "Picked up some interesting new information earlier today, although like everything else we learn, it's hard to know what it means."

"Tell us," Claire said, reaching for my hand.

"I mentioned to Mark last night that I was going to take a stab at running down Munoz's girlfriend. The detectives investigating his murder wanted to talk to her at the time, but they couldn't locate her. Paid all her bills in cash, didn't talk much to the neighbors, and no trail at DMV or with Immigration. Also, no match to the fingerprints they lifted from her apartment. They pegged her as an illegal flying under the radar. I figured maybe she'd been printed somewhere in the last seven years, so I had a tech I know run the fingerprints again. Still no luck. And then I started thinking about the hooker."

He hesitated, glancing uncomfortably toward Kate.

"Hooker," she said. "Prostitute. Whore. Call girl. Scarlet woman. Come on, Reggie. I'm seventeen."

"Okay, okay," he said holding his hands up defensively. "Sorry. According to the file, whoever killed Munoz wiped the room clean, but the crime-scene guys were able to lift a partial from Munoz's belt buckle. Not enough to get a match but something they hoped to use as corroborating evidence in the event they turned up a suspect. I figured the technology might be better now, so I sent the partial from the file down to the same tech and asked if he could do anything with it. And lo and behold, he did a Rain Man for me. One look at the partial and he calls me and he says that it's still no good for the database but that he recognizes it. There's a loop or a whorl or whatever that's exactly the same as one of the prints from the girlfriend."

"You're kidding me," I said.

"Nope. Dead serious. This guy has a photographic memory for that sort of stuff. He estimates the odds at about a thousand to one that the girlfriend and the hooker are the same person."

"Wait. You're telling me it never occurred to the cops who investigated Munoz's murder that the hooker and the girlfriend might be the same person?"

"Two biggest differences between good police work and bad police work," Reggie said, shaking his head. "Doing your leg work and double-checking your assumptions. The guy behind the counter at the motel said the girl was a hooker, and the homicide dicks took his word for it. They must have figured he was an expert on hookers."

"I don't get it," Kate objected. "Munoz sounds like a slick guy. Why would he take his girlfriend to a fleabag motel?"

Reggie looked embarrassed again. Claire intervened before Kate could get huffy.

"It's okay, Reggie. Really."

"Guys get turned on by all kinds of stuff," he muttered. "Although if we're right that the girlfriend set him up, the motel was probably her idea. She tells him she has this hot fantasy about being a streetwalker, and he hits the bait. It's not a difficult scenario to imagine."

Kate looked a little pink. It didn't make me unhappy to learn that she was still naïve about some things.

"You have a picture of the girlfriend that you can match up against the footage from the motel security camera?" I asked, breaking the awkward silence.

"Of the girlfriend, yes," he said, reaching into his jacket. "Munoz had one in his desk at work. But nothing to match it to. Munoz registered for the room, and the girl kept her face turned away from the camera."

He handed me a snapshot of a young woman in a bathing-suit top and cutoff jeans. She was wearing dark glasses and looked considerably younger than she had when I met her, but I recognized her immediately. The girlfriend was Theresa Roxas.

30

"Run it down for me again," Reggie said.

I was at the chart on the wall, walking him through the connections while Claire and Kate listened. My weariness had vanished.

"Theresa was the one who passed me the Saudi information," I said, touching one of the boxes Kate had drawn earlier. "She was introduced to me by Alex. Walter and I suspect the Saudi information actually came from the U.S. government, by way of Senator Simpson. Narimanov confirmed the government link and said that Alex had been trying to back-check the information through Washington."

Reggie rocked backward in his chair, fingers laced behind his head.

"I like the fact that this Roxas woman is a direct link between Munoz and what's happening now." He gestured to the chart. "It tells me you're on the right track with all of this. But I still got a big problem understanding the logistics of what happened to Kyle."

"The logistics or the motive?" Claire asked.

"Both, but let's stick with the logistics. I'm going to start by assuming that Munoz was a good guy. Anyone have a problem with that?"

I glanced at Claire and Kate, and then shrugged.

"Fine. Then I'm further going to assume that it wasn't Munoz who moved the car. You lure a guy into a motel room to whack him, you don't let him run out for cigarettes. All the parking-lot camera saw was a big guy in a camel-hair coat. Could have been anyone."

"Okay," I said.

"So, these people have got this carefully choreographed operation going on to discredit and murder Munoz, and in the middle of it, they take time out to have one of their people dress up like Munoz and drive his car all the way up to your neighborhood. And their objective is to kidnap a child who they couldn't possibly have expected to find on the street at that time of night."

"Maybe they were looking for my dad," Kate offered in a small voice.

"I don't buy it," Reggie said. "Your schedule's never been predictable, has it, Mark?"

"Not really."

"And if they were there for you, what would have put them on to Kyle? They couldn't have been expected to know what your family looked like. On top of which, why bother mixing you up with Munoz at all? If they wanted to hit you, too, why not do it another day? Why make things so complicated?"

The answer hit me like a bullet. It was the mention of family that did it.

"What?" Kate demanded apprehensively, her eyes fixed on me.

"They weren't there for Kyle, or for me. They were there for Claire." I sagged against the wall, my knees weak. "They'd researched my family. They knew Claire left the apartment at the same time every night to go to work. But she didn't go that evening, because I'd flown to London on short notice."

The shock I felt was reflected on Claire and Kate's faces.

"Reggie?" Claire breathed.

"Makes sense," he answered softly. "They'd painted Munoz as a violent woman abuser and put him together with the car on the security video in the right time window."

I shook my head at him, loath to have him speculate on the details, but Claire caught the gesture out of the corner of her eye.

"Enough," she said angrily. "Stop trying to protect us from the truth. I want to know exactly what Reggie thinks was supposed to have happened that night."

"You sure?" he asked.

"Yes."

He reached for a cigarette and then caught himself.

"My best guess is that Roxas—the girlfriend—lured Munoz to the motel and kept him busy in bed while a guy wearing a similar coat took the car. He and an accomplice or two drove uptown to grab Claire. Could have gone a couple of different ways from there, but, bottom line,

Claire and Munoz were supposed to have been found dead together the next morning—in the motel, or in the car, or somewhere else. Cops looking into it would have figured things went south somehow with the hooker, so Carlos went out looking for entertainment. He grabbed Claire off the street, and then things got away from him. Murder-suicide. Maybe they even planned to have Roxas put a call in to 911 as the hooker, saying some john she picked up went crazy and tried to beat the crap out of her, and that she had to flee down the fire stairs. It wouldn't have taken a lot to sell the story, given the security video and his supposed history."

I felt sick to my stomach.

"Gallegos told me that Carlos's enemies wanted to discredit him, to embarrass his political allies. The Venezuelan press hammered him for having been with a hooker when he died. Imagine what they would have done with this story."

"Suppose you're right," Claire said. She was ashen and breathing heavily, but she looked stronger than I felt. "Why Kyle?"

"Maybe they improvised—which confirms they had a motive beyond just discrediting Munoz." He glanced at me pityingly. "Only one common result of hurting a man's wife or child. To incapacitate the man."

"It had to have been something I was working on," I whispered. "Something they wanted me to leave alone."

"And they didn't want to come right out and kill you," Reggie added, "because the police would have dug into possible motives. This way they discredited Munoz, knocked you for a loop, and maybe even sent a message to some third parties about what happens to people who don't play ball. It all fits."

"And if I hadn't flown off to London unexpectedly, it all would have worked."

Our stunned silence was broken by Reggie's cell phone. He checked the number and answered it, stepping into one of the bedrooms to talk.

"Gallegos," Claire said urgently. "You need to get to him, Mark. You need to find out who told him to keep his mouth shut."

"He won't tell me."

"So, make him."

I didn't have to ask what she meant. Kate was biting her lip, looking troubled.

"No. Gallegos is innocent. Even if I could make him talk, he'd likely only give us another Venezuelan. And we don't want that guy. We want the guy behind him, the person who was pulling the strings."

"We start with whoever Gallegos gives us and work our way up the line," Claire insisted.

"How? These people are diplomats, Claire. Whoever leaned on Gallegos probably isn't even in America." I shook my head. "There's a better way."

"The bribe," Kate said. "The one that Carlos turned down."

"Right. The bribe was shares in an undervalued oil company. I make it even money that I tumbled onto the scam somehow and started asking questions. We need to go through my old files and see what pops out. If we can figure out which oil company it was, I might be able to follow the money back to the source."

Claire nodded hesitantly and then glanced at our chart on the wall.

"You suspect that Simpson used Theresa Roxas to get the Saudi data to you. Does that make him the source?"

I rubbed my neck, trying to imagine why Simpson would have been bribing Venezuelan diplomats.

"No idea."

"And what about Alex?"

"What about him?"

"He lied to you about knowing Theresa Roxas," she said, her face hard. "Does that tell us anything?"

"Only that someone leaned on him as well," I answered, feeling pained. "But I have to believe he would have come clean with me if he'd been able to establish that the Saudi information was false. He was a friend."

"Is that why Rashid was killed?" Kate asked. "To prevent him from telling you the truth?"

"Maybe," I said, beginning to feel overwhelmed again. The more we learned, the more complicated things got. "Or to prevent him from telling me something about Carlos Munoz's murder, or Kyle's kidnapping, or something else we haven't figured out yet."

"We need to think more about this Saudi connection," Kate insisted. "We need to figure out . . ."

Reggie walked back into the room and cleared his throat, his expression grim.

"I have some news," he said. "It's not good."

Claire and Kate rose simultaneously and came to me. I put an arm around each and pulled them tight.

"The call I just took was from the guy leading the search team in Staten Island. He got lucky and bumped into a couple of old-timers who like to fish out that way. They knew exactly where Vinny's boss had been dumping cars. Search team pulled the BMW out of the water about an hour and a half ago."

"And?" Claire asked breathlessly.

"And there were human remains in the trunk."

Kate buried her face in my shoulder, and I felt Claire trembling.

"Were they able to make an identification?"

"Take a day or two for dental," Reggie answered. "But the remains were wrapped in a Gore-Tex coat, and the coat held up well. Technicians rinsed it off and found a name written in the lining. Your name, Mark. I'm sorry."

Three Days Later

31

We buried Kyle on Monday morning, at a cemetery half an hour north of the city. The grave we'd picked out sat on a flat shelf at the top of a long rise, with views of the Long Island Sound over the bare branches of a grove of maples below. A local minister conducted an open-air service beneath a cloudless sky, an ocean breeze carrying the smell of salt. It seemed like a good place to lay our child to rest.

Afterward, everyone wanted to shake our hands and express their condolences. I was surprised by how many people came. The *Times* had run a small story on Sunday that included the details, and we'd invited some family and friends, but I hadn't expected much of a crowd. In the end, though, more than a hundred people turned out—neighbors, colleagues, even one of the Columbia kids who'd helped me post flyers all those years ago. And there was at least a dozen wreaths. I was relieved to see that one was from Mariano Gallegos. Given everything that had happened, I'd been worried about him.

"Who's that?" Kate whispered, when there were only a handful of people left.

Claire and I both glanced in the direction she was looking. A broad-shouldered guy with a pot belly was hovering about ten yards away, a kid a few years older than Kate shuffling his feet next to him.

"Kyle's old baseball coach," I said, placing the man's face. "Jon something. He owned a shoe store on Broadway." I made eye contact and waved him over. "The younger guy must be his son."

Father and son came to an awkward halt at the edge of conversational range.

"Jon Rosenthal," the older man stammered. "This is my boy, Steve. You might not remember us. Steve and Kyle played ball together."

"In the West Side League," Claire responded gently. "You coached. Of course we remember."

"I wasn't sure it was right for us to come. It's been a long time."

"We're grateful," Claire assured him. "It means a lot to us."

"I just wanted to let you know how terrible I felt for you all these years. It was something I could never stop thinking about. I'm so unbelievably sorry about what happened, but I'm glad you finally found him. Kyle was a really good kid. Everybody on the team always really liked him. . . ."

He broke down mid-sentence and began sobbing. His son threw an arm around him and hugged him fiercely. It was an experience I'd had before, bumping into Kyle's old friends and their parents in our neighborhood. The encounters had all been charged with bitterness for me. No matter how sincere the grief expressed, I knew the innermost emotion of any parent in my presence had to be joy that their own child was well and with them. Today was different somehow. I looked at Steve. He'd grown tall, with his father's shoulders and an athletic build.

"You still play ball?" I asked quietly.

"At Maryland," he mumbled, his gaze fixed on the ground between us.

"That's Division One, isn't it?"

"Yes."

I took a step toward him and reached out to touch his arm.

"Thanks for being here today. And good luck to you—to both of you. You take care of your father now, okay?"

He looked up and nodded. I watched as they walked away together, glad they'd come. They disappeared behind a stand of pines shielding the parking area, and my eyes drifted south, toward the sound. A flock of wild turkeys was grazing along the tree line below, and the sun was glinting off the distant water. There was only one thing left that I had to do for my son—one thing that Claire and Kate and I were determined to do together.

"You ready?" I asked.

They both nodded. We turned as one and headed toward the parking lot.

32

"October eleventh," Claire said, reading from one of my old appointment books. "You had breakfast with a guy named Jens Solheim."

I hunted through the S boxes stacked on one of the trestle tables lining the perimeter of the large workroom, looking for Solheim's file. We'd stopped by the hotel after the funeral to change clothes and then continued on to the Queens warehouse where Amy stored my old records. The top floor of the former factory was partitioned into lofts that were usually rented out to law firms dredging through discovery material. High-speed wireless Internet, a Nespresso machine, a Bloomberg terminal, and an Xbox 360 hooked up to a fifty-inch plasma display were all part of the standard package. Being there reminded me of the long hours I'd spent proofreading prospectuses at the printers when I was a young investment banking associate. Like the warehouse, the printers kept hotel-quality facilities on the premises as a competitive lure. Video games got old fast in the small hours, and the tedium had made me agitate for a switch to research. I found the file I was looking for and flipped it open.

"Solheim was CEO of a Norwegian company named Axion. He wanted my European guys to initiate coverage. Said Axion was planning to acquire a bunch of refinery assets with financing from a syndicate of Scandi banks. I forwarded a summary of the conversation and his request to our downstream guy in London. No follow-up indicated."

"Axion," Kate said, tapping away at her laptop's keyboard as Claire watched over her shoulder. They were both seated at a round conference table in the middle of the room. "Was trading at twenty-five on the

Oslo exchange when you had breakfast with Solheim. Got as high as thirty-six the following year, and then faded back down to the low twenties."

"Market cap?"

"Around four hundred million krone."

Roughly fifty million dollars at the former exchange rate, making them a bit player in the industry.

"Mergers or acquisitions?"

"Bought a condensate splitter in Rotterdam in 2002 and were acquired by Norsk Hydro in 2006 for thirty-three krone per share." She looked up with a curious expression. "What's a condensate splitter?"

"Low-tech distillation tower. Heats up superlight oil recovered from natural-gas fields and separates out naphtha and kerosene. The naphtha gets used as a feedstock for plastic, and the kerosene becomes jet fuel. What about Solheim?"

She pecked away for another minute.

"On the advisory board of the Norwegian School of Economics and a director of the Kon-Tiki Museum in Oslo. Daughter got married a couple of years ago. Nothing else that jumps out."

I glanced at Claire, who nodded in confirmation. I vaguely remembered Solheim. Scandinavian businessmen tend to come in two flavors— intellectual Euro prissy and bluff Viking conqueror. The former are easier to sell to international capital markets, but the latter are more likely to hit the ball out of the park—or to pitch the herring in the barrel, or whatever the equivalent Scandi saying is. Solheim had been the prissy type.

"Mark down Axion and Solheim as unlikelies," I said. "What next?"

"Umaru Kutigi," Claire read, struggling with the pronunciation. "A call at nine-fifteen."

"Hard g," I said, heading toward the K table. "Kutigi's a Nigerian. Used to work for one of the industry rags."

The disposable cell phone I'd bought rang as I was pulling his folder. I checked the display and saw my office number. I'd asked Amy to pass along messages before she went home.

"Give me a couple of seconds here." I tucked the file under my arm and put the phone to my ear. "Amy?"

"Hi. Everything okay?"

Amy sounded forlorn. She'd been keen to help out at the warehouse, but I'd insisted she not get involved in anything that might make her a target.

"Fine, thanks. And you?"

"Busy. You got a lot of calls today. Everyone wants to know how you are, and why Walter's angry at you, and what really happened with Rashid. There are a lot of crazy rumors flying around."

I didn't give a damn about rumors.

"What else?"

"Narimanov phoned. He'd like you to get back to him whenever you feel up to it. And Susan stopped by."

"Let me guess," I said, interpreting Amy's tone. "Walter's not feeling any friendlier toward me."

"No. Walter wants you to know that you're not welcome at Alex's funeral on Wednesday, or at the chapel beforehand. I'm sorry."

I sighed. Not just because I wanted to say good-bye to Alex—I'd hoped hearing the news about Kyle might soften Walter toward me. I was anxious to know whether he'd discovered anything about Senator Simpson's link to the Saudi data, and—by extension—to Theresa Roxas.

"Susan tell you anything else?" I ventured.

"Like what?"

"Like what Walter's been up to the last couple of days."

Amy didn't respond. The good and bad news about her as an assistant was that she almost never gossiped. Good, because I could count on her to be discreet, and bad, because she rarely passed along tidbits from the secretarial grapevine.

"I wouldn't ask if it wasn't important."

"He was in Washington over the weekend," she confided reluctantly.

"Did Susan tell you who he saw?"

"She doesn't know. He made all his own arrangements, which is unusual. She only found out he went because his driver complained to her about having to wait around at Teterboro late last night to pick him up."

I racked my brain, trying to think of anyone else who might be able to shed light on Walter's movements. There was a chance he'd tapped some of his senior NASCAR associates for government contacts, but I strongly doubted any of them would tell me if he had. And I hated to ask Amy to snoop for me—I knew how uncomfortable I'd made her already.

"Okay. What about the service for Rashid?"

"I spoke to his assistant in Vienna. Everything's up in the air because the Saudi embassy can't find out when the city plans to release his body."

"Why not?"

"She wasn't sure. Some kind of problem."

The medical examiner's office had a big backlog. I knew, because Reggie had had to bribe someone to get Kyle's remains released to us in time for a Monday funeral. Five hundred bucks and a case of Jack Daniel's. It was a nasty little transaction that I hadn't shared with Claire or Kate, and that I was grateful to Reggie for handling. But Rashid's murder had to be a top priority for the city. I couldn't believe the medical examiner or anyone else involved would deliberately drag their feet. I'd have to see what Reggie could learn.

"Is that everything?"

"Yes. I'll be home if you need me."

"I appreciate it, Amy. Thanks."

I hung up and checked my watch, debating whether to return Narimanov's call. I didn't want to get sidetracked, but I had to give some thought to the future. I knew how curious he must be about Rashid, and how keen he was to get his hands on the Saudi information. It was just before seven. If I tried him back, I'd likely get his voice mail, which would let me be responsive without getting tied up in a long conversation. I glanced over at Claire and Kate, who were sorting through a stack of take-out menus that had been in a basket by the coffee machine.

"I have to make one more quick call," I said.

"What do you feel like for dinner?" Kate asked. "Japanese, Chinese, or Indian?"

"In Queens? Indian. And don't forget to order for the guys downstairs."

It turned out that Joe's nephew was a cop also, and was more than willing to earn a little extra cash as a bodyguard. He and his partner had driven us from the hotel to the funeral and back, and were currently stationed just inside the warehouse door. I wasn't taking any chances with security. Kate extracted three menus and held them up.

"Punjabi, Bengali, or Tamil?"

"Whoever makes chicken saag and peshwari naan."

She opened one of the menus and began studying it. I turned away and dialed my phone.

"Narimanov," he said, picking up on the first ring.

"Mark Wallace," I replied, disappointed that he'd answered. He probably had his office number forwarded to his cell.

"Mark. Hold a moment." The phone went silent for a few seconds. "Are you there?"

"Yes."

"I was very sorry to hear the news about your son, and to learn you'd been injured in the bomb blast at the Four Seasons last week. Is there anything I can do?"

"It's kind of you to ask, but no, nothing, thanks."

"Are you sure?"

"Yes. But I'm going to be out of pocket for a couple of weeks. I have some family matters to attend to."

"Of course. Take whatever time you need."

I hesitated, feeling guilty because of his graciousness. In his place, I wouldn't have been able to resist interrogating me. Despite my desire to get off the phone, I decided to volunteer an update.

"Thanks. Just FYI, I've become less happy about the provenance of the Saudi data, but I found a couple of hours yesterday to spot-check it against some of the information you gave me, and the technical details are bang on."

"Which leads you to conclude what?"

"Hard to know."

"I see. And who else have you discussed this with?"

"No one," I said, a little put off by his question. "Why?"

"Back-end oil futures are up almost five dollars today. I'm hearing that the hedge-fund community is buying heavily."

"Shit."

Narimanov's silence felt like an accusation.

"I gave Walter a preview of what the Saudi data implied a couple of days ago," I admitted, "when I was trying to enlist his help to check the information through his political contacts. I didn't tell him anything very specific—just that it looked like we might be headed toward short-ages. I warned him not to rely on my analysis and made clear that the information hadn't been vetted."

"Perhaps he found someone to confirm your analysis."

I wished again that I knew what the hell Walter had been up to in Washington.

"Perhaps."

"I'll see what I can find out. Get back to me when you can."

The line went dead. I dropped my phone back into my pocket uneasily. Five bucks was a big move to miss, and my relationship with Narimanov was too recent for him to have complete confidence in my integrity. Claire and Kate were still absorbed in ordering food, so I sidled over to the Bloomberg machine and punched up a market summary. Longer-term oil futures had been up on heavy volume, just as Narimanov had told me, but I noticed that the equity markets had finished roughly unchanged. It didn't make sense. If the hedge-fund guys were expecting an oil spike, they should have been hammering the stock market.

"Food will be here in twenty minutes," Claire announced. "Shall we get back to Kutigi?"

I opened the folder I was carrying and did my best to put Walter out of my mind.

33

"One-thirty," Claire read. "Mac Bunce."

It was past midnight. We'd worked our way through two and a half months of entirely routine calls, meetings, and meals, not finding anything particularly promising to follow up on. We were up to late November, only three weeks before Kyle had been kidnapped. We were all feeling tired and down, but none of us wanted to stop.

"Mac," I said. "Nice guy. Good old boy. Was head of E and P at Chevron forever." I pulled his file and checked the date, seeing a three-line summary of our chat. "We talked about the sale of some offshore leases in the Gulf of Mexico by Pemex to a company named Petronuevo. I made a note to myself to follow up with Petronuevo and filed details of the conversation under both Petronuevo and Pemex."

The table with the B files was directly behind where Claire and Kate were working. I tossed Mac's file on the table between them and put my hands on Claire's shoulders. She leaned forward, resting her head on her arms, as I began kneading her muscles.

"Petronuevo." Kate snorted. "Oil people have no imagination. Every other company I've looked up is named Petro-something."

"Lot of foreign oil companies started off as government monopolies. Governments tend to call things what they are. U.S. Postal Service. British Airways. Deutsche Telekom. Pemex, by the way, stands for Petróleos Mexicanos."

"Boring," she muttered. "If I had an oil company I'd call it Fred. Visit Fred's to get rid of that empty feeling. Fred will keep you warm at night. Let Fred lubricate you."

"Enough," Claire protested, sounding half asleep. "You're going to make your father blush."

"Fred's slick," I offered, sensing her need to blow off steam. "Fred's rich. Fred can be hot."

"Exactly." Kate laughed. "Who wouldn't want Fred?" She clicked a key on her keyboard and her expression changed. "This is weird."

"What?" I asked, as Claire lifted her head.

Kate rotated the laptop toward us.

"Look," she said, touching the screen with the tip of a pencil. "Petronuevo. First trade was on the Madrid Stock Exchange on November seventeenth, opening at one point three euros. Hung around between one and one point three for six months, and suddenly took off like a rocket. Last trade eight point seven, on June twenty-fifth. Then it vanishes."

"Must have been acquired," I said tersely. "Pull the news stories."

She switched to a LexisNexis window and typed in "Petronuevo." Most of what came back was in Spanish. I reached for her trackpad, and she pushed my hand away.

"Just give me a second. I know how to do this."

She filtered the articles by language and began scrolling through the English headlines. The bones of the story were simple. Petronuevo had been a privately funded start-up that had bought some offshore oil leases from Pemex and then done an initial public offering to raise the capital they needed to dig exploratory wells. The IPO had brought in about ten million dollars. Six months later, three of the wells had come back as gushers. Repsol, the biggest oil company in Spain, had announced a tender for the company a month later that was worth almost three hundred million dollars, giving all the initial investors in Petronuevo a thirty-to-one return in less than a year. The story Gallegos had told me at breakfast rang in my ears—Carlos and his associates had been offered shares in an oil company that owned fields that were worth more than the market knew. Carlos declined, but his associates accepted. I hustled over to grab Petronuevo's file, Claire and Kate right behind me. The folder contained eight or ten sheets of yellow paper covered with my handwriting.

"What does it say?" Claire demanded.

"Mac, my friend at Chevron, had an opportunity to bid on the leases that Petronuevo bought," I said, summarizing as I read. "He declined, because the geology didn't look encouraging, but he passed the offering documents along to one of their analysts. Chevron has some kind of proprietary mapping software that they use to collate all the information they receive. The analyst input the data, and the software kicked out an exception report."

"What kind of exception?"

"Each lease was for a block of around five thousand acres. The geology at the edges of one block should match the geology at the edges of the blocks around it. One of the Pemex blocks didn't match. The analyst checked it out and discovered that the information for the block had been rotated ninety degrees. Mac thought something funny was going on, but he didn't want to ask questions because Chevron does a lot of business with Pemex, and he didn't want to risk pissing them off."

Kate looked dubious.

"So, someone screwed up the numbers. It sounds like an easy mistake to make."

I remembered thinking about it at the time.

"No. Absolutely not. The whole point of the geological data is to generate a detailed seismic map of the ocean floor. To do that, you take dozens of individual observations and stitch them together with the help of really precise GPS fixes, working from the bottom up. You can't rotate the composite map without making the exact same mistake with every single observation."

"But if you were faking the data . . ." Kate began.

"Then you'd probably do it the other way around," I said. "Figure out what you wanted the big picture to be, and then manufacture the individual observations to suit. And if you were working top-down instead of bottom-up, then it would be easy to rotate one of the blocks, because it would only involve a single mistake."

"But why would Pemex fake data?" Claire asked.

I continued scanning my notes.

"That's what I was trying to understand at the time. Pemex is a government company. Given what we know now about Petronuevo, my guess is that there were Mexican officials invested in it as well. Maybe the entire transaction was originally designed to put money in the pocket of some corrupt Mexican officials, and someone invited the Venezuelans along for the ride."

"So, what did you do?" Claire whispered.

"Two things. I put a call in to Pemex and spoke to a guy in their leasing group named Ernesto Guttero. He said he was busy with another project and asked me to give him a couple of weeks to look into it. And I phoned Petronuevo directly, but I never got past some PR flack." I cast myself backward in time, trying to remember the conversation with Guttero. He'd been friendly, accommodating. We'd shared a laugh about something. I looked at Kate, a half-formed fear rising within me. "Check Guttero, please. See if there are any news stories from around that time."

She dashed back to her computer.

"Ernesto Guttero from Pemex," she announced a moment later. "News item in *La Prensa* dated two weeks later. I'm running it through Google Translate. . . ." She looked up, the color drained from her face. "He was hit by a car while he was crossing a street and killed instantly. The driver didn't stop."

I put a hand on the trestle table to support myself.

"What next?" Claire said, her voice fierce. "Try to find out who Guttero talked to?"

I shook my head as I gathered my thoughts.

"No. Pemex is a huge organization. We could dig around there forever without really figuring out who did what. The key here is Petronuevo. Petronuevo was the conduit for the bribe. Whoever funded the company originally was the one who set this whole thing up."

"How do we find out who that was?"

"Petronuevo did an IPO, which means they had to prepare a prospectus. The prospectus will identify all the original investors."

"Can I pull that up online?" Kate asked.

"A prospectus for a Spanish issue? I'm not sure. But there's an easier way." I took my phone from my pocket and dialed Morgan Stanley's New York switchboard. "The big investment banks keep copies of domestic and international prospectuses in their in-house libraries."

"Morgan Stanley," the night operator answered.

"Peter McKenzie in Hong Kong, please."

The phone clicked twice and then began ringing.

"Research."

"Peter," I said, recognizing his voice. "Mark Wallace."

"Mark. Long time. How've you been?"

"Can't complain. Listen, I'm sorry to ring up out of the blue, but I need a small favor. . . ."

34

"Thanks so much for your time," Claire said, her voice tinny and muffled on the cell phone's speaker. "You've been really helpful. I'll let you know if we end up taking the space."

"Do," a woman replied. "It'd be nice to have some new neighbors."

I heard the sound of a door being opened, and then Reggie's hoarse whisper from the second cell phone.

"Claire's coming out."

I glanced at Kate, who was sitting next to me in the front seat of our car. We were in an open-air garage in White Plains, New York, twenty miles north of the city. The two cell phones were balanced on the armrests between us. The prospectus Peter McKenzie had e-mailed me from Hong Kong identified the firm that originally funded Petronuevo as Ganesa Capital. According to their corporate records, Ganesa had a single small office on the fifth floor of an ugly concrete building three blocks away from where we were now parked.

"You get everything?" I asked Kate.

She looked up from the computer in her lap and nodded.

"Where are you, Reggie?" I asked.

"We're just stepping into the stairwell." His voice sounded from both speakers now, distinct on one and muted on the other. "I'm going to give you to Claire."

"Were you able to hear?" she asked.

"Yes. No problem." Claire had her phone clipped to her skirt at the small of her back and hidden by a jacket. "You want to review names?"

"I think I have it. The woman I spoke to is Sue Dye. Her boss is Mike

Paulson, and he manages SureView Insurance. The building maintenance guys are Rahim and Joe."

SureView was on the fourth floor of the building, directly below
Ganesa.

"Right," Kate confirmed, following along on her screen. "And the
temp agency they use is People Now, on Mamaroneck Avenue."

"So, what do you think?" I asked nervously. "You ready to tackle
Ganesa, or you want a little more time to recover?"

"I'd rather get it over with," Claire said.

"Any sign of trouble, or anything that doesn't feel right, and I want
you out of there immediately. You have difficulty leaving and you shout
for Reggie. He'll be right outside in the hall. Agreed?"

"Agreed."

"Give me to Reggie again, please."

"Mark?" he said.

"You're going to take care of her if there's a problem, right?"

"Absolutely. Don't worry about anything. She's doing great."

I heard their footsteps on the stairs, and then another door opening
and closing. My palms were sweating, Reggie's assurances regardless. I
couldn't believe Claire had talked me into letting her do this.

"She's headed in now," he murmured.

"Hi," Claire said. "Rachel Whitson. I'm temping downstairs at Sure-
View Insurance."

"Ellen Cho," a woman answered. "Nice to meet you."

"Sue asked me to come up because we noticed some water dripping
into our phone closet. She talked to the building guy—Rahid?"

"Rahim."

"And he said that he and Joe would be up in about ten minutes. But
Sue wanted me to let you know, in case you have a leak."

"I haven't noticed anything."

"My husband's a plumber. You mind if I just check the sink in your
pantry?"

"Please."

"Your pipes are dry," Claire said a minute later. "And there's no water
puddling under the dishwasher. But I'm turned around. If the pantry's
here, where's your phone equipment?"

"There."

"Should we take a quick look? I really like your hair, by the way. Do you get it done locally?"

I was amazed by how calm she sounded.

"Thanks. At a place called Isobel's, on Main Street in Dobbs Ferry."

"You live there?"

"For about six years now."

"My husband and I are in the Bronx. We're always talking about moving out, but it's hard, because we have so much family nearby."

"Dobbs Ferry is only fifteen minutes from the Bronx on the Saw Mill River Parkway. It's a nice place. You should drive by and take a look."

"You're right, we really should. Your equipment closet seems dry also. It must be something in our ceiling—maybe a drain line from somewhere. So, how do you commute here from Dobbs Ferry?"

Fifteen minutes later Reggie and Claire were in the backseat of the car. I leaned over the front seat to give her an awkward hug and a kiss.

"You were great."

"Thanks." She took a yellow pad from the seat pad and began sketching. "It's even smaller than we thought. Reception area, conference room, office, pantry, equipment closet. The door to the office was shut, but I could hear a guy talking inside. And I didn't spot any special security gear—no cameras or anything like that."

The guy she'd heard was presumably Karl Mohler, president of Ganesa. We hadn't been able to learn much about Mohler or Ganesa other than his name and the location of the office. According to their corporate registration and the Petronuevo prospectus, Ganesa ran offshore investment funds, which meant it was almost entirely unregulated.

"Small could be good or bad," Reggie said. "Less people to worry about, but anybody you bump into is likely to ask what you're doing. In a big office, everybody assumes someone else knows why you're there."

"You're the guy who doesn't like the alternative," I reminded him.

"The alternative," he repeated. "You mean breaking and entering?"

"Enough," Kate said, rolling her eyes. "We've been over this a million times. What about the equipment closet?"

Claire flipped a page and began sketching again.

"It was like you said. A white TV cable connected to a box mounted on the wall, and then a red computer cable connecting that to another box, and then another red cable connecting that to a panel with a whole bunch of blue wires coming out."

"Modem, router, switch," Kate said, leaning over the seat and pointing to each of the items Claire had drawn in turn. "Was there a brand name and a model number on the router?"

"Cisco two-five-oh-two."

"Good," Kate said, turning around and tapping at her laptop again. "Connection's slow through my cell phone, but I should have the manual in a few minutes."

Reggie's phone rang. He checked the number and then answered it.

"Uh-huh," he said, motioning to Claire for her pad and pen. "Right. Right. Got it, thanks."

He hung up and tore the piece of paper he'd written on from the pad.

"Ellen Cho. Lives at one-oh-eight Northmeadow Avenue in Dobbs Ferry, New York. Two cars registered to the address—a black '06 Audi A4 sedan and a red '03 Volvo wagon. I got plate numbers on both. I'm betting she's the wagon."

Claire had learned that Ellen parked in a lot two streets over. I turned the key to start my engine and dropped the transmission into gear.

"So, let's go find it," I said.

Reggie, Kate, and I stepped off the elevator and onto the fifth floor of Ganesa's building forty-five minutes later. Reggie pointed right, indicating a dark wood door that had GANESA CAPITAL spelled out in stenciled gold letters, and then led us left, toward the fire stairs. Once in the stairwell, Kate perched on the steps and opened her laptop while I stripped off my winter coat. Reggie examined me critically. I was wearing a red polo shirt with a Verizon logo, khaki pants, and tan work boots. Reggie had supplied the shirt, courtesy of a friend in the city's Special Investigation Unit. SIU was the outfit that did all the wiretap work for the NYPD.

"You look too white-collar," he said. "You need a tattoo or something. Maybe a beer gut."

"Not much I can do about that now. You got the belt?"

He lifted a small duffel bag from his shoulder and handed it to me. I extracted a leather lineman's belt loaded with tools and a dangling line tester and strapped it around my waist.

"Too tight," he said. "Loosen it up a little bit, so it hangs down some."

I did as he suggested.

"Better. You good to go?"

I took a deep breath and nodded.

"Kate?"

She gave him a thumbs-up, eyes fixed on her computer screen.

"Okay, then."

He took his phone from his pocket and dialed.

"Ellen Cho, please. . . . This is Sergeant Landon of the New Rochelle Police Department. I believe you own a red Volvo wagon, New York plate number CSN one-one-three-six. . . . Probably not. It's just that one of our patrol cars found your license plate in the parking lot of a 7-Eleven off the Post Road this morning, and we wanted to let you know that we have it, and to make sure that you drove the car out that way. . . . Really? Has anyone else driven the car? . . . Well, I hate to say it, but that actually is kind of troubling, because the two things that occur to me are that somebody stole your plate, or maybe even that someone stole your car. . . . I'm absolutely sure. I've got the plate right here in front of me. When did you last see the car? . . . Uh-huh . . . Right. That's exactly what I think you should do. If the car's there, don't worry about it. One of my guys lives out in your neck of the woods, and I'll have him drop the plate off this afternoon on his way home. On the other hand, if the car's missing, you should probably head over to the White Plains police department as soon as possible and file a report. . . . Right. They'd be the ones to handle it. . . . You're welcome. We're happy to help. Have a nice day."

He hung up and looked at me.

"She's on her way."

I exited the stairwell, duffel bag in hand, and began walking slowly toward Ganesa's office. A flustered-looking Asian woman in her mid-thirties opened the door when I was about ten feet away.

"Hi," I said. "You with Ganesa?"

"Yes."

"Verizon," I said, pointing at the logo on my shirt. "People downstairs had a leak and their phone system shorted out. Conduit carrying your lines got wet, too. We need to run a few quick tests before we try to power their system on again."

"My boss is on a call, and I have to go run an important errand. Can you come back in twenty minutes?"

"Folks downstairs are out of business without their phones. And I'd hate to bring their system up and take yours down."

She hesitated a moment and then nodded.

"All our equipment is in the closet to the left of the pantry. You need me to show you?"

"No. Everything comes out of the same chase on this side of the building. And I think I've been here before—your boss is Karl somebody, right?"

"Mohler," she confirmed. "Make sure you pull the door closed behind you when you leave, please."

"Will do."

She hurried off toward the elevator as I stepped into the reception area. The decor was generic—beige walls and carpet, mahogany-veneer trim, and a couple of framed posters from Monet's water lily series, one of which looked to be hung upside down. The interior door that led to Mohler's office was still closed. I made my way to the equipment closet as quietly as possible, both hands pressed to the sides of my belt to prevent it from clattering. The router was where Claire had indicated, and looked exactly like the picture in the manual Kate had shown me. I picked it up, tipped it facedown, and gently inserted a paper clip into the pinhole in the back, performing what Kate had called a "hard reset." A hard reset restored the router to its factory settings—including the factory issued password, which Kate had also found in the manual. The power light on the front of the router cycled from green to red to flashing yellow. Flashing yellow meant it was rebooting. Setting the router down, I reached into the duffel and pulled out a compact wireless access point with network and power cords wrapped around it. The access point went on the shelf next to the router, the network cord connected it to the switch, and the power cord went to an available outlet. I did a quick scan, making sure everything looked right, and then took my phone from my pocket and texted the word "done" to Kate. Everything else was up to her. Our plan was that she'd connect to the access point wirelessly from the stairwell, log in to the router with the default password, and then alter the settings so she could riffle through Ganesa's records over the Internet, hopefully learning who Mohler worked for. The green transmit light on the access point began flashing—Kate had connected.

"Can I help you?"

I jumped involuntarily. A guy I assumed had to be Mohler was standing in the hall outside his office door, blocking my exit. He was a few inches shorter than me, skinny, and had a pointed nose that made him look like a rodent. My first thought was that I could probably take him in a scuffle. My second was that it was just me and him in the office, and that it might be a heck of a lot easier to just bang his head against the wall until he told me what I wanted to know. The original original plan—before breaking and entering—had been exactly that. Reggie had nixed it, and Claire made me promise to play it cool.

"You surprised me. People downstairs had a leak, and their phone system shorted. We're just checking your equipment to make sure you don't have a problem when we bring them back online."

He glanced over his shoulder toward the empty reception area.

"Who let you in?"

"I bumped into your assistant in the hall. Ellen? She said it would be okay."

He nodded expressionlessly. I couldn't tell if he was curious or suspicious or just bored. The worst case was that he'd recognize me. My image hadn't been in the media for ages that I knew about, but some people were good with faces. If he did, I was going back to plan number one. One of the tools on my belt was a twelve-inch crescent wrench. I tried to remember the Scottish word Narimanov had taught me—"*laldie.*" A beating with a pipe wrench. I reckoned the tool on my belt would serve in a pinch.

"The Internet went down in my office. You know anything about that?"

"I pulled the cable for a second to test it. Everything in the chase got wet. Should be back up now. Sorry I didn't give you a heads-up—your assistant said you were on the phone."

He took a couple of steps forward and peered into the closet. The wireless access point I'd installed was in plain view. I wondered if he knew what he was looking at.

"Seems dry to me."

"Leak was *downstairs*," I said, letting myself sound a little peevish. It was probably a mistake to be too polite. I unclipped the line tester from my belt and turned my back to him. "Be done here in a minute."

I attached the leads to one of the phone blocks and peered at the display on the tester, willing Mohler to walk away. Fifteen seconds passed with agonizing slowness. If he asked me to explain what I was doing, I wouldn't have any choice but to hit him, because I didn't have a clue. I heard the door to his office close just as the phone on my belt began vibrating. Kate had responded with the same message I'd sent her— "done."

It took only a few seconds to unhook my gear and pack up. Kate and Reggie were waiting for me by the elevator.

"Any problems?" Reggie asked.

"I saw Mohler."

"You get any kind of read on him?"

"Little man in a little office. There has to be someone bigger behind him."

Kate touched the bag that held her computer.

"We'll know soon," she said.

35

We stopped by Ellen Cho's house to drop her license plate in the mailbox and then drove back down to the city. We were working out of the warehouse instead of the hotel, because it was more spacious and the Internet connection was faster. Claire fussed at the Nespresso machine, fixing coffee for everyone, while Kate booted up her computer and confirmed that she still had remote access to Mohler's network.

"Huh," she said, after a few minutes of tapping on her keyboard. "That's strange."

"What?" I asked, exchanging a concerned glance with Reggie. "You can't get in?"

"Getting in was no problem. I'm looking at the activity log on his router. I set it to record all his incoming and outgoing Internet connections, so we could see if Ganesa was exchanging information with anyone external. I figured that if Mohler were a front for someone else, like you said, then maybe their networks were connected."

"And?"

"No links to any outside servers, but I am seeing someone browsing on a bunch of weird Web sites."

"What kind of weird Web sites?"

"Hard to say for sure," she muttered, cheeks flushed. "But the two places that seem to be getting the most page requests are PinkTushy dot com and SchoolgirlPunishment dot com."

"Schoolgirl Punishment" didn't sound like an advice site for parents. "Porn?"

"Easy enough to find out." She typed something rapidly and hit the enter key. "Yuck." She spun the computer toward me.

Inch-and-a-half magenta letters spelled SCHOOLGIRL PUNISHMENT at the top of her screen. Below was a photograph of a fully clothed guy with a naked woman draped over his lap. His hand was uplifted over her bottom, and his mouth was twisted into the exaggerated grimace of a silent-movie villain. The woman was wearing white knee socks and had her hair in childish braids, but her face was turned to the camera, revealing her to be in her mid-thirties. Her expression was one of extreme boredom.

"Ganesa's a two-person outfit, as far as we know," I mumbled, feeling a little flushed myself. I'd seen porn before but never in the company of my daughter. "I doubt Ellen Cho's the one looking at this stuff. So, in addition to being a stock-market manipulator and an accomplice to murder, I'm guessing this makes Mohler a pervert."

Claire joined us, carrying coffee.

"Can he be arrested for looking at stuff like that?" she asked disgustedly, tipping her head toward the screen as she handed cups to me and Reggie.

"No," Reggie answered. "Not unless there are minors involved. And I don't want to shock anyone, but taken by itself, this sort of thing doesn't make Mohler that strange a dude. One of the things you learn in my line is that lots of otherwise mild-mannered people are into all kinds of freaky stuff. Patrol cops see it all the time, because they get called out when people forget to close the drapes or when sex games go wrong. The homicide guys are the ones with the really weird stories, though. They dig deep on people who didn't know they were about to check out, and who didn't have time to tidy up beforehand. Spanking porn is on the mild end of the fetish scale."

"Which is one of the things that made you wonder if Alex committed suicide," I said uncomfortably, remembering our conversation on the park bench. "Because you figured he might have been into something strange and dumped his hard drive to tidy up."

"Possible."

"I'm kind of offended to hear you call this stuff mild," Kate burst out angrily. "I don't see how porn promoting violence against women is any less bad than porn involving children."

Reggie glanced upward, looking as if he wished he was somewhere else.

"World's a complicated place," he said. "When it comes to sex, the only bright line I know to separate right from wrong is consent. Children can't consent."

"And women who are abused or dependent can?"

"Enough," Claire interrupted. "We can have this debate another time. The only question that interests me right now is whether this tells us anything useful about Mohler."

"Maybe," Reggie replied, looking relieved to be let off the hook. "Porn addiction generally suggests a loner and a guy who feels bad about himself for some reason. Mohler could be the life of every party and never miss a night's sleep, but it's a better bet that he has something gnawing at him. It's also likely that he has other addictions. Guy strike you as a boozer, Mark?"

"Possible," I said, still half thinking about Alex. Reggie's description fit Alex to a T. Maybe Reggie was right to suspect that he'd ditched his own hard drive. "He didn't look like the healthy type."

Reggie's phone rang before he could follow up.

"Sorry," he said, checking the display. "I got to take this." He put the phone to his ear and stepped away.

"We'd know more if we could see Mohler's e-mail," I said, glancing back to Kate. "Any possibility of that?"

"Not yet," she answered, shaking her head. "Connecting to the router is like connecting to a switchboard. I can eavesdrop on the conversations that Ganesa's computers are having with each other and with outside computers, but persuading them to talk to me is a whole different level of complexity. It might be easy, or it might be really hard, I can't tell yet. Gabor sent me a step-by-step procedure to try."

"You're back in his good books?"

"Totally. The T-shirt was exactly the right thing to send him. He e-mailed me a picture of himself wearing it."

I was glad to hear it. At Kate's request, I'd laid out a hundred and fifty bucks for a vintage Pretenders concert T-shirt that she'd found online at a shop in London. The seller had drop-shipped it to Budapest, along with a faxed note from Kate that apologized for missing lunch with Gabor's mother. Another miracle of the digital age.

"Let me guess. Gabor's my age, pudgy, balding, and looks like he could use a bath."

"Not quite. Twenty-five, skinny, and dreadlocks. But yes to the bath. Kind of a grubby rock-star nerd look. I showed the picture to Phil and he got all jealous."

She didn't sound particularly unhappy to have upset him. Claire headed back toward the pantry. I turned to follow and my eye stopped on the clock mounted over the door. A half-formed thought caught me up short.

"How long has Mohler been browsing on these porn sites?"

She pressed a few keys on her computer.

"Pretty much nonstop for the last hour. He's on something called Hot Crossed Buns right now."

The time was a few minutes past four. The stock market closed at four. Not many money managers I knew ignored the close if they were near a screen, regardless of how kinky they were.

"He have any other pages open? Maybe something financial?"

She dragged a couple of fingers across her trackpad as I hunched over to watch. She was scrolling through the log file too fast for me to pick much out, but I managed to spot a couple of the Web addresses she'd mentioned and a couple she hadn't. LeatheredMaidens.com and BirchHollow.com were two she'd omitted.

"Porn and more porn, as far as I can tell. Nothing that looks financial. Why?"

"Just another thing that seems odd," I said, wondering exactly what kind of business Mohler ran. "Let me know if you make any more progress."

"Will do."

Reggie was still on the phone, so I joined Claire in the pantry.

"More coffee?" she asked.

"Not yet, thanks. Kate's incredible, isn't she?"

Claire smiled.

"I remember when she was ten and we got the new VCR. . . ." Claire trailed off uncomfortably.

"And Kate was the only one who could figure out how to program it, and Kyle got furious. I remember, too. It's okay to remember."

"I know." She crossed her arms and leaned against the counter behind her. "I'm worried."

"About what?"

"About what's going to happen if we get this whole thing figured out but we can't prove it, because we took too many shortcuts."

It was the same question I'd asked Reggie in the car by the river, after our trip to Staten Island.

"I'll take care of it. I promise."

"By beating someone with a bat?"

I winced. It wasn't something I'd wanted her to know about.

"Reggie told you?"

"He's worried also. We're all worried. For the same reasons, and for different reasons. Whatever happens, I want you to remember that Kate needs you."

"Kate?" I asked, my heart aching.

"And me," she said, biting her lip. "We're a family."

I leaned forward to give her a kiss, and she put her arms around me. I suddenly felt better than I had in days.

"Who was on the phone?" Claire asked, looking over my shoulder.

"Friend on the job with a couple of updates," Reggie replied, walking toward us. "The tech who matched the partial on Carlos's belt buckle to Theresa gave the news to the homicide boys. Homicide put out an APB and sent her photo and prints to Immigration and Interpol. If we're lucky, they'll get some kind of hit."

"But they only know her as Carlos's girlfriend, right?" I said. "Not as Theresa Roxas?"

"Right. But that's fine for now. She's likely moving around under some other name anyway. The department makes Theresa as a connection between Carlos Munoz and Alex Coleman, and two things are going to happen. First, our degrees of freedom will go way down, because Chief Ellison will consolidate everything under someone more politically reliable than me, and we'll be left out in the cold. Second, he'll shine a big bright light up my backside, and your backside, and do everything he can to make our lives miserable." He tipped his head toward Claire. "Pardon my language. But unless we're willing to toss the whole thing to Ellison, and to give up on the kind of stuff we pulled today, I think we should continue to keep our mouths shut."

Claire nodded her agreement.

"Okay," I said. "What else?"

"Picked up some odd news on Rashid. His secretary's right that there's some sort of tug-of-war going on over his remains. My guy couldn't find out exactly what the issue was, but he heard that the State Department was involved."

"You have any guesses?"

Reggie shrugged.

"I'm clueless."

"Ta-da," Kate announced loudly, holding her arms over her head. "Your daughter's a genius."

"We already knew that," I said, starting toward her. "What geniuslike thing have you done now?"

"Figured out that Mohler has a personal firewall on his PC, which makes it really tough to break into, but that he's also running backup software. His entire document folder is getting copied to a stand-alone network hard drive every fifteen minutes. And the backup drive is completely unprotected."

"Wow. Why would he protect his PC but not his backup?"

"Gabor predicted that I'd find a whole mix of different security protocols on the network, when I told him it was a small business. Most small businesses don't have their own IT person, which means they have different technicians working on the network at different times, and even that people sometimes install stuff themselves without thinking about the security implications. I bet that Mohler or Ellen Cho bought the backup drive at Staples and just plugged it in without thinking."

"Incredible. Can we see his mail?"

"One thing at a time," she chided. "Documents first, maybe mail later. I'm copying the backup files to my Google account now, but if you get your laptop out, I can log you on simultaneously, and you can start looking through his records right away."

"You're the best," I said, kissing her on top of her head.

"Never forget it."

I looked at Claire. She smiled at me, and I smiled back.

36

"Shit," I said, tossing my pencil at my computer screen. "I'm an idiot."

"I already knew that," Kate shot back deadpan. "What idiotlike thing have you done now?"

It was just after eight. Claire and Reggie had left ten minutes before to pick up dinner from an Italian place a few blocks away.

"Spent the better part of four hours trying to figure out Mohler's bizarre trading strategies without ever spotting the obvious. Come look."

She carried her chair around the table we were working at and sat down next to me. I picked up my pencil and touched the eraser to my screen.

"Thanks to your genius, I was able to copy all Mohler's positions and transactions for the past six months into an Excel spreadsheet. He's operating in thirty-four different accounts, so I copied each one to a separate page. The first thing I noticed is that he only trades on the first business day of every month."

"Is that unusual?"

"So-so. There are a lot of money managers out there who practice something called 'technical trading,' which means they make buy and sell decisions based on statistical measures, like the moving average price of a stock and the daily trading volume, and pretty much ignore fundamental information, like how much money a company happens to be earning at any given point in time."

"Wait a second," Kate objected. "That's crazy, isn't it? How can you invest in a company and not care how much money it makes?"

"Two reasons. First, because you assume that any news a company might release is already reflected in the price of the stock—"

"There's something wrong with that logic," she interrupted, frowning.

"You're not the first to think so. There's an old Wall Street joke about two economists walking to lunch. The first spots a ten-dollar bill on the sidewalk and tries to point it out to the second. The second refuses to look, asserting that if there were a ten-dollar bill on the sidewalk, someone would have picked it up already."

"I thought jokes were supposed to be funny."

"Nice. At any rate, the second reason technical traders don't bother with fundamentals is that they believe that stocks go in and out of favor, like women's fashion, and that it's more important to figure out what stocks other investors want to buy than it is to have an opinion on what stocks they actually should be buying."

Her lips moved silently for a moment as she parsed my explanation.

"So, they just follow the crowd, no matter how stupid the crowd might be."

"Pretty much. You remember the whole dot-com bubble?"

"Not personally, but I've heard of it."

"The dot-com bubble was this weird period where people paid crazy prices for Internet companies that didn't have any realistic prospect of making money. Fundamental traders recognized that the stocks had no value, sold them short, and got murdered. Technical traders didn't care that the stocks were junk. They bought them because other people were buying them, and made buckets of money on the ride up."

"But the dot-com bubble collapsed, right?"

"Right. In the long run, stocks tend toward the value of their discounted cash flow, which for many of the dot-com companies was zero. But it's a basic trading aphorism that the markets can stay irrational longer than most people can stay solvent. The fundamental guys were wiped out years before the bubble burst. The technical guys who were long on the way up sold out and went short when the market started going down, just because everybody else was selling. They made money both ways."

"So, are you a technical guy?" she asked dubiously.

"No. I pay attention to technicals, because they drive so much flow, but I'm a fundamental guy at heart. The real problem with technical trading is that it's easy to get whipsawed, which is what happens when you're constantly buying on small up moves and selling on small down moves, and losing a little bit of money each time. All of which brings us back to Mohler. One way the technical guys try to avoid getting whip-sawed is by not reacting to every small up and down move, and only trading at fixed time intervals. Once a day is pretty standard, and once a week isn't unusual. Mohler trades once a month, which is less common but still regimented enough to make me suspect he had some kind of technical program going."

"And does he?"

"Nope. That's why I'm an idiot—because I kept looking for the pat-tern I wanted to see and ignored the one that was staring me in the face. Check it out," I said, clicking over to a second Excel workbook. "These are all Mohler's trades. This particular box here lists a group of trades he did in Intel about a month ago. You notice anything unusual?"

"No."

"Mohler's buying in some accounts and selling in others. If he was a technical guy, he'd be getting a buy signal *or* a sell signal, not both. When I dug a little deeper, I noticed that all of his buying was through one broker, and that all of his selling was through a different broker."

"Which tells you what?"

"The benign explanation is that he's stupid. He's paying two spreads and two commissions to buy and sell the same security, when he could just be moving stock between the accounts and saving himself the transactions costs."

"But he's not stupid?"

"I don't think so." I dragged my cursor down the screen and high-lighted a box at the bottom. "Look. This number here is the net profit of all of his purchases and sales of Intel in all his different accounts on this particular day."

"Zero?"

"Zero. Exactly. And it's the same with every stock he trades, every time he trades. He buys in some accounts and sells in others, always through different brokers, and the net always works out to zero."

"I don't get it."

"You will." I tabbed to another section of the workbook. "This is the profit and loss generated by each of the thirty-four accounts, listed month by month for each of the last three years."

"Four of the accounts always lose money," she said hesitantly, "and the other thirty always make money."

"And the net of the money lost and the money made?"

Her eyes flicked to the far right-hand column of the spreadsheet. "Zero?"

"Right. Which only makes sense because Mohler isn't really trading. All he does is buy stock through one broker and sell it through another. . . ."

"And then put the losing trades in the first four accounts and the winning trades in the other thirty," she finished in a rush. "It's like the whole IPO thing with Petronuevo. It's all just a way of moving money from one pocket to another pocket."

"Bingo. And not just moving money. Mohler's making payoffs to people and simultaneously laundering the money so the gains look legitimate. All of which explains why he can spend his entire day looking at Internet porn. He doesn't care if the market goes up or the market goes down. All he has to do is allocate the winners and the losers to the right accounts at the end of the month."

Reggie and Claire entered, laden with carryout food. Kate stood up to intercept them.

"Let me deal with that," she said. "You have to listen to Dad. He's figured this whole thing out."

"Hardly," I protested.

"Almost," she insisted. "You were only wrong about one thing. You're not an idiot at all."

"Okay," Reggie said, pushing his empty plate away fifteen minutes later. "Bottom line, we know what Mohler's doing."

"Right," I said. "The problem is that we don't know who he's doing it for. There aren't any names in his trading records."

"Any luck breaking into his hard drive?" Claire asked, glancing toward Kate.

"Nope," she replied glumly. "I'll check with Gabor again when he wakes up, but whatever kind of firewall Mohler's running is doing what it's supposed to do. No matter what I try, his machine just doesn't respond."

"So, what are our options?" Claire persisted.

"Beyond breaking in and just grabbing his computer? A couple of things, I guess. We can send him a virus and hope he's dumb enough to open it, and that he's not running any antivirus software. That would let me into his computer. And we can keep an eye on his incoming and outgoing mail. We might learn some names that way."

I stood up from the table where we'd been eating dinner, feeling restless and frustrated.

"No. I don't want to lose momentum. Kate's supposed to be at school. And the more time we spend screwing around with Mohler's records and his network, the more likely it is that someone figures it out and comes right back at us. We need to keep the initiative."

"I like that idea," Reggie said.

"What idea?"

"The idea of trying to get these guys to come back at us. The one thing we know about this gang is that they're not shy. Maybe we can use that against them, to set a trap."

37

The LaGuardia Motor Court in Queens is an architectural throwback to the 1950s—a rambling, pink-painted, two-story wooden structure that surrounds an asphalt parking lot on three sides, with rooms that open directly to the central lot at ground level and a long, open-air gallery above. My room was upstairs. Four steps carried me from the cigarette-burned nightstand to the peeling veneer of the wall opposite. Another four carried me back. I pushed the yellowed curtain from my window for the tenth time and checked for activity outside. The view was of the half-empty parking lot, a narrow, brown finger of the East River, and the raw concrete buildings of the Rikers Island penitentiary beyond. The only change in the last two minutes was that the lights of the prison had come on, gleaming with a false cheerfulness through the wintry mid-afternoon gloom. A plane roared low overhead from the adjacent airport, making the floor joists tremble. I doubted anyone got much sleep at the LaGuardia Motor Court. The carpet underfoot seemed to seep desperation, and there was something crusted on the curtain. I let the curtain fall, electing to wipe my hand clean on the leg of my jeans rather than wash it. Lord knew I didn't want to enter the bathroom for any reason. Reggie had been at pains to explain that he was familiar with the LaGuardia Motor Court only because it was owned by the nephew of a city councilperson, and hence one of the dumps where the local court system housed jurors unlucky enough to be sequestered. He'd recommended it as a place that had good sight lines and a management that was simultaneously adept at cooperating with law enforcement and at ignoring most of what transpired. I was too nervous to care much about the ambience, although I felt a vague sense of relief that I'd never been sequestered.

My phone rang as I resumed pacing. I answered it and heard Amy's voice.

"Everything okay?" she asked.

"Fine," I said, spotting a cockroach the size of my thumb on the ceiling. "What's up?"

"Susan called. Walter wants to see you."

"That's a surprise." Alex's funeral had been held that morning.

"I know. I asked what it was about. All Susan knew was that Walter's at home in the city, and that he wants you to stop by as soon as possible."

The hubris that led Walter to believe I'd drop everything and hustle on over to his town house after the way he'd treated me was offensive, and I was more than a little tempted to insist that he call on me instead. Regretfully, I couldn't afford the luxury of holding a grudge. I still wanted to know who he'd seen and what he'd learned in Washington.

"Not going to work for me. Tell her that I'll call in later to set something up for tomorrow."

"You sure?"

"Waiting won't kill him." A shadow fell on the window curtain; someone was in the gallery just outside my room. "Text or e-mail me if you have anything else," I whispered. "I have to go now."

I hung up without waiting for her answer and moved silently to the door, imagining I could sense someone on the other side. I touched the gun in my pocket to reassure myself. Reggie and Claire had been united in insisting that I carry it, much to my surprise. I took a deep breath and jerked the door open.

Mohler was hunched over on the other side, head angled as if he'd been trying to eavesdrop. He was wearing a black trenchcoat with the collar turned up and a Clouseau-like herringbone hat. Startled by my sudden appearance, he leaped sideways, his stupid hat falling to the ground. My nerves had been stretched taut, but it was impossible to feel intimidated by him. My initial impression came back—he was a little man in over his head. I picked up the hat and offered it to him.

"I know you," he said, snatching it from me and working his fingers along the brim. "You're the guy who was in my office the other day. The telephone guy."

"And I know you," I answered. "You're the guy who surfs spanking porn all day and transfers money between numbered accounts once a month."

His lips twitched, exposing crooked front teeth.

"You're fucking with the wrong people. You have no idea what kind of trouble you're in."

"Maybe not. But I know what kind of trouble you're in. So, why don't you come on in, and we'll talk about it?"

"There's nothing to talk about."

"Then why are you here?"

His lips twitched again, but he seemed to have run out of bravado. He entered the room slowly, head darting from side to side. There was nothing to see except the bed, the nightstand, a low chest of drawers, and a green tartan–upholstered chair. I flicked on the overhead light, shut the door, and sat down on a corner of the bed. I figured it had to be marginally cleaner than the chair.

"You're not any kind of cop," Mohler said, turning to face me. "You wouldn't be alone if you were. Which makes you—what? A shakedown artist?"

"An interested party."

"An interested party who broke into my computer system," he said, reaching into his shirt pocket and pulling out a hard copy of the e-mail I'd sent him. "And who's threatening to expose me to the SEC." He ripped the printed e-mail into pieces and threw it to the ground. "And what's the SEC going to do about it? My customers and my accounts are all offshore."

"Then why are you here?" I repeated.

He moved toward me, eyes wild, and I realized how near he was to hysteria.

"Because you don't understand what you're doing. Haven't you wondered what kind of people set up this sort of operation? And what they might do if some small-time nobody threatens to blow it for them?"

"I've wondered about who they are. Why don't you tell me?"

He took a step backward, toward the door.

"And end up dead? I don't think so."

It was the reaction we'd expected.

"You'd be more persuasive if you brought some of these bad men with you," I said, deliberately provocative. "All I'm seeing is a broken-down stock jockey."

He flinched as if I'd slapped him and began digging a hand purpose-fully in his other pocket. My heart rate jumped. The unmanageable risk at the core of our plan was that Mohler proved to be violent himself. It was why Reggie and Claire had insisted on the gun. I rose, groping for my weapon, but Mohler beat me to the draw.

"Take it," he said, thrusting a fat white envelope toward me. "That's ten thousand dollars. It was all the cash I could get on short notice. I can get more, lots more, but you have to be patient. You have to work with me on this."

I pushed the envelope away and settled back down onto the bed, try-ing not to betray how scared I'd been.

"Why?" I demanded. "So these guys you claim to work for won't kill me? Stop bullshitting me. If you had that kind of muscle at your dis-posal, you wouldn't be trying to pay me off."

Sweat shone on his forehead. He held the envelope out again, his hand trembling.

"Work with me, because we're in this together now. If they knew I'd been careless, they'd kill me, too."

I took the cash from him and tossed it on the bed.

"Sit," I ordered, pointing to the chair. "You have to answer a few questions before we strike any kind of deal."

He collapsed onto the chair.

"First, tell me how you got involved in this whole thing."

He edged forward and began working his fingers nervously along the brim of his hat again.

"Why do you care?"

"Because I want to know who I'm becoming partners with."

He nodded rapidly, as if eager to persuade me of his cooperativeness.

"I was working as an account rep at Dean Witter back in the mid-nineties. I signed a couple of geriatrics as clients and did a few trades to try to make them some money."

"But it didn't work out," I prompted, having heard similar stories innumerable times before. "So you did a few more trades and lost more money. Someone complained."

"Right," he said, sounding bitter. "The compliance guys at Dean Wit-ter accused me of churning. They ratted me out to the SEC. The SEC investigated, and suddenly it was securities fraud because there was a problem with some statements. I got a call from the U.S. Attorney, offering me two to four years in jail if I took a deal and threatening me with five to seven if I didn't."

"What did you do?"

"I was still trying to figure it out when I got a call out of the blue from some lawyer I never heard of. He said he could get me off, and that I had friends in high places. I didn't know much, but I knew I didn't have any friends in high places."

"Let me guess. Your problems went away."

"Right. The SEC backed off, so the U.S. Attorney dropped the case. I even got severance from Dean Witter. It was sweet."

He smiled at the recollection, still gleeful at having put one over on the powers that almost crushed him.

"But your new friend wanted a return favor."

The smile vanished, replaced by a look of resignation.

"I was kind of into the whole thing at first. Nice office, good salary, no pressure. Once a month I have to figure out how to allocate trades between a bunch of different accounts, to move the right amounts of money back and forth. It was easy. But it's been the same thing for ten years now, and I got to admit, it gets kind of old."

"No special projects?" I asked, thinking of the Petronuevo transaction.

"A little private equity sometimes. Most of the time I don't even get to read the paperwork. I just sign where I'm told to sign."

"Told by whom?" I asked, circling back to the only question I genuinely cared about.

He shook his head, looking scared again.

"Fine," I said, trying another tack. "Just explain how it works."

He nodded rapidly again.

"I get most of my instructions on the phone. And there's a guy who comes around to collect signatures. Mr. Smith, he calls himself, like it's a big joke."

"Nice guy?"

He shook his head sharply.

"Not a nice guy?"

"It's why we have to be careful. You don't know these people."

"Tell me."

He dropped his eyes to the carpet nervously.

"Smith wanted me to sign some legal papers a couple of years ago. They were in French. I asked how I was supposed to sign if I couldn't read them. 'With a pen,' he told me. I said no. I'd signed all kinds of stuff before, without ever reading any of it. But it was the way he was always treating me, like I was a complete nobody. It made me mad."

"What did he do?"

Mohler glanced up and fixed me with a pathetic smile.

"He put a knife to my throat and made me hold my left hand in a desk drawer, and then he slammed the drawer shut." Mohler held the hand up, so I could see it. Two of the knuckles were badly misshapen. "I don't ask any more questions."

I almost felt bad for him.

"How do you get in touch with Smith if you need to speak with him for some reason?"

He opened his mouth to answer, but a noise from the door interrupted. A key turning in the lock. The door opened, and a man entered. Mohler moaned in fear. The man was wearing a baseball cap pulled low and had a wide, shiny scar stretching from his mouth to his left ear.

38

The man with the scar stepped forward silently. Reggie and Joe Belko were immediately behind him, guns drawn.

"You heard?" I asked, reaching around to the small of my back and unclipping Claire's phone from my waistband.

"Everything," Reggie said, removing the Bluetooth earpiece he'd been wearing to monitor our conversation from the next room. He looked at Mohler. "How about it? Is this the guy who broke your hand in the drawer? Is this Mr. Smith?"

Mohler was staring at the man with the scar like a rabbit transfixed by a snake, seemingly unable to speak.

"These guys are with me," I assured him. "Your friend likes to keep tabs on other people's e-mail. We were expecting you to be followed. There's nothing for you to worry about as long as you tell the truth."

Mohler nodded jerkily, the color drained from his face.

"How about you, Mark?" Reggie asked. "You seen this guy before?"

"Twice that I know of," I confirmed, the recollections popping in my memory. I pulled the gun from my pocket, the elation I'd felt at the success of our plan giving way to rage. "Once at the counter in the diner, when I met with Gallegos, and once in the lobby of the Four Seasons, just before Rashid was killed." I pointed the gun at the man who called himself Smith and put my finger on the trigger. "So, how about it? Who do you work for?"

"Whoa," Reggie said, holding up a hand. "Hang on there. First things first. This is way too small a room to risk any crossfire. Mark, you come around over here and stand between me and Joe."

I edged wide around the man with the scar, eyes locked on his face. He looked bored, like a guy waiting for a bus. I wondered how much more interested he'd seem if I pistol-whipped him in the side of the head.

"Better," Reggie said, when I'd positioned myself as he'd suggested. "Basic rule of any shoot-out is to have all your weapons pointed in the same direction."

Mohler staggered sideways, as if convinced the shooting was imminent.

"Now," Reggie continued, addressing himself to Mohler and Smith, "I want you guys on your knees, backs toward me and hands behind your heads."

Both complied, Mohler starting to cry, Smith still wearing his mask of indifference.

"Good," Reggie said. He holstered his gun under his shoulder and reached for my weapon. I opened my mouth to protest, but he shook his head firmly. He checked the safety and then dropped it into his coat pocket. Bending forward, he began frisking Mohler. "Either of you guys give us any trouble and my partner there will put a bullet through your knee. Nobody's even going to notice a single shot in a place like this."

The tears were running down Mohler's face freely.

"Clean," Reggie concluded, moving from Mohler to Smith. "But what have we got here?" He pulled a gun from beneath Smith's coat and held it up to examine it. "Ruger 40 S and W." He removed the clip and then ejected a bullet from the chamber. "Hollow points. Nice." He thumbed the loose bullet back into the clip, passed both pieces of the gun to Joe, and resumed his search. His hand came out of the coat again a moment later, this time holding a walkie-talkie.

"Joe," he said, frowning. "Do me a favor and go to the window and tell me if you see anything."

Joe took a step backward and lifted the edge of the curtain an inch with the barrel of his weapon.

"Red Explorer," he reported tersely. "Wasn't there a few minutes ago. Backed into a spot on the far side of the lot. No plate visible. Two guys in the front seat. I can't get a good look at them."

"My associates," Smith said, speaking for the first time. His English was unaccented, but his clipped diction made me think he was foreign. "Both carrying HK53s. It's a military weapon. Fully automatic assault rifle. Gets through an extraordinary amount of ammunition. They've both got extra clips in tactical bags."

My heart began racing again. We'd worked up contingency plans in case things went bad, but none that anticipated going up against guys with machine guns. The only exit from the room led to the exterior gallery, and the gallery was lined by a simple rail-and-post balustrade. There wasn't any way out of the room without the guys in the parking lot seeing us, and once they'd seen us, we were completely exposed. Reggie and Joe had suggested the motor court in part because of good sight lines. But sight lines worked both ways.

"You want me to call 911?" I asked hoarsely. Secrecy was less important than not getting killed.

"No time to roll the right firepower," Reggie said tersely. "And I don't want a couple of sleepy patrol cops to get shot to hell. Don't worry. We've still got options." He took a half step forward, pivoted delicately on the ball of his left foot, and kicked Smith hard in the side of the chest. Smith tumbled sideways, smashing his head on the corner of the bed frame. Blood gushed from a gouge in his forehead as he lay stunned on his back. Reggie dropped the walkie-talkie onto Smith's chest, unholstered the gun from beneath his arm, and then pointed it at Smith's face.

"You tell your buddies to stand down, or you're dead."

Smith lifted himself on one elbow, wheezing. Blood ran diagonally down his cheek and was channeled to his mouth by the scar. He licked his lips and smiled, a sheen of blood on his teeth.

"I thought you were the good cop," he sneered. "The one who didn't hurt people."

Smith must have heard my conversation with Reggie in the car after our trip to Queens. He'd been the one eavesdropping on me, the guy who'd been in my apartment. If the circumstances had been different, I would have kicked him, too. I didn't want to interfere, though—I was praying Reggie could get us out of the mess we were in without any shooting.

"Unless they threaten me," Reggie barked. "And right now I'm feeling very threatened. You need another demonstration of my willingness to hurt you?"

"Not going to make any difference. I walk out of here with Mohler or we're all dead. My 'buddies' have explicit instructions. I don't come out within five minutes, they blow everything and everyone in this room straight to hell, including me. Nothing I say now can change that."

"Bullshit," Reggie said. He cocked his revolver with his thumb, the cylinder rotating to put a loaded chamber under the hammer. "I'm going to count to three."

"Count to any number you want. But you might want to take a moment to say your prayers first. You'll be killing yourself as well." His gaze shifted from Reggie to me. "Could be a good time for you to put in a last call to that wife and daughter of yours. They're at the Meridien, aren't they? I was looking forward to seeing them again. Your daughter's gotten very attractive. Too bad for me. My associates will have to send along my regards."

I started toward him, but Joe grabbed my collar from behind and dragged me back. Reggie took a two-handed grip on his gun and spread his feet slightly.

"One," he said.

I shook myself loose and peered cautiously out the window. The two men were still in the front seat of the red Explorer.

"We got any hope against these guys?" I muttered to Joe.

He rapped a knuckle against the exterior wall, eliciting a hollow thud.

"Depends. If Smith's telling the truth, we're fish in a barrel. Bullets will go through this wall like cardboard. One guy stays in the parking lot and hoses the room high. The other guy runs up the stairs while we're all hugging the carpet and hoses the room low. Game over. Different story if they want Smith back. They try to come through the door, we might give them a few surprises."

"What if we open up on them now, when they're not expecting it?"

"Fire a handgun through a car windshield at thirty yards and you got deflection and penetration problems. Maybe one chance in ten of hitting your target, even for a top marksman. More likely to just make them mad."

"Two," Reggie continued, eyes locked on Smith's.

"Listen," Joe whispered, leaning toward me. "There's a window in the bathroom. You should be able to get out that way. You got Claire and Kate to take care of. No reason for you to hang around and take chances."

"What about you and Reggie?"

"I'm too old to be climbing through windows, and Reggie's too big. We'll make our play here."

A low groan made me glance toward Mohler. Urine was spreading from the crotch of his pants. Dying in a crappy motel room was bad, but not as bad as abandoning my friends.

"I'm staying," I said. "Give me a gun."

Joe reached into his coat pocket with his free hand, pulling out Smith's Ruger and the loose clip. I rammed the clip home and flipped the safety off with my thumb, just like Reggie had shown me.

"You got to pull back on the slide to load the first shot," Joe instructed, pointing to the top of the gun. "Shooting starts and you hit the floor and wait for a target. Aim low and count your shots. You got a ten-round magazine. Try not to let go of your last round until you absolutely have to."

I nodded and looked back to Reggie. The tendons tightened on the back of his arm as he began to apply pressure to the trigger. I believed he was about to fire, and also believed that we'd all be equally dead shortly thereafter, just as Smith had said. I felt terrified and calm at the same time, one half of my brain screaming to run and the other half analyzing my situation. I needed to get in touch with Claire, to warn her to leave the Meridien and to tell her how much I loved her. I reached for my phone.

"Guys getting out of the car now," Joe announced from behind me. "Both look to be wearing body armor. I can't tell about HKs, but they got some kind of assault rifles."

"Last chance," Reggie crooned softly.

Smith laughed. Reggie took a deep breath, his chest expanding.

The staccato hammering of automatic gunfire from outside made me dive to the floor, both arms locked over my head in an instinctive effort to protect myself. Mohler shrieked, and I figured he'd been hit, but I realized almost simultaneously that I wasn't hearing any impact noise from bullets. Somebody was shooting at something, but not us. I lowered my arms as the firing ceased and saw Mohler scuttle, crablike, into the bathroom. Reggie, Smith, and Joe were all frozen in the same postures they'd been in a moment ago.

"What the fuck happened out there?" Reggie demanded, his eyes still glued on Smith.

"White delivery truck on the east side of the lot," Joe responded urgently. "Rear door rolled open and some guy opened up with a weapon on a tripod. Maybe a BAR. Both bad guys down. Shots penetrated right through the body armor. Had to be large caliber. Truck's pulling out now."

"Plate?"

"Obscured. Writing on the side reads WEST END STORAGE. Also a slogan and some kind of phone number that I can't make out."

I got up unsteadily and joined Joe at the window, ebbing adrenaline leaving me shivery and nauseated. His description hadn't done justice to the scene below. Smith's men had literally been ripped to pieces. A blood-soaked leg had come to rest almost immediately beneath us, a brown construction boot still neatly laced to the foot. I gagged and turned away as a woman began screaming in one of the downstairs rooms.

"Our lucky day," Reggie said, his voice clipped. He sounded amazingly composed, and I wondered how he did it. He tipped his gun toward Smith. "Who shot up your pals?"

"Go fuck yourself," Smith said, sounding a lot less confident.

"Watch him," Reggie said to Joe, stepping over Smith's legs and heading for the bathroom. He pushed open the door and swore. "Mohler's gone." He went inside, reappearing a moment later. "Skinny bastard must have wormed his way through the window and jumped. There's a Dumpster right below. Probably half a mile away by now."

"So, what do you want to do?" Joe asked.

"Secure the area and call in the cavalry," Reggie replied, stooping to cuff one of Smith's wrists to the bed frame. "All we can do. We fucked up, and now we got to deal with the consequences. We straight on our story?"

Joe nodded and I followed suit, trying not to betray how unsteady I felt. We'd rehearsed a version of events that minimized the illegalities on our part, anticipating the likelihood that capturing Mohler and whoever might be following him would end the cowboy phase of our investigation. I was sorry we'd lost Mohler but glad to be alive, and particularly glad to still have Smith. There were some things I wanted to talk to him about.

"Okay, then," Reggie said as he straightened up. "Joe, you cover me. I'm going to head below and take charge of the scene." He glanced at the

Ruger still dangling from my hand. "Thanks for sticking it out with us, Mark. You got to lose that gun when the reinforcements arrive, but for right now, why don't you keep an eye on Smith?"

"No problem."

"Be careful," he added in a lower voice, brushing past me on his way toward the door. "Keep your distance. I want your finger off the trigger and the safety on. We don't need any more accidents. We have enough explaining to do already."

He patted me on the shoulder and vanished outside. Joe stood guard in the open doorway, his back to the hinged side of the frame, eyes sweeping from Smith to the parking lot below and back. The woman downstairs was still screaming.

"I'm okay here," I said to Joe. "You keep watch on Reggie's back."

He nodded hesitantly and moved to the gallery railing. I squatted down in front of Smith, the gun in my hand concealed from Joe by my body. My finger was on the trigger, and the safety was off.

"See my wife and daughter again, you said," I hissed to Smith. "When have you seen them before?"

Smith wiped blood from his face with the back of his hand, his cold, gray eyes fixing on me.

"Tough guy," he snarled. "Who would've guessed?"

"Because I didn't run out on my friends?"

"Because you already lost one kid. And now you're risking the other."

I tilted the gun by my hip, pointing it at his face.

"You know something about what happened to my son?"

"I know what's going to happen to you and the rest of your family."

The urge to pull the trigger was overwhelming. But Smith dead wouldn't be able to tell me who was responsible for murdering Kyle or provide me with the information I needed to protect my family. I forced my hand to relax, flipped on the gun's safety, and jabbed Smith in the mouth with the butt.

"Consider yourself lucky that I need you alive."

He shook his head like a boxer tagged by a punch and then spit blood and a broken tooth onto the floor.

"Difference between us," he said, giving me the same vermilion-hued smile he'd given Reggie. "I don't need you for anything."

A siren sounded in the distance. I glanced toward the door and

Smith lunged forward, snatching the gun cleanly from my hand. He spun the weapon upside down and had the barrel to my throat before I could react. I grabbed his wrist, feeling his thumb scrabble for the safety. A shot rang out as I twisted sideways, the bullet missing me by inches. I threw my body on top of his, pinning the gun flat between us. He fired twice more before I could get a clean hold on the weapon, each shot giving rise to a burning pain in my side. We struggled for what seemed an interminable time, Smith with a death grip on the gun despite having one hand cuffed to the bed. I wondered where Joe was. I finally worked the weapon free, hearing it fire a fourth time as I wrenched it from Smith's grasp.

"Freeze," Reggie screamed. He was standing over us, gun out and pointed straight down. I rolled onto my back and let the Ruger slip to the floor. Smith lay beside me lifeless, the wound in his chest just beginning to bleed.

39

"You hurt?" Reggie demanded.

"My ears are ringing," I said thickly.

"No surprise. What about the rest of you?"

"I think I'm all right," I said, exploring my chest tentatively. My shirt was torn and singed, but everything else seemed intact. "Maybe a contact burn . . ."

The words died in my throat as my eyes traveled to the open door. Joe was on the floor of the gallery, back propped against the railing and legs stretched out in front of him. His gun was on the ground next to him, and he had both hands pressed to his left thigh. Pain creased his face. I started to my feet, but Reggie held me down by the shoulder.

"Stay down. I don't want you keeling over. We got too many casualties already."

He turned his head to the door. "You doing okay out there, partner?"

"Fine. That first shot just put a little nick in the leg. Smith dead?"

"Either that or doing a hell of a good imitation," Reggie replied. "I need another minute here. You think you can call 911, let them know we're on-site? Be the perfect finish to a shit day if one of us got blown away by some trigger-happy rookie."

"I'm on it."

Reggie returned his attention to me, probing through the hole in my shirt.

"I checked it."

"Let me check it again."

The closest of the multiple sirens sounded as if it was only a block or two away. On top of all the questions and fears racing through my mind, I suddenly wondered what kind of trouble I was in.

"Listen," I said, wincing as Reggie probed a little harder. "I know I fucked up. But this is self-defense, right? I haven't got anything to worry about here, do I?"

"One thing for a cop to shoot a bad guy," Reggie said, his voice hard. "Whole different thing for a civilian to do it, particularly when the bad guy was cuffed to a bed and the civilian had a motive. Chief Ellison is going to take that bright light I was talking about and shove it right up your ass, no matter what Joe and I swear to."

"So, what do we do?"

"Go to plan B," he said, taking the Ruger from my hand and pulling me roughly to my feet. Glancing down, I noticed a pool of blood spreading outward from Smith's body, the carpet fibers too worn or cheap to absorb it. My head was buzzing, and I felt faint. I'd killed a man. It was a different thing from having hurt someone. No matter that Smith had deserved it—my body was rebelling against the act. My tough talk in Reggie's car suddenly seemed laughable.

"You feeling light-headed?" he asked.

"No," I lied, ashamed to own up to my weakness. I took a shaky step sideways, away from Smith's body.

"Good. Because the second half of plan B is your disappearing through the bathroom window, like our friend Mohler. Much better if we tell everyone that you took off before the shooting started."

"So, who's supposed to have shot Smith?"

"Me. That's the first half of the plan."

He squatted down before I could object, pressed the Ruger to the side of the mattress, and fired a fifth shot. The gun's report was muffled by the bedding, but the coverlet caught fire, releasing a wisp of acrid gray smoke.

"Why the hell did you do that?"

"Gunpowder residue." He wiped the gun down with his sleeve. "It's standard procedure to check."

"This is crazy," I objected incredulously. "This is never going to fly. You were in the parking lot when Smith grabbed my gun. People will have seen you there at the same time that they heard the shots."

"Haven't got much choice, have we? You already said it—you fucked up."

The look he gave me was withering.

"I'm sorry. . . ."

"I told you to be careful. What were you doing that close to him?"

"Asking about Kyle . . ." I trailed off, shamefaced.

"No help for it now," he said, sounding a little less harsh. "And don't worry about witnesses. Old police maxim: The worse the scene, the less reliable the witnesses. Given the slaughter we got down there, the witnesses won't be worth a damn. Hell, half of them are going to swear that I killed those men. Big black guys are exactly what most people imagine when they get scared shitless. Even other big black guys. Whatever Joe and I say will stick."

"All of which puts you on the hook for killing Smith instead of me. I can't let you do that."

He laughed grimly.

"You're a smart guy, but you don't understand anything about police politics. We got me, three dead bad guys, and a decorated cop with a bullet in his leg."

"Ex-cop."

"Even better. A respected former officer who was wounded trying to help his old partner close the unsolved case that haunted him in his retirement. Press will eat that shit up. Every blue suit from the top down—including Deputy Chief Ellison—is going to line up behind us and help paper over any cracks. Hell, I might even get a medal."

I wasn't sure how to respond.

"You going to put that fire out?" I asked, pointing at the smoldering coverlet with my chin.

"Nah. More confusion the better."

The nearest siren abruptly fell silent, and I heard car doors slamming.

"RMP's here," Joe announced. "Couple of uniforms sizing things up. We're out of time."

"Go," Reggie said. "You left when Mohler left. Find somewhere to scrub your hands, and make sure you ditch that shirt."

I looked down at Smith again. His eyes were open and glazed. I felt sick for having killed him, and equally sick that he wasn't going to be able to tell me what I needed to know.

"Go," Reggie repeated, giving me a shove toward the bathroom door. "Don't worry about it. Joe and I will take care of everything."

. . .

Reggie had wanted confusion, and he got what he wanted. Vectoring south and west through the gritty residential streets behind the motel as I tried to figure out where I could hail a cab, I saw pretty much every type of emergency vehicle in the city of New York pass me by. Police cars, fire engines, ambulances, Emergency Service trucks—even a lost-looking Con Ed van with a flashing yellow light. Maybe Reggie had pulled a fuse for good measure. I kept my face tucked into the collar of my coat, not wanting to attract attention, but none of the vehicles so much as slowed as they raced toward the motel.

I eventually caught a cab about ten blocks away, beneath the overpass for the Grand Central Parkway. The driver negotiated a series of confusing ramps and had us on the Triborough Bridge three minutes later, headed into Manhattan. I called Claire at the Meridien and explained the bare bones of what had happened, speaking low so the driver wouldn't hear me through the plastic partition.

"Are you okay?" she asked.

"Yes and no. I'm not hurt, but I'm feeling awfully shaky."

"What about Joe?"

"He seemed okay. I took off before I got much of a look at him."

She was silent for a long moment, and I felt I had a good sense of what she must be thinking.

"I screwed up, Claire. I know that. But Mohler's not likely to get far, and we have Smith's body, and the bodies of two of his men. The police will be able to identify them. It shouldn't be too hard to figure out who they were working for."

"We have to put a stop to this," she said, sounding on the ragged edge of control. "You could have been killed. Joe or Reggie could have been killed."

"I know," I said, trying to contain my own distress. "But we weren't, and it's in the hands of the police now."

"It has to stop."

I gazed down at my lap. My suit pants were torn at the knee where I'd caught them climbing through the bathroom window at the motel. I'd done a lot of things I hadn't expected to do that day. I'd killed a man. No matter how I felt about it, I couldn't walk away now until I was done.

"It will," I said. "I promise. Everything's going to be fine. You still got Joe's nephew there?"

"And his partner. They're playing cards with Kate."

"Good. You and she should get your gear packed, okay? I don't like the fact that Smith knew where we were staying. I want to change hotels, maybe move over to the Waldorf. They must have good security— they've always got diplomats staying."

"Fine," she agreed, still sounding upset. "When are you going to be home?"

"Maybe half an hour. Be ready to go. I don't want to take any more chances."

My phone rang forty-five minutes later, as I was getting out of the taxi in front of the Meridien. Crosstown traffic had been terrible. I checked the screen. The number was unfamiliar.

"Mark Wallace," I answered.

"It's Reggie."

"How's—"

"I'm on a taped line," he interrupted immediately. "Joe and I are both all right, but everything went to hell at the motel after you climbed out the window. The detectives who caught the case want to talk to you."

I pulled open the lobby door and entered the hotel.

"Of course. You got any idea yet who the guys in the parking lot were?"

"I can't talk about that. The investigation's being run out of One Police Plaza. Deputy Chief Ellison is supervising. He wants to send a car to get you."

"Shit. Ellison the only senior guy you got in that department?"

"No. But he's taken an interest."

"Great." I spent a moment thinking about everything I needed to get done in the interim. I had to wash up, ditch my shirt, and move my family. "Tell the chief that I've spent a lot of time at One Police Plaza. I can get myself there. Figure an hour, hour and a half, maybe."

I heard a familiar voice in the background. It sounded like Lieutenant Wayland.

"Be better if we had a car pick you up," Reggie said flatly. "Powers that be are anxious to chat."

"Doesn't work. I got a couple of things to get squared away first."

The same voice spoke again, angrily. Reggie cleared his throat into the phone.

"You at your apartment?" he asked, suggesting the lie to me.

"Will be soon," I replied, following his lead. It didn't matter to me if Wayland dispatched a couple of cops to hang out in my lobby. "See you in an hour."

"Right."

I hung up and stepped into an available elevator, hoping like hell that Reggie was right about how his department was going to respond to everything. It hadn't sounded like anyone wanted to give him a medal. I touched the button for my floor as two men boarded behind me. One pressed the button for the third floor. The other turned toward me, a gun in his hand.

40

"This is a good time for you to be very calm, Mr. Wallace," the man holding the gun said. The weapon was small, but the opening looked like the mouth of a cannon. My heart was pounding, but my only thought was of Claire and Kate.

"You going to shoot me, shoot me now," I said, the words coming out with surprising firmness. "I'm not taking you to my family."

"We prefer not to shoot you," the second man said. "And we're not interested in your family. We want only a few minutes of your time. Our superior would like to speak to you."

They were both big and swarthy—Italians maybe, or Greeks. The guy with the gun spoke like an American, but the second man had a familiar, nasal accent I couldn't place.

"This superior of yours have a scar on his face?" I asked, thinking they might not have heard about the shoot-out. "Because if he does, you're on a fool's errand. He's not going to be talking to anyone."

"You can find out for yourself," the man with the accent said. The elevator doors opened on the third floor. "Shall we?"

I didn't see that I had any choice. He led me off the elevator and to the right, the man with the gun following. The floor was all function rooms, vacant in the pre-dinner interlude. Passing an open door, I saw a uniformed Hispanic man setting a banquet table with glassware and thought about yelling out for help. The guy behind me must have followed my gaze.

"No call to get any civilians involved," he whispered, nudging me with his weapon.

We walked to the end of the corridor, passed through a metal fire door, and ended up on the landing of the emergency stairs. The man with the gun spun me around and pushed me against a wall, holding me by the collar while his companion searched me. The only thing he seemed interested in was my phone.

"A disposable," he remarked, taking it from my pocket. "I would have expected something more high-end from someone in your income bracket. Any particular reason?"

Despite the weapon to my back, it struck me that neither man had been particularly threatening thus far. They sounded almost conversational, entirely unlike Smith. It made me wonder if I was dealing with another outfit altogether.

"I had something more high-end. Someone reprogrammed it as a listening device. You know anything about that?"

He shrugged, looking thoughtful.

"The man you're meeting might. Let's go."

We walked down the stairs and exited the building onto Fifty-sixth Street. A white delivery truck was double-parked a few yards away, gold lettering on the side advertising an appliance dealership in the Bronx. I remembered Joe's description of the vehicle at the motel and came to an abrupt halt on the sidewalk.

"You're the guys who shot those men in the parking lot. You just changed the sign on the side of your truck."

"Lot of trucks like ours in the city," the man behind me said crisply. He pressed the gun into my side. "Keep moving, please."

I glanced left and right as much as I could without turning my head. The sun had set, but the street was crowded with pedestrians, and I could see a police car on the corner across Sixth Avenue. It was the best opportunity I was going to get to make a break for it. An expression I'd heard once came back to me: The enemy of my enemy is my friend.

I took a deep breath and stayed close to the man in front as he edged between two parked cars and opened the passenger door to the truck. He tripped a lever to fold the seat forward, hoisted himself up, and ducked through a dark curtain into the cargo area. Fighting back my fear, I followed.

A hand gripped my arm and guided me as I stepped through the curtain. A sickly red light illuminated the area beyond, and it took a moment for my eyes to adjust. The interior was partitioned, the rear section hidden from view. The space I was standing in was about eight by ten. Three captain's chairs were bolted to the floor in front of a counter that ran the length of the side wall, the space above filled with racked electronics. The center chair was occupied by a man with a shaved head who appeared to be in his early fifties. He was wearing an open-collared button-down shirt with the sleeves rolled up and khaki pants. The red light made him look ghoulish.

"Sit," he said, gesturing toward the chair to his right. "Please."

He had the same accent as the man still holding my arm. The passenger door slammed behind the curtain, and the truck's engine roared to life. Being in the truck seemed like a much worse idea than it had when I was on the sidewalk.

"I'd like to know who I'm talking to first."

"Shimon," the bald man said, indicating himself. He pointed to the man standing next to me. "And Ari."

"You're Israelis," I said, the names helping me place the accents. "I don't get it. What are you doing here?"

The vehicle jerked forward without warning, and I would have fallen if Ari hadn't caught me.

"Sit," Shimon repeated. "We'll talk. I'd hate for you to get injured. A mutual friend of ours always spoke very highly of you."

"What friend is that?"

"Sadly, a friend who isn't with us anymore. The name you knew him by was Rashid al-Shaabi."

Ari had to help buckle me into one of the captain's chairs, the combination of movement and surprise making me clumsy. Shimon touched a button on the console over the counter; the red light winked out and a dim fluorescent came on. It was an improvement, but the entire situation still seemed surreal.

"Rashid was an agent of the Israeli government?"

"We don't talk about things like that," Shimon replied solemnly. "But I can tell you that he was an Israeli citizen. The medical examiner here just released his body to my government. His will stipulated that he be buried in Jerusalem."

"At Har HaZeitim," Ari added quietly. "The Mount of Olives."

"I heard the State Department was involved," I said, feeling stunned by the magnitude of Rashid's deception. He'd been a confidant of almost every influential Arab leader for the past thirty years. "The OPEC people must be going crazy."

"They ripped his office in Vienna to pieces." Ari snorted contemptuously. "And a team of Saudi security people tried to kidnap his secretary."

"Helga?" Helga was an old friend. "Is she okay?"

"Not to worry," Shimon assured me, leaning forward to pat my knee. "Someone tipped off the Austrian police. She's fine."

"It's hard to believe. Rashid always seemed completely dedicated to OPEC."

"Rashid was dedicated to moderate pricing and production policies that promoted stable economic growth," Shimon said, shrugging. "Policies that are good for everyone, producers and consumers alike. You of all people should understand that."

"Until there are shortages," I said, thinking of the Saudi production data that Rashid hadn't had time to discuss with me. "Then it's every man for himself, with each drop being auctioned or allocated for political purposes."

"True."

I wanted to ask what Rashid had thought of the Saudi data, but the shoot-out at the motor court was still foremost in my mind. There was only one reason for Shimon and his men to have been there.

"You were at the motel because you were following Smith. You killed his men to avenge Rashid's death."

Shimon squinted at me. I felt a flicker of the menace he'd projected earlier, mixed with something I couldn't identify.

"Mohler went to the motel to meet with you. Why?"

"I barely knew him," I said, realizing why Ari had grabbed me at gunpoint. Rashid had died in my presence, and I'd been seen meeting covertly with a man linked to his killers. Shimon wanted to make sure I wasn't secretly in league with Mohler and Smith. "I'd broken into Mohler's computer system and learned he was committing financial fraud. I threatened to blackmail him, because I wanted to learn who he was working for. The only name he gave me was Smith's. I'll tell you everything, but first I have to know: Who was Smith working for?"

Shimon glanced at Ari, face impassive, but it was enough for me to place the undercurrent I'd sensed a moment earlier. Confusion. Shimon didn't know what I was talking about.

"The man with the scar," I explained. "He was using the name Smith." My words seemed to fall into a vacuum. I looked from one to the other. "You know who I'm talking about, don't you?"

"We'd never seen him before today." He pointed to the electronic equipment over his head. "It's your good luck that we were monitoring local radio communications and overheard him talking to his men. And that we travel prepared."

I was suddenly equally confused. If the Israelis hadn't been hunting Rashid's killers, then what had they been doing at the motel? The facts shuffled and reassembled in my head, the answer unexpected.

"Mohler. You went to the motor court because you were following Mohler. Why are you interested in him?"

"I'd prefer you answer the same question for me," Shimon said curtly. "Why did you break into Mohler's computer? And what makes you believe this man Smith was involved in Rashid's murder?"

We both knew something the other didn't. Regardless of his civility thus far, I was willing to bet Shimon didn't play well with others and that he wouldn't think twice about pumping me dry of information and then dumping me.

"Terms first. I tell you what I know, and you tell me what you know."

Ari produced a gun. Shimon was silent for a moment, eyes fixed on me. I was almost positive he'd negotiate, but uncertainty wears poorly when you're looking into a loaded weapon. I hoped I looked calmer than I felt.

"No," Shimon said eventually, waving Ari's gun away. "I accept Mark's proposal. This is a complicated situation, and we're more likely to get to the bottom of it if we pool our knowledge." He reached out to pat my knee again. "I don't believe Mark would betray us. Rashid trusted him. And after all, he knows what kind of people we are."

It felt like the umpteenth time I'd explained it all, the only advantage being that I had enough of a handle on the various threads at this point to be concise. I separated my narrative into twinned tales: Petronuevo,

Munoz, and Kyle on the one hand, and the Saudi data and Rashid on the other. Neither Shimon nor Ari took notes, so I assumed I was being recorded.

"There are two links between what happened seven years ago and what's happening now: First, Theresa Roxas. She was Munoz's girl-friend, and she was the one who gave me the Saudi information. Second, Smith. He instructed Mohler to set up Petronuevo, and he was at the hotel when Rashid was killed. We figure out who either of them are working for, and we know who's behind this whole thing."

Shimon swung gently from side to side in his chair, looking preoccupied. The truck had parked, which was good, because the movement in the windowless space had been making me seasick.

"And the motive for Rashid's murder?"

"Maybe he knew something about the Petronuevo transaction, or maybe he was going to tell me something about the Saudi data."

Shimon scratched his head and sighed.

"Or both. Petronuevo isn't a name I recognize, but Rashid might well have known more. I can tell you that he thought the Saudi data was a clever fake, stitched together from pieces of genuine information. Our own best estimate is that the fields have another fifteen to twenty-five years before they begin to run down, dependent on the economic climate."

"Which still doesn't leave much time for a transition," I said.

"We've shared our conclusions," he said, voice tinged with frustration. "With your government, and with others. Regretfully, we weren't believed, because we couldn't reveal our source. People suspect our motives—everyone knows we want more American involvement in the region."

I understood the problem. It was a difficult situation with potentially dramatic consequences for the global economy, but I didn't have time to give it any more thought just then.

"I've lived up to my half of our bargain. Now tell me why you were following Mohler."

Shimon's eyes narrowed as he switched on the menace again.

"I feel compelled to warn you—"

"That if I open my mouth about anything you tell me, you're going to shut it for me. I get it."

"As long as we're clear," he said, permitting himself a grim smile. "The organization I work for has close ties to a similar organization in Germany. A few days ago, a colleague of mine received a visit from one of our German friends, a man I'll call Hans. Hans told us that his people had recently captured an ex-Stasi hoodlum wanted for murder. The Stasi prisoner suggested a deal—his freedom in exchange for information about the people who actually perpetrated the Nord Stream attack."

"Not the Ukrainians?" I asked, too drained of adrenaline to feel much shock.

"No. A team of former East German Special Operations soldiers, current whereabouts unknown. The Stasi prisoner had purchased supplies for them—surface-to-air missiles from Pakistan. Our German friends were able to verify the purchase of the missiles and to trace the money back to its point of origin."

"Let me guess," I said, sensing another piece of the puzzle about to fall into place. "The trail led back to Ganesa, and to Karl Mohler."

"Right. We'd only just put him under observation."

I closed my eyes for a second, visualizing the note cards Kate had taped to the wall of our hotel room and feeling a surge of cold satisfaction. I'd been right to suspect that everything was linked—Ganesa to Nord Stream was the final connection. But there were still any number of details I didn't grasp.

"Why you?" I asked. "Why didn't the Germans work through the FBI, or follow up themselves?"

"Our German friends aren't ready to involve your government yet— or their own, for that matter. There are complicated political considerations. The expedient course was to foist the matter onto us. We're discreet, we have assets on the ground, and we have unusual latitude in our methods."

I'd seen their methods, and I could imagine the political considerations. Germany needed Russia for energy—that was the whole point of the Nord Stream pipeline. The politicians who'd stuck their necks out would be reluctant to circulate proof that the Russians had acted wrongly against the Ukrainians, and doubly reluctant to admit that the actual culprits had been their own compatriots. I kneaded the back of my neck, trying to stay focused.

"So, there are two possibilities. Either this was a genuine terrorist attack, carried out for reasons still unknown, or—"

"It was a provocation," Shimon interrupted, "intended to give the French and Russians an excuse to hit the Ukrainians. We lean toward a provocation."

"Why?"

"A handful of small things. It's particularly striking to us that the French and the Russians seized so many documents implicating the Ukrainians. Given what we know from the Germans, and the fact that none of the seized documents can be independently verified, it seems likely that the documents are forged. And as compelling forgeries take time to prepare . . ."

"The entire operation had to be planned well in advance."

"Hans and his people reached the same conclusion. It's another reason that they're proceeding cautiously."

It made sense on some levels. But I had one big objection.

"If the attack was a provocation, then Russia damaged one of its premier pipeline facilities and murdered a lot of its own senior people just to have an excuse to go after the Ukrainians. That doesn't feel right to me. The Ukrainians aren't that big an annoyance."

"Unless the Russians didn't know it was a provocation," Ari suggested.

His implication took a moment to penetrate.

"You think the French would do something like this on their own?" I asked incredulously.

Shimon shrugged.

"Possible. They tend to get carried away from time to time. You remember the *Rainbow Warrior*?"

I did. The *Rainbow Warrior* had been a Greenpeace ship protesting French nuclear tests in the Pacific back in the mid-eighties. Mitterrand himself had approved a covert operation to blow it to smithereens in Auckland, New Zealand, because he was unhappy about the criticism. The Kiwis—and almost everyone else—had been less than amused.

"Remind me: Who did the actual dirty work on that operation?"

"The action branch of the DGSE, the French intelligence service. Two of their people were caught by the New Zealand police. The experience might have taught them to work through intermediaries."

The DGSE. The same people who'd tried to suppress the Euronews footage of the attack. French foreign intelligence creeps, Gavin had called them when we talked on the phone. Jackbooters. I started to ask why the French would want to hit the Ukrainians and suddenly recalled my last conversation with Rashid.

"Rashid told me that the French foreign minister had visited Riyadh and pushed the notion of a coalition to take over America's security role."

"It's an elegant scheme if you think about it from their perspective," Shimon said, half admiringly. "They killed two birds with one stone. The Russians are indebted to France for their assistance with the raid, which translates into preferential terms for French industry on Russian oil projects. And they get to showcase their military competence, which buttresses a bid to supplant the United States in the Middle East."

"France is one of the countries you shared your analysis of the Saudi oil fields with?"

"Correct. It seems they believed more than they let on and are making a bid to position themselves for the inevitable shortages."

My brain was spinning. I closed my eyes again, trying to see Kate's note cards. Something still wasn't right.

"Back up a minute. Mohler funded the Nord Stream attack. So, if we're right that the attack was sponsored by the French, then Mohler was working on their behalf."

Shimon nodded.

"But Theresa Roxas gave me the false Saudi data, and the most obvious reason for someone to want the data circulating is to make Senator Simpson our next president. Simpson's campaigning on a bigger U.S. presence in the Middle East. Which is diametrically opposed to what the French are trying to achieve."

"Maybe Mohler and Roxas are working for different people," Ari suggested, his tone troubled.

"Unlikely, because they were both involved in the murder of this man Munoz, Roxas as his girlfriend, and Mohler as the agent for Petronuevo. All of which raises the question of why they're pushing different agendas."

I opened my eyes. Shimon and Ari both looked uneasy.

"There's a knot we haven't unraveled yet," I said, thinking out loud. "We still need to figure out who Smith and Roxas really worked for. Senator Simpson, the French, or some third party."

"My people can look for Roxas," Shimon volunteered. "But we have limited resources in this country. We found you only because you paid for your hotel room with a credit card. Unless she does something similar, it could be difficult."

My credit card. Shoot. Smith must have discovered my location the same way. I felt like an idiot. I glanced down at the hole in my pants. The police had likely gotten tired of waiting for me at my apartment building. If Wayland had run my records as well, he'd have men waiting at the hotel. I still needed to ditch my shirt and wash my hands.

"Don't bother," I said, making an effort to put the complication from my mind. "Roxas isn't her real name, and the cops already have Interpol on the case. I have a better idea—two, in fact. First, Mohler's offshore accounts. I know the banks and the numbers. If you can tie the accounts to their owners, we'll know a lot more about his operation."

"What country are the banks in?" Ari asked.

"Caymans."

"That should be doable."

"Great. Second, Mohler told me he had trouble with the SEC, and that someone made his trouble go away. I'd like to know who his lawyer was."

Shimon rubbed his jaw, looking thoughtful.

"Because the lawyer had to be paid."

"Right. The difficulty is that Mohler got off, which means that his records were sealed. You have any influence at the SEC?"

"Not directly," he said hesitantly. "We have friends in the local community who might be able to help, but I'm reluctant to get amateurs involved. They get excited, and excited people talk. We prefer not to attract attention."

I decided not to voice the observation that machine-gunning people in parking lots was a bad way to keep a low profile.

"I know someone who can help," I volunteered, recalling that Walter wanted to meet with me. Walter had influence everywhere. There had to be some way I could persuade him to use that influence on my behalf. "Someone who doesn't get excited, and who doesn't talk. I can go see him right now, but I have a couple of small problems I have to deal with first."

"Such as?"

"The police are looking for me. They might be at my hotel. I need to change clothes and wash up before they find me. And I have to talk to my wife," I added, realizing how concerned Claire must be.

"Relax," Shimon said, smiling, as he patted my knee a final time. "We're good at dealing with problems."

41

We drove from the Lower West Side, where we were parked, to Times Square. Ari left the truck to shop while Shimon connected me to Claire on an untraceable line. There were advantages to hanging out with spies.

"It's Mark," I said, when she answered. "Everything's fine. I'm sorry I've been out of touch."

"Thank God," she replied, sounding shaken. "I've been so worried. Where are you?"

"Not on this line." Shimon had made clear that untraceable didn't mean untappable. Anyone could be listening at Claire's end. "I'm sorry."

"The police were just here," she said, lowering her voice. "Some senior officer named Wayland pushed his way in. He saw the note cards taped to the wall and took pictures. I couldn't stop him."

I was too far down the road to worry about the police.

"He ask you any questions?"

"A bunch. I refused to answer and told him to get the hell out."

"Good for you. And?"

"And he was rude, but he got out. He left some men in the hall with Ken and Dan."

Ken and Dan were Joe's nephew and his partner. Extra men in the hall were good, because they provided Claire and Kate with additional security.

"Understood. I'm sorry about the change of plan, but I think it's better if you and Kate stay put for the time being. My best guess is that I'll be home late. I've got another errand to run, and then I have to stop by One Police Plaza to answer questions."

"An errand?"

I knew how curious she must be, but I couldn't take any chances.

"I'm making progress, Claire. That's all I can tell you."

"And you're sure you're okay?"

"Absolutely."

"That's all I need to know," she said, her voice strong. "I love you. Be careful."

"I will. I love you, too."

42

I heard the truck pull away behind me as I climbed Walter's front stoop. Shimon had wanted me to wear a listening device, nominally for security in case of a mishap, but more probably so he could stay posted on what I learned in real time. I refused, in part because I wasn't worried, and in part because I still thought he might ditch me. It seemed like a better idea to retain cards he didn't have. The compromise was that Ari would keep watch from the pavement opposite.

Walter's home comprised a pair of identical hundred-year-old brownstones, reconfigured as one internally while leaving the land-marked façades unchanged. I'd been inside just once before, nearly ten years ago. The decor was Ralph Lauren throughout, the effect that of an English men's club without the ill-patched parquet floors or the smell of boiled cabbage. I pressed the bell. His street was quiet by New York standards, tree-lined and low-rise, but I still couldn't hear the ring from outside. I pressed it again, a chill wind making my ears ache with cold. The temperature had dropped.

The housekeeper who answered recognized my name but seemed reluctant to let me in. I couldn't blame her. The tracksuit bottom and collarless knit shirt Ari had bought me made me look like an aging rapper. She relented only when I offered to show her my driver's license. Taking my coat, she led me to a ground-floor study. I followed, wondering why Walter had called and how he was going to receive me. I didn't give a damn about his opinions at this point, but I needed him to help me.

The study was empty, and the housekeeper lit a pre-laid wood fire before leaving me to wait alone. The room was paneled in chestnut and furnished with an overstuffed leather sofa and matching end chairs. I warmed myself in front of the burgeoning fire, studying the painting over the mantel. It was of a hunting dog with a dead bird in its mouth. I was willing to bet it was worth a fair bit more than the fifty bucks I would have given for it at a yard sale. I turned when I heard a hand on the door.

"Mark," Walter said, entering the room. He was dressed in a gray suit and a navy tie, and he looked tired. "Thank you for coming."

"Of course." The courtesy was encouraging. I gestured to my own clothing. "Wardrobe malfunction. Sorry to bring the tone down."

He pursed his lips, refraining from comment.

"Drink?"

I started to refuse and then realized how badly I needed something—my nerves were ragged.

"Scotch, if you have it."

A panel in the wall folded down silently, revealing an illuminated bar beyond.

"Johnnie Blue? On the rocks?"

"Fine."

He poured for both of us. I settled on the leather couch, and he took the end chair next to me.

"Cheers."

We touched glasses and drank. The ritual felt forced, and I had the sense he was delaying. Delay was unlike him. Walter believed in frontal assaults.

"I want to begin by apologizing," he said. "I was wrong to fly off the handle at you last week. I'm sorry if I've caused you any distress, personally or professionally."

"You were upset," I said, concealing my surprise. I'd never heard Walter apologize before. "It's perfectly understandable."

"You're kind to say so, but it wasn't. If there's anything I can do to make it up to you, now or later, just say the word."

Curiosity about his change of heart took a backseat to heaven-sent opportunity.

"I appreciate it. Truth be told, one of the reasons I came here tonight was to ask for a favor."

"What favor?" he asked, a touch of the usual wariness returning to his eyes.

"There's a guy named Karl Mohler who worked at Dean Witter sometime in the mid-nineties. The SEC investigated him for churning but let him off the hook. I want to know who his lawyer was."

Walter seemed fully alert.

"Why?"

"I can't tell you. That's another part of the favor. And the last is that I need the answer right now. Please."

He stared at me for a long moment. Just when I felt confident he was going to balk, he picked up the phone on the end table to his right and dialed a number. Something strange was definitely going on, but as long as it kept working in my favor, I wasn't inclined to ask questions.

"Susan," he said into the phone. "Get hold of Pete Ricken for me." He glanced at his watch, and I checked mine as well. It was six-thirty. "No idea. Try him at the office first. If he doesn't answer, try his home and then his cell. I'll hold."

We sipped scotch in silence for sixty seconds. Pete Ricken was the chairman of the SEC.

"Pete," Walter said curtly. "Thanks for taking my call. I'm hoping you can do something for me. . . . Right. Your people investigated a man named Karl Mohler for churning a few years back. He worked at Dean Witter at the time. I'd like to know who represented him. . . . No. Your guys gave him a pass. . . . If the information were publicly available, I wouldn't be calling you, would I?" There was a longer pause, and when Walter finally replied, each syllable sounded like a rock bounced off a metal pole. "Let me make sure we understand each other, Pete. You help me and I help you. If not, my entire community reverses its position on your merger with the Fed. You understand?"

It was vintage Walter hardball, made potent by the fact that Ricken and his agency were so vulnerable. Everyone in the industry had known for years that the SEC was woefully incompetent, a fact Congress and the general public had become aware of only in the wake of the recent market collapse. Ricken and the career bureaucrats who worked for him were engaged in a frantic backroom struggle to avoid becoming an unloved ward of the vastly more capable Federal Reserve. The hedge-fund community had supported Ricken thus far, happier to be underregulated. Their reversal might tip the scales. I was more than a little surprised that Walter would push so hard on my behalf. Whatever mojo I had was running strong.

"Mohler," Walter repeated, his tone more genial. "M-O-H-L-E-R." He looked to me for confirmation and I nodded. "Exactly. . . . Of course . . . I'd be happy to help her out with that. . . . You're welcome." His voice hardened again. "And Pete, I'd like that information tonight, within the hour. You have my number."

He hung up and snorted.

"His wife wants to be a trustee of the Kennedy Center. Wait until he finds out that the minimum trustee contribution is half a million a year."

I laughed.

"Thanks."

"Don't mention it."

He fiddled with his glass, swirling his ice cubes, and the sense I'd had before came back stronger. There was something on his mind, but he couldn't figure out how to get to it. His uncharacteristic indecision gave me the opportunity to put a few questions of my own.

"I heard you were in Washington this past weekend. You learn anything interesting?"

He took a pull at his drink and nodded.

"The Saudi data came out of the CIA and was distributed to the Senate Select Committee a few months ago. CIA analysis jived with yours, but they graded it unverifiable and downplayed it."

"So, why'd Senator Simpson run with it?"

"I asked him. Him and Clifford White together, in the senator's office. Their response was that it didn't matter whether we had five years or twenty years or fifty years. Energy security was a problem that needed to be dealt with, as a matter of national urgency."

"Did they own up to being the leak?"

"No. And they denied knowing this woman Theresa Roxas, or having a private relationship with Alex."

"You believe them?"

Walter tossed back the rest of his scotch.

"I believe Clifford White would pour brandy on your leg at a cocktail party, set fire to you, and then look you in the eye and try to persuade you that you'd been hit by lightning. The senator's harder to read. You want a refill?"

"No, thanks."

He got up to pour himself another. I glanced at my watch again, wondering when Ricken would call back, and how long it would take Walter to get around to whatever was really on his mind.

"Alex sent me a letter."

I snapped my head sideways to look at him. He had his back to me. "When?"

"Postmark was Wednesday. It arrived Friday, but I didn't see it until Saturday lunch."

Alex had died early Wednesday morning.

"What did it say?"

"A number of things." Walter turned toward me, and I saw pain in his eyes. "One of them had to do with Torino."

Torino was the fund Alex had started just out of college. I kept quiet, giving Walter time.

"Alex wrote that he'd done some insider trading. Inadvertently, at first. One of his investors gave him a tip. He bought shares and made money. It happened again. By the third time, he knew there had to be something illicit going on, but he was losing money elsewhere and needed the gain."

"I'm sorry," I said, meaning it. "That must have been a tough thing for him to carry around."

Walter looked at me searchingly.

"He never told you?"

"No. The last time we got together, he mentioned that he'd made mistakes when he had Torino, but I didn't know what he was talking about."

"So, you weren't aware that he was being blackmailed."

Blackmailed. Shit. That explained why he'd been so upset when we had drinks, and perhaps even why he'd felt that he had to kill himself. Another idea occurred to me, and I suddenly felt weak.

"Is that why he lied about knowing Theresa Roxas?"

Walter nodded.

"I have Torino's investor list," he said, drawing a sheaf of folded papers from his jacket pocket. "I've highlighted the names I don't know in yellow. You spent a lot of time with Alex back then. I was wondering if you might know more."

Walter was on the hunt as well, I realized, for whoever had driven his son to suicide. I stood up, the rage strong in my breast, and took the pages from his outstretched hand. I already knew what I was going to find. It was the third name on the second page. I pointed it out to him with a trembling finger.

"Ganesa Capital. The name of the guy who runs it is Karl Mohler."

Walter looked stunned.

"How . . ." he began. His phone rang. We both looked at it.

"Pick it up," I said quietly. "Mohler's a nobody. The lawyer is the connection to the person behind all this."

He lifted the receiver from the hook.

"Walter Coleman. . . . Right. . . . Right. . . . I will. Thank you."

He hung up and looked at me, murder in his eyes.

"Struan, Ogilvy and Cohn. They're a Washington firm."

"We need a list of the principals."

"We don't," he said. "I already know. It's the firm where Clifford White used to work."

43

One Police Plaza in lower Manhattan is an unadorned brick box that looks like an oversized Lego plunked down between the Brooklyn Bridge and Chinatown. A couple of plainclothed cops grabbed me out of the security line after I showed my identification, taping brown paper bags over my hands and escorting me to a basement exam room. It was late, and the long, scuffed corridors were almost deserted. A male tech wearing green hospital scrubs checked me for gunpowder residue, swabbing around my thumbs and vacuuming my shirt. I cooperated passively, unconcerned: Ari had given me special goop to clean my hands with, and the shirt I'd worn earlier was long gone. I was thinking about my conversation with Walter and trying to figure out my next step. Shimon and I had discussed it on the ride downtown: White didn't seem to have the financial wherewithal to finance an operation like Mohler's, so either he was just another link in the chain or he had access to a hidden pool of capital. We had to persuade him to talk, but the evidence linking him to Mohler was circumstantial, which made it hard to threaten him with exposure. Shimon had demurred at my suggestion that we simply grab White and frighten the truth out of him—White had powerful political connections, and the Israelis couldn't risk the repercussions if he subsequently complained.

The tech completed his task, not having made eye contact. One of the two cops who'd picked me up in the lobby made a quick call from the wall phone, and then he and his partner walked me back to the elevator and took me up to the fourteenth floor. Lieutenant Wayland was waiting in the elevator lobby, looking sharp in a freshly pressed white shirt and dress blues. Wayland dismissed the plainclothed cops and led me toward Deputy Chief Ellison's office.

"Let me explain what's going on here," he said, his voice resonant with satisfaction. "I took pictures of that mess you had taped to the wall of your hotel room. We've got you and Detective Kinnard for making false statements to the police and criminal conspiracy to conceal evidence of crimes. I'm betting we'll get Belko as well. Kinnard's out, he and Belko will both forfeit their pensions, and you can forget about ever working in the securities industry again, because conspiracy is a felony. And that's just for starters."

I kept quiet, reserving my energy for Ellison. Silence must not have been the response Wayland wanted. He rounded on me suddenly, face inches from mine. The hall was empty save for the two of us, darkened offices on either side.

"You and your pals are in a world of hurt," he hissed. "Your only option at this point is to come clean and pray for leniency. Am I making myself clear?"

He was clear but wrong. The last four hours had given me options he didn't know about.

"Your boss will be the one to make that decision," I said, shouldering past him and continuing in the direction we'd been headed.

I thought he might grab me from behind and try to bounce me off a wall, but Wayland's new breed of cop evidently stuck to verbal intimidation. He speed-walked past me to regain his position of leadership, jaw clenched and face flushed.

Ellison's office was at the end of the corridor. He was on the phone, so Wayland and I took seats in an anteroom with an unoccupied secretarial station, a long row of file cabinets, and a view of the East River. The chairs were hard plastic. Wayland was fidgety, cracking his knuckles and rolling his shoulders as though he could hardly wait to have at me. A light winked out on the secretary's phone, and Wayland popped to his feet.

"After you," he snarled.

The interior space was large and dark, the only light from a green-shaded desk lamp. The chief sat behind his desk in shirt sleeves, cuffs rolled up and tie pulled down. A bottle of Jack Daniel's stood at his elbow, a half-full glass beside it. He picked up a folder and tossed it toward me.

"Read and sign."

"Read and sign what?" I asked, lifting the folder from the desk.

"Official statements by Detective Kinnard and former Detective Belko about certain events transpiring at the LaGuardia Motor Court today. Your signature confirms your agreement with their recollections."

Wayland grabbed the folder from me before I could open it.

"This is wrong, Chief. Wallace has to make his own statement first."

"You shut the fuck up, Lieutenant," Ellison roared, supporting himself on his knuckles as he half-rose from his seat. "Do something useful for a change. Go get Kinnard."

Wayland looked stunned. I was less surprised, because I had a better notion of who Ellison had been on the phone with. I took the folder from Wayland's unresisting hand, scanning the contents as he slunk away. Reggie and Joe had said what they'd agreed to say. I lifted a pen from the chief's desk without asking and signed a brief declaration at the bottom of both statements, affirming that they were true to the best of my knowledge. Ellison was busy pouring himself another drink when I looked up. He didn't offer, and I didn't ask. Reggie joined us a minute later, Wayland skulking behind.

"Joe okay?" I asked quietly.

"At the hospital, resting," Reggie answered. "He's going to be fine."

"Enough," Ellison rumbled, looking at Reggie. I had the impression that he was struggling mightily not to explode again. "Back in the four-one, Irish, when you and me were probies, Sergeant Wyszynski taught us three rules about getting by in the department. You remember?"

"Do what you're told, don't run your mouth to citizens, and never fuck with the brass."

Ellison knocked back a slug of whiskey from his glass and then wiped his lips with the back of his hand.

"You broke all three rules on this one. And much as it galls me to say it—because I dearly hate being fucked with—you're going to get a pass. I'm going to buy the bullshit story you and your ex-partner told me, and I'm going to figure out how to put the best possible spin on it so everyone comes out smelling like a rose. You go back to looking for missing people, Belko goes back to fishing, and Mr. Wallace goes back to whatever the fuck he does when his friends aren't getting killed. But only if you all swear to keep your mouths shut, now and forever." He pointed a stout forefinger at Reggie. "Agreed?"

Reggie nodded guardedly. Wayland, behind him, looked as if he might spontaneously combust. The chief turned his gaze on me.

"And you. I heard from the mayor that he got four phone calls about you tonight, inside of an hour. One from a prominent local business-man, one from our esteemed governor, one from our junior senator, and one from 'an influential foreign ambassador.' I'm a little curious about that last category. I heard about guys getting skyhooked out of the shit by all kinds of people, but never by 'an influential foreign ambassador.'"

I shrugged. Walter and Shimon had both been busy on my behalf, as promised. Ellison glared at me a moment, as if he might demand some further explanation, but I kept quiet, and he let it go.

"Live and learn, I suppose. You're not planning to write a book about all this at some point, are you, Mr. Wallace?"

"No."

"Or get yourself a guest shot on *Larry King Live*?"

"No."

"Or whisper into a well in the middle of the woods at midnight when you're a hundred years old?"

"No."

"Good. Because the mayor and I reviewed that possibility, and we agreed on certain contingencies. So, if I hear one echo of one word from that well . . ." He shook his head and smiled, communicating the plea-sure he'd take in punishing any indiscretion I might commit.

"You won't."

"Okay, then." Ellison lifted his glass and used it to make the sign of the cross in Reggie's direction. "Go with God, Irish, and take the Jonah with you. Talk to Belko, make sure he's on board. And know this. You give me the tiniest excuse at any point in the future—the *tiniest* fucking excuse—and I will crush you like a bug. There's no room in this depart-ment for a detective with a wild hair. Understood?"

"Understood."

The chief polished off his whiskey and then looked at Wayland.

"Lieutenant," he said, "don't just stand there. Open the door."

Reggie and I didn't say anything until we were outside. He pulled out his cigarettes and offered me the pack.

"Thanks, but one every twenty years is my limit."

"I enjoyed that," he said, tipping his head toward the building behind us as he lit up. "I haven't seen Ellison get bent over in a long time."

"Being political cuts both ways. You worried about retaliation?"

"Nah. Open secret that he failed his last physical with a bad ticker. They'll give him a big send-off at the next Academy graduation. I can stay clean for six months." He buttoned his coat. "Come on. My car's over on Madison. We'll buy a bottle of Jameson and go visit Joe in the hospital. You can tell us both how you fixed the mayor. He'll get a kick out of that."

Shimon's truck was parked across the street. I glanced at it and then back at Reggie.

"I'm sorry," I said. "I can't."

He looked at me quizzically.

"You need to get home? I'll run you up to the hotel first, and we can talk on the way."

"No," I said. "It's over."

He took another hit from his cigarette, staring at me.

"Over, over? Or over for me and you?"

"Over for me and you."

"You promised to keep me in the loop," he said quietly. "I don't know where you've been the last couple of hours, or who you've been talking to, but if you're getting ready to do something crazy, you have to talk it through with me first."

"I wish I could," I said, feeling bad about not being able to confide in him. "I'm more grateful to you than I can ever say, but the situation's changed."

"You gave me your word."

"And I'll keep it if you want me to. But I'm involved in stuff now that you can't be involved in, with people you can't know. You have to believe that I'm thinking about your best interests here, Reggie. I don't want to compromise you."

I must have glanced toward the truck again involuntarily, because he turned his head and followed my gaze. Ten seconds ticked past. He put his cigarette in his mouth and turned up his collar.

"I read about Rashid in the afternoon paper," he said. "Some kind of Israeli spy, huh?"

"I guess."

"Which tells me something about the guys who saved our bacon this afternoon, and about the identity of the 'influential foreign ambassador' who called the mayor on your behalf, right?"

I shrugged, hoping he wouldn't press. There was no way I could put Reggie and Shimon together without unforeseeable and potentially disastrous consequences. They were operating by an entirely different set of rules.

"Things go to shit, and how can you be sure you won't be the fall guy?"

"I know too much at this point."

"Great. So they'll put you in the river."

"I don't think so."

"Well, maybe you aren't thinking clearly."

I caught his arm by the sleeve and shook it gently.

"This is what's happening," I said. "This is what I have to do. I'll tell you what I can, when I can. Right now, you have to walk away."

He pursed his lips and then sighed deeply.

"You talk to Claire?"

"Not yet. But I'll bring her up to speed tonight, before I go any further."

"Make sure you listen to her," he said, looking at the van again. "She's a smart woman." He extended his hand. "And remember that I'm around if you ever need backup."

"Thanks," I said, taking it. "I appreciate it."

"Good luck." He broke our grip and punched me lightly on the shoulder. "Call me when you're done. We'll have a beer."

44

Walter got up to answer his front door, leaving me alone in his study. I was sitting in one of the club chairs, staring into the embers of a dying fire. His house staff had been dismissed for the day. Voices sounded in the hall. Clifford White entered the room, Walter behind him. White was wearing a navy suit and a red tie; his wispy gray hair looked wind-blown. He arched an eyebrow when he saw me, lips compressing. The loathing I felt at the sight of him was a physical sensation.

"I didn't realize Mr. Wallace would be joining us. Are you getting him involved on the political side now?"

"A miscommunication," Walter said, closing the study door and leaning against it. "Or, more precisely, a misdirection. The truth is that I don't have anything urgent to communicate regarding Senator Simpson's campaign. But Mark has a subject that he'd like to raise with you."

"I'm managing a bid for the Republican presidential nomination," White objected warily, turning his back to the fireplace so he could see us both simultaneously. "I don't have time for extraneous matters."

"I think you'll have time for this. Mark?"

I extracted a single sheet of paper from my inner jacket pocket. I'd dressed formally, in the black suit and black tie I'd worn to bury my son. I unfolded the paper and slid it across the coffee table toward White.

"What's this?" he demanded, fumbling for his reading glasses.

"A photocopy of a signature card for a Cayman bank account. I believe that's your signature, Mr. White."

He gave the form a cursory glance. It was authentic—Shimon and his people had worked quickly.

"So?"

"So, the money in that account came from a firm called Ganesa Capital. The principal of Ganesa is a man named Karl Mohler. You know him?"

"No reason why I should. My finances are handled by advisers."

White was slick, absent any tells that I could spot.

"Mohler had SEC problems a few years back. Your former firm, Struan, Ogilvy and Cohn, represented him. Maybe you know him from that connection."

"Regretfully not. We represented a lot of people." He tossed the paper back onto the coffee table, took off his glasses, and looked at Walter. "I have no idea what Mr. Wallace is driving at, but I'm done here. I don't have time for nonsense."

Walter stared back at him silently.

"Mohler's an interesting guy," I continued. "His firm provided the funding for the Nord Stream terrorism, his associates were responsible for the murder of Rashid al-Shaabi, and a woman he'd worked with in the past provided me with the same counterfeit Saudi depletion data that Senator Simpson is counting on to get him elected president."

"Mr. Wallace sounds delusional," White said coolly. "I'm leaving now. Step away from the door, please, Walter."

It was the reaction I'd expected. I was itching to signal Walter to comply, sick of White's denials, but the deal I'd done with myself was that I'd make every effort to cajole White into cooperating peaceably before letting matters progress.

"Some of it I can prove, and some of it I can't," I admitted. "One thing I know for sure is that you're involved with Mohler up to your neck. And you should know that Mr. al-Shaabi's friends—his real friends—agree with me. They're very upset, and they're inclined to respond. I'm the only one who can help you with them at this point, and I'm willing to help only if you admit your culpability and confess the details."

White deigned to turn his head in my direction, a sneer on his lips.

"I'm a former deputy cabinet secretary. I'm not scared of a gang of Jew hoods who've put two and two together with your assistance and come up with seventeen." He looked back to Walter. "Move, or you'll be hearing from the police."

Walter glanced at me.

"Mr. White," I said softly, honoring my commitment to myself despite my revulsion for him. "I feel morally compelled to urge you to reconsider your position."

"Really," he said, mimicking my intonation. "And I feel equally compelled to urge you to kiss my ass."

I shrugged, and Walter stepped aside. White pulled the door open forcefully. Ari was immediately outside, blocking his exit. White took a startled pace backward. He looked toward Walter.

"What . . ." he began.

Ari swatted him lightly on the side of the neck, behind his ear. White staggered, lifting a hand to touch the spot. His index finger came away spotted with a single drop of blood.

"Who the hell is he?" White rasped at Walter, voice conveying more anger than fear. "And what the hell did he just do?"

"I'm a friend and colleague of Rashid al-Shaabi," Ari announced, stepping into the room. "A man who wept at his death." He shoved the door shut with his elbow and then opened his hand to reveal a miniature syringe. "You've been poisoned, Mr. White. And unless you receive the antidote very soon, you'll be as dead as my lamented friend within fifteen minutes."

White looked from Ari to Walter to me contemptuously. He drew himself up, smoothed his clothes, and then rushed the door. Ari caught him by the arm, spun him around as if he were a child, and shoved him gently back into the center of the room. White backed to the fireplace, eyes wide.

"You're lying. This is a trick. You wouldn't dare poison me."

"Wrong," I said. "I warned you to reconsider. Ari, please tell Mr. White exactly what's about to happen to him."

"The poison is a neurotoxin," Ari explained calmly. "It acts at the extremities and radiates inward. Your hands and feet will begin tingling, as if they're going to sleep. Your limbs will tremble and weaken. Eventually, the poison will reach your chest." He drew his finger in a wide circle around his body, spiraling inward. "Your diaphragm will stop, and you'll feel as if you're suffocating. Your heart will race, trying to deliver more oxygen to your brain, but the paralysis will continue spreading, and your heart will seize. From the time you stop breathing, you'll have four or five minutes left to live. Four or five excruciatingly unpleasant minutes."

"That's bullshit," White yelled, saliva flying from his mouth. "You wouldn't dare."

"The reason we use this particular poison is that it's impossible to identify without an extremely broad and very expensive toxicology scan," Ari continued. "Most doctors just assume a heart attack, particularly with a decedent your age."

"You mentioned a pain in your left arm," Walter interjected emotionlessly. "You clutched at your chest before you collapsed and complained of a crushing sensation. I dialed 911 immediately, but the paramedics arrived too late to help."

"You wouldn't dare," White repeated weakly, as if it was a mantra. "You wouldn't. I'm an important person."

"Wrong tense," I corrected curtly, anxious for him to start talking. "We already have. You're wasting time, Mr. White, and you don't have much time left. You need the antidote if you're going to avoid permanent nerve damage. Tell us the truth about your connection to Mohler."

White glowered at us. Sixty seconds passed. His hands began clenching and unclenching, and I could see his left leg starting to shake.

"None of it was my idea," he blurted furiously. "It was all Narimanov. Now give me the antidote."

Narimanov. My world spun a final time and then righted itself. I'd been worried that I wouldn't know the truth when I heard it, but Narimanov's name resonated instantly. He was involved in the energy business, he had political influence, and he had more than enough money to back the schemes we'd uncovered. He'd even courted me—and, God help me, I'd liked him and seriously considered working for him. I wondered what sort of monster could smile and chat with a man whose son he'd had killed.

"Why?" I demanded.

"Narimanov's ex-KGB, like Putin. He was trained as a deep-cover agent, his mission to penetrate Western business circles. Former KGB men run everything over there now, and they hate America because we stripped away their empire. They want their empire back, and they think now is the right moment to make America pay. I've told you what I know. Give me the antidote."

White was leaning heavily on the mantelpiece, seeming unsteady on his feet.

"Sit," I said, pointing to a chair. "Conserve your strength. You're not getting the antidote until you've given us more details. Why provide me with the false Saudi information? And why back Senator Simpson for president?"

White complied without protest, slumping into a chair. His legs were twitching uncontrollably, and he looked terrified.

"Nothing's ever straightforward with the Russians. It's like that stupid chess game Narimanov plays, all feints and fakes and unexpected attacks. The Kremlin is trying to establish a global monopoly on energy supplies. Narimanov and other Russian government agents control vastly more reserves in South America and Africa than anyone knows. They've bought people everywhere: politicians, businessmen, and journalists. The Middle East is the big prize. Simpson's role was to stir things up, to make the Gulf States unhappy enough with the United States that they'd consider looking elsewhere for a protector. But the Saudis and Kuwaitis and the rest would only take Simpson seriously if it looked like he had a shot at winning. Your job was to publish the Saudi data and to make the case that shortages were imminent. Walter and his club were supposed to provide Simpson's financing. We thought it would be enough to secure Simpson the Republican nomination. He's a gifted natural speaker with a good conservative voting record, and he's not entirely stupid. The only hard part was trying to get him to keep his dick in his pants. He's like every other goddamned politician I've ever known, hot for anything in a skirt."

"But at the right moment, you were planning to pull the rug out from under him," I said.

"Simpson went on a congressional junket to Thailand six years ago. There are pictures of him with underage girls. Two of the girls are stashed in Hong Kong, ready to testify against him. And the Saudi information has fake digital watermarks that link it back to a radical environmental group. Once Simpson had served his purpose, he and the Saudi information were both going to be discredited." Sweat ran down White's forehead and into his eyes. He pawed at the handkerchief in his breast pocket but couldn't get hold of it. "Give me the antidote," he implored. "Please. I can't feel my fingers."

"And Rashid was killed because he was going to expose the Saudi data as false prematurely?"

White glanced fearfully at Ari and nodded.

"We didn't know you had a relationship with him. We thought you'd rely on the information Narimanov offered you for confirmation. When Narimanov heard the recording of you talking to Rashid, he decided Rashid had to go."

I'd accepted that I was likely responsible for Rashid's death, however inadvertently, but it rocked me to hear it confirmed.

"But you were the one who gave the order," Ari suggested, "weren't you? You were Narimanov's blind. You gave all the orders. No one else even knew he was involved."

"I had to do it," White mumbled, managing to sound a little ashamed. "I had no choice. He got a hook into me years ago."

"As we have a hook in you now," Ari responded fiercely. "Did the French know the Ukrainians were innocent?"

"No. The Russians planned everything. Narimanov laughed about it. All they had to do to manipulate the French was to pretend to take them seriously. The Russians knew the French wouldn't be a problem in the future, because they control France's gas supply."

"And Theresa Roxas's real name?" I asked.

He flopped his head toward me, the movement jerky and uncoordinated.

"Doris Carabello. She's an engineer with Pemex. Narimanov put her on the payroll when she was an engineering student. He's used her on a bunch of different jobs. Please. I'm begging you. I can't move my legs. I've told you everything. Give me the antidote."

I glanced at Ari. He gave me a small nod, and I looked back to White.

"You've told me everything about the present but not about the past. You still have to answer for my son."

White's mouth opened and closed wordlessly, his head slumped against the back of his chair. A sob racked his chest.

"Narimanov wanted me to stop investigating Petronuevo," I prompted. "He decided to murder my wife. You gave the order. My wife didn't show, so your men took my son instead. Right or wrong?"

White nodded once, his eyes screwed shut.

"Who'd you give the order to?" I asked. "Who killed my boy?"

"Anton Rastin," White whispered. "A Czech with American citizenship. Narimanov found him for me. He has two men he works with, ex-soldiers."

"Anton," I repeated, touching my face with a finger. "He has a scar here, right?"

White nodded fractionally. His breathing had become labored.

"They were all killed in the shoot-out at the motel yesterday. They paid for what they did. Now, please, please, give me the antidote."

I looked at Walter. He was stone-faced.

"You have any questions?"

He shook his head, and I turned back to White.

"You were right at the beginning," I said. "We lied."

"You didn't," White moaned. "I've been poisoned. I'm dying. Help me, please. I'm begging you."

"You're right that you've been poisoned. The lie was about the anti-dote. It doesn't exist. You're dying, and there's nothing anyone can do about it."

White's face contorted with horror. Shimon and I had argued the point for hours. The only way the Israelis would get involved was if there was no chance of White telling anyone what we'd done to him, and the only way to ensure that he kept quiet was to kill him. Eventually, I'd agreed. I tried my best to summon some remorse. White was a human being, after all. Maybe I'd become hardened: It was difficult to feel much compassion.

"He's stopped breathing," Ari said quietly, nodding toward White's chest. "The two of you might want to step out for a few minutes. This isn't going to be pleasant."

Walter and I exchanged a glance.

"No," I said, speaking for both of us. "We've each lost a son. We're in this until the end."

Nine Months Later

45

I nudged the screen door of the adobe farmhouse open with my knee, carrying Claire's and Kate's bags out into the dirt courtyard. It was a fine warm morning, air perfumed by the lavender rooted in the shade of the courtyard walls, and sun brilliant in a cloudless sky. Beyond the walls were endless rows of grapevines, tendrils heavy with purple fruit.

The house and the surrounding fifty acres were a slice of an old California rancho, half an hour north of Napa, that had been purchased by a thrifty migrant couple back before the area became wine country. The husband had restored the dilapidated house and outbuildings, while his wife revived the kitchen garden and planted lilacs, manzanitas, azaleas, and other flowering trees and shrubs wherever they'd take. They'd grown various cash crops in the early years—wheat, oats, and barley—but as time went by, and the wine boom gathered momentum, they'd leased most of the land to local vintners.

It had been a grandson who related the history to me, and who explained why the family was selling. His grandparents had died of old age, well after the succeeding generations had abandoned the land for the city. He was a UCLA-educated venture capitalist with a prominent Sand Hill Road firm, equal parts proud and ashamed of his humble heritage. The family didn't want to spend cash on maintenance but couldn't bear to see the place get run-down. I had the sense he was more interviewing than selling us, wanting to make sure the property was delivered into good hands. Despite our urban background, Claire, Kate, and I somehow passed muster. We found a housewarming gift in the kitchen after we closed the deal—a planting journal the elderly couple had kept over the fifty years of their residence, detailing what had flourished and what hadn't, and packed with agricultural tips and advice. Claire had already become adept at translating it, leaning on one of our inherited farmhands for help with the colloquialisms that defied her Spanish dictionary.

I heard the screen door open again as I was loading the bags into our car, and turned to see Claire and Kate walking toward me. They were both wearing jeans and T-shirts and dusty boots. Kate had a silver locket around her neck, a farewell gift from Phil. He'd visited us in San Francisco before heading off to Vienna for a semester abroad. He and Kate had parted friends, and they still chatted online frequently. She'd put him in touch with Gabor, her hacker friend from nearby Budapest. Phil and Gabor had discovered a mutual interest in electronic music, and Kate had been amused to learn that they were planning to meet up at an outdoor festival in Prague. I was glad her first real relationship had worked out well for her but not entirely unhappy that they'd been separated before things went too far.

"I wish you could be there tonight," Claire said, standing on tiptoe to give me a kiss. "The dancing is really magnificent."

The San Francisco Ballet was kicking off its new season with a twilight performance of Balanchine pieces in Golden Gate Park, and Claire was making her debut as their new pianist.

"I'm sorry," I apologized, hugging her tight. "I might catch the end. If not, I'll definitely see you at the party afterward."

Kate suddenly snapped her fingers and ran back toward the house.

"What now?" I said.

"Her sweater," Claire guessed, shaking her head tolerantly. "I think she left it on a chair in the kitchen. She's really nervous."

The following day would be Kate's first as a freshman at UC Berkeley. Our plan was to spend the night in a hotel in the city and then drive across the Bay Bridge to move Kate into her new residence hall. The previous week had been almost entirely consumed by speculation about her new roommate, with occasional heated digressions on the subject of what she should wear. My opinion hadn't been sought.

Claire touched the corner of my mouth with a finger.

"You're frowning," she said. "You're thinking about Kyle, aren't you?"

"It's hard not to," I admitted. "I keep wondering where he would have gone to college, and what it would have been like to take him for his first day."

She kissed me again.

"I know. I wonder the same thing."

It had somehow become okay for us to be sad together, the shared sorrow paradoxically staving off our individual despair. I still grieved for my son and worried about the world I was leaving my daughter, but I felt optimistic at times, as well—about my marriage, and other things.

"Sorry," Kate called, letting the screen door slam as she darted out of the house. She gave me a quick peck on the cheek and then grabbed at Claire's hand. "Come on. I want to make sure we have enough time."

"She dialed around San Francisco and found a store that has the red sandals she's been looking for," Claire informed me, eyes rolling, as she let herself be dragged away. "In the Mission District."

"Footwear's important," I said, my tone chiding. "I remember the shoes I wore on my first day of college."

"Really?" Kate asked, curiosity bringing her to a halt. "What were they?"

I grinned at her, and she smacked her forehead with her hand.

"Okay," she muttered. "I get it. You're mean."

"I remember my pants, too. They were these really nice boot-cut corduroys—"

"Mean," she shouted, tugging at Claire's hand again. "So mean. Come on. Let's go, Mom."

I waved and blew kisses as they drove away and then headed over to the barn to do some work. I was installing a wire fence on the north side, digging the post holes by hand. One of the farmhands had taught me the proper technique so I wouldn't destroy my back. Let the tools do the work, he'd cautioned, and slow down: *lentamente*. It wasn't a race. It felt good to be working in the sun—loosening the soil with a pointed bar and then scooping it free with the hinged digger.

I took a break at around one, making myself a sandwich in the kitchen and sitting on the front porch to eat it. I hesitated when I was done and then stood on my chair to reach up overhead. There was a small trapdoor in the porch ceiling, to provide access to the dead space between the wood joists and the rafters. *"Para fumigación,"* the farmhand had said and shrugged, when I asked about it. *"Termitas."* I pushed the trapdoor open and felt around until I found the oversized Ziploc bag that I'd secreted a few weeks previously. Removing it, I sat down again. The bag contained two items: an eight-year-old Christmas card with a picture of my family on the front, and a color photograph of my son, Kyle, dead in the trunk of Mariano Gallegos's car. Both items had been found by the police in a drawer in Anton Rastin's home, along with Alex's missing hard drive. Reggie had swiped the card and the photo from the police property room after they'd been processed.

I took the card from the bag first, touching the picture of my family before I opened it. The card was addressed to Alex and contained a chatty letter from Claire, updating our friends and family on our year. The letter opened with the news that she'd won a spot as an interim pianist with the City Ballet, and went on to say how excited she was to be performing again, despite the fact that she'd have to work evenings. Reggie had informed me that the card had Alex's fingerprints on it, which was only to be expected.

I replaced the card and withdrew the photograph. Kyle was wrapped in my coat, lying on his side so that his face was only partially visible. He looked like he was sleeping. The M5 marque and the top edge of a diplomatic license plate were visible at the bottom of the picture; a light post and a bit of the George Washington Bridge showed at the top left. Alex's fingerprints were on the photograph also, which was less expected.

Reggie and I had been sitting in the front seat of his car when he showed me the card and the photo. After I regained my composure, we worked out several versions of what might have happened. White's men—Anton Rastin and his associates—had to have known where I lived, and what my family looked like, and when they could expect Claire to leave our building. One possibility was that the Christmas card had nothing to do with their knowledge—that they learned what they needed to know by observing us. Another was that White discovered that Alex and I were close and had Alex's home or office searched for information about me. And yet another was that White had Rastin lean on Alex, and that Alex gave the card up voluntarily, because he was afraid Rastin would reveal his insider trading to the SEC or to his father.

Doris Carabello's fingerprints were on the photo of Kyle also. The two sets of prints—hers and Alex's—similarly lent themselves to several different explanations. Narimanov wanted Alex to sell me on the Saudi data. White would have instructed Doris to pressure Alex, but Alex's trading indiscretions at Torino were years past, potentially difficult to prove in retrospect and certainly outside any statute of limitations. It's possible that Doris gave him the photo as a threat, to underscore the viciousness of the people she represented. Or that Alex guessed at Doris's involvement in Kyle's death and demanded information about Kyle as the price of his cooperation. He knew how badly my family needed closure. Or maybe Doris shared the photo with him to remind him of his own complicity in my son's murder, and to drive home the leverage she had over him. What seems certain is that Alex, consumed by guilt, wrote the anonymous e-mail to Reggie and then committed suicide two days later.

I rinsed and racked my lunch dishes in the kitchen and then built a small fire in the living room fireplace. I fed the card and the photograph into the flame individually, stirring the ash to make sure they burned completely. Clifford White was dead. Doris Carabello and Karl Mohler had vanished, presumably victims of Narimanov's ruthless tidiness. Alex's true role in Kyle's death would likely never be known, unless he'd confessed more to his father in his letter than Walter had revealed. In retrospect, I couldn't help wondering if a confession might not have been responsible for Walter's abrupt change of heart toward me. Walter was ruthless to the core, but even he would have been shocked to learn that Alex had played a role in my son's death.

Regardless, I didn't plan to ask any more questions. It was time to move on: The Alex I wanted to remember was the friend I'd had before the pride and greed of his father's milieu had destroyed him, not the shattered wreck who might have betrayed me. Amy had captured my feelings when I told her that Claire, Kate, and I were moving to California to start over: "That's good," she whispered, hugging me tight. "Let the dead bury the dead. Matthew eight: twenty-two."

"Amen," I'd murmured back. "Amen."

I was setting one of the corner posts when I glanced up and noticed a distant dust trail moving toward me. It was late afternoon; the wind had risen, but it was still hot. I put away my tools, wiped sweat from my brow, and squatted down in the shade of the barn to wait. A white Toyota Land Cruiser pulled up a few minutes later. Ari was driving, Shimon in the front passenger seat. They both got out and looked around, their eyes masked by sunglasses. My muscles protested as I stood up.

"What do you do for water?" Shimon asked.

"You're a farmer?"

"More than you." He snorted. "I grew up on a kibbutz."

"There's a big lake a mile east that feeds an aquifer directly under our property. I had a study done before I bought the place. Water's never been a problem here, even in drought years."

"It's lovely," Ari said approvingly. "Mazel tov."

"Thanks. You want something to drink?"

Shimon shook his head, arms folded.

"What we'd like is to know why we're here."

"Unfinished business," I said easily, not having expected any pleasantries. "You disappeared without telling me how you fixed Senator Simpson."

The senator had held a press conference the week after White died, to announce his withdrawal from the presidential race for personal reasons. One of his reasons had been distress at the untimely passing of his closest aide. He'd closed with an impassioned appeal for donations to the American Heart Association.

"A quiet word here and there about the senator's libido," Shimon said. "The Republicans don't want a Bill Clinton."

"And relations between America and the Persian Gulf States?"

"Fluid," Ari suggested.

I smiled, but Shimon looked annoyed.

"Unchanged. The French withdrew their security proposal to the Saudis. They seem quite put out with the Russians these days." He took his sunglasses off and rubbed his eyes. "There is some reason other than your curiosity for me to have traveled seven thousand miles to see you, isn't there?"

I nodded, gesturing toward an old windmill a few hundred yards away. The blades were spinning slowly, the iron shaft creaking on ancient bearings.

"The windmill drives the pump that lifts water from the aquifer. I had an engineer out here the other day, to talk about replacing it with a more modern windmill so I could do a little cogeneration at the same time. I mentioned that I planned to install a solar array as well, so I could get myself off the grid. He laughed. Oil's cheap, he explained, because of the financial crisis. It would take forever to get any kind of payback on my investment. His advice was to do nothing."

Shimon shrugged.

"We made another round of the Western governments, identifying Rashid as the source of our Saudi estimates. No one wants to talk about an energy problem twenty years from now. They're all preoccupied with unemployment and stimulus plans and budget deficits."

"They'd focus if they really understood the consequences. We're running out of time."

"So, what do you want us to do?" Ari asked.

"Send me Rashid's information. The real information. I still have an audience."

"Possible," Shimon said, frowning, "but this is a political problem—"

"I read the news accounts of Narimanov's plane crash," I said, deliberately interrupting him. "And I made a few phone calls. It's interesting. The plane dropped off radar almost a hundred miles away from the crash site, and the search-and-rescue team never found Narimanov's body. There's a German air base nearby. I'm not usually a big conspiracy theorist, but it made me wonder: What if the crash was staged, so the Germans—or their friends—could secretly grab Narimanov?"

Shimon stared at me, his eyes hooded.

"Mohler was feeding money to dozens of bank accounts," I continued. "White told us that Narimanov controlled business and political leaders all over the world. If Narimanov was secretly in custody, whoever held him would have leverage over everyone he'd been bribing."

"Tread lightly here," Ari advised softly. "Very, very lightly."

"Let me be very clear," I said. "I'm not threatening anybody with anything. Nothing I know or suspect goes any further, ever. But I want you to know that I've established a nonprofit organization to promote awareness of impending energy shortages and to lobby for more action on alternative energy strategies. Walter Coleman gifted us an endowment. It would be nice if the business and political leaders who were on Narimanov's payroll were encouraged to be supportive as well."

"That's it?" Ari asked.

"That's it."

He glanced at Shimon and then back at me.

"You have information on this organization?"

I fished one of my new business cards from my hip pocket.

"Sorry," I said. "It's a little damp."

Shimon put his sunglasses on again and nodded curtly.

"I'll tell my superiors about your organization," he said. "I'm sure they'll approve. I wouldn't be surprised if you got a number of calls in the near future, offering donations or help. And I'll have a word with Rashid's executor in Jerusalem. My recollection is that he left some papers for you. I'll see that they're sent along."

"Thanks."

Shimon turned and began walking back toward his car, Ari trailing behind. He glanced at the fence posts I'd set and came to a halt.

"You're planning to keep livestock?" he asked.

"Goats," I replied. "A mutual friend suggested they might be a good idea."

Acknowledgments

After finishing *Restitution,* my first novel, I sat down with my editors—Peter Gethers and Claudia Herr—to discuss my ideas for a second. For a quick moment they locked eyes, and then Peter asked quietly: "You are aware that the second book is the hard one, aren't you?"

His question brought to mind *Holes,* a book I'd read to my children years ago. Stanley, the teenaged protagonist, is sent to a youth labor camp, where every day he's forced to dig a large hole in a dry lake bed. At the end of his first day, one of the characters tells him that the second hole is the hardest. At the end of his second day, the same character informs Stanley that the third hole is the hardest. And so on.

Garden of Betrayal wasn't more difficult to write than *Restitution,* but it also wasn't any easier. Which is worrisome, because my long-term plan had been to emulate Winston Churchill, who allegedly dictated his books from the bath, or to become like John Grisham, who—according to an interview I once read—composes each of his tautly constructed legal thrillers in an economical nine months, leaving him the rest of the year to vacation with his family. The truth is that I missed the deadline for *Garden* by a good six months and seem destined to the work habits of Dorothy Parker, who once remarked that she didn't write five words but that she changed seven.

The good news this time around was that I had a terrific team in place to lean on. Peter and Claudia continued as my excellent editors at Knopf and were hugely influential in shaping the initial outline and in persuading me to tweak the final manuscript to reflect the cataclysmic financial events of the last two years. Kathy Robbins, my agent, along with David Halpern and Rachelle Bergstein, both of her office, once again provided invaluable advice and criticism throughout every phase of the project. And, as before, Jennie Yabroff was there to read every word, and she was both ruthless enough to let me know in no uncertain terms when those words weren't good enough and encouraging enough to make me want to keep going. I'm enormously grateful to all of them.

I also particularly want to thank my erstwhile former colleague Steven Strongin, head of research at Goldman Sachs, who took time to explain his views on the energy markets when I was trying to work out the original outline. I'm grateful for the education and hope I put it to good use. Lest anyone think this book reflects his views, however, let me simply say that to the best of my knowledge, Steven has yet to install solar panels.

Else I benefited from the support of any number of friends, and particularly that of my family—Cynthia, Zoe, Nikki, and Matt. Cynthia, my wife, was particularly good about sympathizing when I muttered darkly about uncooperative characters and nice enough never to point out that my problems were definitely of my own making. And the kids have been enthusiastic about my midlife change of career—evidently being a writer has more cachet in teenage circles than being a banker. Go figure.

Finally, I want to thank everyone at Knopf for their superb work in packaging, promoting, and distributing both *Restitution* and *Garden:* in particular, Sonny Mehta, Chairman of Knopf; Anne Messitte, Publisher of Vintage Anchor; Jason Booher, who designed the jacket of this book; and Maria Massey, who acted as production editor. Knopf is a terrific place, and I'm lucky to have been picked up by them.

A NOTE ABOUT THE AUTHOR

Lee Vance is the author of the novel *Restitution*. He was a trader at Goldman Sachs for more than twenty years before retiring as a partner in 2000 to write full-time. He lives in New York with his wife and three children.

A NOTE ON THE TYPE

This book was set in Minion, a typeface produced by the Adobe Corporation specifically for the Macintosh personal computer and released in 1990. Designed by Robert Slimbach, Minion combines the classic characteristics of old-style faces with the full complement of weights required for modern typesetting.

Composed by Creative Graphics, Allentown, Pennsylvania
Printed and bound by Berryville Graphics, Berryville, Virginia
Designed by Virginia Tan